The Loneliness of the Time Traveller

The Loneliness of the Time Traveller

ERIKA RUMMEL

INANNA poetry & fiction

Toronto, Ontario, Canada
www.inanna.ca

We gratefully acknowledge the support of the Canada Council for the Arts and the Ontario Arts Council for our publishing program. We also acknowledge the financial support of the Government of Canada.

Cover design: Val Fullard

The Loneliness of the Time Traveller is a work of fiction. All the characters portrayed in this book are fictitious and any resemblance to persons living or dead is purely coincidental.

Library and Archives Canada Cataloguing in Publication

Title: The loneliness of the time traveller / Erika Rummel.
Names: Rummel, Erika, 1942- author.
Identifiers: Canadiana (print) 20220224196 | Canadiana (ebook) 2022022420X | ISBN 9781771338783 (softcover) | ISBN 9781771338790 (HTML) | ISBN 9781771338806 (PDF)
Classification: LCC PS8635.U56 L66 2022 | DDC C813/.6—dc23

Printed and bound in Canada

Inanna Publications and Education Inc.
210 Founders College, York University
4700 Keele Street, Toronto, Ontario, Canada M3J 1P3
Telephone: (416) 736-5356 Fax: (416) 736-5765
Email: inanna.publications@inanna.ca   Website: www.inanna.ca

The Loneliness of the Time Traveller

LYNNE

NOSTALGIA. IT started a week ago in New York, at a farewell party the Shearers gave me. Maybe I should call it a good-riddance party because I wasn't popular at Argus Investments. My success left a bitter taste in the mouths of my colleagues. *Bitch!* they said behind my back, but I caught them in the act. *Bitch* was hovering in the air.

Stockbrokers are realists. They believe in statistics, in calculable risks, in tangible facts. They don't believe in telepathy and the ability to read a person's mind. But that's my forte. Thoughts are visible to me, whether they come out as words or remain tucked away in people's minds. I see them swirling around their heads, little puffs of vapour merging with other people's thoughts, turning into clusters, becoming trends. I know what people think, about me, about currencies, about real estate, tar sands, copper mines, steel production, oil platforms. That's how I made my money on the stock market, predicting the next big thing, spying on the thoughts of traders and investors, watching the aura of greed tremble in the air and build toward a boom, or the fears gather and burst the bubble. That's how I knew it was the right time to leave Argus Investments and cash out. The market was at its peak. The downward slide started two days after I sold my holdings. The

1

rancour among my former partners was palpable. They resented my perfect timing. I could see the question in their eyes, casting an opaque shadow: *How the fuck did she know? It couldn't have been pure luck. She must have a hook-up*—I do. Reading people's minds is my hook-up.

So the Shearers put themselves out and gave me a party. They thought it was a good investment. I might be useful to them in future. I could see the idea sticking up from Dan's head like the crest of a Mohawk: *Let's keep on friendly terms with Lynne. She's got connections.* Smiles were painted on every face around the table and reflected in the gleaming silverware. Thoughts coiled around every head, wound tightly to prevent them from unravelling and turning into slippery words. It was a perfectly staged party. There were enough flowers for a wedding or a funeral. The caterers had planned the dinner to the last delicious detail, although gourmet food and vintage wines are wasted on this crowd. They are hungry only for stock market news.

"So what's up next, Lynne?" Dan Shearer asked me.

The conversation around us stopped as people leaned in to hear my answer.

"Just moving on," I said.

They thought it was a metaphor, as in: moving on to a new company, to new investments. No, I meant it literally, as in: transmigration. I suppose Dan Shearer would call that a hook-up, too. If he believed in paranormal phenomena such as time travel and switching bodies.

When I reach the point of ennui, when success no longer keeps away boredom, I make my move. It's a natural cycle. The current begins to flow in the right direction, the winds pick up, impatience runs in my veins like sap. It's the season to slough off my old body and slip into a new skin, to enter new territory. I know the danger, but I can't resist the call. Reading people's minds and migrating into their bodies are, shall we say, related activities. One is only a brief incursion—a hit-and-run operation to prey on their thoughts. The other involves all-out war, a battle for total control, the permanent occupation of a foreign body. You become them. They become you. Timing is crucial in transmigration. The battle begins when the body's owner has reached a low point and is ready to cede control to Death. That's when I make my move and contest his take-over bid. It's an operation that requires a high level of competence. I've honed my transmigration skills over more than two centuries and still can't say that I've perfected the method. It's always risky. You have to take into account a large number of variables when you challenge Death for control over a body. You have to time your entry exactly and strike with military precision. One mistake, and you are in a disaster zone. Death wins, you die. But there is glory in fighting Death, a poetic beauty in the glint of danger, the rush of blood, the terror of an uncertain fate, and in the end, the exhilaration of victory. I've never lost a battle yet. I am a survivor.

"Not giving anything away?" Dan said and smiled a knowing smile.

I was tempted to say, "Not at this point. I'm still shopping around, waiting for a suitable body to slip into," then watch the expression on Dan's face. But why antagonize people? I smiled back at him.

"Sorry, Dan, but that's confidential for the time being."

I don't remember the rest of the conversation because my attention was arrested by a painting on the opposite wall. When Dan leaned forward to talk to me, it came into full view and hit me between the eyes—that's what it felt like, a violent knock, someone demanding to get into my head. What I saw was a large white canvas. In the upper left corner was a tangle of green letters like graffiti marking gang territory. In the centre of the painting, a gash spurted tiny blood-red letters that said *LA to NY, NY to LA*. It looked like an itinerary, and I recognized the thing that had punched me in the head: nostalgia. I'd moved to New York from Los Angeles twelve years ago. Was I nostalgic for L.A., for a time when my interests were more genteel, when I studied history at UCLA and worked as an intern at the Clarkson Rare Book library? Yes, those memories played into my nostalgia, but for some reason the painting on the wall had triggered a longing for something further back. It was nostalgia for my first life, in London, two centuries ago. I wanted to go home. I wanted to see Jack again. For some inexplicable reason, when I looked at that painting, Jack's name flared up in my brain, a lick of fire. I ran hot and cold. I could feel his mouth on mine, making me shiver with pleasure. I could hear his voice in my ear, an urgent whisper making my heart beat faster: Come back, Lynne!

Perhaps the cliché is true, and you can't go home again. In my travels I've always moved on. I don't know how to reverse the flow of time, or let's say, I tried it once, in Los Angeles twelve years ago, and it didn't work. What's needed, I think, is a token of the past, a channel to guide me back, an artifact from that period. A page of writing infused with the taste and touch of Georgian London would be best, I decided then. I knew exactly where to get it, but I botched the operation. I suppose thieving isn't one of my talents. Or else, it was just bad luck that I couldn't get my hands on that piece of paper twelve years ago. When I looked at that painting in Dan Shearer's apartment, I made a decision: I'll give it another try. I'll find a way to go back home to London, to my first life. And that meant a trip to L.A. and the Rare Book room in the Clarkson Library.

LA to NY, NY to LA. The words on the painting were *my* itinerary. There is a manuscript in the vault of the Clarkson Library that will serve as my magic carpet, my ride home. It's a woman's memoir, Adele's account of her life with me, of our life I should say, because she was my first victim, my first attempt at transmigration. We shared a body. And we shared in a crime. I need to run my fingers over the lines Adele wrote and let the ink seep into my pores. And then, Old London will enter my bloodstream, and I will be transported. I am sure of that. The question is: will I be able to get my hands on the manuscript this time?

IN THE arrival lounge at LAX, a man in a chauffeur's uniform is holding up a sign: *Dreamvillas.com.*

I flag him.

"Miss Addington?" he says.

I nod. I have completed the itinerary suggested by the painting in Dan Shearer's living room: NY to LA. The nostalgia has gone viral and is clogging my chest.

The chauffeur takes me to a waiting limo. I settle back as he eases into the airport traffic, passes the gaudy Theme Building, a flying saucer on legs, and turns into Century Boulevard. The first windblown palms come into view, and the sprawl of Los Angeles— shopping plazas, car lots, low-rise factories, office buildings—a Legoland stretching for miles to the left and right of the highway. Then I spot a break in the pattern, an irregular shape, the Palladian roofline of the Clarkson Library, and my mind moves back twelve years. History books were my shibboleth then. I had moved into Ginny's body, a graduate student writing a thesis on "Entertainment in 18th Century London." That may have planted the seeds of nostalgia in me. I thought I might do better than just write about the subject Ginny had picked. I might be able to resurrect the past, enter it, conjure up the feel, smell and sound of another century, breathe life into the characters, become one of them. I came close, but in the end I couldn't pull it off. Circumstances were against me.

I'm still caught in the memory loop when the driver slows and turns into the circular drive of a seaside villa. A young Latino steps up, opens the car door for me and takes charge of my luggage. The butler, waiting his turn on the front steps, shows me into the foyer. His name is James Warren. Sounds like a stage name. I give his brain a closer look, and sure enough, he's a temp, an out-of-work actor who has taken on a cameo role in the current episode of my life. There are a lot of lines floating in his brain, everything from Shakespeare to *Downton Abbey*. He's too young for the part of a butler. The role requires someone middle-aged and portly, like Anthony Hopkins in *The Remains of the Day*. James has the narrow face and elastic body of a greyhound. He isn't particularly talented, but he has mastered the butler steps, one foot in front of the other, moving with dignity, and he has memorized a few butler gestures, like the old-fashioned head bow he gives me before taking me on a tour of the premises.

The walls in the principal rooms of the villa are hung with large Rothko-like canvases in primary colours. Whoever decorated the house is in love with abstract expressionism. And with hard surfaces. There is a preponderance of marble, glass, and stainless steel. Even the flower arrangements have something rigid about them, as if they could never wilt. In the living room, James points a remote control at the floor-to-ceiling windows. The opaque blinds rise silently and reveal a five-star view of the bay and the Santa Monica Mountains. Another click, and the wall of glass parts like the Red Sea, allowing us to pass through to the terrace.

Here the tour ends. James winds down and launches into the "we aim to please" finale:

"If you have any questions, concerns, requests—anything at all, Miss Addington—don't hesitate to let us know."

I do have a request. Dreamvillas.com offers personal shopping.

"There's a book I'd like you to get for me," I tell James. "*A Tale of Caution* by Adele Collingwood."

As I say it, the name resonates in my brain: Adele Collingwood, my first alter ego, the body I inhabited in the eighteenth century. *A Tale of Caution* contains her reminiscences. Thinking of Adele, I feel halfway home already, back in Old London. I'm not sure she would welcome me back. She used to call me her evil twin. But I can't leave the past alone. My nostalgia has jelled into a plan and an agenda.

James notes down the title of the book.

"It's a two-volume set," I tell him.

"I will see if—"

I cut in: "*If?* Excuse me. The word you want is *when*." I've learned my lesson over the centuries: Keep the underlings in line. "*When* will you get the two volumes for me, James?"

I can see he's peeved, but his voice remains level. "As soon as possible, Miss Addington."

He gives me an abbreviated bow, a nod really, and leaves.

Those books will serve me as props. Volume One contains the printed text of *A Tale of Caution*. Volume Two contains a facsimile of the manuscript from which the text was transcribed, the one I failed to steal twelve years ago. I hope I'll be more successful this time. I can't wait to see the familiar handwriting. I know that a facsimile isn't good enough for my purposes, that it cannot serve as a channel to the past. I need to get my fingers on the real thing. Even with the manuscript in hand, it won't be easy to travel back in time. Adele's memoirs are inaccurate. She has altered the story of her life to make herself look good, and those inaccuracies may get in the way of my journey and block my path or trap me in dead ends.

Of course, I don't know exactly what Adele has written. By the time she started on her memoirs, I'd moved on. We stayed in touch, but we no longer shared a body. I didn't even know she was writing her memoirs until she came to my house one day, the little rat, and showed a chapter to my husband, trying to out me. Luckily, he didn't believe her. He thought she was mad when she talked of an incubus who had possessed her body for some years and had now moved into the body of his wife. He was afraid she would publish this "rubbish," as he called it, and embarrass his family. He burned some of the pages and locked away the rest. For all I know, she rewrote those pages afterwards. I only found out that the memoir, or a part of it, survived when I read an article about it in the *Journal of Rare Books* twelve years ago. The manuscript ended up in L.A., in the Clarkson Library, not far from the university where I was a student. Patricia Baron, the Head of Research, was preparing a scholarly edition of the text, the article said. The moment I read that information, I started thinking about the possibilities Adele's manuscript offered me. To begin with, I visited the Clarkson—a library specializing in English literature—to take a look at the manuscript. I went through the usual procedure meant to keep ordinary people at bay. Librarians can be possessive about their treasures. I filled out an application for a reader's card, providing all the right information. I was a graduate student at UCLA. My thesis was on entertainment in late eighteenth-century London, based on first-person accounts. The holdings of the Clarkson were of particular interest to me, I wrote in the space provided, and listed the titles of several rare books and manuscripts, which I had culled from their catalogue. Success! I was admitted into the privileged circle of the Clarkson's readers, but immediately hit a roadblock. The librarian at the desk informed me that Adele's manuscript was not available, pending restoration.

"And when will the restoration be completed?"

She studied the information on her computer screen.

"Actually," she said, "we are still at the stage of evaluating whether restoration is feasible." She looked at me over her reading glasses. "It all depends on the library's budget. To be honest, it will be a long process."

In other words, it might be years before the manuscript was put into circulation, if at all.

"Sorry," she said. "There's nothing I can do about that."

So my plan of action wasn't going anywhere, but on the way out I saw a notice posted on the bulletin board inviting applications for an internship at the library. They were looking for a graduate student to assist Patricia Baron, the Head of Research—the woman who was working on Adele's memoirs. I applied and beat out the other candidates with my detailed knowledge of eighteenth-century life, "almost as if I had experienced it in person," as the chair of the selection committee put it so perceptively.

Six weeks later, I started my internship and cozied up to Patricia Baron in the hope of getting the inside track on the manuscript, but she was cagey about her work and showed me only bits and pieces. She had discovered Adele's manuscript tucked away in a copy of Percy Stockdale's *Sixteen Sermons*. The discovery was her claim to academic fame. A previously unknown eighteenth-century autobiography written by a woman! It was a scoop. Patricia wasn't going to share her glory with an intern or give anyone else a chance to poke around and muscle in on her territory. That's why she kept the manuscript out of circulation on the pretext that it was too brittle to handle. The fewer people saw it the better for her, and to establish her intellectual ownership and exclusive rights to the text, she wrote a learned article describing the manuscript and its contents. From her synopsis, I could tell it wasn't a straight autobiography. It was Adele's attempt to whitewash the past. Or to erase the unpleasant memories she had of her guardian, Percy Stockdale, who had come very close to guessing our double existence. The old man was too nosy, and he paid the price. That's why Adele wrote her life or rather rewrote it, as far as I could judge from Patricia's summary. She cut out what would have been incriminating and added a feel-good ending. I'm not saying that Adele made anything up. But she didn't tell the truth either. It was a hybrid, a combination of fact and wishful thinking, a censured and enhanced version of the events. According to Patricia Baron's summary, Adele's *Cautionary Tale* was written in the confessional style of a private diary. Although its professed purpose was to warn readers, it was not entirely clear that the author intended to publish it. It was, at any rate, incomplete or missing pages, she said—the pages my then-husband burned to keep them from becoming public, the part he locked away?

Adele's intentions were clear enough to me. She meant to show— to the public or perhaps only to herself—that she was not to blame for what happened. But she *was* to blame, at least partly, and when I get my hands on the manuscript, I'll be reading between the lines, looking for the kernels of truth hidden there. I absolutely need the truth to get back to my first life. Lies won't work as a conduit to the past. They might send me in the wrong direction.

A few years ago, Patricia Baron published Adele's memoirs in a two-volume edition, including a facsimile of the text. As far as I know, the original manuscript is still in the vault of the Clarkson, but it will require some scheming to get at it. Until then, the printed version will have to do. It won't harm to prep by going over the facsimile. I just have to wait for the butler to do his job and get me the set. Something may click even if the text isn't the original. I wonder how long it will take for James to deliver the books to me at the villa. The sight of Adele's handwriting will have a visceral impact, I hope, and get the adrenalin flowing. It will feed my nostalgia and fan it into a passion.

Transmigration is a great rejuvenating experience, but it has one big drawback. It flattens the emotions. With every transmigration, the chemicals at work in your pleasure centre become more diluted. Entering a foreign body is a military operation, and the person attacked tends to use the scorched earth method. You conquer the land, but the fields are barren. Your victim has blocked the theta waves in her limbic system and destroyed the hypothalamic effect. The body you take over comes with impaired emotions. After a few transmigrations, you become very calm, too calm. You find yourself in a state of emotional repose, and you start missing the ripples, the excitement that goes with emotional engagement. I'm not entirely without feelings, but they are mostly second-hand, generated by memories of emotions I had in earlier lives. That's why nostalgia is such a wonderful thing. It opens the sluice gates. Memories of past feelings rush into my brain, and I am almost whole again—alive, thinking, and feeling.

Seeing the facsimile text with Adele's handwriting will set the mood, I hope, and will take me back to my first life, to London in the 1700s. I need to keep the memories coming until I can get my hands on the manuscript at the Clarkson Library. I have great hopes for that moment. I can't wait to run my fingertips over the lines Adele has written, feel the molecules of the past, make them brim with the fluid of life. Adele's words will be the pathway to my first existence, I'm convinced of it. Her memories are my memories after all. Our thoughts came from the same cortical folds, were fed by the same vascular system, were connected by the same neural pathways. Those memories will lead me back to London, to Adele. And to Jack.

My longing for Jack has been there all along, I realize now, dormant and buried under layers of history. Now it's pushing up, breaking through, coming to the surface. Nostalgia makes the desire run hot in my veins like lava. I want Jack. I loved the hair on the back of his head. I loved his cracked voice, gravelly as if it was exhausted by too much living. I loved the smoky taste of his skin, the hands that stroked me and broke me loose. I loved the food he ate, the ale he drank, the filthy floor he stepped on. I loved everything he was and did. I want to touch the pages that contain his name and mine, follow the duct of the letters Adele has written with her own hand, slip inside and travel along that escape route to Old London, and be whole again. I want to feel the way I felt then, with every fibre, with every cell, with every drop of blood. I want to feel passion.

But I can't make it happen instantly. For one thing, it's Sunday, and the library is closed. For another, it will take time to put my plan into action and get at the manuscript. In the meantime I'm left to contemplate the view from the terrace of the villa. I should be enjoying the Californian sun, pour myself a drink, kick back and watch the surf washing ashore wave after indigo wave, leaving a mother-of-pearl fringe on the pale sand. The rhythm is supposed to be soothing, but it's not working for me. I am restless. The problem is: I'm stranded with myself. There are too many rooms in this villa, too many windows looking out on an empty landscape, a swimming pool without swimmers, a perimeter wall guarded by lonely camera eyes, a private beach undisturbed by footprints. This villa is meant for people craving privacy. I need company. The air is never devoid of thoughts. If I can't read other people's minds, I am stuck with my own, condemned to reading the insides of my brain, the litter of decades. The trash heap of memories is mounting in my head, hopes and regrets, loathing and desire, memories that have started corroding my cranium walls.

Of course, I'm not completely on my own. The villa comes with a staff of four—James the butler, Rosa the maid, a cook, and a gardener/handyman—but reading their minds is about as exciting as reading the label on a bag of chips. My God, their interior landscapes are boring. When the limo delivered me to the house this morning, they were all lined up in the hall to greet me. I could see that Rosa was suffering from depression. Or an unhappy love affair. The two states are hard to tell apart. They produce similar effects, slowing down the brainwaves. The fog in her mind was thick and brown like molasses. She should be on meds, really. The others had swept their minds clean except for a few service thoughts, fluff that evaporates quickly and leaves a stale air in the room. The gardener was the worst of the lot. His mind was like a cage from which the bird has flown. James as well. He kept his eyes politely vacant during the house tour. But I'm not complaining as long as he has the necessary job skills. That's what matters.

I unpack my suitcase, check messages on my phone, look at the tourist brochures laid out on the coffee table—where to dine, where to shop. I'm impatient for James to bring the books, but I guess I can't expect miracles.

I'VE ORDERED dinner for seven o'clock, and at seven, on the dot, James rolls in a service cart and starts setting the table in the dining room. His eyes wander in my direction, discreetly checking me out through the double doors. Above his head, a thin cloud appears and spreads out, a wisp of disapproval. *Those jeans. So last year.* He compresses his lips at the sight of my chop-cropped hair. *Somebody help that woman. She's clueless when it comes to fashion.*

Better keep your thoughts under control, butler-boy, or you'll feel the pain when it comes to handing out gratuities! I've worn the executive uniform long enough—Armani suits in powder-gray with pencil thin skirts and lightly padded shoulders. Hermes scarves. Stiletto heels from Prada. That phase is over. Finito. Not sure what I should be dressing for now. Something retro to blend in with historical research? For the time being I'm slumming it.

James pushes back the connecting doors to the dining room.

"Dinner is served, Miss Addington," he announces, bending slightly from the waist, and gives me a spiritless, perfunctory smile.

"Any progress with the book order?" I say.

"I'm sorry, Miss Addington. I was unable to obtain a copy of the set. The first volume is available, but the second—the facsimile—is a collector's item, apparently. I've placed an order with an on-line seller who specializes in out-of-print books. They'll keep me posted."

"You got the first volume?"

"I thought—"

"Don't think, James. Just do as you are told. Isn't that the first thing they teach you at butler school? I asked you for two volumes. You say one of them is available."

He gives me a distant look. "I will get the first volume to you right away, Miss Addington."

"Good," I say. "And by the way, where have you gone to school?"

"Beg your pardon, Miss Addington?" He sounds wary.

"Where have you received your training?"

"I have a degree from USC."

"Not known as a school for butlers," I say in my snarkiest voice.

He doesn't rise to the bait. He keeps a prudent silence, but a moody edginess trails from his shoulders as he pauses at the door and wishes me bon appetite.

I let him go.

I sit down to my lonely dinner—well, yes, I'm lonely but I refuse to feel sorry for myself. That's how it is. You make money or you make friends. I opted for money and find myself short of friends just now. That may also explain my nostalgia, my craving to go back in time, to my first life when I was poor and had friends.

And passions. I want to be with Jack, who knew how to get my blood roiling. To feel again, I am willing to fight on two fronts, to challenge Time and Death, to face the unknown. Will there be friction when I go against the flow of time? Will I be stripped of my willpower and burn up like a comet falling through space? What if I turn into pure energy and have no body left to enjoy life with? What if I come through singed and withered, bloodless, shrunk to the size of an embryo? For a moment I am deeply afraid, but my fear of the unknown is tempered by a longing for the well-known, for Old London, for my first life, for Jack. The longing for passion has turned into an irresistible force. I want to go on that journey, that pilgrimage, but I need a guide to find my way back, someone to channel my desire: Adele.

The skin on my arms crisps as I think of Jack. I can feel his presence, his voice drawing me on, calling me home. I fell hard for him when I was sixteen and a serving girl at the Bullfrog. I can see the taproom now, the haze of smoke, the clatter of tin plates, the air overheated, pungent with sweat, urine, puke and the yeasty smell of sex. Jack grabs my wrist as I squeeze by his table and makes me spill the jug of ale I am serving. I am good at swatting away the grasping hands of men. No one gets anything for nothing. Not from me. I keep on the lookout for gropers, protecting my bum and my breasts from their dirty paws, but Jack is too fast for me. He grabs my arm. "Come'ere," he says and pulls me down on his lap. I snatch back my arm and see the mark his fingers have left on my flesh, like a branding. I give him a defiant look and struggle up, but he won't let me go. Something in me snaps awake, a sharp desire for that man, who keeps me in an iron lock. "I like that girl," he says to the drunken brawlers at his table and they snort their approval. "She's got pluck," he says. He has the voice of someone with an unsootheable desire to live, of someone wild and untameable, a dangerous man. My heart starts pounding. "Next time I want a nicer welcome, you hear?" he says. His face has gone hard. There is a sneering menace in his voice now. He reaches up, and for a moment I think he is going to slap me, but he's on to the next surprise: tucking a stray lock of hair behind my ears. It's like a caress, as if he wanted to make up for the threat in his voice. "I'll wait for you outside," he says, and nods his head in the direction of the door.

At closing time I go with him to his room, a windowless corner in the attic of a tenement, with slapped-up walls. We don't bother to undress. We just tug aside what's in our way and make love on the floor with a furious, chaotic passion. The night is warm and the sweat trickles down my spine and glistens on Jack's forehead. That's the last thing I remember before he makes me forget my existence and melts me down to liquid ore. In the morning I look into his face and see that he has the beauty of a wild beast, a tiger.

Jack was fatal to any woman careless enough to fall in love with him. He was a man with crime burned into the circuit of his brain, with violence in the marrow of his bones. He was quick to anger, quick to lash out, and if there happened to be a knife in his hand— but I don't want to go there, no. I was infatuated with Jack. I still am. He was a god to me. The tunnelling, echoing sound of the past is leaving me open-mouthed with desire. No one else, in all my lives, has ever come close to Jack—except Sam Kelley, the caretaker at the Clarkson Library. He held an odd fascination for me. Wonder if he still works there. I met Sam on my first day as an intern at the Clarkson, twelve years ago.

I arrived at the library early, drove up to the steel gate which kept out the unauthorized, and pressed the button of the intercom. A voice barked something vaguely Good Morn-ish. The gate rolled back. I drove though and parked in the visitors' lot. My instructions were to go to the caretaker's office—the Porter's Lodge, they called it—sign in and pick up a staff parking permit.

The caretaker was waiting for me at the door.

"I'm Sam Kelley," he said.

Inside the door, an old dog was sprawled on a mat. Sam nudged him with the toe of his work boot. "And that's Gordie," he said.

The dog was a mixed breed. His short legs suggested a dachshund. The rest—curly chocolate brown coat, pointed snout and antenna ears—was anyone's guess. Sam bent down and gave Gordie a vigorous body rub. The dog closed his eyes in ecstasy.

I followed Sam into his office, to the counter that divided his workspace from his living quarters. From the cracked voice on the intercom I'd expected an older man. But Sam was young, my own age, on the burly side, with a corded neck and hands hardened by work. He gave me a probing look. As our eyes met, I was struck by the high intensity, the blow-you-to-pieces force I saw there. I could feel it even though he kept his goods under wraps and covered the surface of his brain with a blanket of custodial chores. Some people are better than others at hiding their thoughts. Sam was a master at keeping them close, but he couldn't hide his cobra energy from me. It surrounded his head with a pulsing red aura.

"Sign here," he said and slid a form across the counter. "The receipt for your office keys and the parking tag."

I gave Sam a hungry look and signed.

He ran his fingers through his buzz cut, turned the page around and read my name. "Lynne Addington?" he said, raising his brows as if questioning my identity. My identity! I almost laughed out loud. I've changed identities many times, although I've stuck with my first name, "Lynne." Whatever it says on the ID of the body I take, I tell people to call me Lynne. For nostalgic reasons. Nostalgia will screw me up one day. It's the chink in my rational armour.

Sam handed me the keys and the parking tag. His touch sent a charge like static electricity through my arm. The custodial wrap covering his mind lifted for a moment. There, right behind his eyes—silky blue eyes that looked sensitive, almost tender—sat a storm cloud of aggression, desire, and resentment at not getting what he wanted *now*. Further down I saw a rich vein of artistic notions, which, frankly, caught me by surprise because he showed no outward signs of aesthetic sensibility. He wore a rumpled T-shirt and fraying jeans. His living room—the corner visible from the counter—was dowdy, the walls unadorned. The only hint that Sam could be whimsical was a watch dangling from Gordie's collar. *Watch dog*, get it? But Gordie was clearly too old for the job. When I passed him on the way out, he wearily lifted his head and gave me an asthmatic snuffle. He had the placid eyes and quiet manners of a pensioner. I could not imagine him raising a single bark no matter what went on.

The Clarkson could have used a guard dog. The neighbourhood was seedy. It had been a vision of grandeur once, but most of the stately homes built at the turn of the last century had been demolished to make way for the Santa Monica Freeway. The wealthy tycoons left. Working class blacks moved into the area in the 50s and Latinos in the 70s. Over the next decade the district went downhill, slumped in on itself. The garbage thickened and congealed. Black mould crept over the buildings. Riots grazed the streets in '92. The Clarkson was a walled oasis in a desert of crumbling houses, a pillared mansion stiff with dignity and surrounded by an acre of pristine lawns and neatly raked gravel paths. But just down the street from the library were two weathered boarding houses with cracked roof tiles and right next to the library, an abandoned building with most of its windowpanes broken, and one frame sagging on its hinges and flapping noisily above the driveway.

Sam and I became friendly after a couple of weeks. As it turned out, we had things in common beyond that first elemental attraction. We were both gamblers, and we decided to keep a running bet on the odds of that window frame coming loose and crashing down. The rotten casing was visible from the window of Sam's bathroom. Once or twice a week we went in there and ascertained that the frame was still hanging on, then placed our bets: a five-dollar bill each, weighed down by a stapler. Sam bet on the frame hitting the sidewalk between nine and five. I bet on it staying up. At the end of the day, I checked in with Sam. He said, "still hanging in," and I pulled the two fivers out from under the stapler. From time to time we renewed our bet.

Although I saw Sam almost every day on my way to the parking lot and often stopped to chat, he remained an enigma. Rumour had it that he went scavenging at night, entered abandoned buildings, made off with copper pipes and brass door plates, and sold them for scrap. Other stories circulated about him. He had accessed a porn site on one of the library computers and charged the Clarkson for the viewing time. A CD collection disappeared from a colleague's office—Sam had stolen it, according to the lunchtime gossip, but there was no solid evidence linking him to the CDs or the porn site. The day I heard about the theft, though, I reconsidered the meaning of the artistic corner I'd seen in Sam's mind. It's not unusual for thieves to have a creative side. I would have liked to take a closer look, but Sam's brain was like a fortress. I was surprised. Nothing like this had ever happened to me before. I couldn't breach his defences. I couldn't get a clear reading of his thoughts. When we met to inspect the hanging window frame, his brain was gauzy, veiled with sexual desire. He never harassed me. He kept his excitement to himself while we were standing side by side at the wash basin, looking across the wall of the Clarkson at the wooden frame creaking in the wind. Once or twice I came close to taking the initiative and making a move on Sam, but the venue wasn't right. The state of Sam's bathroom put me off—the yellowed rim of the toilet, the crud in the wash basin, the pearls of oily deposit on the shower enclosure. Sam's sheddings were everywhere. They cancelled the effect of the after-shave lotion lingering about him in the morning, a scent that normally gets me going.

One morning Sam tagged along to the front door, pointed his chin at the library building and said: "So what're you doing in there all day?"

"Working on an eighteenth-century whodunit," I said.

"You interested in crime?"

"It's relevant to my area of specialization: the social history of London in the eighteenth century," I said. "That's why the Clarkson hired me."

He looked at me belligerently. "They pay you to read a crime story?"

"It's work," I said, "but you are right. I get paid for what I enjoy doing, reading about Old London. The more detailed the descriptions, the better. It's like time travel, you know? It kind of transports you back to the eighteenth century."

There was an amazing explosion in Sam's head when I said that, a red-hot warning flare shot out, raining down rocks and ashes.

"Is that so?" he said and lowered his eyes, trying to stem the flow of lava. I couldn't make sense of his reaction. "You want to go back to the old times?"

"In a way, but it's also part of the research I'm doing for my thesis," I said. I expected him to ask what my thesis was about, but he only said "Oh, yeah?" and turned his back on me, retracting all his thoughts into the dense black outline of his head. I couldn't decipher his thoughts at all. I had never come up against such recalcitrance before, never met anyone as capable of holding his secrets.

"Well, have fun with your book," he said. "I wouldn't mind checking it out one day, but I guess they don't lend books to people like me."

"They don't lend that particular item to anyone," I said. "It's a manuscript, and it's brittle. They don't want too many people handling it. That's one of the reasons why we are preparing a modern edition. When it comes out, I'll give you a personal copy."

"Personal—what's that supposed to mean?"

"With a dedication," I said, air-writing the words: "To Sam, my friend and fellow gambler."

"Uh-huh," he said, and closed the office door on me.

Not all of our morning conversations were as tense. Most of the time we just laid our bets. He grunted "Okay." I said, "See you later," went to my office and buckled down to my task, which didn't involve the manuscript—not yet. I was supposed to proofread it once Patricia had done the transcription, but she was taking her time. Meanwhile she gave me joe-jobs, pointless tasks like checking the stacks for misplaced books, compiling bibliographies, entering data on a spreadsheet, that sort of thing.

IT'S NINE o'clock Western Pacific time. Midnight in New York, and I'm jetlagged.

I undress and get into the shower. The stream of water washing over my face, pearling over my shoulders and down my back, cannot rinse off the memories of the past.

I towel off, get into the thick terrycloth bathrobe provided by the villa, and sit down on the bed. The mattress is so thick I feel I'm climbing an altar and offering my body to the god of narcolepsy. Take me now! Half a dozen pillows are piled on the bed. They come in variants, from plump and down-filled to flat and allergen-free. I pat and grope them and choose a medium-soft filled with down. I close my eyes, but in spite of being tired, I can't sleep, no matter which way I cradle my pillow or arrange my legs.

My thoughts wander back to the Clarkson, to the day I started my job as an intern when Patricia Baron gave me an introductory tour of the library and showed me Percy Stockdale's *Sixteen Sermons*.

"It's one of our treasured possessions," she said fervently. "There are only four copies extant. One is here at the Clarkson, another is in the British Library, number three is at the Folger, and number four at Hamilton House in Scotland. But our copy is of special interest. It may have belonged to Adele Collingwood."

Her words ran through my brain like wildfire. Yes, I remembered Stockdale giving Adele a copy of his sermons, and here it was. Her fingers touched those pages! I thought as I looked at the book Patricia had placed in front of me.

"What's the evidence for her ownership?" I asked. My voice sounded scorched.

"The manuscript of her memoir was tucked into the back of this book. It took me eight months and an incredible amount of research to verify that it was her handwriting."

So that's how Adele's manuscript was preserved—folded into the back of Stockdale's book, I thought. The idea of a return journey was planted in my mind at that moment, twelve years ago. It was a tiny seed, but it grew rapidly in the fertile soil of my imagination. I stopped listening to Patricia. The thought of the secrets that might be spelled out in the pages of Adele's manuscript took my breath away. When Patricia's voice faded in again, she was talking about the research she had done to identify the author of the manuscript.

"I knew that Adele Collingwood had published a number of essays under a male pseudonym," she said.

"Adam Leddy," I said, blurting out Adele's pen name. The idea that a book touched by Adele was right here in front of me had blindsided me. I wanted to bite my tongue. How could I explain my knowledge of Adele's pen name to Patricia? I was a graduate student, an intern, an apprentice historian. Only a specialist would know that bit of information. But I got off the hook.

Patricia gave me a pleased smile. "I see you've read my article," she said. "I started off on the wrong track at first. I speculated that the manuscript had been written by Percy Stockdale, the author of the sermon book. I jumped to the conclusion that the pages tucked into the back of the book were his work as well. But I eliminated that possibility after looking at samples of his handwriting. His writing is robust and well-spaced. The writing in the manuscript is small and cramped, the hand of a woman jarred by strong emotions. From my research into Percy Stockdale's life, I knew that he was Adele Collingwood's guardian. That led me to consider the possibility of her being the author of the manuscript. It was no more than a hunch at first. Then came the break-through. The owners of Hamilton House provided me with copies of her correspondence, and that clinched it. Her handwriting is quite distinct, and it matches the writing in the manuscript."

"The argument for her authorship is totally convincing." I said to Patricia, pretending that her article was the sole source of my knowledge about Adele.

Self-congratulatory thoughts rose from Patricia's head like streamers and blew triumphantly in the current of the air-conditioning.

"Thanks," she said and went on to talk about her work on the manuscript while I drifted off and thought of the years I had spent confined to Adele's body, looking through her eyes silently, unable to speak my own words or make my own moves. It was my first transmigration, and I was too inexperienced to take full control, or perhaps Adele was too strong for me. We had to suffer each other. Most of the time she had her will. A few times I got the better of her. It was a never-ending struggle. I wanted her to go in search of Jack. The memory of my first life was ebbing or melting into Adele's consciousness. Only my passion for Jack remained pure and undiluted, but Adele resisted me stubbornly.

My thoughts returned to the present. "I've made a start on transcribing the text," Patricia was saying. "Actually, I'd like to include a facsimile of the text in the edition, either facing the printed pages or as a companion volume, but reproducing them on quality paper is a costly proposition, and I'll have to raise more funds before I can go ahead with that plan."

"A facsimile edition would be great," I said mechanically, but all I could think of was getting my hands on the manuscript. I had a notion that touching it would somehow transport me back in time and land me in Old London. If I could put my hand on the pages, Adele's DNA might enter through my fingertips and allow me to be one with her again.

"I still have a lot of questions about the manuscript," Patricia said. She was still on the same topic, and I wondered if there was anything in her head beside books and manuscripts. She had professional ambitions, I could see. They surrounded her, a gaseous aura spouting tiny flames. They gave her a spinsterish glow. She hasn't had a man in a long time, I thought.

"I would like to get a better handle on the genre," she was saying. "It's hard to pin down what kind of book it is. A diary or creative fiction? An unfinished novel or a fantasy? I'm inclined to call it an autobiography with fantastic touches. "

Yes, Adele's life would seem fantastic to people who knew nothing about transmigration.

"But you'll have a chance to form your own opinion," Patricia said. "Once I'm through with transcribing the text, I want you to check it against the original."

Yes, yes! I was eager for that moment, but judging by the proprietary air Patricia projected whenever she spoke of the manuscript, she had a hard time letting go and sharing it.

"I'm looking forward to checking the text," I said.

"Consider it a palaeographical exercise," she said. "Deciphering Adele Collingwood's handwriting is hard work."

Adele's crabbed handwriting was a challenge, I knew. We corresponded for a while after I left her body and moved on. I got used to her scrawl eventually.

Patricia finally reached the end of her speech—it sounded like a speech, a set piece, a lecture she had given a few times. I could see that she was one of those people who had difficulties departing from a prepared text. Her aura was devoid of impulses, not a whiff of spontaneity.

"All right," she said, moving on to the next point on her agenda. "Let's go and have a look at the manuscript."

My skin tingled with anticipation. I felt the lure of the past. It was like visiting an old friend after years of separation, and now that I had tracked Adele down, I meant to visit her often, as often as it took to re-enter her sphere and become one with her. I didn't expect it to be easy to join Adele or to succeed on first try, but a plan was forming in my head. I wondered how difficult it was to get into the Rare Book vault and at the manuscript.

Patricia took me through the stacks, past rows of works on the literature and cultural history of eighteenth-century England, which was a specialty of the library. That could be the first hurdle. We hadn't met anyone in that part of the library. No one was browsing the shelves, and I suspected that the area was off limits to readers.

An elevator at the back took us downstairs to the shelves containing the political and military history and to the Rare Book vault.

Here was the second hurdle: a keypad mounted beside the door. Discreetly shielding the pad with her body, Patricia punched in a combination of numbers. The door didn't budge. The light on the keypad blinked red.

Patricia was flustered. "I must have gotten the numbers wrong," she said. "It's a new system. They installed it two days ago."

She moved back to the keypad and tried again. "I'd better concentrate on what I'm doing here," she said. "You have three chances to get it right. After that, the mechanism freezes, and you have to call Security to reset the system. That would be a little embarrassing."

Patricia's aura had been of no help to me during her first attempt. She had used tactile memory which leaves no visible traces. But now she was putting her mind to work, and the combination hovered in the air, forming an arc around her head: # 13796 ENTER. The light on the pad went green, and the door buzzed open. I made a mental note of the combination. One obstacle removed!

Patricia waved me through into a high-ceilinged room with bookcases on three sides and a narrow metal staircase going up to a catwalk. In the middle of the room was a table that could have come from the refectory of a Franciscan mission. In fact, the whole room had the sacral air of parchment and old leather. It took you back centuries and made you forget that you were in Los Angeles. The temperature in the room was glacial, a perfect fit for Patricia's mind. Her aura had turned a deep blue. A reverential mist formed in the upper regions of her brain, like arctic incense.

"I'll get the manuscript," she said, and climbed up the stairs to the catwalk. I watched her, counting the steps she took and the shelves she passed. She stopped at the third bookcase on the left and picked out a baize-covered box. She brought it downstairs and placed it on the oak table. Half a dozen chairs were arranged around the table. In front of each chair was a foam pad set out like a place mat, as if dinner was about to be served on especially fragile plates that needed cushioning. The centre piece was a basket blooming with white cotton gloves.

I sat down expectantly. Patricia undid the Velcro fasteners on the box, took a pair of cotton gloves from the basket, and with her hands sheathed to protect the manuscript from oily secretions, lifted out a bundle of papers. They were folded over, as if Adele had intended to put her memoir into an envelope and mail it to posterity.

Patricia unfolded the top sheet and placed it on the foam pad in front of me. I reached for a pair of gloves, but she held up her hand, stalling my motion in mid-air.

"I'd prefer if you didn't touch the paper," she said, and I wondered whether Patricia herself would turn out the greatest hurdle to jump. I was dealing with a zealot. Books were her religion. "It's very fragile," she said. "I am reluctant even to unfold the sheets. They are brittle, as you can see. And I'm afraid to expose them to the overhead light for any length of time."

I think she was afraid also of the light in my eyes. She granted me only a peek at Adele's handwriting and pointed out a few characteristics. I rapidly scanned the words on the page before me, looking for my name, and there it was, half a dozen lines from the top: *Lynne, a dead woman walking.*

I felt something coming to life within me and pulsing rapidly, but the sight of Adele's handwriting was not enough to lift me out of the present. The page remained black and white, the letters stuck to their two dimensions, and I stayed on the outside looking into Adele's world as if it was on display in a shop window.

Patricia gave me no more than a minute to look at the manuscript before she replaced it in the box. I badly wanted to feel the dried ink on the page. My unauthorized fingertips itched with longing for the life-giving touch of the manuscript. I had pushed back the sleeves of my sweater in anticipation, in the hope of resting my arm furtively on the edge of the paper Adele's hand had touched, but when I looked up into Patricia's uncompromising eyes and felt the cold draft of the icy aura surrounding her head, I knew I was up against powerful odds. I pulled down my sleeves, dejected. I had to wait for a more propitious moment, when I could lay my hands on the manuscript unobserved and find out whether touching it would do the trick and transport me to Adele's world.

"I've had a microfilm made," Patricia said. "You can work with that when you check my transcription." I knew it! She would never allow me to touch the manuscript. It was a holy object to her, an icon. "In fact, that's what I am using myself," she said. "I don't want to touch the manuscript unless absolutely necessary. The images on the microfilm are very clear, you'll find—I don't anticipate any need for you to go back to the original."

Her words left me helpless for the moment, but my desire to commune with Adele had taken root. What had begun as a sentimental wish to pay her a visit turned into a determination to make my way back to the book vault, to read the manuscript on my own terms and renew the bond I had with Adele. I would find a way to resume life with her.

On the way out of the Rare Book vault, Patricia punched the CLEAR button. Knowing the combination and the procedure to unlock the door was a first step toward realizing my desire for a private visit with Adele, but the rest was problematic. To reach the elevator leading to the vault, I had to cross the stacks.

As we walked back, I said to Patricia:

"Are the stacks public-access, or will I need a pass?"

"You'll have to apply for a pass," she said. "Talk to Doris Langer, the head librarian. But I don't know if she'll go for it. She's rather strict about stack privileges."

"She doesn't trust interns?"

"It's not about trust," Patricia said. "It's about statistics. Numbers matter when you apply for grant money. That's why Doris insists on a paper trail—to document library use. She doesn't want people wandering about in the stacks, casually consulting books. She wants readers to fill out a request form so that we can record every single time a book is taken off the shelf, even if a reader just wants to look at the title or the Table of Contents. The other consideration is re-shelving. If you allow too many people into the stacks, helping themselves to books and putting them back again, they are bound to end up in the wrong slot. It's better to let the librarian on duty take care of it."

Doris Langer rejected my application for a stack pass. She was apologetic.

"It's nothing personal, Lynne," she said. "It's our policy." She repeated the explanation Patricia had given me.

That complicated matters. If I couldn't get into the stacks, I couldn't get to the elevator leading to the vault, or to the keypad unlocking the Rare Book room. The path to the pages infused with the elixir of life, with the attar of Adele's DNA, remained an obstacle course. I was up against complications, but that only made me more impatient to touch the manuscript and more determined to find a way to do it. I dreamed of the moment when my fingers would finally trace Adele's writing. I wanted the ink to rub off and dye my fingertips. I wanted to tear off the corner of a page and chew it, digest the past and make it part of my endocrine system. That's how obsessed I was with making bodily contact with the manuscript, with Adele, and through her, with Jack.

I plotted for weeks, thinking of ways to get into the restricted area. My first plan was to steal or forge an access card, but as it turned out, there was no card involved. The stacks were separated from the public reading area only by a counter running the width of the room. Access was through a turnstile and controlled by the librarian on duty. If your name was on "the list," you walked through and picked what you wanted off the shelves on the main floor or on the floor below, where the entrance to the vault was located. The list of people authorized to enter the stacks and serve themselves was short: Sidney Tate, the director of the library. Doris Langer, the supervisor. The two librarians on desk duty. Patricia Baron, the head of research—five people in all. You couldn't bluff your way in.

I came up with an alternative plan: a sleep-over at the library. I would stay in my office after-hours, wait for the cleaners to leave, and make my move when there was no one around to keep me from passing the turnstile and entering the stacks. I knew the combination that would get me into the Rare Book room, and once there, I had a choice: spend the night with Adele and Jack— surely his name appeared on those pages—or go one step further, take away a page of the manuscript and hold on to it forever. Take away a page, I decided, being in a grandiose mood. Although the nostalgic longing I felt then was nothing compared to the malaise I'm suffering now, it did have a besetting quality. The glimpse I had of Adele's handwriting when Patricia showed me her memoirs was enough. The ghost of the past rising into the chill air of the Rare Book room had drawn me on and set me on the homeward journey.

After thinking the details through once more, I carried out my plan. First: I couldn't have my car sitting in the parking lot after hours. That would be a giveaway. So on D-day I arrived at the Clarkson by cab.

"My car's in the garage," I explained to Sam who stood at the door of the caretaker's lodge and saw me getting out of the cab. "Something's wrong with the locking mechanism."

In the reading room, I went through the usual routine for staff members. I walked up to the counter and placed a check mark beside my name on the attendance sheet kept by the librarian on duty. The problem was how to sign out, when I had no intention of leaving the building at night, but I had thought of a solution. Dave and Silvia, the two librarians, worked the counter in shifts. They changed guard at noon. I signed out at 11:30, telling Dave who was on duty that I had a dentist appointment. At 1:00, I returned with the lunch crowd. By then Silvia was on duty. She glanced up briefly from the computer screen and let me pass. She assumed I had been eating lunch outside, at one of the picnic tables in back of the building, or gone for a smoke. No one signed in and out for smoke breaks. I had counted on slipping through that loophole. At the end of the day, there were two check marks against my name, in and out.

I had taken the first hurdle in a stride. Everything was on track—I anticipated no more problems until next morning when I would have to find a way to sign in without betraying the fact that I had spent the night at the library. I thought that part wouldn't be too difficult. I'd emerge from my office mid-morning when there was a fair amount of traffic, saunter to the librarian's desk and place a check mark against my name on the attendance sheet. David would be on morning duty. If he asked questions, I would give him a bland smile, the sort that dissolves the investigative spirit, and say I'd forgotten to sign in on arrival. It was a little iffy, but I thought I could pull it off. I tried to convince myself that I had no reason to worry. Signing the attendance sheet wasn't monitored that closely, I hoped. Someone in personnel presumably checked the pages and transposed the data to a spreadsheet, but only because administrators liked to gather information and analyze patterns. They took no existential interest in the check marks. They didn't care about specific persons, about Lynne Addington, for example, being or not being in such and such a place. They only did the numbers: ninety-two percent of the staff was present eighty-nine percent of the time, with an error margin of nineteen out of twenty. Something like that.

Nevertheless my nerves tingled on the day of the planned sleep-over. I made small talk. I tried to look unconcerned. Anxiety began to distort reality. The conversations around me registered as mocking noises. People seemed to give me suspicious looks. My reading of their thoughts was muddled. "Manuscript" and "library" shimmered on their brains in sinister hues. I fought off premonitions of failure. But everything went according to plan, and by the end of the day I knew I had won: I'd signed in, I'd signed out. The staff had gone home, and I was hiding in my office. Drum rolls went off in my head. Well done, Lynne. Congratulations.

My office, like the rest of the working spaces in the library, was on the lower level of the Clarkson, off a narrow corridor painted a glossy washroom white. It suggested a joyless existence and a life of toil. There may have been a rationale behind putting the stacks and the offices underground. The architect probably thought of the weight of the books, or the need to keep old prints and illuminated manuscripts out of the glare of daylight. Maybe he also thought the lower level provided an atmosphere conducive to study—a vault of silence, a safe house for ideas. I don't know who chose the space, but the burrow where I spent my working hours didn't compare with the airy rooms on the upper floors of the Clarkson, which were furnished with period pieces and precious art, but used only for official functions.

My office was windowless, the furniture oppressive: a hulking desk, a bookcase empty except for *Webster's Dictionary* and a copy of *The Chicago Manual of Style*, leftovers from the pre-Google world, two metal filing cabinets stacked one on top of the other, as if they had been warehoused, and a locker—the type lining high school corridors. I had brought some of my own books and added them to the two on the shelf. I hung a print of Vauxhall Gardens above my desk, but the illuminated galleries and arcades and triumphal arches of the old amusement park couldn't disguise the dreariness of the room.

At five, I locked my office door from the inside. For a while, I sat at my desk, fiddling with a stack of learned periodicals, looking through an article here and there without seeing the words. The inside pressure in my head was building. Then, when I heard the cleaning crew come into the building, I hid in my locker. I squeezed in, fitting my body into the boxy space, twisting my neck, pressing my arms against my sides. Encased in metal, immobilized, I listened to the cleaners' voices, the squeak of running shoes on linoleum, a boom of laughter, the muffled noise of the floor polisher coming closer and receding again, the scraping of chairs, doors opening and closing. Someone came into my office, ran a vacuum over the wall-to-wall carpet, bumped against the locker where I was hiding, moved around the room, dusting perhaps, and left, turning the key in the lock. The whole cleaning operation took a couple of hours. Then the movements ceased, the voices receded, and there was silence.

I got out of the locker, breathed deeply to replenish the oxygen which had thinned in the confined space, wiggled my shoulders to get rid of the shooting pains in my neck, opened the office door, and stepped out into the corridor. The road was clear. I was on my way to the stacks when I heard a faint noise and realized that I had moved too soon. I wasn't alone after all. I instantly retraced my steps and was about to dive back into my office, when Sam turned the corner, and I was caught in the searchlight of his eyes. Blinded. Rooted to the spot. Maybe even crouching a little, to get out of the glare.

I hadn't prepared for this, for Sam making the rounds, or whatever he was doing. The machinery in my brain did clunky turns. I managed to churn out a sentence.

"I got locked in," I said. Did he accept my explanation? I thought I could make out some wavering lines of disbelief, but I wasn't sure. Damn it. I couldn't get a reading on the man.

"You are never locked in," he said. His voice sounded loud, maybe because he was so close to me. The corridor was narrow, and we were practically standing toe to toe. "The exit doors open from the inside. That's building code. In case of fire."

"I know that," I said. "But I didn't want to trigger an alarm. I was just about to phone and ask you to let me out."

"What were you doing here so late?" he asked.

"Catching up on work. I thought I'd leave with the cleaners, but

I went to the washroom, and when I came back, they'd left and locked the building."

He rucked up his brows. "Are you a natural liar, or do you practice a lot?"

"Why would I be lying to you?"

"I don't know. But you are."

I wanted to sneer. I wanted to be ironical and say: You think you can read my mind? But the words piled up in my brain. Something blocked the exit route, tightened my throat, and incapacitated my voice. I was in Sam's power. Not because he had caught me in the act—I had done nothing wrong, I hadn't gotten that far. I was trapped in his fiery aura. The flames were engulfing me. My skin felt scorched.

"Let's go then," he said.

"I need a cab."

"I'll get you a cab."

He took my arm and marched me down the corridor like a prisoner. Sam's touch was full of intimations, and at last I understood what was blocking my throat: desire. It radiated from Sam's body and was absorbed by mine. We were breathing the same air, mixing up our breaths, causing a storm, redoubling our mutual desire. It was unquenchable.

Sam disarmed the back door, and we stepped outside. He reset the alarm behind us. As we walked to the Lodge, his hand cupped my elbow, crowding me, making me walk with uncharacteristic little steps in a thrust and drag motion, dance steps to the pounding rhythm of my heart. If I go as far as the Lodge with him, I thought, I'm lost. I won't know how to fend him off or even if I want to fend him off. I don't know why I thought that, but the night struck me as apocalyptic, the end of something, the beginning of something else.

We rounded the corner of the library building. When we emerged from the shadow of the hedges lining the path, I saw a pickup truck parked in front of the Lodge.

Sam released my arm.

"Couple of friends dropped in," he said. "Or else—"

He stopped and looked at me. Or else what? Or else we might have become lovers?

"—I would have taken you home myself."

"That's okay," I said. "Just call me a cab."

I don't know how I made it to the Lodge. My thoughts were unsorted. Sam went in to make the call, leaving the door ajar. I stayed out on the steps and listened to TV noises, a football game, rapid-fire voiceover, cheering crowds. Someone was pounding the table. I heard a man's laugh and a woman's voice asking, "Where're you going?"

When Sam came out, his aura had gone pale, but the memory of our desire was still warm in my body and gave me a faint ache in the ribcage. He rolled back the gate at the end of the driveway and waited for the cab with me. We stood silently on the sidewalk. He did a kind of balancing act, with the heels of his shoes hanging off the curb. He concentrated on the acrobatics of bouncing on his heels and never once looked my way. I tried to make conversation but he kept a stubborn silence. It was eerie, as if he was planning something—hitting me, hitting on me?—but couldn't make up his mind.

When the cab pulled up, Sam watched me get in. He had his fists buried in his pockets and looked sulky as if I had spoiled it all, or as if he had made an irreversible mistake letting me off lightly like that.

I gave the cabbie my address and settled back, but something made me turn and look at the gate, shut now, keeping us apart, Sam and me, and I knew that he hadn't let me off, that the danger wasn't past. Something large, something of cyclonic proportions, was afoot. I was spooked by my own thoughts. It was not in the nature of transmigrants to have such intense feelings.

I DIDN'T risk another attempt to get into the book vault. I thought I'd wait and see, come up with a better plan perhaps. Occasionally Patricia talked to me about the contents of Adele's memoirs and mentioned what she considered interesting events in her life, but nothing she said was new to me. I was familiar with all the details, and the bits Patricia considered fantastic were entirely real to me. She carried on with the transcription of the manuscript until Cole appeared on the scene and disrupted her work ethics.

Cole Stevens, a Canadian from Alberta, came for the summer to do research on Jacobean furniture. He showed up at the library every morning, trying to charm the staff with his look of helplessness. His brown eyes were slightly out of alignment, one higher than the other. They begged for affection, begged you to take him by the hand and do everything you could for him. He had an annoying mannerism, a little awkward shamble when he came up to you to talk. "Help!"—that old Beatle song was Cole's mantra. The shamble and the trusting eyes and the fresh and innocent smile he put on, as if he had just flipped snow off his cap, they were all part of a larger act. He was playing the Northern ingénue. Or so I thought at first. Later I realized that the shamble had a counterpart in Cole's brain, a wilderness of words conceived and aborted, ideas half-constructed and dismantled again, thoughts suppressed, snowed under by inhibition, but still alive and struggling to get out. The survivors circled the periphery of Cole's brow, now-you-see-them, now-you-don't. They twinkled and flashed to the tune of "Help!" How did the lyrics of that song go again? Something about "appreciate you being around." Well, maybe I'm being unfair in my assessment of Cole because he didn't sufficiently appreciate my being around, back then.

We met twice a day in the neon-lit staff room, furnished with odd tables and chairs, two lumpy couches and end tables strewn with old copies of the *Clarkson Monthly Review*. We all gathered there at noon, bringing along brown-bagged lunches. At three, we came together again like sheep to the fold, and drank coffee or tea from Styrofoam cups. We held on to our cups and mimed an earnest interest in each other's research and family crises. The fug of pretense was worse than cigar smoke. The dominant shade of thought was oatmeal, the colour of boredom.

The scholars who consulted the holdings of the Clarkson joined us in the afternoon ritual. Everything was drearily predictable, including the movements of the visitors. They arrived in the morning, came into the Reading Room with their laptops, sat down, placed their book or manuscript on the foam pads provided, pushed their glasses up to the top of their heads, and peered myopically at the text in front of them. They turned the pages gingerly under the watchful eye of the presiding librarian, made their notes in pencil as required, and left again in the afternoon. There was a procession of bloodless professors and scraggy graduate students, all going through the steps of the ballet dictated by the protocol of the library. The thoughts emanating from their heads were invariably of the thin kind, polite wispy cirrus clouds of history and spidery webs of literary criticism that got swept up by the purifying current of the air-conditioning and dispersed, leaving no trace. Cole was the exception. His Beatles mantra took up permanent residence in the room, hunkered down with him at the desk, followed him to the lunch room, highlighted his head and shoulders, drawing a thick outline around them. It gave him weight and made him look purposeful as long as he kept his shamble under control. It's possible that the snow in Cole's mind was confined to the academic sphere, that his tendency to get stuck in thought and fall silent covered only the subject of Jacobean decor, that he was perfectly capable of making pronouncements on more practical things, the agenda of a department meeting, for example, or the items in a committee report or the draft of a vision statement. I assume there were patches of solid ground and fluency of speech in his brain. His successful career in administration—he's a dean now—points in that direction at any rate.

Patricia liked Cole. I could see that at a glance. She was easy to read for me. If she wasn't in combat mode, those thoughts of hers appeared on the periphery of her head neatly printed, reflecting a life-long habit of orderliness, of compartmentalizing her inner space. I noticed that she kept her distance from me. It looked like professional reserve, but it was aversion. She had developed a dislike for me. Although she hid her feelings under a well-modulated voice, they were perfectly visible to me. The writing was on her cranial wall. It seeped to the surface and rode the length of her blonde hair, escaping like steam from a boiling kettle. I was definitely rubbing Patricia the wrong way, and when Cole came shambling up to me in the lunchroom and introduced himself, I saw the reason for her dislike. Her thoughts flared up and flashed me a message in megapixels: *Keep off my man.* Patricia's jealousy was coming at me so thick and fast that the room seemed suddenly short of oxygen. Her overwhelming urge to edge me out and push me to the wall caught me by surprise. I don't know why she fought me so hard. She was older than me, in her thirties, but she was also better looking. A bit too full-figured, maybe, but not unpleasantly so. Her heart-shaped face, her soulful gray eyes and rosebud mouth would have inspired Gainsborough or any other painter of aristocratic women. It did inspire Cole Stevens. That was clear to me even if it wasn't to Patricia. He gave me a few wayward thoughts, a few maybes, ifs, and wouldn't it be fun all rolled into a ball, but he quickly allowed those ideas to sink to the bottom of his mental heap of snow. No, Patricia need not have worried. I was no competition for her. I'm the bony type. I love trashy food—potato chips, buttered popcorn, bacon and eggs—but the fat doesn't take hold. My arms and legs remain stringy, my face always looks peckish. That's not to say that men ignore me. Waifs and strays appeal to them. It makes them feel superior. Or maybe they respond to my desire. They feel the licking tongues of fire and grow hot. Not Cole. The igloo walls of his brain insulated him from my body heat. I could tell I didn't stand a chance, and I accepted that. Cole wasn't my type, or at least not my first choice. I much preferred Sam, and I had no intention of antagonizing Patricia. I kept my eyes and thoughts to myself or rather on Patricia's introduction to the edition of *A Cautionary Tale*, which she had finally relinquished to me for proofreading. She was still working on the text and tweaking the footnotes.

All through July and August I watched the Cole/Patricia liaison evolve. You didn't need to be a mind reader. It was there for all to see. Cole bunked with a friend in Culver City and pedalled to the library on a trail bike, another prop to support his rugged Northern image. After a few weeks, he left the bike at home and took up Patricia's offer to give him a ride back and forth. That was the start of their synchronization. The two of them emerged from the car in the morning and walked to the library entrance in lockstep. At noon their eyes met discreetly across the Reading Room. They went to the door in a coordinated movement. Their steps merged in the corridor, with Cole moving ahead energetically as they approached the lunchroom. He held the door for Patricia and waved her through gallantly. Inside, they targeted two side-by-side chairs and proceeded to the harmonious unwrapping of their lunches, and so on throughout the day, until they ducked back into Patricia's car, leaving me to theorize about their parallel after-work moves, culminating perhaps in synchronized orgasms.

This routine continued through the summer to the last Friday in August, the date of the annual Clarkson Lecture. It was an event staff was expected to attend. Chairs were set up in the large drawing room on the main floor, to receive the audience— faculty and students from UCLA and patrons of the library for whom the lecture was the preamble to a gratitude dinner. By the time the distinguished speaker, Arthur Haines, had delivered his lecture and finished answering questions from the audience, it was almost seven.

Patricia who had introduced Haines and after the lecture went up to the podium to thank him, now stepped down and came around to where Cole and I were sitting.

"How's it going?" she said to me. She had been away all day, on hostess duty, giving Haines a tour of L.A. He was still at the lectern, talking to colleagues and former students who had come up to say hello.

"Everything's okay," I said to Patricia. "I've finished proofreading your intro to the edition. I'll give it back to you tomorrow."

Jealousy was burning through Patricia's cortex, as she glanced at Cole sitting next to me. The proximity of our shoulders bothered her a great deal. I got up, but Cole rose as well, reducing the distance between us further, bumping into my shoulder as we filed out into the aisle.

"So far I've only a few queries," I said to Patricia, keeping up the patter. "One is about the format of works frequently cited."

Patricia nodded and was about to answer, but Haines had shaken off the last of his admirers and was ready to head for dinner. So she just said "we'll talk about it tomorrow" and moved off with Haines in tow.

Cole did his little shamble, his conversational overture, and said: "Trish told me about the manuscript she's working on."

Trish? They were on "Trish" terms?

"The Adele Collingwood manuscript you mean? The memoir?"

"That's the one," Cole said. "Fascinating story. A woman who thinks she is possessed by an incubus, an incubus named Lynne." His mouth broadened to a grin.

I grinned back. "Actually, Patricia isn't sure about that name," I said. "The handwriting is tricky. It might be Cynne rather than Lynne. If you had an incubus, wouldn't you want it to have an exotic name?"

"I don't know," Cole said. "I haven't given much thought to incubuses. Or is that *incubi*?"

He followed me out. "Any chance of getting a ride with you?" he said.

"Patricia didn't invite you to the gratitude dinner?"

"She asked me, but I declined. Sitting through the lecture was all I could take. That's enough Haines for one day." A green spike of professional envy flashed from Cole's head, disturbing the tangled nest of his thoughts.

"Okay," I said. "I'll give you a ride. Let's go."

At the gate I stopped to check on my bet. Sam was standing at the door. "You're late," he said and gave Cole a dark look.

"I had to stay for a lecture," I said. "How's the window holding up?"

"It's holding up."

"Good," I said, followed him inside, and pulled the two fivers out from under the stapler.

"You know what?" Sam said, giving me a fixed look. "I'm getting tired of this game. I'll lay you one more bet tomorrow, but let's make it a c-note."

"You want to go out with a bang?" I said.

"Yeah, I'm feeling lucky."

I didn't like the way he looked at me, like a weightlifter about to drop the dumbbells and walk away from the competition. Maybe I'll start a new game with you, I thought.

"Okay," I said. "We'll make it a hundred tomorrow and call it quits."

In the car, I told Cole about my bets with Sam. "He's upped the ante," I said, as we drove past the gate out into the street. "I'd better inspect that window before I place my bet tomorrow. Mind if we stop on the way and check it out?"

Cole gave me an amused look. "I'm in no hurry," he said. I could see a wisp of interest rising and settling down into a circle of flirty thoughts orbiting his head.

I drove down the street and parked at the 7-Eleven. We got out and walked back to the abandoned building. When we reached the overgrown driveway, I saw that the front door was ajar.

"Hey, let's go in," I said on impulse. "The window's on the second floor. We can get a better look at it from inside."

"Are you serious?" Cole said, eyeing the derelict building. "The place looks like a hangout for drug addicts."

I shrugged and headed up the front steps. Something small, curled up at the bottom of Cole's brain, came to life: a willingness to take risks. It was a poor and neglected thing, glowing feebly, but it was enough to make him follow me slowly up the steps.

I pushed open the door. There was a pronounced smell of urine. Dust motes were floating in the air lit up by the setting sun. Rags were piled in one corner of what had been the living room. I stopped and listened. Profound silence.

Cole stood just inside the door, undecided.

"Come on," I said, and he followed me upstairs.

In the hallway, a mattress was leaning against the wall, sagging under its own weight. The loose window was at the end of the corridor. I sidled past the mattress and inspected it.

"Good for another week at least," I said.

Cole stood at the top of the stairs, looking apprehensive, but I was determined to get at the place where his courage was hiding. I wanted to fan that little risk-taking flame, just for the heck of it. "Let's have a look around," I said.

"Nah, let's get out," he said.

I ignored him and pushed at the door nearest me. It led to a small room connecting to another, larger one, and doubling back to a third room—a gallery of rooms circling the second floor. After a moment, I heard Cole's steps trailing after me. His adrenalin had kicked in.

The last room had a few broken-down pieces of furniture pushed up against the wall which was covered with graffiti—mostly encouragements to fuck, graphically illustrated. The word "JOHO," done in large looping letters, appeared over and over again as if someone had practised his signature. Near the ceiling, curiously out of reach, I spotted a man's face drawn in rough strokes. For a moment I thought I recognized the shadowy portrait. It touched off a memory, something way back. No, something recent. The face outlined on the wall reminded me of Sam Kelley. In a flash I imagined an after-dark existence for him, break-and-enter, slashing upholstery, ripping down curtains, breaking bottle necks, ripping hood ornaments from cars. I saw him spray can in hand, marking light poles and newspaper boxes, hopping fences and climbing fire escapes, looking for blank surfaces. All of a sudden I felt a craving for adventures of the criminal kind. I wanted to run with Sam, but my radiant body heat reached only Cole.

He had stepped up to the window.

"Great view," he said sarcastically. The window faced the highway, and Cole was looking down on the I-10 crawling with cars locked bumper to bumper in the homeward bound traffic. The scene was tinted bronze by a fireball of a sun, and I made my move.

Thinking of Sam, I stepped up close to Cole, and with Sam fuelling my body heat, I put my arms around Cole brazenly and ground my thigh into his back. I gave his brain no chance. I spoke directly to his crotch, which kicked up under my hands.

He turned. He didn't fight me. A few words of surprise floated up, but I cut off his breath, crowding my tongue between his lips. He didn't resist. He was willing to play the monkey, but I could tell it would be a disappointment. In the end, it was still Sam I wanted. Maybe Cole had second thoughts, too. We let go of each other at the same time.

"I don't know what came over me," he said. The sentence came out of his mouth perfectly formed. Maybe it was his standard exit line.

"The incubus," I said. "That's what came over you."

"Right," he said and pulled his lips into a sheepish grin. Embarrassment, the colour of lent, radiated from his eyes, spread fog-like and descended. The aura spread to Cole's mouth and ears, but there was no time to indulge in embarrassment because we heard a noise downstairs, someone opening the front door, crossing the room, coming up the stairs.

Cole grabbed my arm and pulled me behind the door. We squeezed up against the wall. Surely whoever was coming up the stairs—a tramp, a druggie, a tagger—had already been alerted to our presence by the creaking floors as we dashed behind the door. Or maybe not. He was making his own noise on the wooden stairs: boot steps accompanied by clicking sounds.

Cole's body was pressed against mine, his cheek was wedged against my ear. My hair was streaking his face. The sound of the steps came closer. Through the gap between the hinges and the back edge of the door I saw him: Jack. There was rage in his eyes. He had a knife in his hand. Even if I hadn't seen him, I could feel his presence like thunder in the air. The knife glinted in his hand. I felt the blade cutting into my skin, my mouth opened to scream, but at the last moment, as my lips formed a howl, I realized my mistake. It wasn't Jack. Of course not. It was Sam walking past the room to the window at the end of the corridor. He didn't carry a knife. He was holding a screwdriver. Gordie was with him. That's the clicking sound I'd heard—the dog's unclipped nails on the floor. Sam walked past the room where Cole and I were hiding. The clicking slowed down and stopped. Gordie's head appeared nosing around the door that shielded Cole and me. His asthmatic breath sounded like an engine, going softly, regularly. He looked up at us, mildly questioning our presence in that confined space. From the corridor, Sam called out sharply "Gordie, come'ere, where the hell are you?" and the dog turned and waddled off to join his master.

What was Sam doing out there in the corridor? Checking the window, as I did? Or were the rumours true? Was he a scavenger? Or was he tampering with the window, improving his odds in tomorrow's bet? I heard metal scraping against wood, the creaking of a window frame. There was a dull thud, followed by a faraway tinkling of glass. Gordie gave a muffled woof. Then the steps resumed. The pair, Sam and the dog, passed our hiding place and descended the stairs. The street noise picked up for a moment as Sam opened the front door and stepped out. Then silence returned.

The sun had sunk below the horizon and was just a glow when Cole and I separated, letting the fear escape from between our bodies like a hot breath. We went out into the corridor. The drooping frame was gone. It had fallen off its hinges. I leaned out the window and looked down on the shattered remains, the bits of glass and wood littering the driveway below.

"I guess Sam didn't want to risk a hundred dollars," I said to Cole who was watching me, impatient to get away.

"Right," he said. "It's better not to take any risks." I wasn't sure, did he mean with me or with bets? It was too dark to see the expression in his eyes. His words were hanging in the air. They had a jittery glow and wouldn't stand still. I could see the humiliation coming. Cole was going to disown me and shake off the scene as if it had never happened, as if his prick had never hardened under my touch. Before he could say another word, I said:

"Don't worry. I won't tell *Trish* about this."

"Right, we won't tell her," he said. That idiotic "right" of his was starting to get on my nerves. The word barely registered in the air. It was no more than a misting over. He was already battening the hatches of his brain against temptation.

I don't know why I'm still angry at Cole. Because he didn't develop a crush on me? Yes, that's what it is. I never cared for Cole, but I can't take failure. I keep scratching the sore spot. I replay the scene now, twelve years later, in bed at the Dream Villa. Instead of nuzzling my pillow and going to sleep, I think of Cole and me hiding behind the door, dreading discovery. What could I have done differently? Nothing.

The morning after the encounter in the abandoned house, I stopped at the Porter's Lodge and said to Sam: "I see the frame's come down overnight."

"Uh-huh," he said. He had his aura under control. He didn't give away a thing.

"So all bets are off?" I said.

"Yeah," he said. "That's it for us." As he said it, I felt a momentary relief, the sense that I had escaped danger, or punishment. I couldn't define it. I looked at Sam for an explanation. The red-hot energy was there, surrounding him, but no blazing eruptions and no fireworks, not even firecracker-size, just a band of blinding light held in place by gravity. Sam was unreadable. The relief I had felt for a moment changed into something like remorse over the move

I'd made on Cole, a feeling that puzzled me then, and for which I still have no explanation.

Remorse presupposes moral considerations, and that's outside my frame of reference. Transmigrants don't feel remorse. Perhaps I'm mistaken, and it was regret, which isn't a feeling so much as the realization that one has made a mistake, left a task incomplete or, on a grander scale, missed an opportunity and left destiny unfulfilled. Perhaps Sam felt it too, that we had missed out on something, but I couldn't decipher him. Over the course of my lives I had met a few people who were hard to read, who somehow managed to camouflage their thoughts. They were people with superior self-control, loners who made it their business to keep others out and had built a firewall around their brains, but I had never experienced a failure of that magnitude before. I was locked out of Sam's thoughts.

I didn't see much of him during the rest of the summer and the fall. He didn't come to the door of the Lodge when I drove through the gate, and I averted my eyes in case he did. He flustered me. He roiled my gut and filled me with sensations I thought were outside the parameters of a transmigrant's body. The whole thing spooked me.

THE PHONE rings. It's James, apologizing in his domestic baritone for disturbing me at this late hour, but FEDEX has delivered the book I asked for, the first volume. Excellent. That will give me something to do—reading the text. It will be a warm-up exercise. It will set the mood and shift the balance of time and place until I get at the real thing, or at least at the facsimile of Adele's manuscript.

A few minutes later, James appears at the door, hands me the padded FEDEX envelope and backs out of the room, no, sidles toward the door without showing me his back. Neat trick. I have to admit he has some good butler moves.

I hold the packet like a birthday gift, fingering it, feeling hard edges through the bubble wrap. Why didn't I order those books long ago? Because I'd moved on. By the time the edition appeared, I was swept away, sucked into a new obsession—the New York stock market. Wall Street drove out all thoughts of the past, recent or long ago. When you play the stock market, you live in the moment. You don't indulge in memories. The desire I had felt at the Clarkson to touch the manuscript of Adele's memoirs, the fixed idea of revisiting her, the risk I ran to get my hands on the original—it all seemed crazy once I moved to New York. It seemed like an aberration of the brain. Why would I want to read Adele's memoirs when I already knew her thoughts and had lived her life with her? Why go back to the old days when I could go forward and have new experiences? And yet, twelve years later, here I am, feeling the same craving for the past that I had when I was an intern at the Clarkson. I'm not sure what triggered the craving this time. The nostalgia started in New York, in Dan Shearer's apartment, when I saw the painting on the wall of his dining room and the inscription: *From NY to LA, from LA to NY.* Can a cryptic line on a painting have this kind of goal-shifting effect?

I open the FEDEX packet.

A CAUTIONARY TALE by ADELE COLLINGWOOD
Edited and annotated by Patricia Baron

I look at the cover image, an engraving of the Tyburn gallows and a throng of onlookers jostling for a view of the condemned man as he mounts the scaffold. The hanging of the criminal has turned into a street party. There's gin-guzzling and brazen lovemaking, babies crying untended, thieves weaving in and out of the crowd, fingering purses. My fingertips start prickling. I want to join the party, or maybe I just want to rescue the man on the scaffold. He is too young to die.

The book is a starting point, a first step on my journey into the past. I feel the need for a ceremonial beginning. I check the contents of the Dream Villa bar, pour myself a Black Russian, and settle on the sofa with the book in my lap. The first sip of vodka hits my throat with pure distilled force and clarifies my vision.

I open the book to Patricia's Introduction. The words are like her speech, trickling across the page, slow and deliberate. Her voice comes back to me, her lecturing hectoring voice rings in my ears.

"For many years the Adele Collingwood Manuscript in the Clarkson remained unidentified and indeed unexamined. It was during a review of the library's holdings that the clutch of papers tucked into the back of *Sixteen Sermons* by Percy Stockdale, the Rector of Hinxworth, came to light...." Yes, yes, I know all that. Fast-forward to the next page.

"The first question confronting the critical reader is the question of genre. My inclination is to categorize the work as a memoir. The text certainly has the characteristics of an autobiography in the sense that..." I'm too impatient to go on with her Introduction. Never mind Patricia's speculations. I know the manuscript is autobiographical, twice over. It's our two life stories squeezed into one manuscript, the way we were squeezed together in real life, Adele and me, her so-called incubus. They say you always remember the first time. This was my first transmigration, a desperate manoeuvre after I lost my life for I don't know what—for being with the wrong man in the wrong place?

I go on to the text, impatient for Adele's own words. They have a strange pull on me, as if Adele invited me to look for clues and discover her subtle presence between the lines. How can that be when I'm dealing with a modern edition, with pages she has never touched? Nostalgia is playing a trick on me. How can there be vibes coming off a text that is the result of optical character recognition? It's a sterile process. And my surroundings, too, are sterile. Nothing to evoke memories of my first life. The straight angles of the furniture, the silence unbroken by words, the deserted beach below—it's a setting that is worlds apart from the noisy, crowded streets of Old London. The conditions aren't favourable, so why am I moved? Longing distorts my mind.

A CAUTIONARY TALE

It is a dreadful thing to be possessed, to be invaded by a spirit woman who commands your body and soul and looks out at the world through your eyes. It happened to me. Pray it will never happen to you.

I am free now, delivered from the tyranny of my incubus, but for a long time my conscience was troubled by the things she made me do. That is why I have drawn up this account of my life, as a warning and a reckoning. What attracted that evil spirit to me? Was it my illness or the medicine I took or the nurse who cared for me? Was it the arrangement of the furniture in my room or the pictures on the wall that beckoned to my ghostly twin? And how do I guard against another assault, for that is my greatest fear: that she will return, seize upon me once again and wreak havoc. The first time she transformed me. The next time she will erase me. It will be death, or worse than death, for no one will notice that I am gone. They will say: "Adele has changed a great deal. I wouldn't have thought it possible. She was always a little contrary, but never quite so brusque, so demanding, so calculating. I liked the old Adele better." That is what they will say when they meet Lynne, a dead woman walking and looking exactly like me.

I was seventeen when Lynne took possession of me, and in the grip of a severe illness brought on by the shock of my father's death. The doctor who attended me could not name my ailment. He could only take my pulse and prescribe ineffective potions. All he saw was a catatonic patient, a silent sufferer lying on the bed, eyes shut, body limp and still. He did not see Death reaching out for me with skeleton hands or the spirit of Lynne wrenching me from his icy grip. True, she rescued me from death, but only to make my body a mule to carry her and my mind a vessel to fill with ideas of her own.

At first I thought I was suffering from nightmares. Lynne's memories rushed into my brain—cloudy scenes of a world peopled with the most abject creatures, beggars and pickpockets, gentlemen of peculiar tastes, easy women and their procurers. In my fevered mind, I saw a young woman standing in the doorway of a tumble-down tenement. She was with a man, a rough character with a shaved head and dressed in a ragged black coat reaching down to his ankles. His left cheek was disfigured by a scar in the shape of the letter J.

He unbuttoned his coat and turned to her.

"Get down," he said.

"That will cost you extra," she said.

He took her by the shoulders and forced her to her knees. "You are Jack's girl, aren't you?"

"What's it to you? Are you going to pay me extra or not?"

"I'll pay you, don't worry."

He fumbled with his breeches and she leaned forward into the folds of his coat.

He started panting.

"I'll pay you all right," he said and grabbed her by the hair. He wrenched back her head. I saw a glint of steel, a rapid movement of his hand, then a gash of crimson blood from her throat.

She struggled up and in her death throes tore at the man's coat. Her nails left a trail of bloody scratches on his naked thigh. With her last breath she called out, "Jack, help me! I don't want to die."

The murderer pushed her to the ground and escaped into the foggy night. For a moment his victim lay motionless. Then I saw her rising up from the blood-soaked ground as if lifted by an invisible force, and suddenly she was at my side, joining me in the battle against Death. I was swallowed up in a storm, gusts of wind beating down on me mercilessly, filling my head with a blinding swirl of, I know not what, dried leaves, grating sand, dust thick like flour. But then the tempest passed, and the doctor, who had given up on me, became hopeful again.

I myself had no understanding of what had happened to me, that I had been invaded by an incubus. I knew I had defeated Death, or rather *we* had defeated death because I sensed a living otherness within me, feeling *her* thoughts and memories mingling with mine in a fever dream. I tried hard to put those dreams and visions out of my mind, but to no avail: they stuck and demanded their rightful place alongside my own familiar thoughts. Shreds of sentences and odd phrases began to ring in my ears, as if a ghostly twin was growing within me and taking up more space every day.

When I told the physician that I had nightmares which pursued me into my waking hours, he comforted me. I need not worry, he said. My situation had been so desperate that he administered a new and experimental concoction of drugs. The dreams were no doubt side-effects that would soon abate.

"Besides, it is natural to experience nightmares at the point of a violent crisis and ultimate resolution of an illness," he said...

He said. Who said? I drop the book. I am drifting into sleep, unquiet memories swirling in my mind as I relive my death. I see my murderer: the man with the shorn head and a scar on his face in the shape of the letter J, the initial Jack carved into his cheek. And now this man takes his revenge, killing me because I am Jack's girl. Jack! I cry. Jack, help me! I don't want to die. But no one hears my cries. Blood spurts, a red smear on the cobblestones. The image turns into a blur, fades to black. Sleep.

ADELE

I WAS FOUR years old when my mother died. My first half-conscious memories are of an undefinable tension between my father and my aunt Martha Collingwood when we visited the Collingwoods in their spacious and well-appointed house in London. It was, my father told me later, on account of my aunt's presumption.

"There was never an air of coming to the aid of a widower trying to raise his daughter as best he could," he said. "No, she believed that a man like me could not be trusted with a child's care, and that she, a childless woman, knew better than a loving father." Aunt Martha's helpfulness was always seasoned with a dose of arrogance, he said. "Her sister had inexplicably and inexcusably fallen in love with me and saddled her with an undesirable brother-in-law. I was a man without standing in society, an inventor, that is to say, no better than a madman. That is what she thought of me, and she never let me forget it."

While my father spoke of Aunt Martha with undisguised bitterness, she always kept a dignified reserve in my presence, but her silence was eloquent. I was a child whose mind was curiously open to the thoughts of others, receptive to the atmosphere in a room, to what remained unspoken. That may have been one reason why the spirit invaded me. My mind was susceptible to the vibrations in the air and to emanations of which other people seemed completely unaware.

My aunt would say only that my father was "impractical," but I knew that was a serious charge. When she spoke the word "impractical," the very air in the room grew dense with the vapours of her resentment. And even if she succeeded in muting her disapproval of my father, the look on her face betrayed her. I knew the signs. The same frown appeared on her forehead, the same tight little grimace when she scolded the maid for idleness. Aunt Martha was a stout woman with a commanding voice who ruled her household like a Russian tsar. Idleness was anathema to her. She herself was never idle. When she sat down on the sofa in the drawing room, she did not rest quietly. She reached over and plumped up the pillows. Next, she contemplated the windows. Did they need cleaning? And the curtains—was it just the angle of the light, or were they getting dingy? When she picked out a book to read, she passed her finger over the bookshelf to check for dust. I can still hear her voice. "Sarah!" she called, and the maid appeared, looking terrified. "Sarah, when was the last time anyone cleaned the bookcase? Do run a duster over the shelves, and while you are at it, straighten out the books. I can't stand it when they are all higgledy-piggledy, one sticking out, the other pushed in." When she stepped out on the porch, the gardener ducked into the tool shed, trying to keep out of her way. But she went after him. "My good man," she shouted, peering into his hideout. "Even a lowly tool shed must be kept in order. I don't like to see cobwebs in the corners or hoes leaning against the wall, where they might fall over and trip a person up." She lorded it over everyone, except her husband. Ian Collingwood was the only man to whose opinion she deferred. The affection she showed him was no conventional display of good marital relations. She was devoted to him. To everyone else she was a hard taskmaster.

My father was unwilling to bend to her will, but in spite of his dislike for her hectoring disguised as good advice, he took me to

London whenever the Collingwoods issued an invitation. They were childless and very fond of me, and he did not wish to deprive me of their goodwill. He made no secret of the fact, however, that it was an ordeal for him to come up from Hanley, where we lived and where he was employed in the Wedgwood ceramics factory.

On such occasions, Martha Collingwood received him in the drawing room of her commodious house and offered him tea and biscuits, which he politely declined. Uncle Ian put in an appearance as well and made desultory conversation for a few minutes. That gauntlet run, my father rose and said to me, "I'll be off then, Adele. Be a good girl and obey your aunt and uncle."

I warily observed the polite exchanges of the adults. I felt comfortable with the Collingwoods, and comfortable also with my father, but not with both parties in the same room, and perhaps that was another opening I gave to the spirit. My soul was divided, split between my father and my aunt, leaving a crevice wide enough for a spirit to enter and make herself at home.

I loved listening to my father's tales, of foreign countries in which he had travelled before he met my mother, of their courtship and their happy life together during the few years fate granted them. His language was strange, his phrases complex and intricate, as if they had escaped a book. Much of what he said went over my head. Sometimes he talked about his work and about his employer, Josiah Wedgwood. He always spoke of him in a tone of veneration. Mr. Wedgwood, he said, was a "seeker" and "wanted to make such machines of men as cannot err."

I wondered what Mr. Wedgwood was seeking and how men could be turned into machines.

"What kind of machines?" I asked.

"Clockworks," he said and told me that Mr. Wedgwood had in his employ some two hundred labourers and a dozen highly skilled foremen, all of whom worked by the bell. The master followed their operations closely and let them know that he took proper notice of punctuality and was willing to reward diligence, while he would dock the pay of those who were careless and committed blunders. He employed a clerk of weight and measure, whose sole job was to weigh out the clay and make sure there was no wastage of material.

"And what do you do at Mr. Wedgwood's factory, father?"

"I find ways of improving the process, of reducing the waves and veins in molten glass, and the blistering in mortars, and I make sure the Jasperware has the right hue of yellow."

When he saw me wide-eyed, he stroked my cheek. "Well, my child, you may not understand every word I say, but you get the gist at any rate."

My life went on in this fashion—quiet days in Hanley, exciting days in London—until my tenth birthday, which was celebrated, as birthdays usually were, at the Collingwoods' house. On that day, my uncle always played the role of a benevolent host to perfection. He patted my head, commented solemnly that I was growing into quite a little lady, and presented me with a gift of money. Material gifts such as toys or frocks or board games were left to the discretion of my aunt and presented by her wrapped up and beribboned in the most intriguing fashion. On my tenth birthday, however, I was informed that my uncle's gift consisted in sending me to Miss Lee's boarding school in Clifton-on-Downs.

"It will cost me fifty guineas a year," Ian Collingwood told me, "and I only say it to teach you the value of things, my dear."

"Oh, but I would much rather stay with father and save you the outlay," I said.

"It is a great privilege to go to Miss Lee's school, you little goose," my aunt said, "and you ought to thank your uncle and show some gratitude."

My father failed to show gratitude as well. Apparently, his wishes had not been sufficiently consulted. It was one of the few occasions on which the veil of courtesy was dropped, and Aunt Martha engaged in open warfare with him.

"Why send her to Miss Lee's school?" my father said.

"I can't imagine why you would ask such a question, Henry," my aunt shot back.

My uncle raised his eyebrows. "I confess I am as baffled as Martha. I thought it was understood, Henry. The subject came up at Adele's last birthday and, if I remember correctly, you did not object."

"It was mentioned in the most casual fashion," my father said, "and I saw no reason to go on about it at the time, but I suppose we must discuss it now. So, if you will be so good and answer my question: Why send Adele to Miss Lee's school?"

"Because she cannot be for ever indulged in childish fancies and never obliged to attend to the things that finish a young girl," my aunt said.

"The things that will make her a coquette, you mean!" my father exclaimed. I saw my aunt frown and wondered what "coquette" meant.

"My dear Henry, you like to be provoking," she said. "Of course, Adele must learn grace and manners, the things that belong to a well-bred young lady. In my day it was enough to learn womanly virtues at home, but today it is thought a great advantage to send one's daughter to a boarding school. Your objections, I must say, are most unexpected."

"I have no principal objection to Adele attending school," my father said slowly, and added after a pause, "and am grateful for your liberality, Ian—" Here he paused again. Expressions of gratitude did not come easy to him.

Aunt Martha nodded a sour acknowledgment. "I dare say Ian has always been very kind to Adele."

"I am grateful for your liberality," my father repeated, "but I strongly disapprove of the school in question, a school that will teach Adele nothing but frippery."

"Frippery? She will learn to deport herself in a manner that will prepossess society in her favour. You call that frippery, sir?"

"I have read the brochure you showed me last year, Madam," said my father with the same icy formality, "and I disapprove of Miss Lee's establishment. It offers to the pupils a smattering of French and a great deal of vanity and mock art. Dancing is de rigueur, but Latin is to be eschewed and thought-provoking literature replaced with pious commonplaces. My daughter, it seems, is to be guarded from the dangers of solid attainment and weighty responsibilities and to pass her days in folly and silly endeavours."

The gap in my heart opened wide, as I looked from my father to my aunt and back again. They were tearing me apart and laying me wide open to evil spirits.

"My dear Henry," Aunt Martha said with dignity. "Surely you would not want Adele to incur the danger of pedantry or exchange the graces of style for the severity and preciseness of a scholar—"

"I would indeed," he exclaimed.

I had shrunk into a corner of the sofa during this exchange and made myself very small, but my aunt took both of my hands and drew me to my feet.

"Child," she said. "You had better go downstairs and ask cook for a piece of that apple pie you like so much."

I did as I was told and was therefore not privy to the exchange that followed, but as my father let slip later, he yielded to my aunt only because it was suggested that he was being selfish and holding me back.

My aunt in turn felt obliged to defend her position to me when she took me to Belvedere House, as Miss Lee's establishment was called.

"Even if what you learn there is trifling," she said, answering in an oblique way my father's arguments, "what you unlearn is by no means inconsiderable."

"What will I unlearn?" I asked.

"Your provincial dialect, for one thing," she said. She was convinced she could hear the Hanley dialect in my pronunciation. "And other tricks you have picked up," she added, "such as slouching, and courtesy-neglecting." My aunt felt that posture was of great importance, and dancing lessons would enhance it, she believed. "In choosing a school," she said, "one must look first and foremost to two points: good housekeeping and a good dancing master. The rest will fall in place soon enough."

By "the rest" she meant presumably the social advantage I might gain from associating with the daughters of good houses. In that point, at any rate, I did not disappoint her, for I soon made friends with Eliza Florsham, and no one, however censorious, could find fault with her sweet nature or her pedigree. The daughter of Mr. Florsham of Grove Hall, Hinxworth, was certainly a desirable friend in Martha Collingwood's eyes, but Eliza's brother, whose acquaintance I made in consequence of this friendship—ah, there was a black mark against his name in my aunt's book.

LIFE AT Belvedere House was a sluggish dream, from which I awoke only when I was asked to spend holiday weekends with Eliza at Grove Hall. It was not her fault that things there did not turn out comme il faut. Eliza was dove-like, of unvarying sweetness, ready to love everyone, smile with them and weep with them. She was a creature born for friendship. I delighted in her company, even if her play was a little too genteel for my taste and her devotion to her pet dog Pug a little too strong. I loved Eliza even if she was too dainty to play tag on the lawn and could not be tempted to do anything that might appear unladylike. No, it was not her fault that things went awry, that her brother Francis had been allowed to grow up without discipline, without correction. When I first met him, he was a naughty boy of fourteen. His character did not present an attractive picture, but are schoolgirls judges of character? No, I saw a lively dark-eyed boy, a natural athlete with supple limbs, a dashing rider. I did not see his truculence or his cruel heart. I was dazzled by Grove Hall, moreover, its sweeping staircase, its galleries, its immaculately groomed lawns. I was enchanted by the terrace, the reflecting pond and the fountain with the marble dolphins. Liveried servants attended us at table, an elegant carriage took us to church on rainy Sundays. And the main drawing room was a marvel of scrolled plasterwork and gilt-edged mirrors.

What if Francis Florsham did not at first do me the honour of noticing my presence? I saw it as a challenge. When he ignored me, I redoubled my efforts to attract his attention, and when he treated me with contempt, I tried to appease him. He, in turn, had no scruples to let me know that I was nothing but a common girl without rank, plebeian in the extreme, and encumbered with an unfashionable uncle and aunt. Of course, a few years later, when Belvedere House had shaped my speech and deportment, when I had blossomed into a young lady and, more significantly, when it appeared that I might inherit the Collingwood fortune, Francis changed his mind. His roving eye now sought me out, and his manner became accommodating, indeed insinuating. I was weak, I confess, meeting his eye without blushing and allowing his hand to rest on mine longer than was proper. Once, in the shrubbery, he snatched my arm and pulled me close and spoke rapidly, of his regard for me, of my lovely form, of I know not what because his touch blocked all thought. I heard nothing more. A thick fog overspread my brain, the blood ran hot through my veins as his arms encircled me. I drooped against him and allowed him to disorder my scarf and run his fingertips down my décolleté and touch the mound of my breasts and would have permitted more if I had not feared that we might be seen from the terrace. Still, I let his lips graze mine and could not help putting my hand against his thighs where his tight breeches sketched out a tempting sight for my eyes. Is this another clue to the puzzle of my life, and was it my hot blood that attracted Lynne? Did the moral flaw in my character which made me susceptible to Francis expose me to the influence of evil spirits as well? Or was this another case of a soul divided, split between good and evil, and Lynne slipping in through the crack in the middle?

There were other illicit encounters with Francis at Grove Hall. He lay in wait for me and took advantage whenever he found me alone.

The north wing of the house had been closed off to reduce the work of the domestics while the master was abroad on business. I had a curious mind, and one day when I saw a door standing ajar, I hesitated only a little before stepping through. The open door seemed like an invitation to look around. I crossed a gallery, where the forebears of the family looked down on me from their ornamental gilded frames. The velvet curtains on the tall windows had been drawn shut, leaving the room in semi-obscurity and giving it a mysterious air. From the gallery I went on to peek into a deserted bedroom and gaze at the empty stone fireplace and the carved mantelpiece above. The furniture was shrouded in dust sheets, the rugs rolled up and pushed against the wall. I walked across the creaking floorboards and lay down on the four-poster bed, its blue damask hangings crowned by a gathering of ostrich feathers. As I was sinking into a delicious dream of courtly love, a voice made me jump:

"Ah, there you are, Adele. How is the excursion going, or should I say, the pilgrimage?"

It was Francis, who had followed, or perhaps preceded me.

"A pilgrimage, I think, since you want me to worship at your shrine," I said pertly, to cover my embarrassment at being caught in a place where I was not supposed to be.

"On the contrary," he said, caressing me with his eyes. "I am ready to make you my goddess."

We were full of classical nonsense then, dignifying our lowly conduct with poetic allegories.

I noticed he held in his hand an ivory statuette, the lithe figure of a dancer on a pedestal of ebony. He set it on the bedside table.

"What a lovely piece," I said.

"And valuable, too. I could get"—he was going to name a sum, but changed his mind—"a great deal of money for it."

"You aren't going to sell it?" I said.

"I might."

"Will your father permit it?"

"I don't need his permission, Adele. I am the heir of Grove Hall, and all this will be mine one day. But my father is a miser, keeping me on a tight leash."

"And so you have decided to help yourself?"

He shrugged. "What else can I do?"

"What if someone sees you taking the piece away?"

"That's where you can help me, Adele. You say you love me, now prove it."

"I don't see how I can help you."

"By hiding the statuette under your skirt. It would be so easy." He plucked at my skirt playfully, and when I slapped his hand away, sneaked his arm around my waist and tried to kiss me.

"Come, Adele, don't be so difficult."

For a while I fended off Francis' advances, as I was in duty bound, but my eyes told him I was not disinclined, and my beating heart, which his hand soon found, encouraged him to renew his efforts until I yielded to his caresses and answered them in kind. In truth, I welcomed them and was thrilled more than alarmed by his indiscretions. He appeared to me a paragon of manhood, handsome and captivating. My errant soul was imperfectly corrected by education, and the thin veneer of good behaviour I had acquired at Belvedere House dissolved under the fire of his eyes.

He pulled me down on the great bed and we wrangled, with him laughing and snatching at my velvet bands, and me shoving him away half-heartedly. When I tried to sit up, he pushed me down roughly and threw himself on top of me. The mattress bounced under our weight, and one of the legs of the bed gave way with a loud crack. I squealed and laughed hysterically—until I heard quick footsteps and saw Eliza standing in the open door, looking at us in confusion.

We got up at once and smoothed our clothes. I began to stammer out excuses, but Eliza put her finger to her lips.

"The housekeeper—" she whispered and stepped into the room. Before she could say more, we heard laboured breathing, and a few seconds later, the rotund figure of Mrs. Colson filled the door frame.

"What was that noise?" she said, catching her breath. "It sounded like wood splintering."

She took in the three of us and the sagging mattress, stepped up to the bed, lifted the coverlet and inspected the broken leg.

"How did that happen?" she said, fixing Francis with suspicious eyes.

"I wish you wouldn't ask so many questions, Colson," he said. "What business of yours is it?"

"It is my business to look after the house, Mr. Francis," she said.

"You can see for yourself what happened," he drawled. "I suppose the three of us shouldn't have sat down on the bed at the same time. The leg gave way. It's a rotten old piece."

I looked at Eliza to see how she was taking Francis' lie—the *three* of us sitting down on the bed together. She bit her lip, but said nothing.

The housekeeper looked around the room and spotted the statuette.

"And what is that doing on the bedside table?" she said. "It doesn't belong there."

"I was going to take it to my room," Francis said. "It's too beautiful to be hidden away where no one can see it."

The housekeeper pursed her lips. "The master wants me to keep this wing closed," she said.

"Then why was the door left open?" Francis said. "Indeed, I was going to look into that. It's gross negligence, Colson, wouldn't you say so? There are some very valuable things here. Anyone could come in and walk away with—this statuette, for example."

The housekeeper blanched and fingered the key ring hanging from her belt, as if to make sure no one had made off with it. "I could swear the door was locked, Mr. Francis," she said in a low voice.

"My father will be surprised to hear that it was left open."

The housekeeper's face crumpled. "You wouldn't get an old servant into trouble, Mr. Francis, would you?"

"Well, Colson," he said haughtily. "If you keep your mouth shut, so will I."

The colour came back into her face. She curtsied. "Thank you, sir. I am much obliged."

He took Eliza's arm, waved to me, and steered us out of the room and down the stairs.

"And I trust you two ladies won't say anything either," he said before sauntering away and leaving us standing at the door of the drawing room.

"I am so sorry," I whispered to Eliza. "I shouldn't have snooped. And then Francis surprised me—"

She pressed my hand and said in her sweet, forgiving voice. "I know, Adele. It wasn't your fault."

But it was my fault, and that moral weakness, I am sure, made it easier for Lynne to invade my mind.

MY RESIDENCE at Belvedere House came to an end abruptly a few days after my sixteenth birthday. I was called into the headmistress' study and there found my aunt looking distressed. On Miss Lee's face, too, could be seen a certain degree of agitation, if her dignified mien could be said to show agitation.

"Your aunt wishes to speak to you, Adele," she said.

"My dear," Aunt Martha said in a voice betraying exasperation, "your father has decided to withdraw you from Belvedere House. I find I cannot dissuade him from his plan, although I am at a loss to see how you can do better elsewhere. We have every reason to be grateful to Miss Lee for the guidance she has given you."

"But why would my father want me to leave?" I asked in some confusion.

"A young lady, who has been educated at Belvedere House, will accept her father's preferences without question," Miss Lee said, and Aunt Martha nodded.

"Yes, my dear, it would not be proper to inquire into the decisions of your elders, but you and I shall take a turn in the garden and have a little talk while your things are being gotten ready."

I saw that matters had been settled, and my opinion was not likely to make any difference. I curtsied to Miss Lee and followed my aunt into the "walled walk," as the path following the periphery of the school property was called.

Once we were out of sight and earshot, Aunt Martha embraced me with more feeling than she had ever shown me before and said, "We are so sorry, my dear, I cannot tell you how sorry. Your father—" She searched for the right words. "Your father does not understand what is wanted in a young woman of fashion and wishes to see you educated after his own peculiar taste."

As it turned out, I had played a pivotal role in his decision by innocently reporting in a letter that I was being instructed in smiling amiably, sitting in a manner that showed off my figure to advantage, and descending the staircase while displaying a due amount of ankle, but no more.

He at once sought an interview with the Collingwoods.

"He brandished your letter," my aunt said, "and protested that you were taught to value appearance over substance, that the school corrupted your mind.—Corrupted? I said. Corrected, you mean. But I could not change your father's mind."

I wished my aunt hadn't told me of their altercation because it deepened the chasm in my soul, forcing me to choose who was right: she or my father. When she saw the tears in my eyes, she sounded a more conciliatory note.

"You will at any rate learn the honest art of housekeeping at your father's house. And if at any time he can spare you, I hope you will come and visit. When you are old enough to go into society, you will of course spend the season with us in London—Your father could not deny you that, as it would be very hard indeed to make you miss out on the attentions of eligible young men."

We talked in this vein, until it was time to bid adieu to my companions and take leave from my teachers and Miss Lee. I made a tolerably composed impression when getting into the carriage with my aunt, but my heart was heavy. The only circumstance that eased my mind was the fact that Eliza Florsham, too, had departed the school a few months earlier on the death of her father and was now living in Hinxworth with her brother, the new master of Grove Hall.

The move back to Hanley was hard on me, I confess. During my stay at Belvedere House I had seen very little of my father and a great deal of the life my wealthy schoolmates enjoyed. My aunt and uncle's house in London could not match the grandeur of their estates, but it was certainly fashionable and spoke of money. Silk hangings, Chippendale cabinets, oriental vases—Aunt Martha spared no expense to impress her visitors. The cottage in Hanley impressed no one. It was small and dowdy. My room was furnished with a narrow bedstead, a plain commode, and a washstand with a mirror in a painted deal frame. A braided carpet covered the plank floor. The rest of the house was similarly furnished, with the bare necessities. In London, there were two maids, a cook and her helper, a valet, a groom, and a gardener—a domestic corps drilled like an army by my aunt. At Hanley, there was one servant, Madge, who was used to being her own commander and paid little attention to my wishes. I am certain that it wasn't my surroundings that drew Lynne to my bedside. The Hanley cottage was too sober, too modest to attract an evil spirit. It must have been something in my flawed mind that drew her on.

I didn't like the house, but I was fond of my father, and his company made life at Hanley bearable. When he took me out of school, he did not mean to end my education. On the contrary, he was bent on providing me with what was to his mind true education. He at once set me to read Plutarch's *Moral Essays* and his *Lives of Noble Greeks and Romans*. He guided me through Hume's *The History of England* in six volumes, brought out his books on the native flora and fauna, and explained Linnaeus' taxonomy. He bade me write summaries and extracts of everything I read, observing the rules set out in Quintilian's *Rhetoric*. In the evening he examined my work, dealt with any difficulties I had encountered in my reading, and taught me the elements of arithmetic. I showed no talent for mathematics and caused him much frustration by my obtuseness, but I succeeded in pleasing him with the compositions I wrote.

"Not bad at all," was his judgment after he read my essay on the topic of Flatterers and Friends. "I see Belvedere House has not completely spoiled your native intelligence and your gift of expression."

I took a certain pleasure in my father's company, but I missed my friend Eliza and, I must admit, the attentions of Francis. My father spurned trivial talk and liked to discourse instead on philosophical themes or on the advances of science. That was all very well, but it did not feed my starving soul, and my greatest joy accordingly was to visit Grove Hall. My father did not object to Eliza's invitations, and the Collingwoods kindly offered to send their carriage to take me to Hinxworth. On occasion, they accompanied me to take the air in the environs of the town. My uncle Ian had developed difficulty breathing, and the fragrant pine woods were said to have a salubrious effect on the heart and lungs.

It was during those visits that Francis Florsham began to importune me in a more urgent fashion. He was now his own master and no longer under the eye of his father, who would not have suffered such dalliance.

The contrast between the splendours of Grove Hall and the plain cottage at Hanley left me with longings, and after the amusing trysts with Francis and the sweet company of Eliza on a weekend, I felt the loneliness of my father's house. Is it any wonder, then, that Francis had little work to overcome my scruples when he appeared one day at Hanley, riding his favourite grey cob? Without obtaining my father's leave beforehand, he invited me to accompany him on an afternoon's stroll in the countryside. It was Madge's half-day off, and she had gone to visit her sister in the neighbouring village. There was no one, then, to deter me from taking my ill-advised pleasure, no one to witness my folly.

"We shall be back in an hour," Francis said. "No one will miss you or be the wiser for it. What a jolly good time we shall have together without Miss Prissy" (he meant his sister) "chaperoning us!"

It was a pleasant summer day, the air soft and genial, made to stir the heart and make lovers sigh. As soon as we reached the open country and came to the first stile, Francis took my hand, pulling me close to him and pressed his lips to my glowing cheeks. We walked to the edge of the wood. He spread his coat beneath a great elm, and before I knew it, we were tumbling on our makeshift bed, and he was taking even greater liberties than those in which I had already indulged him at Grove Hall. His lips were on my neck and on my bosom, his hands were taking heedless pleasure exploring forbidden territory. I allowed my own fingers to trace the contours of his body and found them very pleasing of shape. These follies made time fly, and when I finally returned to the house, heated and out of breath—Francis had discreetly left me at the crossroads and cantered off with a gallant flourishing of his hat—the afternoon had turned to dusk.

Madge had long since returned from her visit with her sister. She took my shawl and eyed me curiously but asked no questions. I was glad that father had not yet returned from work; indeed he was unusually late. We soon discovered the tragic reason for his absence.

Mr. Wedgwood himself came to the house to tell us that there had been an accident at the factory, an explosion that took my father's life.

On hearing his words, I cried out and was faint with remorse. At the very time I had tumbled with my lover and thoughtlessly amused myself, my father had lain dying! The walls seemed to give way around me, and I fell to the ground senseless. It was during my subsequent illness that Lynne slipped into my defenseless body and set up her tyranny.

MY FATHER'S sudden death would have reduced me to utter poverty if my aunt and uncle had not taken me in. The Collingwoods came as soon as they heard of the fatal accident and my illness and took me to their house in London. They engaged the best physician money could obtain to attend on me and were very good to me during the long period of my convalescence. Aunt Martha sat by my bed for hours on end, talking or reading or just holding my hand and stroking my cheek. Ian Collingwood wound up my father's affairs and paid the expenses of his funeral. They treated me like a daughter, and since they had no children of their own, asked me to take the Collingwood name.

I could not do it, not then.

"It feels like betrayal to discard my father's name so soon after his death," I said, "almost as if I wished to consign him to oblivion, when it is my duty to honour his memory forever."

Aunt Martha shook her head. "Romantic twaddle!" I heard her say, but it was the voice in my head—Lynne's voice. She had taken up residence within me by that time and was disparaging my feelings. My aunt merely said:

"No one prevents you from honouring the memory of your father, Adele."

But I was afraid that Lynne would prevent me, that she would make me forget not only my father but even myself. She was crowding out my thoughts and obtruding her own.

"Bear up, my dear!" my aunt said, putting her cool hand on mine. "Take it one day at a time and go forward steadily. You will soon be your old self again."

I nodded and pretended to agree with her. I concealed the anxiety twisting my stomach. It would have been better to seek refuge in my aunt's arms and cry out: "There is no future for me as long as *she* is in me. I can hear her breathing, I can hear her whisper. There is such wreckage in my head, I will never think straight again!"

If I had cried out for help then, at the very beginning of Lynne's tenure, perhaps something could have been done. But I did not confide in my aunt. I could not bring myself to tell her of the spirit within me, and she would not have believed me. She admitted only tangible facts. Of course, she believed in a God enthroned in heaven, but here on earth she wanted the solid proof of her eyes. Everything else was idle imagination. That is why she never liked my father, because he was a dreamer, a man of ideas. And that is why he in turn disliked her.

At first, I merely sensed Lynne's presence within me, but a few months later, after I had settled into my new life with the Collingwoods in London and even conceived a faint hope of returning to my former self, Lynne gave me a taste of her power.

One morning I awoke with a pounding headache. I opened my eyes to find the room spinning and my mind a blur. When I was able to focus again, I saw a young woman sitting in the window seat, a shimmering apparition, there and not there. "She is a figment of my imagination," I thought. Or a ghost. She was clothed in my dressing gown and, as the loosely draped front revealed, stark naked underneath. She was about my height and build, with a head of tangled strawberry blonde hair and a face marred by freckles. Her hands were red and chafed and her fingernails cracked and broken.

She lounged in the most unbecoming manner, showing a good bit of thigh and a dark patch I dared not name even to myself.

"Who are you?" I asked the ghostly intruder.

"Your double," she said, laughing mischievously, and introduced herself. She had been a serving girl in an alehouse and suffered a violent death before slipping into my dying body and pulling me back from the brink.

"I wish I could go back to my old life," she said. "To my lover Jack, I mean. I miss him terribly. But I guess I'm stuck here with you. I'm so weak I can't even get up from this chair, and when I touch myself, it's as if I was touching air—In any case, I saved your life, and you owe me something in return."

Dread overcame me. I could see that she was going to exact a high price for rescuing me. But my more immediate concern was

Lynne's presence. Was she visible only to me, or to others as well? If so, how could I explain Lynne's presence to my aunt or to the maid, who was bound to come upstairs any time now.

I stared at my unwelcome guest with dismay and frantically searched my mind for a way to conceal her or make her disappear altogether.

"Bugger!" Lynne said. "You are trying to pull me back inside. And I see you are succeeding. *Succeeding.* Did I really say that? Dear me! I'm losing myself and getting stuck in your fancy speech." She went on muttering strange hybrid talk, but her cheeks were turning pale and her body appeared to attenuate and shrink under the dressing gown.

When I saw that my efforts had a measure of success, I doubled my concentration. Pressing my fingers to my temples, I said over and over again: "Go back where you came from, Lynne. Go back."

She sighed. Her face had become transparent and misty, and my head began to ache so severely that I cried out.

I could hear Sarah moving about in the corridor. "Miss Adele?" she called. The next moment she entered, looking at me with alarm. "Are you feeling quite well, Miss?" she asked. "I thought I heard a cry."

"A bad dream," I managed to say. "But it's all right now."

She stooped and picked up the dressing gown which was lying in a pile on the floor beside the window seat. I had managed to tuck Lynne back into my head in the nick of time. But it wasn't the last visit she paid me, and every time she materialized, she was harder to recall until she came and went as she pleased. By then she had adjusted her mien to resemble mine and had learned to model her speech after my example. At first, she mingled genteel phrases with her own low cant, but soon she perfected her skills and learned how to speak and act like a lady. It was only when she talked of her lover Jack that she dropped all niceties and lapsed into her old persona, speaking to me of her longing for him in the crudest terms. In all other respects, Lynne was a fast learner—God knows where she is now and what other powers she has acquired in the meantime. I tremble at the thought that she might return and enslave me again.

When Lynne first slipped the confines of my body and appeared to me, you couldn't quite call her my double. Her body seemed to be made of air, but in the process of solidifying into flesh. She still possessed her own features, which were rough but not unattractive, except for her throat which was disfigured by a jagged scar. With every subsequent appearance, however, she grew to resemble me more, or perhaps I began to resemble her. We became an amalgam. The scar on her neck faded, her skin softened, her wide-set eyes drew closer together. Conversely, my brown hair which was rather dull turned a chestnut hue and my long nose lost some of its pointedness. I suppose I was fortunate. What if Lynne had been very plain and doubled my own shortcomings? I admit that she improved my appearance, but in all other respects her influence was detrimental. As she grew stronger and matured, I was forced to admit her to full partnership in my thoughts. Our conversation—if that is the right word for our internal dialogue—resembled a miracle play. I took the part of Wisdom and she played Folly, or I was Dame Virtue and she was The Great Temptress, and we spoke our lines trying to outperform and outwit one another. Those battles would have astonished anyone who could have listened in, but they remained inaudible to the outside world, thank God. Lynne's escapes from the confines of my body could not be concealed, however, and I lived in fear that my secret might be discovered as her outings became more frequent. She kept materializing at the least sign of weakness in me and asserted her independence whenever I was in distress. She had no scruples stealing my clothes and walking around town pretending to be me, doing a plausible imitation of my voice and manners. Naturally I did not let her go without a fight, but I always ended up the loser. She escaped, and I remained behind on the bed, prostrate, exhausted, in a stupor of pain and dizziness, feeling that my body had lost its contours and my mouth had become uncoupled from language, that I was empty, like the skin sloughed by a snake.

Of course I remonstrated with her when she returned. "You are putting me at risk," I said. "What if someone sees me upstairs and a moment later sees you entering the house. Two Adeles would be hard to explain."

She was defiant.

"It's your own fault," she said. "If you didn't fight me so hard, our minds would have fused by now, and there would be no disagreement about where to go and what to do. It's only because you baulk me that I go off on my own."

It took all my intellectual powers to repress her desire for independence. As long as my mind was engaged in serious thought, she was lying low. Lofty ideas seemed to weaken Lynne, or perhaps they held no interest for her, but one cannot always be philosophizing. When my mind was at leisure, when I sat idle or listless, she rose up and flexed her muscle, made a buzz in my ears, and drummed on the membranes of my eyes until they burned. I began to fear a coup d'état. Her outings were brief, but with every materialization, it became more difficult to draw Lynne back inside and confine her once again to my body. The time will come, I thought, when she will silence me altogether and superimpose her thoughts on mine, when the metamorphosis will be complete, when she will usurp my whole being and I will cease to be Adele and become Lynne. She will drag me down into her wretched world of drunks and pickpockets and easy women.

As it was, she importuned me at every occasion to visit her old haunts and her lover, Jack, the worst kind of man, a criminal involved in endless feuds with rival gang members. In one egregious case, he carved his initials into an enemy's cheek. "To teach him a lesson," Lynne said. "The man was a dirty rat. That's why Jack cut him." She told me the story with a snickering pride. "Jack was an artist with the knife," she said and sighed deeply. She missed her lover. He missed her too, she was sure of that.

"Of course, he thinks I'm dead, murdered by the man whose cheek he cut up and who paid him back by killing me Wouldn't it be fun to track my lover down and give him a surprise? Ta-da, Jack! I'm alive!"

I wanted no part in such an adventure. She threatened to go off and visit him on her own, but there were limits to her independence, thank God. She had gradually extended her outings. An hour or so seemed to be the extent of her reach, however. After that, she lost strength and had to come back to replenish her energy by dipping into my pool of blood. She complained bitterly about my lack of cooperation.

"You never pay any attention to my likes or dislikes. That's because you are madly in love with Francis Florsham."

"But you like him, too."

"Yes, but he doesn't compare with Jack."

Round and round we went, arguing who was the better man, Francis or Jack, and whose love was truer, mine or hers. We were fools in love, both of us.

WHEN I was eighteen, my aunt took me into society. She had high hopes that I would leave my mark on London's bachelors during that first season. She prepared meticulously for my coming out and supplied me with enough silk and glitter to become the belle of the balls, had my personal charms run to it. But the admiration of men waits only on beauty, and although my looks were improved by Lynne's admixture, I could not claim to be beautiful.

In my aunt's eyes, it was my character rather than my appearance that made for a stumbling block. She blamed my father for allowing me to develop bad habits—speaking my mind, showing more penetration than was good for a young lady of fashion, and displaying a certain forwardness that alienated the affections of the gentlemen. Even so I was not without suitors. Given the Collingwoods' wealth and my expectations, the young men were willing to overlook my imperfections and my reputation for being difficult.

Nothing came of my aunt's efforts, however. For once I was in agreement with Lynne. We loathed the proper young gentlemen to whom my aunt introduced us. She had the worst taste in men. She did not care about their looks. We did. She cared only about a man's family and financial position. We wanted to be amused.

Lynne shared in my evening entertainments, of course, hovering in my mind and looking out through my eyes. She ogled the young men who asked to enter their names on my dance card and candidly discussed their physique. Her words were like a dull hum in my ears. She gauged the merits of a man by the shape of his posterior and the width of his shoulders, musing what his breeches might conceal and venturing guesses about the circumference of his upper arms. Her verdicts ranged from "a regular cove" to "a hen's ass," the latter to be avoided at all costs. In my view, Francis was the ideal suitor, and Lynne concurred. He was the best man at hand. As soon as my thoughts turned to Francis, she began to sing in her raucous voice:

A lusty lad will kiss a wench, me thinks it is no folly.
Do kiss me, lusty lad, I say. I will, he says, by golly.
I leave my measure pinching, I bid him hang all flinching

and so on, in the same vein.

We encouraged each other. My aunt and her friends proffered a list of respectable suitors. On my own, I might have yielded to the pressure she put on me and chosen one of them. I might have given up on Francis and settled for second-best, but with Lynne supporting me, I baulked. To the great annoyance of my aunt, there was no gentleman of her acquaintance, whose attentions I wished to invite or whose affections I hoped to engage. She warmly recommended William Pepys to me—"of good family and a junior partner in a tin mining concern," she said. "Very eligible, my dear. A young man who has a good head on his shoulders and is coming along very well."

William Pepys was game and might easily have been brought to the point of proposing, had I given him an opening, but I disdained him.

Lynne sniggered when he was introduced to us. One could expect no better from her. But to my shame, I must admit I also laughed behind his back. Can you imagine being saddled with a name pronounced "Pips" and a voice to match it? I almost felt sorry for him.

"And his thoughts look like little furry balls, money mashed up with horsehair," Lynne said, as I was making polite conversation with Mr. Pepys. I had a hard time keeping a straight face with Lynne whispering into my ear. She came out with such peculiar expressions because she could see what people were thinking—or so she claimed. Pepys, she said, had hairy thoughts.

Apart from his squeaky voice, Mr. Pepys was tolerably good-looking, but he could not compare with Francis, who was the measure of all men for me. William Pepys danced well, yes, but Francis danced better. He dressed fashionably, but the cravats Francis wore were ravishing. William could not match Francis' dark eyes, his curly hair, his finely formed person, his gallant speech. No one could. Francis was entertaining, and Mr. Pepys was oh so boring. His brain had room for only two subjects: business and hunting.

My aunt persisted in her efforts, however. Mr. Pepys had her full confidence and support. He came to pay us a morning visit, and I was obliged to receive him, although I would have preferred to remain upstairs. He had come to declare himself, and Mrs. Collingwood left the room discreetly to allow him to open his heart to me.

"Miss Leddy," he said—I still went by my father's name then. "Your aunt has given me permission to pay my addresses to you."

"Perhaps it might have been better to secure my permission first," I said.

He looked embarrassed. "I took the liberty of presuming on your goodwill," he said, "after you honoured me with two sets of dances at the ball yesterday."

I had danced with him twice, but under duress. I had been sitting with the other young ladies, while the gentlemen passed and looked us over as if we were a lot at auction. It was an exasperating ritual. There wasn't much we could do except wait and hope to avoid the most undesirable men—the short, the ugly, the clumsy dancers and the boring talkers—because if you rejected one gentleman, etiquette dictated that you couldn't accept another and had to sit out the whole set. And here I was itching to dance, and there was Mr. Pepys wanting to dance.

He bowed and said, "May I ask for this dance?"

I gave him a gracious smile. The pairs were lining up, and the dance was too good to miss.

"I suppose you thought you had a right to presume," I said when Pepys reminded me of those dances. Lynne's voice was in my ear: "Don't encourage him. He is a silly ass. I can't stand him."

My words were hardly encouraging, but Mr. Pepys persevered and would not let me off. He brought out the worst in me, or perhaps it was Lynne who made me use unvarnished words.

"I cannot say that I enjoyed the ball last night," I said. "The talk was so dull."

He looked surprised and asked what my favourite topic of conversation was.

I looked him straight in the eye and said: "Philosophy." I was sure that would get rid of him, but he hung on. He really must have been in love with me, the poor man.

"Philosophy!" he said and looked startled, but made a quick recovery. "No doubt, you mean moral philosophy. And indeed, I believe that women are more spiritual than men. I dare say, they are not only more capable of discoursing on morals but, what is more important, of exemplifying them in their lives. It does you credit, Miss Leddy, to take an interest in such a noble subject."

But I was merciless. "When I spoke of philosophy, I did not mean to restrict myself to moral philosophy," I said. "Indeed, it is logic and epistemology that engage my special interest."

That was more than he could stand, and he took his leave. After that he always greeted me politely, but never again asked me to dance and made no more calls at our house.

Aunt Martha took it hard that Mr. Pepys had been allowed to depart without declaring his intentions and accused me of deliberately discouraging him and other would-be suitors.

"But, Aunt," I said, "affections are involuntary, and mine have not been raised by any gentleman proposed for my consideration."

"Then you should submit them to considerations of prudence and to the authority of those who have a right to direct your conduct," was her reply.

When I turned nineteen, she redoubled her efforts to see me married advantageously. I, however, was determined to marry only for love and only a man who could arouse passion in me, by which I meant, Francis Florsham.

While we lived in London, I did not see much of him. My aunt did not approve of Francis, and it was difficult to get around her. She took her chaperoning duties seriously. If anything escaped her sharp eyes, moreover, there was an army of old women on patrol, just waiting to be supplied with material for gossip. But I stuck to Francis, and in time found a way to see him in secret.

ONE OF Lynne's constant complaints was that I did not take full advantage of the material comforts my aunt and uncle offered me. She had been poor all her life and was greedy for the good things money could buy.

"They want you to take the Collingwood name. They want you to inherit their money. Why don't you oblige?" she said to me. "What's wrong with you, Adele? No, don't tell me. I know what's wrong. You have no experience of life. You never had to fend for yourself the way I did. You are naïve. Or maybe just impractical, like your father."

She goaded me. We haggled. In the end I agreed to become Adele Collingwood—not because I accepted Lynne's argument, but because I could not stand the sadness in Uncle Ian's eyes. He had his heart set on making me his daughter, and my refusal to let him adopt me and to take his name hurt him deeply. It was as if I refused to return his affection. The poor man needed all the love he could get. He was at death's door. His health had been deteriorating for some months and had reached a point of crisis. He suffered from a fatal shortness of breath and an ulcerated stomach. The attending physician urged him to escape the acid smog of London and move to the country. My uncle had enjoyed our sojourns to Hinxworth and had come to like the place. When the physician pressed him to leave the city, he decided to move there. Hinxworth was a picturesque little town and offered what the doctor had prescribed—clean air.

He purchased a house and hired a London architect to renovate it. My aunt wanted the look of an old country seat, something that gave the impression that the property had been in the family for centuries. At the same time, she was not willing to put up with the inconveniences of an old house, such as damp bedrooms, creaking floorboards and windows with sticky sashes. She wanted something that looked ancient but was modern, and the architect obliged but it could not be done quickly, and three months went by until we moved to Hinxworth at last. The property, which was named Three Oaks after the majestic trees shading the house, had been turned into a suburban villa, a doll house copy of a mansion, with cornices and a red tiled roof, and an entrance adorned with fluted pilasters and flanked by two large bay windows. The rule that the house must present its best front to the road meant that it was facing north and thus we entered upon a dark hall and a sunless drawing room, which altogether foreshadowed the sad times to come.

The operation of closing up the London house, packing the contents, and moving to Hinxworth had taken a toll on my uncle. By the time we settled into Three Oaks, he was too ill to enjoy the country air. My aunt and I made our entrée into Hinxworth society on our own. She went at it with her usual energy and determination, invited the people who mattered and was invited by them in turn. She patronized the charitable bazaars. She attended the monthly meeting of the Lending library. She joined the committee organizing the annual flower show. She shirked no duty and in no time at all we were on everyone's social calendar.

The town offered little in the way of entertainment, but that did not bother me. It offered great opportunities for trysts. In London, I could not get away from the guardians of morality. In the country there were places to hide from curious eyes. There were deserted lanes, dark woods, corn fields, and of course Grove Hall with its maze-like alleys. It was a perfect setting for lovers, and Francis and I took advantage of it to meet in secret.

In any case, Aunt Martha's attention was taken up by her ailing husband, who was now no more than a sickly shadow to her solid body. The dear man sat at dinner, pale and watery-eyed, chewed his food slowly, coughed into his handkerchief from time to time, contributed very little to the conversation and excused himself early. Within a few weeks, he was too ill to get out of bed at all. He languished through the autumn months, nursed devotedly by my aunt, and died just before Christmas.

"Spoiling our plans for a shopping spree in London," Lynne said while I wept. "The only shopping we'll be doing now is for mourning clothes."

In vain I tried to bury her voice. She was strident. "I mean black does nothing for your complexion," she said. "You'll look ashen."

"Who cares about looks at a time like this?"

"Your beloved Francis cares if you look like a scarecrow."

The morning after my uncle's funeral, Aunt Martha sat me down on the tasselled sofa in the drawing room and spelled out what our life together should be henceforth.

"Adele," she said, touching a cambric handkerchief to her eyes. "Here we are, a widow and an orphan, alone in the world. We have but each other, and we might as well make the best of it. Your uncle has, thank God, left us well provided for, and we shall have a comfortable life. I won't put on the air of a grieving widow for the world. Those who had occasion to observe me in my married life will know that I loved and cherished my husband, as a man of his merit deserved, and that I cannot but feel the cruelty of fate, which took him from me before his time. I grieve deeply for him, that is true, but I am not given to displays of emotion and dislike them in others. Nor do I think Ian would have wanted me to pine away and mope around for the rest of my days. I shall, accordingly, gather up my courage and turn my eyes to the future and look for comfort from you, whom I regard as my daughter and from whom I expect filial devotion in turn. And you will get your reward in time."

"I will be at your side when you need me," I said, tears in my eyes, for I did love Aunt Martha in my heart. How could I not love her, remembering all the years of kindness I had from her. The misgivings that had clouded our relationship more recently were forgotten in that moment. "I will always think of you as my mother, and believe me, your approval is all the reward I ask."

Lynne moaned. "What a sentimental fool you are, Adele. Listen to the treacle coming out of your mouth."

"That was very prettily said, and I hope you mean it," my aunt said. "As for my approval, you will have it if you show yourself a little more pliable, for you have become a very self-willed young lady. But I am fond of you nevertheless and mean to do well by you."

We embraced. There were tears and professions of mutual goodwill, only I spoiled it by saying: "But, aunt, you are so very hard on me sometimes."

"What do you mean, Adele?" she said, raising her eyebrows.

"It's just—"

"Well, out with it. What is it?"

"Mr. Quail. I wish you wouldn't encourage him to pay his attentions to me."

Thomas Quail was the local solicitor, and my aunt had recently promoted his suit. She had to concede that he wasn't very lively, but that was not something that counted with her.

"He has good prospects, nice manners and an unblemished character," she said. "You should be pleased and honoured by his attentions, especially now that you are almost twenty-one."

She feared my becoming an old maid. But I was not desperate enough to settle for a tedious lawyer and spend the rest of my days looking at Grove Hall with regret and yearning. I talked back to my aunt.

"Mr. Quail may be all you say, but he does not speak to my heart."

She did not let me get away with that argument.

"Say rather that there is another, who quickens your heart and sustains your hopes."

I blushed. "I won't deny it," I said.

"My dear," she said, "it would do you no good to deny it. You could not possibly resist all followers if your heart was not pre-engaged. Besides, I am not blind. I can see that you have lost your heart to that worthless young scamp, Francis Florsham."

"He has as much merit as Thomas Quail," I said hotly. "But there are people in Hinxworth with rather narrow views. They will not brook any behaviour unless it is sanctioned by Hinxworth custom. Mr. Florsham has seen the world, has breathed a more liberal air—"

"A libertine air, you mean. He has come back from his grand tour on the continent a dandified jackanapes. The Reverend Stockdale, who is a learned man and does not lack wit, quoted me the adage *uomo italianato, diavolo incarnato*, which is to say that those who go to Italy come back regular devils. Mr. Florsham certainly bears out that adage. He is a young scapegrace who will run through his father's fortune in no time at all. Mark my word."

It was no use. There was nothing my aunt or the rector, Mr. Stockdale, could say to persuade me that Francis was less than perfect. We did not go into society during the mourning period following my uncle's death, but that did not keep me from encounters with Francis during an afternoon walk along the country lanes.

"And do you know," I said to Francis when we had taken our seat on a secluded bench by a little stone chapel, "she quoted me a wretched Italian verse, uomo italianato—"

"—diavolo incarnato!" He completed the line, laughing disdainfully. *"An Italianized man is the devil incarnate.* An old chestnut out of Ascham's *The Schoolmaster*, and as hoary as the Tudor Age," he said. "And if you don't look out, Adele, you'll end up like your aunt: a homespun woman with the taste of a greengrocer."

He missed no opportunity to show his contempt for my aunt. Her style was mean, he said, her conversation flat, and all her skill consisted in taking a hand at cards.

"Oh, I won't be like her, ever," I said airily, "but as for the quote: she had it from the rector."

"From that toady of hers!"

"He may be her toady, but I have heard him described as a gentleman of taste and learning."

"I suppose Mr. Stockdale is entitled to be called a gentleman by virtue of his profession," Francis said carelessly. "And he may be learned by the standards of Hinxworth, but I doubt he would cut much of a figure in London or Paris."

"Your sister thinks highly of him."

"What does Eliza know! She is partial to the clergy and a dupe to sanctity and devotion. I wish she were less given to heart-heaving and prayer."

I defended Eliza against Francis' unkind words, but I agreed with him about the Reverend Stockdale. He played the toady to my aunt because she was wealthy and willing to support his causes. That is why we saw a great deal of him. He was after my aunt's money. Of course, Francis himself was not above such considerations either. But I say that with hindsight. At the time I still believed in him, even though Lynne had warned me: "He may be in love with you now, but he'd fall out of it fast enough if you weren't your aunt's heiress. Unlike my Jack. He loved me for myself and would have gone on loving me even if I never brought him a penny."

It was common knowledge that Francis was in debt and hounded by creditors. During his father's lifetime, the assets of the family had been secure. The elder Florsham lived within his means and made sure Francis did, too. But when he died, Francis indulged himself. He bought a fancy carriage, he gambled, he kept horses and hired a master of hounds, he gave lavish dinners and had questionable friends. It took him no more than three years to run through his inheritance, and when he had mortgaged every acre of land he owned, he borrowed from Eliza. Now his creditors threatened to auction off Grove Hall.

Of course, Lynne took every opportunity to compare him with Jack. But even if Francis had been a better man, no one could measure up to her Jack. She never let me forget that I was in the way of her happiness. If she could only steer my body, she said, we would be in London now, searching for him. Why was I so uncooperative? Why did I not help her find Jack?

"How can you be in love with a man like that?" I said, "—a cruel brute who carves his initials into living flesh!"

"It's you who are cruel," she said. "It's you who are heartless."

I was not without heart, but it belonged to Francis. What people said about him was true, however. He was desperate for money, and the mothers of eligible young ladies were not inclined to regard him with favour. Francis had acquired a reputation for fast living, and they closed their drawing rooms to him. When nothing presented itself in the way of suitable marital prospects, he fell back on me. My family connections were not desirable, but I would bring him a large dowry. I in turn was besotted with Francis. He had dallied with me over the years, paying me court when it suited him, and putting me aside when other amusements beckoned, but with all avenues blocked, he found it worthwhile to concentrate his attentions on me or rather on my aunt. His courtesy toward her increased markedly, and at last he formally asked for my hand in marriage.

My aunt received Francis' proposal coldly. I had passed my twenty-first birthday, and she had less sanguine expectations for me now, but she was not prepared to throw me away on a young scapegrace. She turned Francis down and refused to bless my engagement to a man, whom she recognized as a fortune-hunter. Still, she could not discourage me. Francis had made a credible show of being in love—credible, that is, to a young and inexperienced woman, who was willing to deceive herself and see love where there was none. Hard pressed by his creditors, he made a desperate attempt, a last effort to gain my hand and thus the Collingwood fortune. The only way to overcome my aunt's resistance, he said to me, was to present her with the fait accompli of our marriage.

"We'll elope and go to Scotland where the laws governing marriage are less stringent," he said. "We'll wed there."

I had doubts about his scheme.

"Aunt Martha will be outraged," I said. "She will disown me."

"You can write from Scotland and urge reconciliation," he said, "and I will ask my sister to go to her on our behalf and prepare the ground. Eliza is your best friend and will be ardent in our defense."

"We cannot ask for a warmer advocate than Eliza, I know that," I said, "but my aunt may not be open to mediation. She can be very hardnosed, you know. And she is particular about observing proprieties."

"But we shall be properly married, and she can have no objection to our union in principle. Indeed, she must be sensible to the honour intended you. I come of an old and respected family, and she might well take pride in such a connection. It's my embarrassed finances that give her pause." He did not say that my money would deliver him from poverty, but put it the other way round. "If anything, it is my poverty that keeps your aunt from giving her consent."

"She has said nothing about your monetary situation," I said. "She has questioned your sincerity."

"But how can she continue questioning my sincerity once I have pledged my love to you before the altar?"

"Because she believes that your willingness to marry me stems from love for my expectations rather than love for me," I said bluntly.

"What does it matter that she mistrusts me!" he cried and folded me into his arms. "What does it matter, as long as *you* believe that I love you? And you must believe me, dearest Adele."

Swearing to his love by all that was sacred, he overcame my scruples. Or rather, his sweet caresses more than his arguments made him persuasive. Lynne was not taken in by his words, but she was ready for an adventure. That's all it was to her: a thrill. She had no moral scruples. She added her pleas to those of Francis and urged me to elope. She was so happy at the thought of the excitement awaiting her that she seemed ready to burst the confines of my mind and embrace my lover bodily. Her thoughts were crowding my brain. Her words were on the tip of my tongue. I said yes.

What else could I say to Francis, when his vow of love was sweet to me, and when Lynne disturbed my senses, mingling her blood with mine and bringing it to a dangerous boil? I allowed him to kiss me and, fool that I was, murmured: "I do believe you, with all my heart."

"If your love is equal to mine," he said, "you must not hesitate to risk all. And if your aunt should disown you, we shall be poor, but we shall still have one another and be happy together." It was a shameless lie, but it was uttered with the glibness of a practiced liar and therefore succeeded.

"This is what we'll do," he said. "On the day after tomorrow, you'll leave your house early in the afternoon on the pretext of paying a visit to my sister. I shall wait for you on the road in my carriage, and off we go to Scotland."

"I am to leave home without even taking a change of clothes?" I asked, which goes to show Lynne's influence. Material considerations had taken the place of moral concerns with me. Francis had persuaded me. The matter was settled, and all that was left to discuss were the circumstances. I was thinking of stockings and caps and gauze instead of my reputation. That is the extent to which Lynne had vitiated my mind!

"Come dressed for an afternoon visit, my love. Take only what you can bring away without raising suspicion. You might take your jewellery, for example. We'll get you a wedding dress when we arrive at our destination."

"And what if it rains on that afternoon? Aunt Martha will wonder why I would want to walk to the Hall in miserable weather. She'll urge me to take the carriage, and that would complicate matters."

"What if, what if—don't worry, Adele. We must wager something if we want to gain happiness. I say: let's pray for good weather."

"In any case, Aunt Martha will send someone to the Hall if I don't return in time for afternoon tea. And so, we gain no more than a few hours by that expedient."

"That's easily remedied. I'll instruct my groom to deliver a note from you to your aunt, informing her that you will be staying at Grove Hall to keep Eliza company since I am away from home. Say that Eliza will send you home in the carriage, once I arrive. All I need from you is a note written in your hand—three lines addressed to your aunt explaining the situation. That way we'll gain a few more hours before anyone at your house will even begin to make enquiries. By then we will have made our escape and, before anyone can trace us, we'll be safely across the border and married. What can your aunt say or do then?"

It was a clever stratagem, but chance foiled it. This is what happened, as I discovered from Eliza's tearful account and the nagging reproaches of my aunt. Not long after I met with Francis at the appointed place and we set out for Scotland, a servant came to Three Oaks with a note from Eliza. I had told my aunt that I would spend the afternoon with her and left the house under that pretense. By coincidence Eliza did in fact invite me to tea. The maid who answered the door to her servant told him that I was already on my way to Grove Hall. The servant returned to Eliza with this information. She was puzzled, wondering why he and I had not crossed paths. Perhaps I had taken a short-cut through the park, she thought.

She waited for some time and finally grew uneasy. At last, she went outdoors and walked down the gravel path to the gate, keeping a lookout for me. Soon she was overtaken by Francis' groom, on his way to deliver my deceitful message, as had been arranged—informing my aunt that I would spend the evening with Eliza. She stopped the groom and asked where he was going. He looked uncomfortable, but answered the truth: "To deliver a letter to Mrs. Collingwood."

"On whose instructions?" Eliza said.

"The master's," the groom replied.

"But he is away," Eliza said. She was thoroughly confounded by the groom's answer, for the letter, she could see, bore my handwriting.

The groom insisted that the master had given him instructions before his departure to deliver a letter to Mrs. Collingwood at five o'clock that afternoon.

Eliza was not satisfied with his answer. "Hand me the letter, good man," she said. "I am on my way to see Mrs. Collingwood myself and will deliver it into her hands."

The groom, who was cognizant of Francis' scheme, hesitated, but Eliza was firm, and he could not very well refuse to give her the letter.

Eliza at once made her way to my aunt's house. She arrived there breathless and found Mrs. Collingwood in conference with the Reverend. Mr. Stockdale had only just arrived himself, ostensibly to inquire after the lady's health but in fact because he was curious as to what was going on.

"I was returning from a call to a parishioner and riding along the road to Leeds," he said, "when I saw the Florsham carriage approaching at top speed. Good God, I thought, the man is in a hurry. I hope nothing is amiss. I turned my horse off the road to let the carriage pass and glimpsed in its interior a young lady who looked familiar. I hesitate to say—"

He stopped and looked meaningfully at Mrs. Collingwood.

"Not Adele!" Mrs. Collingwood said, and Eliza covered her mouth to stifle a cry.

Once Eliza had added her story to the Reverend's and my lying letter had been unfolded and read, it did not take long for the plot to unravel.

The Reverend offered to take up the chase on horseback. He hoped to intercept us and persuade me to return with him to Hinxworth. Nothing need be said about the adventure, he suggested, as long as all parties agreed to keep it confidential. Aunt Martha had no interest in blackening my name, and Eliza loved me too much to cast aspersions on me or her brother. She, too, wanted my reputation to remain intact in the public eye.

THE REVEREND caught up with us at a blacksmith shop on the outskirts of Letchworth. Francis had called a stop because one of the horses had gone lame. He and I were sitting at a wooden table in the shade of an elm, waiting for the smith to do his job. I was not feeling particularly anxious. I suppose love has that effect. It dulls fear. But the sight of a rider in the distance woke me from my fond dreams and rang an alarm in my heart. At first it was just a blurred image, then it jelled into the Reverend Stockdale, and the next moment he was in the dusty yard, getting out of the saddle.

He did not look angry and greeted us civilly. Francis had shifted on the bench to put a polite distance between us. I could barely gather my thoughts and stammer out a greeting. The Reverend sat down and put his hand on my arm as if he wanted to take possession of stolen goods.

"Now, my dear," he said in his preacher's voice. "This is all a great foolishness, and I warrant neither you nor that gentleman has quite thought through what you are about. Am I right, Mr. Florsham?"

Francis gave him a black look. "We know very well what we are about," he said. "I'll have you know, Mr. Stockdale, that my intentions are honourable. We wish to be married. The lady is of age and may please herself."

"Quite right," the Reverend said. "But she will not please her aunt, who stands in her mother's stead. And it is written: Honour thy mother and father." Here he turned to me again. "Surely you do not wish to distress your aunt, Adele. She has asked me to bring you home. She loves you dearly, you know, and wants the best for you."

I made no reply, and he kept on talking. "Your aunt has also entrusted me with a message for Mr. Florsham, which, with your permission, I shall give him privately."

He got up and asked Francis to step into the road with him. I watched them walking up and down. The Reverend had his hands clasped behind his back and was full of clerical dignity. Francis was angry. He stopped and threw up his hands. When they came back into the yard, he avoided my eyes.

"And now," the Reverend said to me, "may I have a few words with you in private, my dear? Mr. Florsham will oblige us by inquiring about his horse in the smithy."

Francis moved off, and the Reverend sat down at the table again and started on a story. I don't know whether he had rehearsed it ahead of time. His delivery was perfect at any rate.

He sighed. "Adele," he said. "I will tell you the story of a very foolish young man, named Percy. When he was about your age, he was hired as a tutor to the son of Lord Cauley. Instead of looking to his duty, which was to instruct the young gentleman entrusted to his care, he made it his business to moon after the boy's sister, a very pretty young lady, but I am sorry to say, a very flighty young lady and open to temptation. In no time at all she was head over heels in love with young Percy, who recited poetry very prettily and had no qualms about persuading the silly girl to run away with him one moonlit night. Well, many a coxcomb has tried his hand at the game, and many a lady has been fooled by such tricks and been brought to ruin in that fashion. As for the young scamp Percy, I dare say he was in love with the girl, but perhaps he was in love also with the lord's armorial bearings and his money. Whatever kind of love it was, the pair was discovered, and the young man whipped within an inch of his life and thrown out into the street with his clothes cut into bloody strips. Afterward the curate of the house came and picked the young fellow out of the gutter and took him to a lodging house, where he gave him a long sermon and pressed half a crown into his hand. And I think he was a very good man to do so."

I listened silently to the Reverend's instructive tale of youthful folly. Lynne railed, telling him to stop sermonizing. I sat rooted to the bench, my hands over my mouth to keep the screams of my enraged twin from reaching the air.

"And what do you think the morale of the story is?" the Reverend asked me.

"I don't know," I said curtly. "I'm in no mood for parables." Lynne's voice had sunk to an angry whisper burning my throat.

"Then I shall tell you what I learned from it," he said. "No good can come of eloping. But love is ever foolish, and I understand that as well." He paused and said with meaning: "Let me just add: if I were in Mr. Florsham's shoes and had obtained the favour of a fair and accomplished young lady, I would show more respect for her position and court her honestly."

"You have made your point, Mr. Stockdale," I said, "but I cannot agree with your opinion. Mr. Florsham had the honest intention of making me his wife, and I do not see what alternative he had, given my aunt's resistance. She can separate us of course, but she cannot change my feelings for Mr. Florsham."

"Then you will be sorry to hear that Mr. Florsham's determination does not match yours. His ardour has cooled. I had no difficulty persuading him to give you up after I told him that your aunt intends to make over her fortune to the church."

I jumped up. "Is that true?" I cried.

"Is it true that your aunt will make over her fortune to the church or is it true that Mr. Florsham is ready to relinquish you, seeing that no money is to be had from the marriage?"

"Never mind," I said. "I shall ask him myself." And I stormed off to where Francis was standing, slump-shouldered.

"Is it true that you have given me up now that I have no money to bring you?" I asked him sharply.

"Is that what the Reverend told you?" he said.

"Yes, that is what he told me. And what have you to say to that?"

He was silent and looked at the ground. "Adele," he said at last. "I am sorry to cause you distress, but I believe the Reverend is right when he says that we must consider the wishes of your aunt. I was wrong when I persuaded you to elope with me."

"You scoundrel!" I screamed. This time I did not need Lynne to drive me on, although she was clapping her hands and applauding me and thumping my brain, shouting along with me. "You liar! You don't love me at all."

The Reverend had come up to my side and said to Francis: "I suggest you take my horse, and the young lady and I go back to Hinxworth in the carriage."

"Yes," he said, "that will be best." But before Francis could get away, I gave in to Lynne's urgings and slapped his face so hard my palm hurt. As I climbed into the carriage, I looked back and saw that my hand had left a red mark on his cheek. Anger contorted his face. Good riddance, he mouthed, and Lynne said to me:

"You saw the words he mouthed, didn't you? But do you know what he was thinking, your fine gentleman? *Bloody quim!* That's what!"

And so, I was disabused of my belief in Francis. In retrospect I have to admit that the Reverend's meddling was fortuitous. If we had made it across the border, the honeymoon would not have lasted long. Francis would have treated me the way he treated everyone who was no longer useful to him—with contempt. Even if my aunt had given in after the fact and supplied me with a dowry, he would have spent it on himself, and I would have ended up like his sister, destitute.

When we got home from our interrupted journey, Eliza was waiting at my aunt's house, dissolved in tears. She embraced me and whispered: "I would very much have liked to be your sister-in-law."

My aunt was tight-lipped. She said only that she was disappointed. The whole affair was hushed up. Francis left for France in a hurry to escape his creditors. Eliza did not breathe a word of the affair to anyone, out of loyalty to her brother as much as to me. It might have all passed like a bad dream, had it not been for my aunt calling Thomas Quail and amending her will.

She made no secret of it to me. She did not spell out the details, but what she said was ominous. "I'm doing it for your own good, Adele. I don't mean to leave you without resources, but I prefer any gentleman seeking your hand to be attracted by your person rather than by your expectations." In other words, she was going to tie up her money in a way that would make it awkward for any suitor to get at it.

I wondered at the time whether the Reverend Stockdale had a hand in that transaction. Like my aunt, he kept his mouth shut about the affair, but he looked very smug when I saw him next.

"God," Lynne said, "I loathe that man! He has a way of looking at you, I don't know what to call it, but he gives me the creeps."

I knew what she meant. Percy Stockdale was a hypocrite. He always sounded sincerely concerned, but I had seen the glint in his eye—he was holding back an ironic laugh.

LYNNE

I WAKE up at six in the morning, my body still working on New York time, my brain buzzing, filled with thoughts held over from last night's reading. *Monday, Monday!* Time to take action.

Yesterday I read myself to sleep. I must say I had great expectations from immersing myself in Adele's *Cautionary Tale.* I thought I would be up all night cradling the past, feeding my nostalgia, reliving my life with Adele, but I suppose that was asking too much of a printed text. After the first excitement of seeing her and my name on the same page, déjà vu set in. I knew where the story was going after all. A few times, when Jack was mentioned, my heart began to race. His name gave me a jolt. I lit up with desire—that internal heat I feel so rarely and miss so much—but when I turned the page my heartbeat went back to normal, and after a few more pages my eyelids began to droop. No, it takes more than a printed text to change the chemical balance of your psyche and allow you to slip into the past. This volume won't do the trick. If I had the second volume at least. A facsimile is one degree closer to the original than a printed text. It preserves some of the idiosyncrasies of the writer's hand. The loops and tangles of the letters, the dots and commas, the duct of the pen. It would convey something of Adele's mood and character, something I could relish until I get my hands on the original, the pages she handled and breathed on, until I can enter the curls of her letters, slip through the interstices of time, and twin my life with hers again.

I open my iPad and pull up the website of the Clarkson. They open at nine. It's too early to put my plan into action. I look at the staff list. Patricia Baron is still there, I see, still Director of Research, but now also affiliated with the English Department at UCLA, teaching something called the Literature of the Mind, which promises a three-pronged approach—psychoanalytic, philosophical and neuroscientific—that's what the website says, but maybe that's just code for English Lit.

So here is the plan: drive to the Clarkson, look up Patricia and let her neuroscientific light shine on me. Ask casually about the manuscript. See what can be arranged.

I last heard from Patricia ten years ago when she sent an email to unspecified recipients, a mass invitation to attend the launch of *A Cautionary Tale*. I didn't go because I was in New York by then and couldn't bear to be away from the hub, not even for one day. I sent my regrets, and she replied with the unsolicited information that she was about to become Patricia Baron-Stevens. I wonder how she and Cole are getting along now. Are their lives still synchronized? And what about Sam Kelley? Is he still manning the Caretaker's Lodge, and is he still hot?

I buzz James and ask him to serve breakfast and get me a rental car. It will be available within the hour, he tells me.

Breakfast is served. I'm too impatient to dawdle over it. To make the time go by faster, I go downstairs and walk the beach. Black-winged seagulls have gathered by the water's edge. They look at me warily first with one eye, then with the other and make way reluctantly. They skim over the water in a low half-circle and close up again behind me.

The sky is grey and misty, but the sun is starting to burn through the marine layer. A tall wave breaks against the rocky wall at the far end of the beach and shoots up a tongue of glittering spray. I take off my shoes, kick at the sand, jog a bit, find I'm out of condition, and slow down again. I watch the tide coming in, let my thoughts ride on the crest, let them carry me back, whirling, to the summer of my discontent, when I laid my last bet with Sam, when I waited for Patricia to finish the transcription of Adele's manuscript, and she stalled, concentrating her energies on Cole Stevens instead.

Turning back to the house, I see James in the circular drive, waiting beside the rental car, looking my way as if to summon me discreetly. I close down my memories and let them blow away on the offshore winds. Maybe I should call the Clarkson before I go. I give James the T-sign and pull out my phone. I punch in the number for the Porter's Lodge and hang up when I hear Sam's gravelly voice: *Leave a message, I'll get back to you as soon as possible.* So, he's still holding the janitorial fort at the library. I don't leave a message. What I want to say isn't for electronic transmission. And maybe it's better not to announce my visit. I want our first exchange of looks and words to be unscripted, like an accidental meeting. I'm too wound up already, worrying about Sam's reaction when he sees me, twelve years older. Thirty-six. God! Maybe he'll look through me the way men do when they look at middle-aged women. Maybe I'll even have to remind him who I am, and he'll say "Lynne Addington? Oh, yeah," and stall out. What if Sam has a gut now and thinning hair? What if he is married, with two kids and no interest in a sideshow? What if his red-hot aura has faded and turned the colour of rotten meat?

In any case, there's no need to give Sam advance warning of my visit. He'll be around. It's his job to be around. And Patricia? I don't want to get to the Clarkson and find she's in a meeting and has no time to see me. I've been hanging around all morning, I don't want to squander more time waiting. I want life to move at an efficient pace.

I give Patricia a call. She answers the phone and instantly clicks on my name. She's one of those people who need no reminders, who can hold a grudge forever.

When I tell her I'm in town and ask could I drop by, she sounds tentative, but after the first hesitation, a positive note creeps into her voice. I can tell what it is, even over the phone. It's the hope of making a donor of me. Patricia likely has a project on the go, and like every good fundraiser, knows my net worth. So far, I've ignored the Clarkson's annual drive for donations and refused to pay for having my name etched into a shiny plaque on the donors' wall. But hope has taken hold of Patricia. Her phone voice changes from tentative to full engagement. No doubt she thinks that a one-on-one meeting has potential and, if skilfully played, may bring out the donor in me and lead to funding for her current project.

She'd love to see me, she says, the little hypocrite, but she'll be teaching in the afternoon and needs to prepare. What about tomorrow? We could talk at leisure then. Her voice embraces me over the phone in a blur of cozy fellowship. We settle on tomorrow, 10:00 a.m.

I'm surprised at my relief. I realize I wanted to postpone my visit to the Clarkson. I'm not ready to face Sam. Maybe I should go clothes shopping first. Hold it. Did I really have that thought just now? God, I'm far gone! No, no clothes shopping. I'm good as I am. No shallow makeover, and no twenty-four-hour agonizing over "how will I look? What will I say?"

I tell James I won't be needing the car this morning after all. For some reason he looks pleased today. Something is percolating in his brain, something that goes beyond butler-thoughts—I see. He has an audition, no, a call back. A part in a TV serial? Lucky him. He's got an agenda. But what the hell am I going to do with myself between now and tomorrow, 10:00 a.m.? It's a question that doesn't come up often. In fact, I can't remember the last time I checked my Task Manager and had an open slot. I always had plenty of work, and if I wanted a break, I had my choice of social engagements. But I'm out of the loop now and haven't kept in touch with anyone here in L.A.

I go back upstairs and flip through the names on my phone. There's no one on my contact list I'd want to talk to. Maybe I should check stock market figures? Nah. I'm done with that. Watch the news?—The news I want isn't on TV. No, I'll concentrate on the business at hand. I pick up Adele's *Cautionary Tale* again. I see there is a page of Acknowledgments. Patricia expresses her gratitude to the library for permission to publish the manuscript. She gushes over the generous support of the Preston Foundation. They financed the facsimile edition of the manuscript in the second volume, which I'm still waiting for, which has become a collector's item. She thanks fellow scholars and "my dear friend Cole Stevens" for giving her advice and encouragement, and "last not least, Lynne Addington, without whose heroic action the manuscript would not exist today."

My heroic action. *Right*, as Cole would say, although it happened after he went back to Canada. All summer Patricia had been dragging her heels on the transcription of Adele's manuscript.

"I'm almost done," she kept saying when I asked, but the spools on her microfilm reader remained static. I don't think she even looked at the manuscript from one day to the next. She was too busy smooching with Cole. She had given me a couple of make-work assignments, but she didn't bother to check my work. I could have spent the office hours filing my nails or counting the hairs on my head for all she cared. She was in love with Cole. Her aura changed, her gaseous halo took on a new shine and the little dancing flames turned into something like sun flares. As her affair blossomed, the professional side of her brain went into hibernation. I've noticed it before: happy lovers lose all drive. They look into each other's eyes and let the work pile up. Patricia's mind was filled with a haze of sentimental thoughts. The transcription of the Adele Collingwood manuscript was in limbo.

It was only when Cole returned to Canada in September that Patricia sobered up. Her brain functions returned to normal, and the manuscript resumed its place of importance in her mind. By October it had moved to the forefront. The Weisman gallery at Pepperdine University was organizing a pre-Christmas exhibition of manuscripts. The director invited Patricia to talk to a group of benefactors, who had sponsored the exhibit. She moved into gear then. Her nerves vibrated, the air around her head went electric and quivered. Someone among the invited guests might be talked into financing a facsimile edition of Adele's manuscript. Patricia was hoping for an heiress with cultural pretensions, or a media boss bored with electronics and looking for something that wasn't virtual, or an oil magnate with bad conscience about the giant carbon footprint of his ventures. What were the options for raising the money needed for her pet project? Sending begging letters to everyone who had used the library in the past year? Making strategic phone calls and taking a select group of donors to lunch? No, the usual sources of money were tapped out. Patricia counted on meeting new people at the dinner following her talk at the Weisman Gallery and she wanted to offer them something special, something that distinguished her project from all others, lifted it above the flatness of the ordinary. Our relationship entered a new phase. Patricia asked for my opinion. We consulted. We plotted. We schemed. We had to come up with something to make the glucose spread through the donor bodies and fuel their cells. We had to generate excitement with enough bang to translate into funds. I did my best, working with her—to further my own agenda of course. Whenever we talked of the manuscript, I thought how I could get my hands on it. Patricia's talk at the Weisman gallery might provide me with an opportunity if I played my cards right.

"You know what will get them going?" I said. "Show them the real thing—the manuscript."

What was needed, I said, was performance art. Slowly open the baize covered box, let the tension build, pop the jewel, wait for the Ah! Then pump them for money. Handing around the manuscript was bound to stimulate dinner conversation and give Patricia an opening to suggest a facsimile edition.

She nodded slowly. She saw my point and liked the idea. You had to give patrons a song and dance for their money. Showing them the original might do the trick, but she wrangled with her curator's conscience and her protective love for the manuscript. No pawing the original. She drew the line at that. Look, but don't touch.

As soon as I had sold Patricia on the idea of displaying the original at Pepperdine, I suggested taking me along for the evening.

"We can pass the manuscript around propped up in a box, but it's better to have two people keeping an eye on things," I said to Patricia. And in a surge of collegial benevolence, she said yes.

Of course, I was looking for my own Ah! moment. I was thinking of making another attempt to get at the manuscript and filch a page. The memoirs were my magic carpet, my ride into the past, I was convinced of that, but the transformation I had in mind could not take place in public. Touching the manuscript with the dinner guests looking on might give me a rise, but I could not incur the risk of failure to complete the transformation. What would happen to me if I got stuck half-way into the process? What if I sloughed off my present body and could not reach the eighteenth century or could not enter Adele's body? I might end up in limbo, leaving behind a corpse without acquiring a new abode. The solution was to steal a page of the manuscript and attempt the transformation in private, under carefully controlled conditions. I had no concrete ideas how to go about the theft beyond keeping my eyes open and taking action when an opportunity presented itself. There were too many variables to make a definite plan, but at least I would be close to the object of my desire.

The box containing the precious pages was in the car with us when we drove out to the Pepperdine campus. Patricia had decided to pass the manuscript around after dinner on a Styrofoam cushion and allow the guests a look at one of the messier pages of Adele's memoirs.

"Corrections and interlinear insertions lend authenticity to a manuscript," she said. "I want the guests to envisage the moment of creation."

My task was to place the Styrofoam tray on the table in front of our potential donors like a dessert course, serve from the right, clear from the left, move on a few paces, repeat action. Patricia would preside and keep an eye on the proceedings.

The scenario she proposed wasn't auspicious for engineering my escape from the present, but I didn't give up hope. A window of opportunity might open and allow me to pounce. That's what was on my mind when we drove to Pepperdine. I was prepared to pounce. I wasn't prepared to perform a "heroic act."

The rainy season had started early that year. It was pouring when we turned off the coastal highway. The lush grounds of Pepperdine were soggy, the cluster of dorms and academic buildings looked old and mushroom gray under the lowering sky. According to the sign at the campus entrance, the Weisman gallery, where the patrons would gather for the opening of the exhibition, was on the right, but Patricia went straight.

"Oops," she said, "I missed the turn," and pulled over sharply. The back of the car fishtailed. We careened across the road, slid down the hill, and started rolling. Patricia's computer bag hit the roof. The manuscript box whacked the back of my head. The seconds passed like bad film footage with sudden pans and lurching zooms. Then there was a dull thud, and we came to a stop. For a moment I was disoriented. My heart raced, my lungs contracted as if I was being squeezed out of my body, the ex-body of one Ginny Addington, the graduate student of which I had taken possession two years earlier. Her bones rattled. The molecules rearranged themselves. I thought we would fall apart, Ginny and me, but I stopped the disintegration in time, and we reconstituted. Only my left elbow stayed out of sync and hurt. I looked through the cracked windshield. The crumpled front end of the car had come to rest against the trunk of a tree. I thought I could smell the fumes of spilled gas. For some reason the airbags had failed to deploy. Beside me, Patricia was slumped over the steering wheel. Her eyes were shut, a trickle of blood ran down the side of her mouth. Her hip was moored in the seat at an unnatural angle, a bizarre fit.

I pushed against the door on my side. It opened with a groan and stuck, with the lower edge digging into the muddy lawn. I crawled through the opening. On second thought I reached back into the car and felt around for the manuscript box, pulled it out, rappelled up the hill on my hands and knees, stumbled across the road, and dropped down into the ditch on the other side. I had only congratulatory thoughts as I crouched there and fingered the box—until I came to my senses. What the hell was I thinking? I had nowhere to hide it. I looked around. Wet grass. Dripping palm trees. No spot to leave it for later pick-up. No suitable hiding place on my own body. I cursed my fashionably tight pocketless dress. I might be able to read a few pages of the manuscript right here with the old ink streaking in the rain, but what good would that do me? Communing with the dead isn't a matter of passing your fingertips over a piece of paper for a minute or two. It takes concentration and meditation. It takes manoeuvering. It takes time. But that's just what I was lacking. I had to do something fast. I could hear ambulance sirens in the distance. Security must have seen the accident on their monitors and called 911. In a few minutes the medics would be here and take us to Emergency. Chances are they'd find the manuscript box beside me and return it to the rightful owner—the Clarkson. No, the risk of being caught in the act of stealing was too great. The only way to ensure permanent access to my treasure was to possess myself of Patricia's body, to become Head of Research with access to the manuscripts and rare books, and leave my host body behind as a corpse. The smell of gasoline was in my nose. I had no time to spare. Defying the odds, defying my aching body, I scrambled back to the car and dragged Patricia out, pulled her up the hill, heaved her over the berm and into the sheltering ditch on the other side. The sirens were coming closer. Patricia's eyes opened and rolled back into her head. She breathed noisily. Her mouth was slack. Her lips parted, welcoming Death, or me. I contracted my mind into a ball, slaked off my skin, slipped between Patricia's lips, shot up into her brain and nestled in her mind. I powered up, doubling my energy with Patricia's, preparing for a fight with Death who had already mapped out his territory and set up camp in her body cavity. I was taking the coordinates, familiarizing myself with the layout of Patricia's brain and gathering up the main lines, when it hit me: I can't feel the legs. Oh shit, I thought, the connection between Patricia's brain and her legs is severed! I don't want to be a paraplegic. No way. I won't be able to do anything. I'll be stuck in Patricia's half-dead body, helpless forever.

I lit out of her brain, dropped into the darkness of non-being, hoping like hell I'd make it back into my old hide in time, before the onset of decentralization, hoping the protean trick would work a second time. I pushed my way down into Ginny's system, pulled everything back into place, and slammed the pores shut. Home. I was drooping with exhaustion. The baize box was where I'd left it, beside me on the grass, but there was no time for thinking up another plan. An explosion shook the ground and the car went up in a fireball. I heard moaning but wasn't sure whose—mine or Patricia's.

When I came to, I was in an ambulance, lying on a gurney.

"She's coming around," the medic said. His face came into focus. "So how are we doing?" he said, taping the IV line to my arm, giving me a smile seasoned with black ambulance humour. He was the type who'd smile at a corpse.

How was I doing? Not bad, considering the journey in and out of Patricia's system. But what about the manuscript? That was the question on my mind.

The manuscript survived. The medics found it under my prone body, as if I had tried to shield it from the elements. Patricia survived, too, thanks to the fact that I'd dragged her out of the car and over to the other side of the road, but she never recovered the full use of her legs. I thanked the gods I'd made it back into my old body in time. It was a freak idea in the first place to exchange my perfectly good system for an unknown set-up. It was an act of desperation. In any case, the accident scotched our plans. Patricia and I never got to perform our act to impress potential donors, and my so-called heroic rescue of the manuscript did nothing to advance my private scheme. But this time will be different, I swear. I'll come up with a fail-safe plan.

TUESDAY MORNING. I am on my way to the Clarkson for my meeting with Patricia.

And Sam.

The last time I saw him was at the party celebrating my rescue of the manuscript, which came away a little crumpled and smudged but—unlike Patricia—intact.

A reporter from the *Los Angeles Times* had picked up the story of the accident and given it a dramatic twist, turning my unsuccessful grab for the manuscript into a heroic rescue. In his words, I had risked my life pulling Patricia from the burning car. I had saved her and the manuscript. The staff at the Clarkson lapped it up and threw a champagne party in my honour. Sidney Tate, who rarely emerged from the palatial quarters he occupied as the director of the Clarkson, came and shook my hand. Doris Langer, the head librarian, made a little speech praising my courage and my commitment to research. For a moment I thought I might get lucky, and Doris would ask me to take over Patricia's project for the time being. But, no, she was too tactful to delegate the task to me. She pretended that Patricia was going to be back shortly, that her mangled legs would miraculously heal and grow a second set of neural pathways. The project was on hold pending Patricia's recovery.

"Our hearts go out to her," Doris said, and everyone applauded.

I clapped limply. I couldn't get in sync with the bleeding hearts. Compassion isn't in my register. There was no sense in wasting my time at the Clarkson after that. I had failed twice in the attempt to get at the manuscript, and now the whole project was on hold. I was so demoralized I would have liked to quit on the spot, but I held back. I didn't throw my ID tag at Doris Langer, I didn't stomp out, even though I was angry. Not just because I'd failed to steal a page of the manuscript. I was angry also because Sam snubbed me. He came to the party, downed a drink, talked to no one, didn't even look at me, and ducked out again.

Doris Langer said: "Well, that's Sam for you. He's been acting strange, ever since he got out of hospital."

"I didn't know Sam was in hospital," I said.

"That was last year, before you started here. Around the time we interviewed you. He had an accident."

"What kind of accident?"

Doris hesitated. Bits and pieces of words were floating around her, just short of coming together into a coherent thought.

I kept up the eye contact. "What kind of accident?" I repeated.

She cleared her throat. A dark shape emerged from her head. I couldn't make it out. A hook? A wire?

"He tried to hang himself," she said. "But don't repeat that, Lynne. I shouldn't even have mentioned it."

An image of Tyburn and Jack dangling from a noose bleeped up on my mental screen, a grainy image, indistinct and distorted, as if seen through a medium denser than air. It loosened my throat muscles. I was afraid of crying out. Doris was looking at me, expecting me to say something. I blinked away the image and swallowed the cry.

"Of course I'll keep it to myself," I said.

"It was a miracle he survived," Doris said. "He was in intensive care for a couple of weeks. I looked after his dog while he was in hospital, and one day Gordie went off his food—you know how dogs sense when their master is in danger? Well, I think that was the crisis point, but Sam pulled through. When he came home, he looked different somehow, but perhaps you have to expect that in someone going through a harrowing experience like that."

"How can you hang yourself 'accidentally'?" I asked.

"Well, you know," Doris said, giving me a coy look. "Kinky sex. Some people get their jollies that way, and maybe he went too far. But that's none of my business."

Two weeks after the party, I handed in my resignation. I made a show of regret and gave Doris a plausible story. I couldn't stay on, I said, because my fiancé was moving to the East Coast. Chris wasn't exactly my "fiancé." More like a friend with benefits, a one-night stand that had settled into something mutually satisfying. He was a stockbroker, and I did move to New York with him. That much was true at any rate.

Chris had a toothy smile, Irish eyes, and a black mane of hair he kept a little too long for my taste. He was hyperkinetic, always in motion. Wherever we were—a bar, a private dinner, a reception— he worked the room, hugging the women and gripping the men's arms. He was full of buzzwords, casting around for that winning system, that quintessential entrepreneurial science, the newest method of improving everything, his body, his brain, his portfolio. Stress—what stress? Chris loved non-stop action. He was hugely into everything: sexual acrobatics, crazy work schedules, after-hour clubs, the Yankees, batting and pitching stats. In fact, he treated life as a game. He was in it to win the playoffs. The trouble was: both of us were after the trophy. We got into each other's way. The relationship didn't work out in the long run, although the lessons Chris taught me about the stock market did. We had a buffo life while it lasted, parted without rancour and even collaborated on occasion when it was to our advantage, pulling off lucrative deals long after we'd stopped being lovers.

I rarely think about Chris now—but here we are, at the Clarkson.

EVERYTHING LOOKS exactly as I remember it: whitewashed perimeter walls with the Victorian roofline of the library rising above them, a steel-gate into which someone has scratched an indelible FUCK—well, that's new. I press the intercom, give my name and am buzzed in by a voice that is not Sam's, a voice I don't recognize. I pass through the gate and see that the blinds on the windows of the Porter's Lodge are pulled down. The house has a deserted look. Is Sam's answering machine sitting in a vacant room? The story Doris told me about his suicide attempt comes back like an afterimage. The hook. The noose. Is the disembodied voice I heard when I phoned him the ghostly memento of a dead man, a man who has hanged himself, successfully this time? A wave of regret washes over me, a tsunami out of proportion with the short time I've known Sam, but not out of proportion with the liking I had for him. Of course, the suicide is just a crazy idea of mine. It's a malfunction of the system, a problem with the wiring in the brain of my host body perhaps, a kind of short circuit. There had been a few problems with Ginny Addington's body in the beginning. There always are when you take over. You have to correct the foibles of the old owner or get used to them. I thought I had ironed out all the kinks in the Addington system, but maybe there is a faulty connection I have overlooked, one of those annoying glitches that happens only periodically, that you can't pinpoint or repair.

I push Sam out of my mind and go to the administrative wing, where Patricia has her office now. It's actually two offices combined and customized to accommodate her wheelchair and allow her to circumnavigate her desk without scuffing the furniture.

When I come into the office, Patricia doesn't get up. She merely raises her hand in greeting. Otherwise, there is little evidence of her disability. The wheelchair in which she sits is concealed by the desk. A sweater is draped over the back panel to make it look like an ordinary chair. Patricia's upper body movements seem normal and have a certain trained vigour, but her aura lacks the corresponding verve. It is static and grey. Suffering has left its mark on her, has carved its initials into her face, and coarsened her rosebud mouth. She's no longer a Gainsborough girl with rosy cheeks and alabaster arms, pink ribbons fluttering in the zephyr winds. I feel a phlegm of sympathy coating my tongue, but I swallow quickly, taking my warning from the black outline of Patricia's halo, the sign of underground resentment.

Patricia beams a professional smile on me. "Before I forget," she says as soon as I've sat down—although I can read in her neatly printed mind that under no circumstances will she forget the first item on her agenda. She reaches for a boxed set of books on her desk. It is the two-volume combo I asked James to get for me, the edition of *A Cautionary Tale* and the facsimile of Adele's manuscript. It's a deluxe gift set meant for potential donors.

"Go ahead," Patricia says. "Have a look at the facsimile."

The box is covered in baize, like the one containing the real manuscript. Nice gimmick.

I take out the slim facsimile volume. The pages look stunningly authentic. No wonder this has become a collector's item. The paper is artfully distressed. It looks but doesn't feel brittle. The pages are loose and folded over, like the original Adele tucked into the back of Stockdale's *Sixteen Sermons*. There is no title or running head to remind the reader that this is a curated version. It preserves the anonymity of the original, a sheaf of private papers. The letters, in cobalt blue ink, make their way across the page in a slightly downward sloping line, keeping in close formation, jostling each other. Only one thing is missing to make the reproduction perfect: the third dimension. The lines lie on the page, flat. The ink will never smudge or flake off. The edges of the paper contain no trace of Adele's DNA. Not a single cell of her skin has rubbed off on them. But the visual effect is remarkable.

"Stunning," I say.

"Isn't it?" Patricia says smugly, as if I had complimented her, as if she personally had produced the facsimile. "I always meant to give you a copy of the text we worked on," she says, "but somehow I managed to lose your address." —Liar! You had my email address when you notified me of the book launch and when you told me of your marriage to Cole. I'm in your files, Patricia!

"It's been a long time," I say. "Ten years at least since our last contact. You were about to get married—How is Cole by the way?"

Her face goes pale with ineffable pain. An empty space opens up in her eyes where nothing stirs and nothing speaks, but she finds her way back quickly. "No idea," she says. Her hands flutter, waving away Cole's name. "I haven't seen or talked to him in ages. We separated, you know." I read the rest of the story in the cloud of words above her head. The bastard married her only to get the green card. As soon as he had his papers, he left for Oregon.

So far, our spoken sentences have been no more than filler words, but now we are coming down to the contents of our lives.

"Well, things didn't work out for me either," I say and tell her about breaking up with Chris. I don't say that it's been a cordial parting. I can see that Patricia hungers for the camaraderie of bitter feelings.

"Your career has worked out at any rate," she says. "I feel—" She stops. The rest of the sentence trails from her right temple like a flag. She wanted to say "I could have made a better career, too, if it hadn't been for the accident" but her face shuts down before the words can pass her lips. She changes course: "I feel you would have been just as successful if you had stayed in academics. You were one of the most capable interns the Clarkson ever had—perhaps I should say *the* most capable intern."

I swallow that bit of flattery since the conversation is going in the general direction I want it to go: the year I worked at the Clarkson. Patricia is playing nicely into my hand.

"It was great working with you," I say with a forced breath of enthusiasm. "You know, I'd love to see the Adele Collingwood manuscript again. There is something magic about holding a genuine relic of the past in your hands."

Patricia stiffens. Her grey aura turns to concrete. "Unfortunately, we had to take the manuscript out of circulation permanently," she says. "We ask all researchers to use the microfilm. The manuscript was fragile to begin with, as you know, and it was damaged further in the accident. Of course, if you hadn't rescued it—"

Her aura darkens with the memory of that fateful night and the thought that I rescued her as well as the manuscript. She resents owing her life to me.

She looks at me from the bottom of her pain, her face broken up with bitter memories. Then she pulls the pieces back into place. Her aura brightens at the edges as she gets on with her agenda. She makes me an offer: "I suppose we could make an exception for you, Lynne, and let you see the manuscript if it means that much to you."

"Actually, I was hoping for more than just seeing it," I say. "I'd like to spend a day going through the text page by page, savour it. A nostalgia trip, you know."

I need time to bond with the past imprinted on those pages and, if that doesn't work, an opportunity to abscond with one of the pages, make it my pillow for the night, and dream in Jack's paper and ink embrace.

But I can see that there is no room for negotiation. This is Patricia's best offer. She is not prepared to make further concessions, even if it means losing my goodwill and letting me depart without signing on as a donor. There are limits to her venality, apparently. The manuscript, I realize, is the tangible metaphor of our intricate relationship, our competition, and she is determined to win this round. She looks at me, thin-lipped.

"I'm afraid that won't be possible, Lynne. We can't expose the manuscript to light for any extended time," she says.

Fuck you, I think. You want to take a hard line with me? Fine. But don't expect me to play nice. No manuscript, no money.

"That's too bad," I say, making it sound like good-bye, nice seeing you.

Patricia realizes that her chance to pump me for money is slipping away and changes tack. "But you might like to take a look at another manuscript, a new acquisition," she says, flashing the next point of her agenda on the mind screen: her new project, the one that needs financing.

"It came up for auction in Scotland two months ago. A dozen pages in Adele Collingwood's handwriting. It belongs with the memoir we have, a continuation if you will, although it's fragmentary."

I catch my breath. What pages? Did the notes Adele took to Hamilton House survive? She wanted to show them to my husband. She was going to betray me. She thought she could convince him of my ghostly existence, but she misjudged Daniel Worth. He didn't believe in spirits. He thought Adele's notes were pure nonsense, but he didn't throw them out, it seems.

"The owners of Hamilton House put those notes up for sale because they needed money to finance the renovation of their estate," Patricia says. "They have a marvellous collection. You may remember I identified Adele Collingwood's handwriting on the basis of letters in their library. That correspondence was up for auction as well. We would have loved to buy it and add it to our collection, but a bidding war broke out and drove the price beyond our budget range. We did acquire Adele Collingwood's notes at any rate, which may be of considerable significance if my theory is correct, and they are part of her memoir."

My mind is racing. If that is the chapter she showed to my then-husband—

"I'd love to take a look at those pages," I say.

"The manuscript is in prime condition. Apparently, it was kept in a strongbox together with legal documents." Patricia's aura heats up and boils over, spritzing the room with enthusiasm. "I've been thinking of doing for that manuscript what I did for the memoir: produce a facsimile edition with a transcription and notes. The memoir was an enormous success, you know."

"Sounds like an excellent project," I say.

Patricia is all smiles now. "I'd love to have your opinion of the new manuscript."

"I'd be glad to have a look at it."

"Just let me know a couple of days ahead, and I'll have it ready for you in the Reading Room," she says.

I can't wait to verify my hunch that this is the manuscript Adele left behind at Hamilton House.

"How about day after tomorrow?" I say.

"No problem," Patricia says. "I'll have the manuscript ready for you then."

"Thanks," I say and scrape back my chair.

"Before you leave," Patricia says, "—if you aren't in a hurry, that is, I'll take you to Doris Langer's office. She'd like to say hello to you."

"Sure," I say. "In fact, I was hoping to see her."

Patricia wheels out from behind the desk. She shows me her steely resolve to ignore all inconvenience, her will to triumph over circumstance. An aura of balled determination surrounds her like a suit of armour as she cruises into the hall. You have to admire Patricia.

"The place looks pretty much as I remember it," I say, as we make our way down the corridor to Doris' office.

Patricia nods. "Nothing has changed," she says wistfully. "We are all plodding along, keeping to the same old routine. Except Sam Kelley."

My mind goes haywire. "What's he up to?" I ask and irrationally dread the answer. I'm afraid she'll say: He's dead.

"He's handed in his resignation. It was about time. Everyone complained about him. He wasn't doing his job. He has discovered his vocation as an artist, you know. He calls himself Joe Who. Spelled JOHO."

JOHO. My breath catches. I see the letters scrawled in giant looping letters on the wall of the derelict building, where Sam almost caught me with Cole. JOHO, repeated over and over, a whole wall tagged with his name.

"He's made quite a splash with his so-called art," Patricia says.

My brain has stopped working. I can only echo her words and do a slack-jawed follow-up. "Success? As an artist? When I worked here, there were rumours that he was a petty criminal."

"He is. He broke into abandoned houses and sprayed slogans on the walls. Vandalism is a crime as far as I'm concerned." Patricia's aura has gone lemony yellow with annoyance. "But graffiti is considered an art form now. And if you perform dangerous stunts to put your mark on highway overpasses and the like, you are a hero. At least in artistic circles."

"So he quit?"

"He kept asking for leaves of absence, two days here, a long weekend there. Right now, he's in New York for a show. But this time Sidney put his foot down and told him: We can't go on like this. We can't have you take off unscheduled days. We need a caretaker full-time. So Sam agreed to leave by the end of this month. Apparently, he's bought the building next door. He wants to renovate it and turn it into a graffiti gallery."

"You mean the abandoned house across the driveway?" The smell of urine and distempered walls is in my nostrils, the musk of our bodies—Cole's and mine—squeezed behind the door, the echo of tinkling glass after Sam loosened the window frame and made it fall to the pavement below.

"The tear-down, yes," Patricia says. "We are all nonplussed."

I drive home, stunned. Sam in New York! We might have passed each other in the street. Sam the graffiti artist. So that's the meaning of the creative vein I saw when I first met him, that flash image of his core I spotted before he locked the gates of his mind against me. It was this hermetic quality, his ability to lock me out that first attracted me to Sam. That, and his red-hot aura. I wish I hadn't been sidetracked by Cole. But even if I had concentrated on Sam and things had worked out between us, we wouldn't have lasted long. Animal passion is only good as long as it lasts. It leaves no residue. He would have left me after a while. I have no follow-up hold on my lovers. Men sense the second-hand nature of my feelings. With every transmigration, those feelings have become thinner, and now they are just a faint echo, a memory of the passion I had for Jack once, when I was alive. That's why I have to go back in time. I want the glow of firsthand feelings. I want someone to rekindle my fire. I want to go home to Jack and experience once more that primary heat. Will the manuscript notes turn out to be the crucible to transport me back in time?

ANOTHER MORNING at the villa. I am up early, listless, waiting for the hours to pass.

The sun has climbed over the ridges of the Santa Monica mountains and infused colour into the picture. I look down on the beach, expecting an empty landscape of raked sand, and see instead a lone figure wandering the beach. The maid who suffers from depression. Rosa. She stops at the scalloped edge of the water. She is too far away for me to decipher her thoughts, but it looks as if she wanted to walk into the water and keep going until the waves fill her mouth and stop her breathing. Then she turns and slowly walks into the house.

A few minutes later, she is at my door, ready to make the bed and tidy the rooms. I sit on the terrace and watch her through the glass door as she passes a dust cloth over the furniture and puts anything I've moved around back into its original place—like a prop manager in a theatre setting up the next act in a play. The molasses in Rosa's head has thinned out to a grey mist. If she was in a panic when I saw her walking down at the beach, the crisis has passed, but she is still needy, wanting to be loved. I wish her luck. It won't be easy for her to attract a man. She looks bovine. Maybe it's her ankles, thick like calves' shanks. Worse, she's low on spark. Probably a piece of lard in bed.

She comes out onto the terrace and sweeps around the patio furniture in a forgetful sort of way. She doesn't talk, that girl, she's all slow-motion gestures. It may be a language problem. The few thoughts hovering in her brain are all in Spanish. When she is done with her job, she murmurs something. "Enjoy your day," it sounds like. She leaves without looking back, her head circled by fotonovela words—amor, lloras, engañe.

How will I fill the hours of the day? Why did I allow Patricia to make me wait until tomorrow to see the new manuscript? It was a power play. I should have pushed back.

But Patricia's complimentary copy of *A Cautionary Tale* will rescue me from my forced leisure. The boxed set she gave me contains the facsimile of Adele's memoirs. Let's see what that will do for me.

I settle down on the sofa and find the place where I left off in the printed text. The elopement. The Reverend Stockdale catching up with us.

"Percy Stockdale was a hypocrite," Adele writes in her cramped, slanted hand. I stare at the letters, I concentrate on the words, but I get no rise out of them. I read on. "He always sounded sincerely concerned, but there was a glint in his eye—he was holding back an ironic laugh."

Adele and I saw through the Reverend. Most of his parishioners were taken in by his fake cordiality. He was popular in Hinxworth, and he certainly had the trust of Adele's aunt. I guess his style matched her spiritual needs. She often asked the Reverend to escort her on excursions, tours of cathedral towns and country houses. The Reverend obliged. As far as I remember, he declined only once when he was requested to join her on a trip to Wookey Hole, the famous cave near Glastonbury. On that occasion, he pleaded a trick knee, but otherwise he bravely shouldered the duty of escorting Mrs. Collingwood. He had his reasons of course. He realized that humouring the old woman put her in a charitable mood. He used those outings to pump her for money. All he had to do was bring the conversation around to the sad lot of orphans, widows, and cripples. She had taken a liking to Stockdale, and he always came away with pledges to feed and clothe the poor or pay for the doctor's services. I don't know whether he applied the Collingwood money to charitable purposes. If he pocketed it himself, he was clever enough not to be caught.

I remember yawning a great deal when we were in Percy Stockdale's company. Those outings bored the hell out of me. I wasn't into historical sites. I got my education in a seedy inn by the waterside. Brawling customers were my teachers. Ancient coins, topographical sketches, and the sight of medieval ruins put me to sleep, but Mrs. Collingwood liked the genteel company of the Reverend.

"The old goat is sweet on him," I said to Adele. "Watch out. She'll marry him."

Adele refused to believe me. She got angry when I hinted at her aunt's weakness for the Reverend.

"Why are you angry at me? Why aren't you angry at Percy Stockdale?" I said, but I knew the reason for her displaced anger. She was powerless against him, and so she punished me, the messenger.

"You are taking it out on me," I said, "but that doesn't change the facts. The Reverend plays your aunt like a fiddle. You watch and see. She'll give away her fortune to him and leave you empty-handed."

"Don't be silly," Adele said, but a shadow of uneasiness settled on her.

The Reverend visited us every Wednesday. Mrs. Collingwood was a woman of regular habits. She got up and went to bed at the same time every day. She ate, took her tea, read, and went for walks by the clock. She took her constitutional right after the mid-day meal, come rain or shine. Sometimes, she just walked up and down the tidy garden path, checking that the gardener had done his job and deadheaded the blooms or trimmed the hedge. On Wednesdays, the Reverend took the mid-day meal with us and afterwards accompanied her on a walk to the park at Brook's End. It was her charitable day, she said. The most benevolent and philanthropic ideas came into her head during those walks in the park.

And what does Adele have to say about that? I turn back to her memoir and concentrate on her handwriting. I'm still hoping for an uptick.

Brook's End was a place of great natural beauty with a little wood on one side and open meadows on the other and a stream running through, placid at first, then cascading down a waterfall and rushing on through a narrower course, churning white water. Aunt Martha liked going to Brook's End, which she had often visited in the company of my late uncle. His favourite spot had been an overlook, where the rushing water of the stream had eaten into the bank and formed a steep cliff. The spot was named Lover's Leap after a popular tale about a spurned lover who had jumped to his death from the cliff. There had been talk of putting up a railing along the edge for safety's sake, but nothing had been done about it. The place had an aura of dark romance, and my aunt liked to repair to a bench by the water and think of bygone times.

One Wednesday—a fateful day it was—the Reverend called on my aunt as usual. The sky was overcast and threatening rain.

"It's rather blustery outside, Mrs. Collingwood," he said with a little polite hesitation in his voice. "Perhaps it would be better to defer our walk to another day."

I was sitting in the window seat, leafing through a book, and he cast a look my way to draw me into the conversation. He was hoping for my support, but I was not inclined to do him any favours. We were at war since the elopement. No doubt he preferred to remain indoors, making himself comfortable in our drawing room.

"The sky seems to be clearing," my aunt said, determined to keep to her routine, "and I don't mind the breeze."

I remained mute, leaving Mr. Stockdale no choice but to

comply with my aunt's wishes, and off they went together, leaning into the wind.

Immediately upon their departure, I was overcome by fatigue and experienced the kind of pounding headache I recognized as a sign of impatience in Lynne, a sign of her impending materialization. Such incidents had become more frequent in the weeks after the unsuccessful elopement, and I was at a loss how to deal with my unruly twin. She had been taking a great many liberties lately and was becoming more independent and mischievous every day. I had to be ever wakeful. If I let my guard down, she began blustering and pushing against her confines, and whenever possible making her getaway and gallivanting around the countryside. I remonstrated with her.

"You will bring scandal on me, Lynne!"

She brushed me off. "No need to worry about your precious reputation," she said. "I take good care of it and do my trysting where it can't be witnessed. In any case, no one will recognize me, or you, as it were. I go about well disguised. I've bought a hooded cape from a peddler, if you want to know, and a knitted shawl and a dashing black wig."

"And where do you keep your disguise?"

"That's for me to know."

"And where did you get the money to buy those things?" I asked.

She laughed. "Earned it, what else? Did you think I stole it from you?"

I was afraid to ask how she had earned the money. She had the mind of a strumpet. Lately, she had begun to sigh after the local doctor. Indeed, the village was abuzz with tales of trysts between Dr. Worth and a gypsy woman, although I could hardly credit those filthy rumours.

"Is it true?" I asked. "Have you managed to catch the doctor's eye?"

"I wish it were true," she said. Lynne was fascinated by all that was dark and dismal, and the doctor was a morose man. His furrowed brow and his secret sorrow—he was a lover spurned—was all to her taste.

On that Wednesday, then, she left me behind with a crippling migraine and set out on one of her gypsy adventures.

I LOOK up from the book. No, Adele's words won't help me. Not in this case at any rate. Things got exciting only after I burst out of my prison—Adele's body—for an outing of my own. I left her behind on the bed, a slaked skin. She knew nothing of what I witnessed that afternoon, except what I told her myself. I took a shortcut through Brook's End to the barn where I kept my gypsy clothes. It was risky to cross the park while the Reverend and Mrs. Collingwood were on *their* outing, but I thought it was just as risky to go around the long way and leave Adele alone for more than an hour or so. Separated from her bloodstream, I could not maintain my energy, and I was afraid she in turn might recover and gather enough strength to fend me off and bar my re-entry. I had to watch the time and keep my outings brief.

The park was popular with the townspeople, but on that cold and windy day it was deserted. I thought I had given the Reverend and Mrs. Collingwood enough of a head start, but when I came to the footbridge that crossed the river, I saw her sitting on a bench by the water. At that same moment she looked up and spotted me. I was trapped. I had to go to her, pretend I was Adele and come up with an explanation for being at Brook's End.

I wasn't entirely sure I could deceive Mrs. Collingwood. After mingling our blood for some years, Adele and I had grown to look alike, and during my outings, if I didn't wear my disguise, I copied her language and manner as well. I had acquired a certain polish and could pass for a lady if I wanted to. The plan was to make my permanent escape from Adele's body as soon as it was in my power and to leave her behind dead—as dead as she would have been had I not wrangled with Death and rescued her. Of course, I had to make my final escape in a place where her body would not be found immediately, for once I left her form behind and took the life force with me, her bodily remains would decay rapidly. That was my guess. Well, I guessed wrong. Adele survived me! But on that Wednesday, I had other things on my mind: how to face Mrs. Collingwood as Adele. Could I pull it off and make the old woman believe that I was her niece? In the event, there was no need to prove my skills of impersonation.

Mrs. Collingwood got up from the bench and waved to me, then dropped her arm and leaned forward at an odd angle. She took a few steps in a tentative way as if she was exploring the ground, then clutched her chest, sank to her knees and toppled over the edge of the cliff. Her head struck a rocky ledge before she landed in the water. She lay there, half-submerged, with the current tugging at her clothes. I had cried out in alarm, and immediately clapped my hands over my mouth, but too late. The Reverend, who had wandered on discreetly and left Mrs. Collingwood to her reminiscences, caught the sound of my voice and stopped. I ducked out of sight before he could turn around and scrambled away through the shrubs lining the path.

I turn my eyes back to the pages of Adele's memoir. This time I do feel a tug. The memory of that afternoon is taking hold. Can Adele pull me into the past? I hope so. I am all but convinced of it.

> There was great consternation when the Reverend returned to the house with my aunt seemingly unconscious, laid on a farmer's cart in her sopping wet clothes. She was carried inside, and a commotion ensued, with the cook calling for posset, and the maid for caudle, until Dr. Worth came

and pronounced my aunt dead. The death was either the consequence of her headlong fall, he said, or more likely her fall had been the consequence of a fatal stroke.

The Reverend was distraught.

"It was unfortunate that I was not at Mrs. Collingwood's side when it happened," he told us as he stood in the hall, his boots muddy and water dripping from his coat. "I heard a cry and hurried back at once. She must have tripped and fallen and been knocked unconscious. A farmer's lad, who happened by came running and, together, we lifted her out of the water and carried her to higher ground."

The boy told the same story, with embellishments. "There she was in the water, her skirts all abillow, and we had to drag her, the Reverend by the arms and me by the feet, and dropped her on the bank, and the Reverend turned her over and she spewed out a quantity of water—"

"That's enough," the Reverend said. "You need not go into detail, my boy. Don't you see that you are distressing Miss Collingwood?"

"Well, begging your pardon, Miss, so we dragged her to the water's edge, and I ran off to get help 'cause the Reverend was all fagged out and his boots were full of water. I tried to hail a woman I saw walking nearby, but she never looked my way."

That detail about the woman walking nearby struck terror into my heart. No one else considered it to be of any importance, but to me it was matter for grave reflection. Could that woman have been Lynne?

"In any case," the Reverend said, "a woman would have been of no help to us. It was a conveyance that was wanted in the circumstances."

For much of the fateful afternoon, I had lain on my bed, barely conscious, with the curtains drawn tight. At last, just before my aunt's body was brought to the house, Lynne returned and resumed her place within me. As always, her re-entry brought on the most excruciating pain, an unbearable tingling of the skin, a dull ache in the limbs, and a searing flame shooting through my head.

Lynne was in the habit of regaling me with her adventures as soon as I recovered from her agonizing re-entry. She plainly enjoyed the discomfort her escapades caused me. On that day, however, she was subdued and reticent. I let her be because I was stunned by my aunt's death. Later on, however, I recalled the boy's breathless account and began to question Lynne. It was then that she admitted to having witnessed the accident.

She told me the story so coldly that I shuddered inwardly. She had no feelings herself and did her best to quell my emotions as well. The only sensations she allowed were the passions to which her brutish disposition made her prone. She shrugged off the sadness my aunt's death engendered in me and poured cold water on my hot tears. She wouldn't let me grieve. Her first thought was: we are free of all constraints now and might choose our lovers as we please. It was only at night when I hovered between sleeping and waking, and Lynne had grown tired of interfering, that I was allowed to grieve for my aunt's loss. Her dear face appeared before my eyes and a sad longing crept into my heart, but in the morning, Lynne rose refreshed and covered my feelings with scorn.

The wake was hardly over when Lynne accosted me: "What are you waiting for, Adele? We are rid of the meddling old woman, and nothing stands between us and a bit of fun. How about a jaunt, a holiday in Paris? We could visit Francis. Maybe you can talk Eliza into coming along to make it look respectable—seeing that you always worry about your reputation. No one would find fault with Eliza if she wanted to see her brother or you for travelling in her company. It doesn't mean that you have to take up with Francis again. It would be an excuse to get away from Hinxworth for a while."

"You are the very devil, Lynne," I said. "Have you no compunction? No piety?"

"Oh, bother piety!" she said. "You know I don't go in for that kind of thing."

"Quite apart from considerations of piety," I said, "where would we get the money for such an extravagance? You forget the little matter of my aunt's will. I am sure she and the lawyer have thought of terms that will keep us on a short leash. She hinted as much."

"But she also said she wouldn't leave you without resources," Lynne said. "And since you've been as good as gold since the elopement—or should I say, as boring as hell—she may have relented and changed her will back again."

"No, Lynne," I said. "That little excursion to Scotland you made me take—"

"What! You were more than willing—"

"Don't deny that it was your influence that prevailed. I wouldn't have allowed Francis to persuade me if it hadn't been for you. That little excursion has sealed our fate."

"If you ask me, it wasn't the elopement that made her change the will," she said. "It was the Reverend."

A few days later Mr. Quail, the executor of my aunt's will, handed me a letter:

"Dear Adele, (it said) I am very sorry that you fastened your affections on an unworthy individual. The danger your suitor poses to your happiness may be past for the time being, since he has removed himself to Paris, but I mean to discourage Mr. Florsham in perpetuity by taking away what, I believe, is your chief attraction in his eyes: your expectations. I realize that I shall at the same time deprive you of enjoying the benefits of my estate, but I am convinced that it is all for the best. You will lose the counterfeit affection of Mr. Florsham, but I hope you will soon gain the genuine affection of a gentleman who values your true attractions, to wit, your good mind and your courageous heart.

To this end, I have decided to entrust my estate to the Reverend Percy Stockdale, leaving you only a small annuity and the right to reside at the house for life, with the upkeep and the servants' wages charged to him. Should you marry a gentleman who meets the Reverend's approval, the estate will revert to you, apart from certain charitable bequests and a sum to compensate the Reverend for his labours. In this manner I hope to make Mr. Stockdale the guardian of your intentions, prevent you from committing another folly, and ensure that you find an honest and respectable suitor.

I have stood in your mother's stead and feel a mother's love for you. You must believe me when I say that I have always meant well and had your happiness at heart in all my decisions. I embrace you, dearest Adele, with all my heart. God bless and protect you always. Farewell.

Your loving aunt, Martha Collingwood."

The terms of my aunt's testament reduced Lynne to impotent rage. She spewed out a torrent of vile curses that made my blood curdle.

I shared her exasperation, however. My aunt's intentions may have been good, but the results were disastrous for me. She had fallen for the Reverend, as Lynne put it, and trusted him implicitly. The will charged him to "protect my niece's interests and carry on the good work in which he is so laudably engaged, that is, the relief of widows and orphans." In other words, my aunt's testament gave the money into the Reverend's hands, to do with it as he pleased. There were no safeguards.

After the reading of the will, Thomas Quail took me aside. He was apologetic. He had warned my aunt against giving Percy Stockdale a free hand and suggested more stringent conditions. She rejected his advice. In fact, she rebuked him. It was unworthy of him to suspect the clerical gentleman's intentions, she said. Quail did his best, and finally persuaded her to insert the clause that prevented my complete ruin, which assigned me a small annuity and allowed me the free use of the house for life.

THE REVEREND had us under his thumb all right, but he had enough sense not to triumph over Adele in public. Naturally, the terms of Mrs. Collingwood's will were the talk of Hinxworth, but Percy Stockdale played his cards well. He looked sombre at Mrs. Collingwood's funeral, closed his eyes devoutly when the coffin was lowered into the ground, and delivered a sermon on the virtue of charity that had the congregation in tears.

He took on the role of the benevolent guardian and gave a flawless performance, but Adele and I could see the writing on the wall. According to the will, the Collingwood money would revert to Adele if she married a man of whom the Reverend approved. Of course, he would approve of one man only: himself. It was the obvious way of making himself the permanent owner of the Collingwood fortune.

"And he wouldn't be the first old codger to lust after a young wife," I said to Adele.

She agreed with me, but the Reverend was clever and didn't give us any reason to bring accusations against him or arouse the indignation of the Hinxworth matrons. He behaved correctly. He did not cut back on our household expenses, as he could have if he wanted to be mean. He did not dismiss any of the servants, although they had little work with only Adele to look after. He did ask her to give up the carriage, but not to save money. He had a different agenda. He wanted her to be dependent on him. His carriage was at Adele's disposal whenever she needed it, he said. He was so kind and reasonable it was hard to find fault with him, but there was something in his eyes that belied his goodwill. Whatever favours he was doing Adele, we knew he would call them in one day. My own worst fear was that he would guess at our double life and take action. What kind of action? Well, it was the eighteenth century, and everyone believed in the power of exorcism.

I turn back to Adele's memoir. Let's see what she has to say about that.

It started with the Reverend asking solicitous questions about my health. It hadn't escaped his notice that I was often indisposed, he said.

I did not confide in him. I kept silent about the cause of my excruciating migraines: Lynne's outings. I suffered terribly when she went off on her gypsy adventures, and they were frequent now. Her mind was set on men. If she could not have Francis, she wanted another: the strapping ostler at the village pub, for example, or Doctor Worth, who fascinated her. My efforts to repress her caused me a great deal of anguish, and her ability to escape the confines of my body nearly unhinged me.

The Reverend continued his Wednesday visits to the house after my aunt's death and, seeing that he could not induce me to walk with him, sat doggedly in my drawing room and made conversation.

"My dear Adele," he said, "I worry about your frequent indispositions. It's only natural that you should feel the loss of your aunt, and perhaps also"—he paused—"the loss of another person, who shall remain unnamed, but take care that your natural sadness does not turn into permanent melancholy."

"Thank you for your concern, Mr. Stockdale," I said. "I seem to have a surfeit of well-wishers and advisors. Just yesterday, Sarah, my maid, recommended root of lovage, seeds of wild parsnips, myrrh, mistletoe of the oak, and dried millipedes, all pounded and steeped for eight days in two quarts of brandy. And this morning Mrs. Minton took it upon herself to supply me with an elixir of iron filings, gentian, and centaury tops, steeped in rosewater. My mood would improve, she said, if I took four spoonfuls of the mixture every morning and then walked about for an hour."

The Reverend smiled. "I have my doubts about the efficacy of millipedes and iron filings," he said, "and I would not recommend anything steeped in brandy, but there can be no harm in walking about—especially in pleasant company." Did he mean his own company?

I kept silent while Lynne sneered and made disparaging remarks about the Reverend. She adored youthful vigour in a man and recoiled from the signs of age in Percy Stockdale— his mellow eye, his measured step, his greying hair, his wise words. They were all hateful to her. "Of course, *he* doesn't think of himself as old," she said. "He looks into the mirror and tells himself: 'Gray hair is becoming in a man—it makes him look distinguished. And what if I'm not as agile as a young man? I'll make it up to her in experience.' Men are full of such conceits."

While she grumbled, the Reverend started up again.

"It is with good reason," he said, "that St. Paul recommends marriage over celibacy—you know the passage in Corinthians to which I refer, my dear Adele. Very few human beings can do without a companion on their journey through life, always provided their companion is a suitable—"

I interrupted him impatiently: "I did not expect a sermon on the occasion of a private visit, Mr. Stockdale." And Lynne whispered into my ear: "Yeah, tell the old codger to hold his tongue." She had begun moaning and groaning as soon as St. Paul was mentioned, filling my head with her noise.

"I apologize," the Reverend said mildly, "I did not mean to catechize you, my dear."

"In any case," I said, bringing the matter to a head. "If you have such high regard for St. Paul's counsel to get married, I wonder why you did not take it yourself."

Let him come out with it at once, I thought, and propose to me, and I'll give him a piece of my mind to make him understand that I would rather give up the Collingwood fortune than pay for it with my happiness.

"My dear Adele," he said. "You reduce the matter to simple alternatives—falling in love or not falling in love—whereas there are many circumstances that might interfere with a person's wish to marry—as you no doubt know from experience."

"You are alluding to Mr. Florsham," I said. "I assure you I have learned my lesson. I concede that he was not a desirable suitor, so there is no need to go on about him."

"Quite so," the Reverend said. "I, too, find it more rewarding to discuss a question in principle rather than descending to individual cases. Let us talk about the subject of marriage in general, then. In your opinion, what are the characteristics a man must possess to win a woman's heart?"

All right, I thought, I'll play your game for a while. "He must be a man of integrity, to begin with: upright and truthful," I said.

"No one will gainsay you in that point."

"Twaddle," Lynne said, yawning. She was not fond of earnest conversation. Philosophical debates, moral disquisitions, political questions—they were all soporifics to my twin.

"He must, moreover, be intelligent, well educated and well spoken, with interests exceeding his professional calling," I said.

"It goes without saying that he must be polite and considerate?"

"Yes, and kind, too. I would not have a misanthrope."

"Ah," said the Reverend, "you speak of your personal preferences now?"

"Not at all," I said. "In fact, I am citing a list supplied two centuries ago by the great humanist Desiderius Erasmus, a list which is in my opinion unsurpassed."

"Your opinion," he said, "is remarkably similar to the contents of an article I read the other day in a London periodical."

Here he gave me a quizzical look, and I felt the blood rising to my cheeks, for I knew very well the article to which he was alluding.

"It was signed A. Leddy," he said, "—your name before adoption, I understand. Do you know the author?"

I shook my head. I could not utter a word for the constriction in my throat. Even Lynne was cautiously silent.

"Might he be a relative of yours?" the Reverend asked.

"I cannot say."

"I happen to know the publisher of the *Weekly Magazine*—Jeremiah Hurst. He is a friend of mine," said the Reverend, and no doubt registered the look of alarm on my face. "I wrote to him accordingly, asking him for the author's address. I told him I was struck by the acuity of his mind and wished to enter into correspondence with him."

"And have you received an answer?"

"I did. Mr. Hurst tells me that 'A. Leddy' is a pseudonym and that the author happens to reside in this very town."

I took a deep breath and said: "I may as well tell you what you have no doubt surmised already: I am the author of the article. And I used my father's name to honour him, for it was he who encouraged me to write."

"I had my suspicions," he said. "Allow me to congratulate you on the maturity of your thought and on your literary skill. I take it you used a nom de plume not only to honour your father but also because it is difficult for a woman to have her writings accepted for publication, however meritorious. I would however recommend you use a less transparent pseudonym."

His equanimity surprised me.

"You do not disapprove of my writing, then?" I asked.

"Not in principle," he said, and got up to take his leave. "After all I am a writer myself."

He had published a collection of sermons, and I must say he was a polished orator.

"I am at work on a memoir now," he said, "and shall take advantage of your talents to consult you in matters of style, if I may. We shall talk about that another time, however. I have presumed too long on your hospitality."

"What did I tell you?" Lynne said the moment he was gone. "You'd get into trouble with all that meditating and writing. I wouldn't mind the trouble if it was well compensated—but to drown yourself in a flood of useless words for a pittance, I don't know why you do it. I got more out of the men I knew in Bishopsgate than the miserly fee the printer is paying you, and for less work, let me tell you. And with some of them it wasn't even work. I got a deal of pleasure out of it, and they paid me handsomely—speaking of which, I haven't had any for a long time, pleasure, I mean." That night she would give me no peace with her whisperings.

"Watch out," she said. "Old Percy is trying to butter you up. He's thinking *I'll humour her for the time being*. In a couple of months, he'll get on his knees and propose."

She was right. Soon the Reverend's conversation became more pointed. He hinted at his feelings for me, he alluded to the conditions in my aunt's will. He told me that he had made his own will and was pondering the wording. He reminded me that the estate might revert to me, indeed that his own estate might go to me as well under certain circumstances. What circumstances? Marriage. He didn't come out with it, but his intention was clear to me. He was playing the courtship game, and the will was his trump card. If I didn't marry (he meant, if I didn't marry him), I ran the risk of losing out. He might leave the estate to his brother. Or to charity. His lawyer had suggested the addition of a codicil to his will, outlining the contingencies, he said. And all the time, while he was talking of legal matters, he waited for an encouraging word from me. He thought if he played his cards right, I would give in and indulge his old man's fantasies.

Lynne was vocal in her disgust.

"Get rid of him," she kept saying. "Get him out of the way."

"What do you mean—get rid of him?"

I thought of her violent past and became alarmed. I feared she was hatching a dark plot. Lynne's power over me had reached the point where I was no longer able to check her actions. No, I cannot be held responsible for what happened in the end, can I?

Yes, you can, bitch! We were together in this, you and I. —For a moment I'm breathless with anger. Then I come to my senses, or rather I notice what Adele's words and the sight of her handwriting are doing to me. They have aroused me! I'm feeling the past. Her words are taking hold of me. Adele will guide me back to Old London, I am sure of it now. I read on eagerly.

While I was afraid of Lynne, she was afraid of the Reverend. I would not have thought it possible that anyone could affect her thus, but the Reverend had dropped a word that terrified her: exorcism. He mentioned certain tales circulating about a Bristol man who had fits. According to the gossips, a local clergyman cured him by performing an exorcism that cast out the evil spirit within him. I could not tell whether the Reverend was only making conversation when he told me the story or was giving me a hint that he had guessed the true nature of my ailment.

I don't know if Lynne believed in God, but she certainly believed in the devil and the power of dark rites. She sneered, but she was afraid.

"Next thing, the old codger will pray over you, Adele, and light candles and burn incense, or whatever it is exorcists do."

She was afraid the Reverend might succeed and drive her out, make her lose her bodily abode and send her into limbo again. That is why she was determined to get rid of Percy Stockdale before he could get rid of her. She saw her chance when Mrs. Trescot, a friend of my late aunt, invited us to spend a week at her house in London. The Reverend thought the diversion would do me good and offered his carriage and his company. He had business in London himself, he said. I was not keen on his company, but I liked Mrs. Trescot and was looking forward to getting away from Hinxworth, which had become a place of sorrows for me.

Six months had gone by since my aunt's death, and I was now in half-mourning. It had been a relief to take off the crape, that scratchy piece of silk around my neck, which reminded me every morning of the sad day which had robbed my aunt of her life. Now that I was in half-mourning, I could at least wear a gray dress—a drab mushroom colour, but better than the dull black of paramatta silk which swallowed all light.

Lynne had gone into a spin of happiness when our journey to London became a certainty. She rattled my heart and made my temples pulse. The day of our departure arrived. As the carriage left Hinxworth, I could barely respond to the Reverend's polite conversation for all the stirrings within me and all the giddy talk echoing in my head. Lynne was full of London memories. In the afternoon, as our coach rattled through the suburbs of London and then threaded its way through the city, she was straining to see and hear everything. She made my eyes bulge with her curiosity and my mouth gape with her greed to breathe the city air, foul as it was. My ears were ready to burst, but she wanted to catch every sound, the cacophony of rattling carts, the scuffle of vendors and workmen, people shouting and cursing, the bursts of coarse laughter, the rough talk as we rolled through the poorer parts of town, the civilized tones as we reached the fashionable streets and finally, Mayfair and the townhouse of Mrs. Trescot, who had offered me hospitality. By the time we arrived there, I was prostrate with exhaustion from Lynne's harangues. She wanted to go to the Bullfrog, the ale house where she had been a serving girl. She complained vigorously of being confined to my body and strained against her prison. My head was aching intolerably. I could take only a little tea and nibble on a biscuit before excusing myself and sinking down on the bed in my room, half-dead. I was battling Lynne in vain. She was determined to return to her old haunts and find Jack. But even she wasn't bold enough or couldn't devise a way to escape, when I was surrounded by witnesses. She clawed at the back of my head, the bony walls of her prison, screaming "I want out! I want to look for Jack!"

But only I could hear her anguished screams.

"How can you long for such a man—a violent scoundrel?" I said, or rather thought, for she was a party to my thoughts.

"You'd know why, if you had felt his hands run over your body, and the touch of his hands on your breasts," she said, making me wince with pain and the crudeness of her remarks. "Jack was the best lover I ever had. I wish I could see him again."

"He is a criminal. For all you know, the law may have caught up with him. He may be in gaol."

She cried out. She wouldn't hear of her beloved Jack being in gaol. She couldn't bear the thought. She was drowning in a pool of longing.

"I never loved anyone as much as Jack," she said, rocking me back and forth, banging her head against the walls of my brain.

I am rocking back and forth with desire for Jack. I want him back. Now. I want my old life back, I want to slip away from my glass and steel apartment in the villa into the crooked streets of London. The scene comes to life in my brain—I no longer need to read Adele's lines. I remember how we argued when we were finally alone in Mrs. Trescot's guest bedroom.

"I'll go to the Bullfrog and find out where he is," I said.

"Nonsense," she said. "Why would you want to go back to that wretched place? How can you still have feelings for that man? I thought Dr. Worth was occupying your fancy now."

I sobbed in her eardrum. "But that's not love. All I want is a fling with the doctor. And that can wait until we're back in Hinxworth. Right now it's Jack I'm pining for."

I was burning for him. I am burning for him now.

I breathed words of fire into Adele's ear. I made her blood tingle like quicksilver. She did not have the strength to resist me. She could not prevent me from escaping the confines of her body. She was in an agony of fear that we might be discovered leaving the house, but our relationship had reached the tipping point. When I materialized that evening, I no longer worried about staying away too long. I no longer felt like a spirit in a borrowed body, a mere guest dwelling in Adele's mind and body. What part of her was left behind in the bed that night when I materialized? A phantom of a woman, with a residue of life twitching feebly within her? Or nothing but a shadow?

I (or should I say, we) got dressed, put on a hooded cape against the rain, pulled a shawl over my hair and ducked into the corridor. I made my way down the back staircase, slipped into the kitchen and took a knife from the drawer for protection. A key was hanging on a nail beside the back door. I took it down and unlocked the door. I waited on the threshold for a moment, listening to the deep silence of the sleeping house and the mournful rushing of water in the gutter outside. Then I locked up behind me and pocketed the key. I stood in the unlit alley behind the kitchen, bracing myself against the gusts of wind. It was good to listen with my own ears, to see the world through my eyes only. No need to share the hazy image of the world-tinged verdigris, tattered and old in the rain and the mist, and yet I thought I heard Adele's voice ringing in my head, screaming *No, don't, Lynne! We shall be raped and killed!* It was as if we had reversed roles and a part of her had stayed within me, like a fetus, as if she was in *my* bloodstream instead of me being in hers.

I hurried on, through the quiet neighbourhood of Mayfair, into the city, down to the river, along pot-holed streets. The wooden signs above the shops were swinging in their frames and creaking in the wind. Streetlamps became sparse, sights rose up and faded back into the dark, specks of light cast narrow tracks across lanes, leaving the doorways in deep gloom. Even I was afraid now, wondering whether I'd make it to the Bullfrog without being jumped by a robber, but I did make it to the alehouse, rattled the latch, and pushed open the stout door. The taproom was as I remembered it, the air putrid and thick with smoke. There was a press of people, the dull roar of rough talk, drunken howls, a hissing and braying and whinnying from gaping mouths. Well, yes, it was a hell hole of stinking bodies. I hesitated, but only because I realized that I could not go into the taproom, dressed the way I was, looking like a lady.

I slammed the door shut and went around the back, feeling my way down the stone steps that led to the kitchen.

Nellie, the cook, looked up from the pot she was stirring over the fire and wiped off the sweat trickling down her forehead, stinging her eyes and blinding her. She stared at me. Her voice was uncertain.

"What is it?" she said as if she had seen an apparition. "What can I do for you, lady?" "Nellie!" I said. "Don't you know me?"

A light came into her eyes when she heard my voice and she gave me a gap-toothed grin.

"Odds bods!" she said. "It's Lynne! We all thought you were dead. And here you are, all dolled up in fancy clothes and looking like a lady." She gave me an admiring glance. "I hardly knowed you, girl." She wiped her hands on her dirty apron and fingered the fine wool of my shawl. "So you've come back for a taste of the old Bullfrog?"

"Only to find Jack. Can you tell me where he is, Nellie?"

"In gaol. They said he killed you in a black rage."

"Jack? Not he. Someone knifed me to get back at him, but I fought him off and got away!"

"They swore they saw your dead body, and it was Jack who did you in. He'll hang for it, and good riddance, I say. That lad is the very devil."

"Devil take *you*, Nellie!" I shouted. "They'll hang Jack for what he didn't do. I'm alive, I'm right here, ain't I ?"

She shrugged. "Yeah, but even if he didn't kill *you*, he did enough bad work to hang ten times over."

I broke out in tears. I couldn't stop sobbing Jack's name.

Nellie realized that she had made a mistake badmouthing Jack.

"Come now," she said. "I didn't know you were that thick with him. I didn't mean it, you know. Jack weren't that bad."

I wiped away my tears.

Nellie put her arm around me and patted my back. "What's that you got there?" she asked when her fingers brushed against my coat pocket, which held the knife.

"A hard answer in case someone asks me a hard question," I said, and she nodded.

"Want me to get one of the lads in the taproom to go with you?" she said. "You got away once, but you ain't got nine lives, dearie."

"I can look after myself," I said and went out into the night again, slip-sliding on the wet cobble stones, sobbing as I thought of Jack locked up in gaol, trying to keep my wits together. It was a dangerous corner of London, and there were ragged figures peeping out of the shadows and crooked shapes huddled against the walls of rotten houses. I kept a tight grip on the kitchen knife in my pocket. Then I saw a man leaning into the driving rain, wrapped in a greatcoat, his flapped hat pulled low over his face. There was something familiar about him. Was it Percy Stockdale? No, it couldn't be, I thought. What business did *he* have in Bishopsgate? I saw him go up to the doorway of a dingy tenement building and start talking up a whore. The swine! I thought. Giving Adele sly smiles and hinting at his feelings for her! Again, I sensed Adele within me, almost as if she had spoken those words.

A gust of wind was driving the rain. I pulled my shawl close to avoid discovery. I didn't want to run into the Reverend now. I had had enough adventure for one night. But it was too late. He turned and looked around, as if to check whether someone was following him, as if he sensed my presence. Then he spotted me and called out: "Adele?" It was a question. He wasn't sure. But I panicked and ran.

He came after me. I heard his pounding footsteps, his ragged breathing as he overtook me and seized my arm. I felt my borrowed body collide violently with the Reverend's. He let out a shout. Then there was silence. His grip on me relaxed, and he sank to the ground. I looked down on my hand and realized that I had pulled the knife from my pocket and was clutching it. I dropped the blade, heard it clatter on the pavement, got up and ran down the empty street. At the corner I stopped and looked back at the dark shape on the ground, at the Reverend's body, his white hand stretched out in a gesture of helplessness. The whore he had talked to earlier was by his side, bending over him. I ran on and did not stop until I reached Mrs. Trescot's house in the early morning hours. I let myself in and sneaked up to Adele's room, cleaned the muddy hem of my frock as well as I could, wiped my boots, slipped back into Adele's body or rather the shadow outline of her body lying on the bed, and was overcome by sleep as heavy as a coma. When we awoke—the maid was pulling back the drapes to let in the sunlight and eyeing the wet boots on the floor with surprise—I quietly looked up to the ceiling above the bed through Adele's eyes and said to her: "We'll have our peace now, I suppose."

"What do you mean, Lynne?" she whispered, terror in her voice.

And so, I told her I'd knifed him, but of course she already knew. I do think she was in my blood that night, that we were one, and that she recalled what happened, except that she thought of it as a prophetic dream which had come true.

I was so close to success that night in London, so close to taking control of Adele's mind and body. For the first time I had managed to carry her away with me. She could no longer keep me from finding Jack. And then all my hopes collapsed. First Nellie's ominous words—Jack will hang for sure—then the encounter with the Reverend. People have called me unfeeling, abrasive, and self-centered. I may be all that, but I'm no murderer. It wasn't my fault that Percy Stockdale was slumming it in Bishopsgate. And I didn't go after him. He tackled me. I acted in self defense. If he hadn't tripped and fallen against me, he would have gotten away with a nicked finger or a slashed coat sleeve. In any case, I have no regrets. Percy Stockdale got what he deserved.

I turn back to the facsimile in my hands and search Adele's words: Does she dare to write about that night? Does she blame me for what happened?

I had no more power over Lynne. She escaped, and I fell into a swoon, no, fell prey to a nightmare. I dreamed that the Reverend died a violent death. It was a dream unlike any

I ever had before. The damp night air on my face felt real. I spoke in a voice that was not mine and yet I felt it pour out of my own mouth. My whole body was alien to me, but I was able to move my limbs and grapple with an enemy who held me fast. I fought him off, and when he fell to the ground defeated and I ran for my life, it did not feel like a dream. I awoke with a gasp.

Lynne returned at dawn and re-entered my body, yet it seemed she had never left it.

"Did you go to the Bullfrog?" I asked.

"Leave me alone," she said. "I'm tired."

We were both overcome by exhaustion and fell into a heavy sleep. When I woke, the dream was still vividly present to my mind, as if I had indeed lived it. Thinking back, I became convinced, moreover, that the enemy I fled, the man who fell to the ground was Percy Stockdale. It was a foreboding dream. Was the Reverend in danger?

My hand trembled on the railing as I walked downstairs to face Mrs. Trescot over breakfast. My foot faltered on the steps. I was in a vertigo of fear. Had anyone in the house heard Lynne come in last night? Had the maid said anything about my wet boots? I entered the breakfast room in trepidation, but Mrs. Trescot greeted me with a smile and a kiss on the cheek and made only polite conversation. What were my plans for the day? she asked. She hoped the rain would let up. She so wanted to go for a ride in the park this afternoon. Her morning was taken up with tedious affairs, alas.

"A consultation with the housekeeper about certain domestic matters, and after that, an appointment with the dressmaker for a fitting. I would have much preferred to enjoy your company, my dear."

"Don't trouble yourself on my account, Mrs. Trescot. Indeed, I was about to make *my* excuses to *you*. The journey has fatigued me more than I expected. I think I will keep to my room. In the circumstances, you will not mind, I hope."

She did not mind and was quite content not to see me for the rest of the morning. The day crept by, with me agonizing over the Reverend. I had told Lynne the dream I had in her absence.

"I saw him lying on the cobblestones," I said. "He was injured or even dying. What if the dream comes true?"

"I hope it does," Lynne said. "Then we would be rid of him. But we'll find out about that tonight. He is supposed to take us to the theatre, isn't he?"

Lynne had led a blighted life. It had hardened her. She seemed unconcerned, and I suffered in silence.

In the afternoon, as it was still raining, Mrs. Trescot asked me for a little music. I complied, playing a few pieces on the spinet—badly, as I could not concentrate and barely knew what I was doing. Then it was time to dress. We had made plans to go to the theatre in the evening. Mr. Stockdale and his friend, the printer Jeremiah Hurst, were to escort us. The appointed time came, and the Reverend failed to make his appearance.

"Is Mr. Stockdale always this late?" Mrs. Trescot asked, as we were waiting in the drawing room.

"No, he is a punctual man," I said. My innards twisted at the recollection of my dream. I fidgeted with my handkerchief.

Fearing we would be late for the performance, Mrs. Trescot gave orders to ready her own carriage and sent a servant to the Reverend's lodgings to say that we would meet him at the theatre. She was puzzled and finally alarmed when neither the Reverend nor his friend was to be found, and the seats beside us remained vacant. The play, a silly little comedy, barely distracted us, and certainly got no laughs from me.

As we came out of the theatre, a messenger was waiting for us with a note from Mr. Hurst:

"Dear Mrs. Trescot, I refrained from writing earlier because I did not wish to disturb you and Miss Collingwood unnecessarily, but I cannot withhold from you any longer the disquieting news: Mr. Stockdale did not return to his lodgings last night, and a search party has yielded no clues to his whereabouts. Our friend remains at large, and I am at a loss how to proceed from here. I shall, however, take the liberty to call on you tomorrow morning with any news I may receive in the meantime. In the hope of seeing this mystery solved in a fortuitous manner, I remain at your service. Jeremiah Hurst."

Then at last I was certain: What I had experienced last night was no dream. Lynne had carried me away with her. I really was at the Bullfrog, breathed in the noxious vapours of that godforsaken place, grappled with a man, left him dying in the street, and ran home through the rainy night.

Lynne knew what happened to the Reverend and was perhaps instrumental in the turn of events. She was cowed, but she felt neither remorse nor pity. She was apprehensive only of discovery, whereas I feared the wrath of the all-seeing God, the avenger of evil. I could not divorce myself from what Lynne had done. I felt guilty by association.

By association! Adele wanted to put the chief responsibility on me. She pretended Stockdale's death was only a dream vision, but she knew that was a lie, or self-deception at any rate. She was there with me. We acted as one and I remember the argument we had that morning.

"You know exactly what happened last night," I said to her when we were alone.

She clung to her version of the events. I had left her behind as always, she insisted. She had been in her bed, in the grip of a nightmare. "It was you who stabbed him and left him lying in the street!"

"Never mind who did what. If he is dead, you can be sure that someone stripped his body and tossed it into the river," I said. "So, you needn't worry about any telltale evidence."

"I pray he is merely injured, but I fear he will have recognized you, or rather me, and what if you were observed in the act?"

"If he is alive, he'll keep his mouth shut. After all we caught him talking to a prostitute," I said. "If he is dead, and she saw what happened, she too will keep it to herself. No doubt she helped herself to his money, his rings, watch, cufflinks and anything else he had on him that was of value. You need not worry about a prostitute offering to testify before a judge."

"And what about the divine judge?" Adele said. "God does not need human witnesses to pass sentence on a sinner."

"Oh, please, spare me the pious twaddle," I said. "Look around you. Do you see justice anywhere? My lover is sitting in gaol for another man's crime, and you talk to me of divine justice?"

And what does Adele have to say about that?

The next morning Hurst paid us a visit together with the Reverend's lawyer, Mr. Merryweather. He was a corpulent, pink-faced man and appeared at the door of the drawing room like a blustery bird of omen. My last encounter with him had been on another woeful occasion—the death of my aunt and the reading of her will, which put the Reverend in charge of the Collingwood fortune. Mr. Merryweather now informed us of the Reverend's death with a great deal of huffing and puffing as if he was short of breath, although I suspected it was a mannerism he cultivated to impress on his clients the laborious nature of his task.

"A violent death. A robbery turned murder," he said but he did not wish to dwell on the distressing circumstances more than necessary.

Mrs. Trescot clasped her chest and gave out a shriek. I did not have to feign dismay. The lawyer's words recalled the horror of the previous night. Anguish and remorse flooded my mind. Should I confess what I knew?— "What!" Lynne hissed. "Are you mad? Keep your mouth shut, you stupid idiot."

Mr. Hurst wiped his eyes with a crumpled handkerchief and took my hand wordlessly. He was overcome with grief, mourning the death of his friend. I pressed his hand in silent commiseration.

"Of course, you may rely on me for any assistance required, Miss Collingwood," Mr. Merryweather said, bowing to me and breathing heavily. "I am not at liberty to say much about the Reverend's testament, which he has lodged with me, but I can offer you some reassurance. The arrangements made for you at your aunt's death will remain in force, that is, you retain the right to reside at the house on the same conditions as before. The Reverend's heir has been notified, but it may be some time until everything is settled and the will proved, since he lives in the colonies."

I naturally assumed that the Reverend had left his estate to his brother, Captain Stockdale, although I had heard that the two men were not on friendly terms.

"Captain Stockdale has gone to the colonies?" I said, surprised. As far as I knew, the Reverend's brother lived not fifty miles from Hinxworth.

Mr. Merryweather coughed and cleared his throat. "As I said, Miss Collingwood, I am not at liberty to speak of the details of the will. I can only assure you that the Reverend's untimely demise will not affect your annuity and that you may continue drawing on me for the funds."

Mr. Merryweather's reticence about the will was the first inkling I had of Percy Stockdale's estate (or rather my aunt's money) going to someone other than Captain Stockdale, his nearest relative. In the course of the events, I discovered that the beneficiary was his nephew, Andrew Prior. The young man's good fortune soon became known in Hinxworth, and when he arrived in town to wind up the Reverend's affairs, the Hinxworth matrons received him like a new star in the firmament. He was the most eligible of bachelors, and they could not praise him enough. Such an elegant figure! Such a perfect gentleman! And of marriageable age, too.

"Not to mention his money," Lynne said in her matter-of-fact voice. "—the Collingwood money. Here is your chance to get it back. Why don't you go for him, Adele?"

Lynne had been lying low for a time after that disastrous night in London and our return to Hinxworth. I would have savoured the peace and quiet if my conscience had allowed it. I wanted to unburden my soul and tell what I knew of the Reverend's death, but I was a coward. I could not face the consequences—gaol or worse. Lynne brooded over the fate of her lover Jack and interfered with my thoughts only when my conscience seemed to gain the upper hand. Then she rattled and blew up like a storm, sweeping away what resolve I had with an unearthly noise that resembled an animal's howl more than a human utterance. She robbed me of all will to confess. I slumped into resignation.

I TURN the page. There is an illustration. A page from *The Daily Advertiser* which carried Percy Stockdale's obituary.

I'm sure it got the attention of readers. It was full of juicy information: a clergyman robbed and murdered in Bishopsgate (Patricia's footnote: a disreputable district of London), and a prostitute on the scene. The question must have been on every reader's mind: What was the Reverend doing in Bishopsgate?

According to the obituary:

> Mr. Stockdale had made it his mission to persuade disorderly women to abandon their sinful lives. Well-meaning friends cautioned him against an undertaking so fraught with danger to his person, but he shrugged off the risks, hoping for spiritual gains. Mr. Stockdale will be known to the reading public as the author of *Sixteen Sermons Preached on Board of the Intrepid*. A volume of correspondence—*Letters and Recollections of a Life Time*—is awaiting publication. Persons wishing to place their names on the subscription list are invited to visit the offices of the publisher, Jeremiah Hurst, in Paternoster Row.

The Reverend may have been known to the public as a writer of sermons. To Adele and me he was known as a bully and a hypocrite. I could see the thoughts twisting between his eyebrows when he talked to us. He was an operator, always deep in strategy, trying to keep us off-balance and in the dark. When he spoke, his face was animated, his voice had a persuasive edge, his eyes were alive. There was something youthful about him when he talked. But when he was silent and the muscles around his mouth relaxed, he looked like the old man he was—fifty-one, which was ancient as far as I was concerned. There were other signs that gave away his age—the raised blue veins on his hands and the way he walked, stiff and knock-kneed—signs that made his little attentions to Adele repellant. He was after her, and pushing hard, and we couldn't get rid of him. He had money and authority. We had neither. We were powerless against Percy Stockdale, but on that night in London he ran out of luck.

There is a knock on the door. I've ordered lunch for one o'clock. Rosa rolls in the serving table. I guess James is busy with his second career, doing his best at the audition I saw flashing in his mind.

I have ordered up finger food because I'm planning to eat and read. It's one of my bad habits. The habit of a lonely diner. Keep eyes on book, grope for food, push into mouth, leave greasy fingerprints when turning the page or swiping the Kindle screen.

Rosa puts out plates of scallops wrapped in bacon, little quiches, and chicken satays, then hands me a small white envelope on a silver tray.

"What's that?" I ask.

"Ees a note for you, Mees Addington," she says with a smile. She's definitely over her depression. And she's thinking of James. What has James got to do with this? Is he her boyfriend? No, there is something else going on, but I can't make out her Spanglish thoughts.

"Does James have the afternoon off?" I ask.

"No, ees no longer here."

"Fired?"

"No, no. He quit job."

She lowers her eyes, rolls the serving table into the corridor and pulls the door shut behind her, leaving a mist of thoughts that are gibberish to me.

I open the envelope and look at the note, written on Dream Villa stationary.

Hey, bitch. I'm out of here. I've seen a lot of assholes at Dream Villa, but you take first prize. If you need any more fucking books, you can get them yourself. James.

The little shit. I guess he got the part he auditioned for. Let's just hope he doesn't have to play a butler. As for book orders: never mind. I have both volumes now, courtesy of Patricia. I've got the facsimile, and I am hoping to get my hands on the real thing soon.

I line up the plates with the finger food and treat them like popcorn at the movies. I keep my fingers grazing over them, moving the little bits to my mouth. My thoughts are already on the next page of Adele's *Cautionary Tale*. With every line, the past becomes more palpable, so real it almost blots out the present.

ADELE

THE HINXWORTH gossips eagerly seized on the obituary in *The Daily Advertiser*. The sordid manner of the Reverend's death raised questions. What was he doing in Bishopsgate at that time of night? they asked. Was his concern for prostitutes genuine or motivated by less honourable motives than those reported in the newspaper? They examined his past, the peculiar circumstances in which he had acquired his fortune. Why did Mrs. Collingwood leave her money to him? Why did he make no effort to save her from drowning—was her death perhaps convenient and furthering his own goals? Was Percy Stockdale a fortune-hunter, who had courted the widow Collingwood for her money? Then came the news that the Reverend had left his money, not to his brother, as everyone expected, but to his nephew, Andrew Prior.

The nephew too was caught by surprise, as I discovered when I made his acquaintance. He was a clerk in the office of a notary, he told me, and he had been at his writing desk copying out a contract when a letter was delivered, asking him to attend the reading of his uncle's will in the chambers of Benjamin Merryweather, attorney-at-law.

I had received a similar letter. When I arrived at his chambers, I was ushered into the presence of Mr. Merryweather. He greeted me in his usual manner, with asthmatic breathing. His small, pursed mouth gave him an air of astonishment, as if he had just been presented with an incredible piece of evidence and was receiving it with a sharp intake of breath.

Soon afterwards Andrew Prior joined us. I did not know at the time what his relationship was to the Reverend or that he was the chosen heir. I saw a young man, blond, snub-nosed and generally displaying a cheerful countenance that made Lynne stir within me and ask "Well, what have we here?" as if he was put on display for our perusal. His clothes were well brushed, I noticed, and his boots well-polished. "Nice body," Lynne said. "Presentable, certainly, but not very fashionable."

After the introductions had been made and I was given to understand that Andrew Prior was the late Reverend's nephew, Lynne's tone changed. An heir was always attractive. Never mind his sense of fashion.

Mr. Merryweather proceeded to business. He reached for the file that was in readiness before him on the desk and began to read out the terms of the will:

"The Reverend Percival Douglas James Stockdale, rector of Hinxworth, disposes of his effects as follows."

Here he stopped, breathed deeply, filled his lungs with sufficient breath for the task ahead, peered through the lower part of his spectacles, and continued reading from the document in front of him.

"I, the undersigned, bequeath to Andrew Prior, son of Mary Prior, née Stockdale, and of her husband, Thomas Prior, all my hereditaments in land and moneys. As it is my understanding that the said Andrew Prior may have departed for the colonies, advertisements are to be placed in the major newspapers to ascertain his whereabouts and to make him acquainted with the existence of this will. Should it be impossible to contact him within twelve months after my death, the instructions set out in Codicil A shall apply."

The codicil! Lynne almost exploded when she heard the word. I had to press my lips together to quell Lynne's cries. The Reverend had mentioned the codicil to us many times, as an inducement or more likely, a threat. He indicated his willingness to amend his will and make me his heiress under certain circumstances—marriage, he meant.

Mr. Merryweather now held up a wrapper marked "Codicil A" before continuing to read: "Should the said Andrew Prior be found within the period specified, I instruct my solicitor, Mr. Merryweather, to destroy Codicil A forthwith, and bind him to secrecy regarding its contents."

Here the lawyer paused and unfolded the wrapper marked Codicil A. It was empty.

Mr. Prior wrinkled his brow and asked: "You have destroyed the codicil, according to the instructions?"

"No, Mr. Prior, I never received it. I drew up a document of that description for Mr. Stockdale, but he took it away to make changes to it and never returned it to my office. Wherever it may be now, your presence here renders it void in any case."

He gave me a quizzical look, almost as if he regretted that the codicil had become void. No doubt he was informed of the Reverend's intentions and knew perhaps that I might have been the beneficiary of the will if I had accepted the Reverend or if Andrew Prior had not come forward to claim the legacy. Then again Codicil A may have designated the Reverend's brother as the heir, even though the two men were estranged at the time of his death—a quarrel over a point of honour, as far as I understood. But those were idle thoughts. I was out of luck. Andrew Prior was here to claim his legacy.

After a little more huffing, Mr. Merryweather went on with the reading of the will. He lowered his eyes to the document and, running his index finger down the page, read through the list of furniture, books and personal belongings. The last paragraph enjoined the heir to expedite the publication of the Reverend's memoir entitled *Letters and Recollections of a Life Time* and to assume the costs associated with publishing it. On hearing that title, Lynne and I were equally alarmed. Did those recollections include references to my elopement? I certainly would not want to see his reflections on my affairs to become public.

Merryweather had gone on and had now come to the funds and moneys-of-account "as well as a dwelling in Hinxworth, known as Three Oaks and presently tenanted." He paused, contemplating me briefly while I in turn looked at my prospective landlord.

It was clear from Andrew Prior's mien that he had expected neither the property nor the moneyed wealth revealed in the will. No doubt he wondered about the property, knowing that the rectory in which Percy Stockdale had resided was for his lifetime use only. His questions soon made it clear that he had no inkling of the circumstances under which the house had come into his uncle's possession. As for moneys-of-account, he must have realized that the Rector could not, by any calculation, have put by that amount even if he had been exceedingly frugal.

When he gave expression to his surprise at the size of the estate, Mr. Merryweather with a glance in my direction and after some harrumphing and clearing of his throat offered this explanation: The Reverend had come into his fortune very lately through the death of a wealthy friend, Mrs. Martha Collingwood, who had left her estate to him. At the mention of the Collingwood name, the heir gave me a questioning look.

Meanwhile Mr. Merryweather kept hemming and hawing and finally said:

"I hope you will not think me forward, Mr. Prior, when I say that Mrs. Collingwood expected the Reverend to make charitable use of her money."

Andrew did think him forward. "You may safely leave that matter to me," he said tersely. "And who is the present tenant of Three Oaks?"

I answered this question myself. "I am the tenant. Mrs. Collingwood was my aunt."

I could guess what he was thinking: How was it that my aunt passed me over in favour of Percy Stockdale? And under what conditions did I now reside in the house I might have called my own in the ordinary course of things? Perhaps it even occurred to him that the fortune Percy Stockdale had inherited so recently would have gone to me if he had not been found and the mysterious Codicil A had come into play.

Mr. Merryweather coughed asthmatically. "Mrs. Collingwood's will, which made Percy Stockdale her heir, also specified that her niece be given the right to reside in the house rent-free and to enjoy the usage of its furniture, linen, and other chattel on the premises, with the upkeep of the house being charged to the heir—to wit, the Reverend—a duty that has now devolved on you, sir."

"And which I shall fulfil to the letter, and beyond," Andrew said, reddening and bowing to me. It was a most awkward moment. "I certainly hope he'll fulfil his obligations," Lynne said under my breath, and made my breast heave with her indignation.

"If you wish to go beyond the letter, Mr. Prior, that is of course your privilege," Mr. Merryweather said in a reserved tone, as if to say, *but I doubt it.* "In addition to lifetime residence, Mrs. Collingwood's will specified that her niece be paid an annuity of fifty pounds per annum, to be dispensed quarterly, an obligation that also devolves on you. Indeed, I have allowed Miss Collingwood to draw the amount owed for this quarter, pending the proofing of the will and subsequently, your authorization, Mr. Prior."

"Quite right," Andrew Prior said with another bow toward me, but his blush had not subsided as he came to penetrate the meaning of Merryweather's remarks concerning charity.

"Finally," the lawyer continued, "we come to specific behests." He read on: "I furthermore direct my heir to pay my housekeeper, Mrs. Anna Lambsley, the sum of thirty pounds in gratitude for her loyal services. I direct Mrs. Lambsley to dispose of my clothing according to her wishes and keep such linen and household articles as she might need in her retirement. The cook, the cook's helper, the gardener, the houseboy, and the maid are to be paid their wages for six months or until they have secured a new position, whichever comes first. I furthermore wish Miss Collingwood to select from my possessions at the rectory any item or items of furniture, books, ornaments or other personal belongings as a memento of our friendship and a token of my admiration for her many accomplishments."

Mr. Merryweather had come to the end of the will, took off his spectacles, and used them to weigh down the document as if it might fly away otherwise. An uneasy silence descended until I said, to put an end to the awkward situation: "Thank you, Mr. Merryweather. I suppose that is all that concerns me. If there is no further need for my presence—"

"I won't presume on your time, Miss Collingwood," Merryweather said promptly. "I will send you a copy of the will in due time. Everything else, I suppose, can be transacted between you and Mr. Prior directly."

I sensed a general relief that we had gotten through this unpleasant business in a polite fashion.

"I shall write to you, Miss Collingwood, and let you know when I will be in Hinxworth to supervise the removal of the Reverend's belongings from the rectory," Mr. Prior said. "The incumbent will no doubt want to take vacant possession as soon as possible. I will inform the housekeeper of Mr. Stockdale's behests and direct her to allow you to go through the Rectory and select a memento from the Reverend's possessions."

There was nothing further to do or say, and I wished the two gentlemen a good day. Andrew Prior too rose from his seat, but Merryweather waved him back, saying: "Don't go yet, Mr. Prior. We have papers to sign."

Nevertheless, Andrew Prior followed me to the door and kissed my hand gallantly. "I hope there will be an opportunity to talk about all of this when I am in Hinxworth," he said. I nodded but did not reply to his friendly overture and kept my eyes down, as I was fully occupied in repressing Lynne's interference. Her anger had boiled up during the reading and had turned into a firestorm when

Merryweather came to the part inviting me to select a keepsake from the Reverend's belongings. "The bastard!" she hissed into my ear. "Like hell I want to remember him!" Her wrath was burning my innards, but when Andrew kissed my hand, she calmed down.

"Well," she whispered pertly, "here is our chance to recover the Collingwood fortune. He is a handsome fellow, worth the effort." I had no intention of making the effort or go out of my way to be agreeable to Mr. Prior with a view to rousing his interest in my person. If I had been amenable to trading for a wealthy husband in the marriage market, I could have accepted the Reverend's overtures and saved myself a great deal of trouble. Of course, Lynne knew my thoughts and argued back: But the Reverend was an old codger, and Andrew Prior is young and good-looking. She approved of him, although not wholeheartedly. He was too gentle and too polite for her taste, but she clung to the idea that I might go after him, seduce him, and get the Collingwood money back. "Go on," she said, "give him a smile. He's got the money." She wanted me to play the coquette, but I had other business on my mind. Andrew had been charged with seeing to the publication of Percy Stockdale's memoirs, and the obituary had mentioned the prospective publisher, the Reverend's friend Jeremiah Hurst in Paternoster Road. That was going to be my next stop. I wanted to anticipate Andrew. Perhaps Hurst would allow me to read the manuscript if I explained that my aunt and myself might be mentioned in it and that I wished to avoid drawing attention to myself. It was a justifiable request. If I found that the manuscript contained material detrimental to my reputation—a mention of the elopement, perhaps, or speculation about the origin of the frequent "migraines" I suffered during Lynne's escapes—I hoped to persuade Mr. Hurst to suppress those passages.

Thus, I made my way to Paternoster Row without delay.

ARRIVING AT Hurst's printing shop, I stood for a while at the unmanned counter in the front room. When no one came forward to attend me, I went on into the workshop and raised my voice above the din of the presses to attract the attention of the compositors. One of them finally interrupted his work long enough to inquire into my business and when I asked to see Hurst, informed me brusquely that the proprietor was engaged. I used a ruse and told him I had come to subscribe to a forthcoming book, and at once the sullen expression of the workman changed to one of civility. He offered to see whether Mr. Hurst might set aside his present work to attend me.

Not long afterwards, Hurst himself emerged from the back of the shop. He was in shirt-sleeves and had the look of a man roused from deep concentration or else from an afternoon snooze, but he rallied, greeted me politely, and led me past the presses to a slovenly office. Every space on the desk, the two chairs facing it, and the deep shelves lining the walls, were covered with bundled manuscripts and wooden boxes overflowing with yet more paper. "You should have given me warning, Miss Collingwood," he said by way of apology for the state of his office. The basso of his voice always surprised me. One did not expect such a rich timbre to issue from such a small man, for Mr. Hurst was rather delicate in form and figure.

He shifted some of the stacks of paper to make room for me to sit down, but before I could state my business, we were interrupted by a knock and the announcement of a second visitor: Andrew Prior. He greeted me in some surprise, and I felt uncomfortably like an interloper. I knew of course why he had come—in fulfilment of the obligation the will imposed on him, but his promptness was most inconvenient to me, and I cast around how best to explain my own presence.

Hurst looked from me to Mr. Prior and back again. "I see you know Miss Collingwood, but I haven't had the honour of your acquaintance, sir. Have you come on joint business?"

"My name is Prior," Andrew said. "I am a relative of the Reverend Stockdale, whose memoir you have undertaken to publish. I have come to assume the cost of the enterprise in the hope that it will hasten the appearance of the book."

"Heyday!" exclaimed Mr. Hurst, folding his face into a grimace, somewhat between a grin and a cry. "There seems to be a great interest all of a sudden in Percy's *Letters and Recollections*. You are not the only one who wants them printed with all despatch, which has perhaps to do with the method of Percy's despatch. Murder sells copy, you know. A deadly knifing has a peculiar attraction for the populace as long as it isn't their own hide that's nicked by the knife."

Andrew took umbrage at the jocular manner in which the printer referred to the death of the Reverend. "I thank you not to joke about a crime that has cost Mr. Stockdale his life," he said earnestly. "And what do you mean about there being a great interest in the manuscript all of a sudden?"

I too was baffled. I myself had an interest in the manuscript, but I had not made my request to Hurst as yet.

"I mean," said Hurst, "that another gentleman came here yesterday, inquiring after Percy's memoir. He indicated that he had a printer who would undertake the business without delay or expectation of further subscription. And I am sorry to say I gave the manuscript to him."

"I can well imagine that you are sorry losing a job by your precipitate surrender of the manuscript," Andrew said rather sharply.

"I don't think you can imagine it," answered Hurst, turning serious and furtively wiping his eyes. I too felt somber at the thought that a stranger was now in possession of the manuscript and was, perhaps at this very moment learning the secrets of my life. Lynne who had stirred at Mr. Prior's appearance had gone quiet as well, no doubt thinking of the consequences of what we had just heard.

"Well," Andrew said, "since my business here is done, I'd better take my leave."

"Half a minute, Mr. Prior," Hurst said, putting a hand on his arm. "You are not by any chance related to the printer Thomas Prior, who intended to go into business with me, if death had not put an end to all his earthly business?"

"You must mean my father," he replied.

"Your father!" the printer exclaimed. "Then you must be Andrew. Yes! Now that I look at you more closely, I recognize in you the features of my old friend. And to think that both Thomas Prior and Percy Stockdale have died prematurely, cut off by a jealous fate. It is a sad thing to survive one's companions, let me tell you." The printer wept openly now and wiped the tears from his eyes. "If I joked about Percy's death earlier, believe me, it was only to hide my feelings. But let me welcome you properly, my dear young friend, now that I understand who you are." And he embraced Andrew like the prodigal son returned to his father's home.

"Oh, then—," the young man said touching his forehead. "Yes, a faint memory is coming back to me of you visiting our house with my uncle when I was a boy."

"But how comes it," the printer continued, "that you are in London? Percy told me that you had gone to the colonies and was very sorry to lose touch with you so completely."

"I first heard of this at the lawyer's today and can't help being puzzled. I have never set foot outside of England," he said. "I cannot think why my late uncle believed I was anywhere but in London. Indeed, I wrote to him a few years ago, when his sermons appeared, and was gratified at the time to receive a civil response expressing the hope of renewing our acquaintance. But that's as far as the matter went. I never heard of him again and put it down to the manner of gentlemen who write many pleasant things without meaning them and thought that he was perhaps less keen on meeting with an impoverished relative than his polite letter made me believe."

"You are entirely mistaken when you ascribe such motives to Percy," said Hurst. "I can tell you what he had to say about that business, and you will perhaps guess the rest. He was very pleased to receive your letter, he told me, but misplaced your address and applied for that information to his brother, whom he knew to be in touch with you. He received a note from the Captain by return mail, saying that even if you had crossed the ocean and gone to the furthest reaches of Upper Canada, the distance was less than the distance he wished to place between you and Percy—or words to that effect. On receiving that message, my clerical friend used very unclerical language, let me tell you. 'What the deuce can he mean?' he exclaimed. 'What a boorish fellow my brother is! I suppose he means to say that Andrew has emigrated and gone to seek his fortune in the colonies.'"

"How very odd," Mr. Prior said.

"Since you never left London, I can only surmise that there was a deceptive purpose, although why his brother would want to deceive Percy about your whereabouts is not clear to me."

"There was a great deal of animosity between the brothers, I regret to say."

"I know," the printer said. "That was a sorry business. But tell me, Andrew—if I may resume the familiar address, for I called you 'Andrew' when you were a boy—tell me, how is it that you refer to yourself as Percy's impecunious relative, yet are willing to pay for the publication of his *Letters*? For that was your purpose in coming here if I understood you correctly?"

"You did," Andrew said, "but my circumstances have changed a great deal." He cast me a guilty look and reddened before he explained the matter. "Percy Stockdale has made me his heir."

"You—his heir?" said Hurst and shot him a look of surprise. "I would have thought—" He did not finish the sentence and instead gave Andrew a wry grin. "Nay, let that go. I spoke out of turn." He took Andrew's arm in a friendly grip. "So, you are Percy's heir! I knew at any rate that he would not leave his money to that brother of his, who behaved like a scoundrel. As far as I know they were no longer on speaking terms."

"They differed over a point of honour, I believe," Andrew said in a reserved voice, taking umbrage, it seems, at the printer speaking ill of any member of the Stockdale family. "In any case, you didn't think he'd leave his fortune to me?"

"After his brother, you are his nearest kin—his only surviving kin, I believe."

"But there may be someone with a better claim?"

The printer waved him off. "You won't get another word out of me concerning that business, young man. I've said too much already." Both men studiously avoided looking in my direction.

"Then let me ask you another question: who was it that took away Percy's manuscript yesterday?" Andrew said.

"He gave his name as Mr. Jamieson. I was a fool to take offence at his speech which was rather commandeering. I thought I would make him eat humble pie and beg me to take back the manuscript, for I thought—and still think—it impossible that any printer will take on its publication without subscription. You see, our friend Percy was no great genius of letters, although he flattered himself to be a poet worthy of the laurel crown. I humoured his foolish conceit and agreed to publish his sermons. It was hard on my pocketbook, let me tell you."

"That is regrettable, but I would say it reflects the vulgar taste of the reading public, who do not appreciate food for the soul."

"Indeed. They don't go in for preaching and moralizing, and I am a businessman and must cater to the tastes of my customers. I obliged Percy because he was a good friend, but when he came to me with his *Letters and Recollections*, I said to him: 'Percy, let me be honest with you. Who will want to read the letters and recollections of the rector of Hinxworth? If you were a politician and could tell us of intrigue and corruption, there might be something in it for a printer, or if you were to tell us of secret trysts and love affairs—' but he smiled and shook his head. 'No love affairs?' I said. 'Well, then, my friend, let me tell you there are already too many lacklustre letter collections on the bottom shelves of the bookstalls, to add yet another.' Percy was well-off and could have paid for the publication, but he had his pride and asked me to take the manuscript on subscription, for then, he said, I would see that there was a demand for a book like his. He was like that, you know, a little too convinced of his own importance, but never mind that now. I'll get his book published. I owe that much to the memory of an old friend."

I heaved a sigh of relief when I heard that Percy's memoirs contained nothing about trysts or love affairs and were entirely dull. Then he had been discreet, which was more than I had dared to hope. But who was Jamieson? The Reverend had never mentioned anyone by that name in my hearing. Andrew Prior was also at a loss.

"All very well," he said in reply to Hurst's assurance that he would publish Mr. Stockdale's memoir, "but that gentleman—Mr. Jamieson—is now in possession of the manuscript."

"Oh, give him another day or two, and he'll return it," Hurst said.

"I wish I could share your confidence," Andrew said. "Have the kindness, at any rate, to inform me if the manuscript comes into your hands again."

"I will, to be sure—"

There was a knock on the door. One of the workmen looked in and said: "'Nother visitor for you, Mr. Hurst."

He stood back and allowed a tall, sallow-faced gentleman to pass. He was elderly, but straight-backed and with a stiff bearing that said, "I stand on my dignity."

"Ah, there you are, my boy!" he said to Andrew, quite ignoring me and the printer. "I came up to London when I heard of Percy's violent death—which did not surprise me one bit, by the way. He was always one to keep company with irregular types: artists, poets, novelists—and whores, according to the obituary in *The Daily Advertiser*."

This tirade was my introduction to Captain Stockdale, the Reverend's brother.

Hurst looked black and was about to speak up, but Andrew was faster: "I am surprised to hear you talk like this, uncle. Nay, it grieves me to hear you speak ill of your brother. The obituary made it clear that he had been on a mission of mercy, trying to persuade disorderly women to abandon their sinful lives."

"Hah!" the Captain exclaimed. "Persuade disorderly women to abandon their sinful lives? Piffle!"

"Excuse me for interrupting this interesting conversation," Hurst said. "You have me thoroughly confused. It appears that you are Percy's brother, but did you not introduce yourself as Mr. Jamieson yesterday when you took away the manuscript?"

The Captain's brows contracted. "Jamieson? Nonsense! You must be hard of hearing to mangle my name like that. Mr. Jamieson, indeed! I am James Stockdale and announced myself as such when I came to your shop yesterday to inquire about the manuscript. Unlike Percy, I have a sense of piety. I felt it was my duty—regardless of the antecedents—to see my brother's wishes executed. I recall you wrote to me last year to solicit a subscription. No doubt Percy put you up to it, thinking he could trade on our kinship. At that time, I declined, of course. But I was not about to allow my resentment to go beyond the grave. Let bygones be bygones, I thought. And I won't deny that I was curious about those *Letters and Recollections of a Life Time*. I wondered whether Percy had anything to say about me in those memoirs. And then I thought, well, if he does, I wager it's nothing good. In any case I felt it incumbent upon me as his nearest relative to see the book published."

"But you didn't trust *me* to do the job," Hurst said. "Have you changed your mind all of a sudden?"

"Not about you," the Captain said, "but about paying for the publication now that I find the money has gone to my young friend here. When I read the obituary, I reckoned Percy's property would come to me by default if he had died intestate. And even if he had the foresight to make a will, I thought, he would not cut off his brother. But I should have known better. Percy was a man without scruples, and this was his final trick. He bypassed me, as I discovered when I spoke to Merryweather." He turned to Andrew. "Not that I begrudge you the money, my boy, but seeing that you are Percy's heir you might as well pay for his book."

Andrew was not to be goaded.

"I assure you I was as perplexed as you, sir," he said respectfully, "and am quite unable to explain how the Reverend Stockdale came to make his decision in my favour."

The Captain waved him off with studied nonchalance. "It makes no difference. The money would have come to you in the end," he said. The even tone belied the chagrin colouring his cheeks russet. "This final mark of disrespect, this final attempt to harm my interests, only serves to confirm my former opinion of Percy. But I have inured myself to his treatment and shall disregard this insult."

"I am glad to see you philosophical," Andrew said. "As to the Reverend's memoirs. That is in fact why I am here. I offered to pay Mr. Hurst for the publication of the memoirs, when he informed me that he was no longer in possession of the manuscript. I was at a loss how to proceed, but it seems it was all a misunderstanding, and I take it the parcel under your arm is the manuscript I feared was lost."

"So it is," the Captain said and placed the packet he had been holding under his arm on Hurst's crowded desk. "I brought the manuscript away with me, thinking I might find a more competent printer." Here he shot a defiant look at Hurst, who glowered back, but did not deign to answer him. "However," the Captain continued, "I may have underestimated the difficulty of finding a competent publisher for what I see is an incompetent piece of writing. That is the opinion I have formed, at any rate, after a cursory perusal of the manuscript last night. On the whole, it may be better to allow Mr. Hurst to complete the undertaking, especially since he has garnered a list of subscribers and surely expects no more from the heir than to make good the shortfall. In this matter, however, I am willing to respect your wishes—" Here the Captain made Andrew an ironic bow.

Andrew saw a need for diplomacy. "As *you* wish, my dear Captain," he said. "I do believe the manuscript will be in good hands with Mr. Hurst. As I have just discovered he was a friend of my late father and on intimate terms with the Reverend himself. For that reason—and always providing that it meets your approval—I think it best to allow Mr. Hurst to complete the task which was entrusted to him by the author."

"Say no more," the Captain said. Andrew's diplomatic words had smoothed his ruffled feathers.

"I am glad to see you bear me no grudge in consequence of the will," Andrew said, still anxious to appease his relative, "for I need your advice now more than ever. Your knowledge of the world will be invaluable to me when it comes to assuming the duties inherent in accepting the legacy. And it goes without saying that I hope you will share my good fortune and allow me to requite the friendship you have shown me in the past."

The Captain appeared satisfied.

"It's good to find a young man remembering his benefactors," he said, "even when he is no longer in need of favours or money."

Hurst meanwhile had taken possession of the manuscript and held on to it as if it might get lost in the chaos of the room.

"Let me assure you again, my friend," he said to Andrew. "The manuscript will be published with all speed. We must let the world know what kind of man Percy was—a good and charitable man. He had his foibles of course, but who among mortals is without sin? How I wish he had listened to my warnings about visiting Bishopsgate. He could have transacted his business in a safer manner, you know."

"You will greatly oblige me, Mr. Hurst, if you tell me more about Percy's charitable enterprises," Andrew said.

The Captain bared his teeth in an ugly sneer, but said nothing. Lynne was more vocal, and let me know what she thought of

Hurst's praise. "Charitable, my foot!" she cried, and I must say I was curious myself to hear about the Reverend's good deeds, if indeed they went beyond dispensing my aunt's largesse.

"I will, my friend, I will," Hurst said in answer to Andrew's plea. "But at present I am steeped in work that cannot wait even for Andrew Prior, as welcome as that name is to me—" and he waved toward the desk buried under sheets of paper with the margins marked in blue pencil. "The day after tomorrow I shall be at greater leisure and, if you honour me with another visit, we can talk of anything that tickles your fancy."

"Then I'll take my leave and come back another day," Andrew said.

"And I have no reason to trouble you again now that the business of Percy's memoirs is settled," the Captain said and turned to leave as well.

The two men bid Hurst good-bye, but I tarried.

"I apologize for keeping you a little longer, Mr. Hurst," I said, "I have a favour to ask you now that you are once again in possession of the manuscript, and I hope you will not refuse me. Would you allow me to read the manuscript before you proceed to printing it? Let me explain the reason for my request. I wonder whether the Reverend mentions my aunt's name in his memoirs. If so, you will understand that I am concerned about what he had to say, given the peculiar circumstances in which he inherited her fortune and the consequences for my own position—I won't elaborate, but I am sure you understand that there are private matters I would not want to see publicized."

"Of course, I understand, Miss Collingwood, and I have no objection to you reading the manuscript or to hearing any reservations you may have, although I can assure you that Percy's reflections on your aunt are nothing if not respectful and expressing gratitude for her generosity."

"Then perhaps I may take the manuscript with me now with the understanding that I will return it to you tomorrow morning before I leave for Hinxworth. I am much encouraged by your assurance that there is nothing objectionable in it and grateful for your willingness to indulge me if I have any remaining concerns."

We left it at that. Mr. Hurst handed me the manuscript of the *Letters and Recollections*, and I went away, eager to read it.

BACK AT Mrs Trescot's (for I was once more a guest at her house), I immediately retired to my room to peruse the Reverend's memoir. I had been afraid that coming up to London for the reading of the will would encourage Lynne to make another attempt to escape the confines of my body, but for most of the day, first at the lawyer's and then at the printer's office, she kept her murmurs to a low pitch. She may have been cowed by the memory of that last night in London and even regretted the Reverend's death although I had little evidence that she had any conscience. I suppose her silence on our return to Mrs. Trescot's merely indicated that she was as eager as I to read the Reverend's *Letters and Recollections*. I sat down at the writing desk in my room and rapidly scanned the letters he had included in the manuscript. To my relief, I found the contents harmless. There were no telling passages about my condition, and nothing about the attempted elopement. When the Reverend first mentioned to me his plan of writing a memoir and publishing a collection of letters, I felt threatened. No doubt that was his intention. He wanted to frighten me. On his visits he often brought along his notes and occasionally quoted from the letters he wished to include, under the pretense that they might interest me or that he wanted my advice. One of them, I recall, was addressed to a celebrated physician in London, whom he consulted on my behalf. He had noticed that I frequently suffered from "migraines," as I called the condition in which I found myself whenever Lynne made her escape. He sought the physician's advice against my wishes. Naturally I did not want to discuss my condition with anyone. The letter the Reverend wrote and quoted to me contained a great deal of personal information about me which I would not have wanted to see published. He also read to me a letter he wrote to a cleric in Bristol, who obtained a measure of fame, or should I say notoriety, for claiming that he had delivered a man of a demon. In that missive the Reverend inquired into the practice of exorcism, mentioned my frequent indispositions, musing whether I was possessed, and offering his own theories about demonic influences. In fact, he came dangerously close to the truth and half-guessed the role Lynne's materializations played in my migraines. In a third letter, written to a friend, the Reverend referred to my elopement with Francis, although he suppressed all names. He made a point of reading those letters to me, purportedly to consult me about matters of language and style and to confirm the accuracy of his recollections, but of course his purpose was to intimidate me. He showed me the letters, I suppose, preparing the ground for a marriage proposal and hoping to pressure me into accepting him. Marriage was the price I must pay for his discretion. He did not say so directly, but his meaning was clear: Accept me as your suitor, or I will publish those letters and expose you to scrutiny. Marry me, and I will protect your reputation. None of these embarrassing letters were included in the collection he had submitted to Hurst, however. I don't know whether he thought better of it or had given up hope of coercing me into accepting him as my husband. Nor was there anything in his memoirs about my aunt and her will (but that was to be expected since the transaction might raise suspicions about his own motives). But there were quite a few snide remarks about his brother James, although he never mentioned the cause of the rift between them. The point of the letters he included in that volume was, as far as I could tell, to acquaint the reader with the illustrious literary circles in which he moved. They were letters to and from well-known poets and essayists. I knew that he was often in London, but I had no idea he was so well connected and took such a genuine interest in literature.

The letters were preceded by a short autobiography. I expected the Reverend's style to be pompous or at any rate self-important like his manner of speaking, but to my surprise I found the piece well-written and occasionally witty, manifesting the satirical vein which I had observed more than once, but in this case the irreverence was directed against himself or his brother. Now that I had met the Captain, I was rather amused by the Reverend's caricature of the man and the accuracy of his observations—the Captain's surliness and acrimony, his military bearing, his blunt speech. I also came to realize how little I knew of the Reverend's personal life, and how little he had given away about his actions and thoughts, considering the long conversations we had.

The Captain, I learned, was the older of the Stockdale brothers. After the early death of their mother, the boys were looked after by Mary Stockdale, an impoverished relative on their father's side. For three years, she was a loving nurse to the motherless children, but when she left the household to get married, the boys were entrusted to an old parson. He did what he could to drill classical Latin into them and inspire them with Christian morals. It seems, however, that James Stockdale derived little benefit from the parson's instructions. He ran away at fifteen and went on board of a merchant ship. There, as I read, "he continued for some years, showing himself a youth of violent passions and acquiring a bad character even among men not known for moral niceties. His fits of drinking and his unruly behaviour earned him severe discipline on several occasions, but he behaved so well in an engagement with pirates that his former score was wiped clean and he returned home at twenty to a hero's welcome. Our father, gratified that life had made a man of James, bought him a commission in the King's navy, thinking that a lack of education was no blemish in that career. And indeed, James made good and climbed the ladder of promotions and on his retirement called himself Captain Stockdale."

Percy Stockdale never gave his father the least cause for worry, at least according to his autobiographical sketch. He applied himself to his lessons, went up to Oxford University at seventeen, took his exams, and made a successful career in the church. His father was pleased, but his brother only sneered, the Reverend wrote.

"I suppose you were able to pull the wool over the examiners' eyes when you qualified for holy orders," James said, hinting that I had been a womanizer at Oxford. Perhaps I was not quite as virtuous as I should have been, but if so, I will plead my youth as excuse. I had a young man's vices, I admit, but there was no reason for James to insist that I had no vocation for the church and that the church was nothing but a meal ticket for me.

It certainly was a poor meal ticket to begin within. For some years I was one of those wandering curates who move from town to town and perform marriages for a guinea, no questions asked. Eventually I too found employ in the royal navy. I became chaplain on the Intrepid, but after the battle of Minorca in 1756, I lost my taste for war.

After resigning my post as chaplain, I became tutor to the son of Lord Cauley and foolishly dared to lift my eyes to one of the ladies of the house. The entanglement was discovered and led to my removal.

Ah, I thought when I read those words, that is the source of the moral tale the Reverend told me when he caught up with Francis and me—the tale of his own attempted elopement. He continued:

I then went to London to take over another curacy and began my association with the literary crowd in the coffee houses, in which I took much pleasure, perhaps more than I should have—at least in the eyes of my superior who called them fops who waste their afternoons gossiping, and in the evening retire to Drury Lane to raise hell in the theatre pit. My predilections could well have spelled the end of my clerical career, had not my father rescued me by putting in with the Bishop and obtaining for me a position at Long Houghton. That was my toehold on the rung to a career in the church. As luck would have it, one of my friends from Oxford days, young Lord Beveridge, held the right of nominating the candidate for the rectory at Hinxworth and remembering the pleasant time we had at Oxford put forward my name. And so, I became a gentleman of leisure, for the rectory was worth a great deal and had rented property attached to it that brought in respectable money.

He is certainly candid about his own life, I thought, and congratulated myself that he had not taken the same liberty telling of my affairs. Indeed, I had to concede that the Reverend was discreet. He did not mention the origin of the quarrel that had alienated him from his brother, although it was clear that he did not hold him in high esteem. By contrast he spoke affectionately of Andrew and had much to say about his life, which I read with interest. I gathered that Percy Stockdale had been a frequent visitor at the house of Andrew's parents, whenever he came down from Oxford during his long vacations. Mary Stockdale, whom he fondly remembered from the days when she was his foster mother, had married a printer's assistant. The couple made their home in the north end of London, between Marylebone Lane and Wigmore Road, but Percy Stockdale did not mind the long way to the suburbs, when he came to town. He retained a filial affection for his former nursemaid and took a liking to her boy.

Andrew in turn (he wrote) thought his "Uncle Percy," as he called me, a jolly good fellow because I always carried candied nuts or sugar drops in my pockets. When the boy admired my fine waistcoat and elegant breeches, so different from the coarse black stuff his father wore, I told him that was nothing, compared to the fashionable garments of the young lords in Oxford. Even their morning gowns were made of brocade, and the sleeves and hems embroidered with medallions of gold lace, I told him, but Mary Prior did not like it when I carried on in this manner.

"Don't be putting fancy ideas into the child's head," she said, and her husband concurred.

"The boy won't go to Oxford on my earnings as a printer," he said. But I gave Andrew a friendly pat on the head and said:

"Oh, but the boy deserves the best, and who can tell what the future will bring?"

Until his thirty-first year, however, the future brought Andrew nothing remarkable. That is when a letter of his reached me at Hinxworth. We had lost sight of each other for some years, but he had read a notice of my appointment and obtained a copy of my sermons, on which he congratulated me. In the same letter, he told me about his own life, that he had aspired to a legal career, but the premature death of his father, followed within a year by that of his grieving mother, put an end to those ambitions. He had duly notified James and me of Mary Prior's demise, but received no reply. Alas the news did not reach us, as we were both abroad at the time.

Andrew was a clerk in a notary's office then, and as yet unmarried, but only, he said, because he did not have the means of supporting a wife and children. In a word, he was a reluctant bachelor. I resolved then and there to come to his assistance, if for no other reason than to match the generosity of my brother. For James, he told me, had sought him out after his return to England and his retirement from the navy and had given him tangible proof of his good will. He concluded his letter to me delicately hinting at my estrangement from James, which might perhaps prevent me from replying, and expressed the hope that it might be possible to be on good terms with both his relatives—the only family he had. Indeed, he hoped for a reconciliation in the future. In other words, he voiced the proper sentiments that inclined me to renew our acquaintance. Of course, he may have written with a view of obtaining my financial support, I thought to myself, but I was not averse to giving him assistance if he turned out to be a worthy recipient. Thus, I wrote a friendly reply with the promise of further communication when I was next in London. Alas, I misplaced his address. Since he had mentioned that he was on friendly terms with my brother, I applied to James for that information. Indeed, I thought a common interest in our nephew might provide an incentive to return to more cordial relations, but James replied in the most boorish terms, informing me that Andrew had sought his fortune in the colonies. Thus ended my effort to extend a friendly hand to my brother and to renew my relationship with my nephew.

And thus also ended the Reverend's preface, except for a tantalizing and alarming postscript: "Letters describing my service on board of the Intrepid and my years in Hinxworth will be found in Part Two of *Letters and Recollections*."

Part Two! Did it exist or had it only been a vague plan? And if it existed, did it contain those revealing and embarrassing letters describing my condition?

I saw that my sense of relief and gratitude for the Reverend's discretion had been premature and resolved to ask Hurst what he knew about Part Two. The next morning before embarking on my journey home to Hinxworth, I visited the printer's shop once more and handed back the manuscript.

"And was there anything in it you would like to see expunged?" he asked me.

"Nothing," I said. "I found it well written, although perhaps of no great interest to the general public."

"My opinion exactly," the printer said.

"One question, Mr. Hurst," I said. "There is a postscript announcing a second volume to come."

The printer rolled his eyes.

"Percy did mention a sequel, but I declined to have anything to do with it until I saw that the first part aroused an interest in the reading public. In any case I doubt that he had enough material to justify a second volume. Half a dozen letters, maybe. You might find them stowed away in his desk at the rectory. If so, my advice is to pack them off to the attic, but I fear Andrew will be too pious to allow any of his writings, however dull, to languish in obscurity. He will insist on publishing them to do his duty by Percy. Well, it's all the same to me—if he likes to spend his money that way, I'll publish it."

I had nothing to say to that, although I was secretly glad that the Reverend's last will entitled me to a keepsake. Here was my chance to forestall the publication of the second volume in case it contained anything embarrassing to me. I would go to the rectory at the first opportunity, search for the second part, and if it existed, follow Hurst's advice to bury it—in *my* attic!

ON MY return to Hinxworth, I received a note from Andrew which was very much to my purpose. He encouraged me to go to the rectory and choose a keepsake at my earliest convenience. He had already told the housekeeper, Mrs. Lambsley, to expect a visit from me and to permit me to go through the premises. He himself would shortly come to Hinxworth, he said. He had written to Percy Stockdale's successor, asking when the house must be vacated. As it turned out, urgent family business prevented the new rector from taking up his post at once. There was no immediate need to vacate the premises. Andrew therefore came to an agreement with him to rent the house for three months. It was a convenient arrangement and would allow him to go through everything at leisure and decide what to keep and what to leave behind or sell.

Of course, I was determined to steal a march on Andrew and inspect the premises first. I wasted no time therefore to go to the rectory, bringing along a satchel large enough to conceal the manuscript—should I find it—from Mrs. Lambsley's curious eyes. Courtesy demanded that I inform Andrew of the nature of the keepsake I had chosen. My intention was to bring away the manuscript together with a vase or a print or another object of no particular interest—and mention only the latter in my obligatory note of thanks to Andrew.

It was a sunny September afternoon when I knocked on the door of the rectory, a fine edifice built of Bath stone. The façade had recently been remodelled in the Georgian style. The architect, however, had only a feeble grasp of classical forms and exhausted his imagination in a singular-looking porte-cochère with crude Corinthian columns. Ivy was growing up the walls, flanking the entrance on either side.

Mrs. Lambsley herself answered the door and showed me in. She was a plump old woman, always neatly attired in a well-brushed gown, pleated apron, and white muslin cap.

"My dear Miss Collingwood," she said, clasping me to her ample bosom. "What a wonderful man the world has lost in Mr. Stockdale! But you must feel the loss even more keenly than I, seeing that the Reverend was your guardian, if I may put it so, and your mainstay after the tragic death of your aunt."

I opened my mouth to state my business, but closed it again as there was no chance of interrupting the flow of Mrs. Lambsley's words. "Oh Lord, save me from that old rattle," Lynne moaned, as I tried to extricate myself from her embrace.

"Ah, your dear aunt, bless her soul!" she continued. "There was an admirable woman! And to think that she should be robbed of her life by an accident. But 'every human accident is by divine permission,' as the Reverend said at her funeral. It was a touching sermon, and I wish I remembered every word. 'Resistance and repining are in vain,' he said. 'Could tears bring back to life—No, that came later. I should drain the juices of my body,' he said. No, that's not it either. I had it all by heart at one time, Miss Collingwood, it was so beautiful, but memory fails me now—"

I assured Mrs. Lambsley that I remembered Percy Stockdale's sermon very well.

"No doubt you visit her grave often," she said. "*I* do, you know, and can never read the lines the Reverend composed for her headstone without shedding a tear: *She walks amongst the heavenly choir, how selfish then is our grief.*" She heaved a deep sigh.

"Yes, very profound," I said.

"She walks among the angels, that's for certain. Always mindful of those less fortunate than herself—you yourself can attest to that of course."

"I know what I owe my aunt for taking me in after my father died," I said. "I would have been destitute without her help." And would be destitute again if it had been up to Percy Stockdale, I thought.

"She was very kind indeed, and if I understood the Reverend correctly, willing to provide you with a substantial dowry if the right man came around, but now—" she petered off not daring to say more.

"Of course, she thought old Percy was just the right man for you," Lynne whispered. "I almost thought she'd come right out with it and ask you about Francis Florsham. Wouldn't the old bat love to know what happened, but even she doesn't have the nerve."

I was about to make my way past Mrs. Lambsley, but she got a second wind. She had not yet exhausted the subject of my aunt, "that pattern of womanhood" as she called her, and was not to be hurried in the epic description of her virtues and those of her admirer and heir, the Reverend Stockdale.

"But come in and look around," she finally said. "Mr. Prior has told me that the Reverend remembered me in his will and would like you and me to have a keepsake each, but I didn't want to be forward and thought I'd wait to make my choice until the heir comes himself—I expect him any day now, you know. I'd rather he chose something for me himself. I did clean out all the cupboards and closets and took away the clothes so as not to distress the young gentleman when he sees them, because I certainly couldn't keep from crying as I folded away the vests and coats I had seen on Mr. Stockdale so often."

So, Mrs. Lambsley had begun to turn out the content of the cupboard and closets! Then I had come in the nick of time, although she would hardly dare to disturb the contents of the Reverend's study.

On my request Mrs. Lambsley took me into the study, accompanying every one of my steps with a stream of words or perhaps I should say a storm of words because I felt quite windblown by the time I pleaded to be left alone, as I wished to contemplate my loss, or so I said.

"Of course, my dear Miss Collingwood. I can just imagine how you feel standing in the very room where he used to write his sermons—"

"And that is what I hope to find and take away as a memento—his sermons or any other piece of writing in his own hand."

Mrs. Lambsley entirely approved. "Then let me give you the keys to his writing desk," she said. "He always carried them with him, and indeed his writings were treasures. Mr. Hurst sent the keys to me, together with his other belongings, when he was found." She wiped her eyes and finally lapsed into a commemorative silence, handed me the keys, and left, not without much sighing.

The Reverend's desk was an intriguing piece. The top, which was of burled mahogany, opened to reveal a writing pad, two drawers at the back and more compartments to the left and right, each of them locked tight. There were so many keyholes in fact that I wanted to say, "Sesame open!" I eventually found the right keys to fit each drawer, but none of them yielded what I was looking for. There were bills and receipts, household books, and sermon drafts—but no letters, and no manuscript.

Then I set to work on the side compartments, which contained trays lined with tulip wood. They contained stacks of legal papers and drafts of sermons. I almost despaired. It would take me a long time to sort through them, but then I noticed a piece of paper peeking out from under the ink blotter, and on lifting it, found the very thing I had been looking for: a thin sheaf of papers—no more than ten pages—that bore the inscription: "Recollections, Part Two."

The Reverend must have been working on Part Two right up to his fateful journey to London! I pulled out the bundle of pages from under the blotter and began to read, when I heard the wheels of a carriage. They ground to a halt in front of the house. Mrs. Lambsley's voice could be heard next, calling to the houseboy:

"Tom! That will be Mr. Prior, I expect. Go and help with the luggage presently, and be quick about it."

I hastily folded up the telltale title page of the Reverend's manuscript and put it into the pocket of my skirt. Then I picked up some sermon drafts and placed them on top of the manuscript before slipping the packet into my satchel and readied myself to meet Mr. Prior. If he asked me what I had chosen to take away I could tell him: sermons. For good measure, I also took down the print hanging above the desk, a portrait of John Milton looking dreary, and put it in my satchel as well.

That done, I moved to the window and was in time to see Andrew help James Stockdale down from a hired carriage. So, the Captain had come as well! Tom was shouldering their luggage, as the two men stretched their legs.

"Those infernal roads," I heard the Captain say in his cross voice. "I am shaken to pieces!"

"I too feel bruised from all the jolting," Andrew said, "but I count myself lucky when I think of the stagecoach we passed, groaning and creaking along the rutted road." He looked up, saw me at the window, and bowed.

"Miss Collingwood," he called. "What a pleasant surprise to see you here."

I nodded to him in turn and went out into the hall to meet him. Mrs. Lambsley was showing the two men in. She made Andrew a curtsy, quite ignoring the Captain.

"I am Mrs. Lambsley," she said. "Welcome to the rectory, Mr. Prior. For I have no doubt you are the gentleman with whom I had the honour of corresponding. I can see the Reverend in you all over again."

"Very kind of you to say so," Andrew said, looking around at the Captain.

"Nonsense," said the Captain, angered at being overlooked when his age should have given him precedence. "There isn't the least resemblance."

"This is Captain James Stockdale," Andrew said to the housekeeper, who curtsied in turn but did not say another word of welcome. There was an awkward silence, but now Andrew had caught sight of me, and I in turn stepped forward and explained that I had come for my keepsake and indeed had made my choice.

Mrs. Lambsley was hovering. "Will the gentlemen take tea?" she said stiffly, "or would you like me to show you to your rooms first?"

"I'll just see that that young fellow puts my things where I want them," said the Captain gruffly, looking after Tom who was toiling up the stairs with the visitors' bags. "And then I'll have a glass of ale, Mrs. Lambsley, for my throat is parched. None of your tea for me."

"We'll see the rooms first, then," Andrew said, "and afterwards I at any rate will be glad to take tea. I hope you will join us, Miss Collingwood."

I said I would be glad to join them. I would have preferred to go home. Indeed, I couldn't wait to peruse the content of Part Two, but it would have been impolite to decline the invitation.

The Captain had already followed the boy upstairs, and Mrs. Lambsley now offered to show Andrew to his room.

"I thought it right to put you into the master's bedroom, Mr. Prior, you being Mr. Stockdale's heir," she said. "You will find it a handsomely furnished bedroom of good proportions with a bay window overlooking the apple orchard."

Andrew thanked her for her consideration.

"The Reverend often lamented losing touch with you—he had much to say in praise of your mother, you know, and something to say also of the gentleman who has come with you, but I can't say it was to his credit."

Andrew contracted his brow. "Mrs. Lambsley, I thank you to remember the respect due to the Captain's position as the Reverend's brother."

"I didn't mean to speak out of turn," said Mrs. Lambsley, "and hope I haven't given offense. Don't think we aren't grateful to you, Mr. Prior, for engaging our services. We shall all find ourselves without employ soon enough, I expect. There isn't much chance of being kept on here. The new rector is a great gentleman, they say, for whom the Hinxworth stipend is but pocket money. They say he won't be in residence here. He'll hire a curate to look after the parish. Aye, and even if the bishop came himself, he could not match the Reverend Stockdale. We shall never see the likes of him again. Such a charitable man he was, who had a kind word for everyone."

She fetched a deep breath to replenish her lungs, allowing Andrew only to squeeze in a sentence, saying how glad he was to hear it, before she went on:

"And not just kind words, mind you. He was never behind giving a largesse to the harvesters, and when the men brought the tithe, he gave them a right generous frolic: a dinner of sirloin of beef and plum pudding and a shilling each. And how many times did he send Polly to a poor cottage with a dish of meat or a basket of apples to fill dumplings with. And his sermons—oh, Mr. Prior, I wish you could have heard the Reverend's sermons! None of those theatrical performances you see nowadays and high-falutin' words the congregation can't understand, but good and wholesome talk that sent you home a better person than you were before."

"I very much regret the ill fortune that prevented me from hearing the reverend gentleman's sermons," Andrew said, which set Mrs. Lambsley off on another monologue.

"To think of the cruel fate that has taken that dear, dear gentleman from us. We couldn't help wondering enough, cook and me, that the omnipotent God would allow such a heinous crime to be perpetrated on a clergyman of his distinction. I've been in the Reverend's service these fifteen years, and a kinder master one could not wish for, and now he is no more and has left us orphaned—"

The flow of Mrs. Lambsley's words was interrupted by the appearance at the top of the stairs of the Captain, whose wrinkled brow expressed deep dissatisfaction.

"What is the meaning of putting me into that despicable garret," he said, looking down at us from the height of landing. "The lad tells me that a chamber on this floor is unoccupied and of a much more satisfactory prospect."

"I thought a quiet room would suit the gentleman," said Mrs. Lambsley succinctly, her flow of words quite dried up.

"No doubt, the graveyard outside the window makes for a quiet place," said the Captain sarcastically. "And perhaps there are people who wish me there sooner rather than later."

"A misunderstanding, Captain," Andrew said, "which no doubt can be set right immediately, can it not, Mrs. Lambsley?"

"Tom may move Captain Stockdale's things down the hall, if that room is more to the gentleman's liking," said the housekeeper, looking stony-faced.

"It is, and I have already given the lad the necessary directions," said the Captain. Indeed, Tom now appeared beside him, showing a degree of confusion.

"Mrs. Lambsley," he said, "the gentleman—" He pointed to the Captain and stopped, not quite sure what to say about the Captain's unheard-of audacity in countermanding the housekeeper's orders.

"Well, don't stand there and gape, Tom," said Mrs. Lambsley. "If the gentleman doesn't like his room and Mr. Prior has no objections, you may carry his things to the front bedroom."

"No objections!" snorted the Captain.

"Go at once, my boy," Andrew said, "and make sure that everything is done to Captain Stockdale's satisfaction."

"I shall not stay in this house above one night," said the Captain later when we were sitting in the drawing room before a tray with tea, scones and strawberry comfit, and the Captain with a glass of ale, as he had desired. "I shall take my departure as soon as ever I can make the necessary arrangements. I know when I am not wanted."

"But, my dear Captain," Andrew said soothingly, "your company is wanted very much by me, and you have kindly undertaken to remain with me in Hinxworth and allow me to benefit from your advice in handling affairs here. You know that our stay in the rectory is only for a short time. We agreed that it was a piece of good fortune that we were able to rent these quarters—"

"A piece of good fortune, my foot!" exclaimed the Captain. "You call that impertinent housekeeper, that dragon, a piece of good fortune? A woman who has the gall to shut me up in a room the size of a closet, with which a servant might find fault? And to tell me that she thought I might like a quiet room!"

"You were no doubt right to take offense. It was an inexcusable error of judgment on her part. But she has been spoken to, and the matter has been put to right. I believe you are satisfied with your quarters now. The room seems to me spacious and well appointed and making every allowance for your comfort. Surely it is to your liking?"

"That it is. But the housekeeper ain't. And unless you dismiss that termagant on the spot, I shall leave at my earliest convenience. I cannot remain here while that Xanthippe has charge of the house."

"As much as I wish to oblige you, Captain, it is hardly possible to find a replacement for Mrs. Lambsley at once. Nor is it necessary to inconvenience ourselves, when she has been rebuked for the impropriety of her conduct and, it is hoped, been taught to show respect to her betters henceforth."

"A woman who needs instruction in that point is unsuited to the business of housekeeping. Dismissal is the only rebuke to serve the purpose at hand."

"I would be of the same opinion, Captain, if her situation were permanent. But as it is, she and the rest of the household servants have been engaged for a term of three months only, and will be let go at the end of that time without further ado, for by then we shall have wound up our business here. To dismiss her now, without a prospect of replacement, would surely be cutting off your nose to spite your face."

"You may suit yourself, Andrew," said the implacable Captain, "but I won't put up with her, not for a day. Nor do I like the maid —Polly is it? A consumptive creature apt to depress a man's spirits."

Indeed, poor Polly was a most ill-favoured girl: a narrow face with a peaked nose and black, furtive eyes. She had a habit of keeping her lips compressed, saying little, and looking around nervously as if haunted by a ghost.

"She does not have the gift of making a guest comfortable, I'm afraid," I said to the Captain. "She is a nervous girl, but you won't see much of her. She is the cook's helper and served us only because it's the regular maid's day off."

"And God knows what the maid looks like," the Captain said. "I've never seen a more unpleasant lot of servants."

Andrew saw that they had reached an impasse.

"Why not sleep on the matter?" he said. "You may feel differently about the household in the light of day."

"I have no choice but passing the night here. But don't think I'll change my mind, Andrew. You should know me better by now."

It was at this point that I rose and prepared to make my adieus, leaving the two gentlemen to discuss the desirability of retaining Mrs. Lambsley's services. Andrew rose as well, accompanied me to the front door and apologized for the Captain's surliness.

There wasn't much I could say to that. "I hope he will settle in tomorrow. He will find Mary, the regular maid, a very pleasant young woman. Once you have taken matters in hand here, I expect you will want to visit Three Oaks and inspect the premises I currently occupy as your tenant."

"I have no intention of intruding or 'inspecting' the premises, as you put it, Miss Collingwood," he said, "but I would gladly call on you if I may."

"Well," Lynne said, as soon as I was out of the door, "you've done better than I thought." And lapsing into her vulgar language, she added: "You got him hooked!" But I wasted no thought on Andrew. I hurried home, congratulating myself on having found the manuscript of Part Two in the nick of time. I couldn't wait to see what the Reverend had to say in those pages, although Lynne grumbled: "Why waste any more time on this boring stuff? Burn the bloody thing and be done with it." She had no patience for reading books or anything of a literary character. I in turn always found it useful to immerse myself in reading, as it had the effect of putting her into a drowsy state and thus interfering less. So, I ignored her mumblings and, on coming home, sat down to read the manuscript I had taken from the Reverend's desk. I quickly saw that it was only a loose collection of thoughts jotted down on a dozen pages. There were his musings on my condition, and those I burned in the fireplace as soon as I had perused them.

On a page, which bore in one corner the pencilled remark "Include?" he wrote down his first impressions of me:

> I was told that Miss Collingwood had nothing much to recommend her in the way of looks or demeanour, and indeed when I made the round of the parish, as it was my duty as curate of souls, I was welcomed cordially by her aunt, Mrs. Collingwood, but Adele was unsmiling and looked at me rather sternly, as if to take the measure of the man. Mrs. Lambsley, my housekeeper, had referred to her

looks as plain, but she is too severe a judge. Adele does not possess conventional beauty and, unlike others of her sex, does not trade on it. She wore her chestnut hair pulled back into a tight knot, a style more suited to an older woman than one of her age, and yet I found myself drawn to her.

"Oh phooey!" Lynne exclaimed, for the description had roused her from lethargy. "I'm glad we are rid of the old lecher."

Whatever the quality of Adele's features, her speech and native intelligence infuse them with life. She is a young woman with a certain presence. I have heard her called "accomplished," but that is a term of faint praise in the mouths of Hinxworth matrons. They use it when they fail to warm to a woman because she is a little too well-read for their taste, when they mean to say she is too knowledgeable. True, knowledge in a woman is a daunting thing and not entirely desirable. Conversely, a dull companion spoils your evening, as any man can tell you who has been seated at table next to a simpering coquette. And a dull spouse can spoil a man's whole life.

He went on to speculate about my ailment, the frequent migraines I suffered.

I wonder what causes that condition? Is it unhappiness or listlessness, brought on by lack of stimulation, for Hinxworth has nothing to offer a bright mind, or is it a more serious disturbance of the mind? There is that in her eyes sometimes which makes you think that a strange alter ego has taken possession of her, or as if she had a double, another being, quite alien, looking out at you. When I read the account of a Scottish cleric, who described cases of multiple personalities, or possession, which may bring on physical ailments such as blindness or an inability to talk, I thought he might be describing a case similar to Adele's. He cites the example of the man of Gadara (Matt 8) who was possessed by a legion of demons, or Saul, who was troubled by an evil spirit and suffered from depression (1 Sam 16). If that is what ails Adele, the rite of exorcism would be in order. Or is it the effect of Mrs. Collingwood's strict regime, for that woman is a dragon, even if she has a charitable disposition.

Lynne bristled at the mention of possession and exorcism. She was terrified by the idea of being ejected, while I myself would have willingly undergone that procedure, had I not feared being made a public spectacle.

"He is right about your aunt at any rate," Lynne said. "She was a dragon and rode you worse than any demon."

Adele certainly ought to be grateful to Mrs. Collingwood for taking her in after her father's death and one would have expected her to oblige her aunt by favouring a gentleman who had her approval instead of mooning after Francis Florsham. Indeed, given her native intelligence, she might have realized that the master of Grove Hall was a lout and might have guessed at his mercenary motives. Mind you, I do not entirely fault him for considering Adele's dowry. It would be difficult for anyone to forget that Miss Collingwood is an heiress, but I do find fault with his methods, his attempt to seduce her and elope to Scotland. Her aunt was right to withhold her approval and thanking me for rescuing her from Mr. Florsham's clutches.

Here followed the story of my elopement, which would certainly have ruined my reputation if it had become public. I did not need Lynne hissing in my ear to know what I had to do—destroy those pages at once.

The remainder of the manuscript was of no great personal interest to me, although it did explain the reason of the estrangement between the Reverend and his brother. On a page with the pencilled remark "To what extent/in what form to include?" he described the scene that had led to their quarrel.

My brother has taken care to tell the world his side of the story, as I have been told by mutual acquaintances. I visited his house in Agmondesham only once, in an effort to bring about a reconciliation. We were off to a bad start. I found James in his parlour, walking back and forth on the braided rug, much disturbed. The cause of his agitation was a book he had been sent by an acquaintance with the warmest recommendation. He had begun to read it on the morning of my visit and was annoyed to see that the author questioned the wisdom of using military force.

"Now tell me, Percy," he said after greeting me in a desultory manner hardly in keeping with our reunion. "Are we to allow acts of rebellion in the colonies or suffer attacks from foreign powers without fighting back? Because that is what the author suggests."

I saw that he was in his usual pugnacious mood. I tried to mollify him by feigning an interest in his opinion.

"What exactly does the author say?"

He read out a few lines: "*We find by daily experience that men's minds are best subdued by making them feel that it is in their interest to submit themselves.* Submit! The man wants us to submit? Pacifist drivel, I say!"

"But, James," I ventured to say, "what do you say to the arguments advanced by those who disparage the war not for philosophical but for economic reasons? Giving up the American colonies, they say for example, delivers us from the vast expense of administering and protecting those regions, whereas commercial intercourse need not be relinquished entirely and might still be productive of many advantages."

"Rubbish! No man of honour would accept peace when a war can be fought to the glory and the emolument of the Empire."

"But will you always and under any circumstances uphold the desirability of war, even after you contemplate the misery it engenders, for I will not speak of the law of the gospel which enjoins peace on every Christian?"

"Preaching at me, are you?" James said, his complexion florid with anger. "I see you are another of those damned pacifists. But I know what to think of your talk of peace. A coward will cloak his failings with beautiful words and tell you: I shall not fight because I am a lover of peace."

I saw that I was getting nowhere, and this subject was not conducive to the purpose of reconciliation, for which I had come. I therefore assured him that I was no pacifist, but had come in peace, as was desirable between brothers—and I thought he was in agreement with me on that point at any rate.

James recovered from his fit of anger then and remembered his duty, settling into the role of a polite host, but not without a little bluster. This time, however, his venom was not aimed at me, and after he delivered himself of a tirade on the obtuseness of his housekeeper, the high price of beef, and the blatant lack of interest shown by his neighbours in the naval exploits of England, which was his favourite topic of conversation, he calmed down. I knew that James devoted many leisurely hours to perusing books and illustrations of famous battles and was inclined to go on about the glory of the British navy at great length.

It did not take long for the talk to turn to the Battle of Minorca, which had been the beginning of our quarrel, and I welcomed it because it was time to bring the matter out into the open. No doubt James would get into a lather again, but I was determined to take a conciliatory stand and put an end to our disagreement. He was my brother after all.

Predictably he started out with the complaint that people tended to confuse us because of the unfortunate similarity in our names: he being christened James Lyndon Percival Stockdale and myself Percival Douglas James Stockdale. This became an issue in 1756 when he was serving on board of the Intrepid, and I obtained an appointment as chaplain with the 22nd regiment. It was one of life's coincidences that the Intrepid served as transport for the 22nd regiment and thus reunited the two of us, who had long been separated by our diverse callings. Our serving on the same ship led to a confusion that had serious consequences, according to my brother.

When I asked him to elaborate, he answered: "We had better cast the mantle of oblivion over that sorry chapter."

But I thought it was better to have it out and settle the matter once and for all.

"I still don't understand why you are bearing me a grudge, James," I said. "It was an ill-fated battle, and I'll admit that neither Admiral Byng nor I did myself proud."

"Indeed," he said with acerbity, "some men have no courage and would betray their country to save their skin, but whereas the Admiral was court-marshalled for his actions, you got away scot-free and threatened my record on account of my middle name being the same as your first name and the confusion this caused in careless people's minds."

"I cannot see how my actions could have harmed your name. They may not have been gallant, but they were not dishonourable," I said and invited him to cast his mind back to the events of 1756 and compare what we remember.

"You are not suggesting that my memory is faulty?" James said. "Let's see now." He wrinkled his brow and looked for inspiration at the sabre hanging above the fireplace, as if it were his Muse. "The Intrepid carried your regiment to Gibraltar in April and hence to Minorca. Within a day of setting sail from England, you landlubbers were seasick to a man."

"We were packed into the hold like so many parcels of merchandise and rolled up and down by the swell."

"And you complained more loudly than any of the men— of the motion of the ship, of the stench, of being confined below deck on orders of the captain who wanted you out of our way. Your constant complaining made me ashamed and reluctant to acknowledge you as my brother. Then we got to Minorca. Let me see, that was—"

"On the twentieth of May," I said.

James was nettled to find himself anticipated.

"No need to prompt me," he said. "The twentieth of May it was, and I shall never forget the date when we engaged with the enemy. The dawn had hardly broken and the line advanced when we had three ships on us at once."

"At dawn? As far as I remember, the manoeuvres leading up to the battle were lengthy and the engagement hesitant at first. There was no combat taking place at all in the fore noon."

"Zounds! Are you saying I don't know what I saw with my own eyes?"

"Nay, James, I will defer to your memory in that point since it is immaterial to the grudge you are bearing me, or so I assume."

"Quite right, you hadn't shown your face on deck by then. The soldiers were stationed on the forecastle and gave the French some volleys of small arms, but they sheered off, the wind being in their favour. Aiming their heavy pieces at our hull and rigging in turn, they sought to disable us. We heard the whizzing of balls but kept our station properly. At length they achieved their purpose and the foretop mast was clear shot away and came down with a prodigious crash, pinning a number of men under it."

"I certainly remember that calamity, and you do me wrong when you say that I kept below deck. I was on the forecastle, for in battle the chaplain is expected to be a soldier as much as a man of God. I myself was caught under the rigging and struggled free to help those who were struck down by the mast. Three of us were straining to lift off the splintered beam, and others were dragging the wounded from beneath."

"If that's so, you didn't keep at it for long, for I saw you backing away and taking cover, your countenance betraying fear and horror."

"I won't deny that I was terrified and backed away when I thought I could offer no more help."

"You shunned your duty, which was to minister to the dying if they could not be helped to safety, for a great many had their limbs smashed and the lifeblood draining out of them."

It was indeed a lamentable scene. The whole ship shuddered under the impact of a shot to the hull and threw us all into disorder and confusion. To the present day I remember the shrieks of agony and despair as the water began to flow in plentifully through a gaping hole in the hull. Some of the fellows fell on their knees and prayed to God, others had earlier fortified their courage with strong liquors and found comfort in their stupefaction. One wretch, who had his left leg shattered by a musket ball, implored us to put an end to his life rather than suffer him to drown, for the ship was sinking fast. Some of the sailors were hoisting out the lifeboat and bringing it alongside the ship.

"Everyone who was able to walk or crawl did his utmost to get into the lifeboat and quit the ship," I said.

"And you were among the first to leap into the boat, while those of us engaged in the rescue of the wounded reluctantly abandoned our efforts. There was no time to spare, and the boat, already crowded when I was taken onto it, put off directly."

I remember the scene as clearly as if it had happened yesterday. As soon as we were clear, the Intrepid began to drift and bore down on the other ships in our line, dashing against the side of the Phoenix with a sound horrible to the ears. We saw the two vessels pitched up high one moment and swept sideways the next, while the other ships laid back to avoid a like fate and our line, now disordered, fell prey to the enemy's strategy.

"And that was the reason for the unfortunate outcome of the engagement," I said. "No individual act of courage could have changed that."

"Whatever the outcome of the engagement for Admiral Byng, it was an unfortunate day for me," James said. "Others observed your cowardly behaviour, and as we were of the same stature and you had exchanged your clerical habit for a sailor's coat better suited for action, some persons rendered a confused account of the events, getting us mixed up, and I have been defending my reputation ever since."

"Without wishing to excuse my cowardice, allow me to ask whether you have any indication that I encouraged the misunderstanding."

"That is my impression."

"Then you are under a wrong impression."

And so, my attempt at reconciliation ended with the Captain stubbornly insisting that I had purposely encouraged the confusion of names, and me strongly denying that I was in any way responsible for it.

It was an interesting story, but of no concern to me, and I confined those pages to the flames with the rest of the manuscript. I was not depriving the world of a great work of literature, I told myself. I was merely suppressing indifferent musings that might cause mischief. It was one of those rare occasions where Lynne and I were in perfect agreement. What a relief it was to see the pages of the Reverend's manuscript go up in flames and subside into ashes.

THE FOLLOWING day I received a note from Andrew informing me that the Captain had taken ill. He would therefore have to delay his visit to Three Oaks—a delay he regretted very much, he said, as he had much enjoyed our conversation and was looking forward to seeing me again.

"There you go," Lynne said with great satisfaction. "I could see that he likes you. Soon he'll be running after you. Too bad the old codger is keeping him from paying us a visit."

I must say I too had been looking forward to Andrew's visit although I did not share Lynne's crass motives. I merely found his company pleasant. My friend Eliza who happened to be at my house when I received Andrew's note, said at once:

"The poor old man! It is a wretched thing to fall ill and not have the comfort of one's own home. You must call at the rectory, Adele, and ask if there is anything we can do to comfort him."

I thought it was a little forward to call on a gentleman I hardly knew, but Lynne was all for it. "If he can't come to us, we'll go to him," she said.

"You think it proper for me to call in the circumstances?" I asked Eliza. Why ask her, Lynne hissed in my ear. Just do it! It's a perfect excuse to ingratiate yourself with him.

For once my dear friend and my evil spirit were in agreement, although for very different reasons. Eliza was all compassion. Visiting the sick was an act of Christian charity. "We should both call on him," she said. "Besides, it's a courtesy to Mr. Prior, who is your landlord after all. Surely you wish to maintain good relations with him." "You see," Lynne said, "even she can see the advantage of staying on his good side."

In truth I did not need her to urge me on, but I was uneasy nevertheless. "I'm in two minds," I said to Eliza. "My position is peculiar, to say the least. The terms of the will oblige Mr. Prior to be my benefactor and allow me to reside in the house rent-free. I wish I could decline his largesse—"

"Are you out of your mind?" Lynne shouted in my ear, although she understood perfectly well that I did not mean or rather could not afford to go that far.

"Alas," I said to Eliza, "poverty forces me to accept the arrangement, but I deeply regret it."

Eliza patted my hand. "You mustn't fret over that," she said. "It is your aunt's money after all, and it was her wish that you should remain at Three Oaks. Mr. Prior is merely following her instructions."

As I went upstairs to fetch my cape and umbrella, for it threatened to rain, Lynne kept harassing me. "You see? Even Miss Goody-two-shoes is on my side. Even she thinks you should be nice to him."

"If I'm uncomfortable with the visit, it's on your account," I said to her. "You are so unpredictable. I am afraid you will misbehave in his presence and make me blurt out something unbecoming."

"Misbehave? What can I possibly do, locked up inside you?"

"You know how to make yourself felt, Lynne, and how to disturb me. That's why I'm glad that Eliza will keep me company. I need her support."

"I am aware of that," she said. "You invite her to spite me. I hate that sanctimonious twerp. And she is so boring, she puts me to sleep."

That was the effect I was hoping for. I had discovered that Eliza was a useful ally in my attempts to keep Lynne in check. She found Eliza tiresome, but at the same time she was cowed by her moral authority.

FORTUNATELY, IT was Mrs. Lambsley's day off and we were spared her fulsome speeches on the occasion of our visit. It was the maid who opened the door. Mary was a plump girl of twenty, with a pleasant smile, glowing pink cheeks and a general air of healthy vigour. If looks can sway a man's opinion, I thought, the Captain should be pleased to be attended by her.

Mary announced us and withdrew to make tea, as requested by Andrew. When I had introduced my friend Eliza to him and we were all settled comfortably, I asked what had brought on the Captain's illness.

"He seemed hale when I met him on the day of your arrival," I said.

"It is rather puzzling," Andrew said. "He certainly was in good fettle when we went to bed that first evening, but during the night I was awoken by a sound—a moan coming from below stairs. I quit my bed, opened the door of my chamber, and finding the corridor deserted, stepped out on the landing. On leaning over the banister, I saw a thread of light under the door of the study. I must confess I was alarmed. My first thought was of robbers. You may laugh if you please, but I armed myself with a pair of fire tongues before creeping downstairs to reconnoitre."

"Oh dear," Eliza said. "I don't know how you found the courage—"

"To tell you the truth, Miss Florsham, I was terrified, and my hand trembled when I opened the door of the study. To my surprise I saw the Captain, who I thought had long gone to bed, slumped on a chair beside the writing table. The drawers of the desk stood open as if ransacked by a thief. I rushed to his side, thinking an intruder had attacked him."

"Then he was injured?" I asked.

"Not in the ordinary sense. He raised his head with an effort and looked at me dully as if he did not know me. 'What are you doing here?' I asked him. He breathed laboriously and explained that he could not sleep and came downstairs. The writing table had attracted his attention, for he recognized it as an ancient piece that had once stood in his father's study. As he was inspecting it more closely, a spell of faintness overcame him. He could not remember what happened next, he said to me, and leaned his head back wearily. Pearls of sweat were standing on his brow, and his breath came in gasps. Needless to say, I was alarmed, but he would not hear of my calling the servants, especially not Mrs. Lambsley, for whom, as you know, he has conceived a dislike. He asked me to fetch him a glass of water, insisted that he was feeling better already, and barely permitted me to lend him an arm and accompany him back upstairs. I offered to keep him company but he waved me off. 'That confounded woman has upset me,' he said. 'A good night's rest will set me right again.' Such was not the case, however. The next morning I found the Captain in a worse state of health. He staunchly denied that anything was amiss, but his fevered look told another tale, and I sent Polly for the doctor, the Captain's protestations notwithstanding. Dr. Worth came at once and told me that there was a fever about with symptoms much like those displayed by the Captain, but when I described the circumstances in which I found him, he said he could not exclude the possibility of the Captain suffering from the aftermath of a stroke."

"That would be serious indeed."

"The Captain is of course eager to return to his own home, but his wish cannot be granted at this time. In his present condition, the doctor said, a journey could prove fatal. The Captain must have complete rest until the prescribed medicine can take its salutary effect. Even so it will be some weeks until he is strong enough to withstand the rigours of coach travel."

"You can trust the judgment of Daniel Worth," I said. "He is a most competent physician."

"I will do my best to persuade the Captain to remain," Andrew said, "but he is a stubborn man, I fear, and used to having his own will at all times. He won't hear of keeping his bed during the day and has ensconced himself in a chair. 'That will do me,' he said. 'I'm comfortable enough.' So, I gave up trying to make him stay in bed.

I suppose he can get his rest sitting up as long as he does not exert himself, takes his medicine, and gets the idea of returning home out of his head. The matter is confounded by the strong dislike he has taken to the housekeeper."

"Mrs. Lambsley?" Eliza said, surprise in her voice. "But she is the soul of a woman!"

"She has given me no cause for complaint, but it appears that she has conceived a prejudice against the Captain, and I cannot deny that he has reason to be offended by her conduct. She has not treated him with the respect he deserves."

"But can't you contrive to keep her out of his way and have the maid look after him?" I said. "Surely the Captain can't take exception to Mary Watson? She is a very good-natured young woman."

"Indeed, she engaged the Captain's sympathies at once," Andrew said and smiled at Mary, who had come with the tea things. "We have just been speaking of your good services, my dear. How is the patient?"

"Quite well, sir, but the Captain will tell you himself. He has asked to speak to you. And the ladies as well, when I told him that you had visitors."

"I wonder if that would not be too much excitement for a sick man," Andrew said.

"Captain Stockdale won't agree with you there," Mary said. "He complained a great deal to the doctor that he was shut up alone in the sickroom and found the time passing very slowly."

"Then we must pay a visit to the sickroom at once," Andrew said. Eliza and I agreed readily.

The Captain looked pale, but his voice was as strong as ever when he greeted us. "Come in, come in. I don't know what's worse, the pain in my backside from sitting so long in this confounded chair or the boredom of sitting here on my own."

"I hope we can cheer you up, uncle," Andrew said.

"The doctor has just left and what he said didn't cheer me up at all. I asked him when I would be able to return to my house in Agmondesham. 'Another three or four weeks will restore you sufficiently to allow for travel,' he said. Three more weeks! There was another question I meant to ask him, but the thought of three more weeks confined to this room made me forget everything else."

"Would you like Tom to go after the doctor and call him back?" Andrew asked.

"No, no," the Captain said. "It'll keep." There was embarrassment in his voice. "Besides, the man doesn't strike me as the conversational kind. Yesterday, he very rudely cut me off in the middle of a sentence to tell me that he must be off to complete his rounds. I didn't take it well at all, let me tell you, and would have known how to answer him, except it doesn't do to get on the wrong side of a man who has your life in his hands. And so, I bid him good-bye very coldly."

I smiled inwardly because I suspected that the Captain had treated Daniel Worth to one of his ill-tempered rants. The doctor in turn was a man of few social graces. His Scottish burr did nothing to improve that impression. The people of Hinxworth accordingly kept their distance from Daniel Worth. He was respected, but not liked, and apt to inspire fear in his patients rather than confidence.

"No, my question can wait," the Captain said, but after some hesitation continued: "Or perhaps you can answer it, Andrew. I was wondering whether the fever can give a man delusions."

"Have you felt yourself subject to delusions?"

"Aye, there's the rub," said the Captain dryly. "You can't tell whether a delusion is a delusion."

"Suppose, then, you give us an example," Andrew said.

"For one thing, the maid—Mary Watson—when first I laid eyes on her, my heart almost misgave me. You will think me a silly old man, ladies, but I thought I was looking into the eyes of an old love of mine, a woman I knew ever so many years ago. Mind you, I recovered my wits fast enough and knew my error, but even so I was struck sufficiently by the resemblance that I made a fool of myself asking the girl if her mother's hair was flaxen like hers.

And a very queer look she gave me and said she didn't remember her mother.

"She was orphaned as an infant," Eliza said, "and taken in by the Watsons as a foster child. They are farmers, very kind people who treat her like one of their own."

"That's what Mary told me, when I asked. Now what do you think, is that the sort of trick memory can play a man who is labouring under a fever?"

"I see no reason for concern," Andrew said. "You may of course ask the doctor's opinion, but no doubt he will tell you that a sudden remembrance of times past brought on by the glimpse of a familiar feature or tone of voice is not outside the realm of common experience."

"And it is well known that a fever heightens the senses and stimulates thoughts that lie dormant otherwise," I added, and Eliza nodded reassuringly.

"I am glad you think so," said the Captain. "But the fever has affected my mind, I dare say, for I am quite taken with that girl, and I'm not usually the sentimental sort. I mean to say"—he hastened to clarify—"if ever I had a daughter, always speaking as an unmarried man who knows nothing of such things, she is the sort of daughter I would wish for."

"Oh, but your paternal feelings do you credit, Captain," Eliza said. "Mary is a good and honest creature and a worthy recipient of your sentiments."

Andrew seconded her. "She seems a very proper young woman."

"And," Eliza added, "the sort of person who does not look merely to the sixpence she earns, but does her work conscientiously and will tend you with an innate sense of charity."

"Humph," said the Captain, "I dare say, if that is true, she is a rare bird."

"I would not, at any rate, call it a delusion to think kindly of Mary Watson," I said.

"No," he said, "more an old man's folly than a delusion."

We took our leave then, wishing the Captain a speedy recovery, and Andrew escorted us to the door. Lynne was in a congratulatory mood. "He was ogling you," she said, "and you blushed very becomingly. Well done!"

I too was gratified, I must admit, but at the last moment our conversation took a dangerous turn. At the door, he said:

"By the by, Miss Collingwood, I understand that the Reverend was working on the second part of his memoirs. I was hoping to find the manuscript here, but so far I haven't been successful. I've gone around the rooms and examined each piece of furniture, starting with the writing desk in the study, which seemed to have put the Captain into a fever. I investigated the contents of all the other chests of drawers in the house, peered into all closets, and went through numerous boxes in the dusty attic. Alas, they contained nothing in the way of a memoir. I meant to ask you: has the Reverend ever spoken to you of that second part and do you have any suggestion where I might look for the manuscript next?"

I cringed. "Now, keep your head," Lynne said sharply. For a moment I saw in my mind the pages of the manuscript burning in the fireplace, then I managed to say:

"I am afraid I can't be of any assistance to you, Mr. Prior. I know only that the Reverend was disappointed with the reception of his book of sermons, and that Mr. Hurst was not optimistic in his projections for the volume containing his memoir. I may be wrong, but I believe the Reverend abandoned plans for a second volume as a result and, for all I know, discarded the remainder of his letters."

Lynne silently applauded my handy lie. We were both relieved to hear that Andrew's search for the second part of the memoir had been unsuccessful—I had been uneasy in case the Reverend had kept a second copy or there were more pages which had escaped my notice in my hasty search. I hoped at any rate that my reply to Andrew Prior would discourage him from any further efforts to search the Reverend's papers, but the remainder of the afternoon was spoiled for me.

LYNNE

I HAVE another half hour to kill before going to the library for my appointment with Patricia. I pick up Adele's book again and read on, but it's all about Andrew. Andrew the Good. Such an earnest man, so courteous, so full of good will. So boring. I don't know what Adele saw in him, other than the money of course. I encouraged the affair but I didn't enjoy it. Andrew annoyed the hell out of me with his flawless manners and his head full of maxims. There was no colour to his ideas, no spurts of originality, just a steady flow of humdrum thoughts.

I skip a few pages, trawl through the scenes until I light on Daniel's name. He was my romantic interest at the time. I was aching to get back with Jack but if I had to settle on a man in Hinxworth, Daniel Worth was my first choice. Of course, realistically speaking, I had no way of acting on my choice. I was chained to Adele. We argued about that endlessly.

"I wish I had a body of my own," I said to her.

"So do I!" she said. "I didn't ask to be twinned with you, and whenever you escape, you take liberties with my body and use it as if it were your own."

"*As if* it were my own—which isn't the same as *being* my own," I said. "I hate this second-hand life. By the time my feelings are filtered through your blood, they no longer deserve that name. They are little more than puppy licks."

"If that is the case, I don't know what your feelings would be undiluted. You are a cauldron of passions, as is."

"Those aren't passions!" I said. "They are frustrations mixed with impatience. They come from the head, not from the heart. The problem is: you know nothing about true love, Adele. Indeed, I wish you would show more interest in my so-called passions and take your lead from me on occasion. At least I could have some fun then, even if only at a remove."

She shuddered. "I know only too well what happens when you take the lead." She was thinking of that night in Bishopsgate. Remorse swamped her brain and almost pulled me under as well. That's what happens if you share a bloodstream and aren't in control.

"You and your bloody conscience!" I said. "I can't stand another round of guilt mongering. I wish I had found a more congenial body to inhabit."

"If you don't like your present abode, you are free to leave."

"I just might," I said.

That's where Daniel Worth comes in. I thought of him as a kind of magus in touch with the beyond, a man who might lend me a hand getting my own body. I remember the day I heard the gossip about his experiments, which got up my hopes. We were walking home from the rectory. Adele and her friend Eliza had paid a courtesy visit to the Captain who was sick at the time. Adele was upset because Andrew had asked about the second part of the Reverend's memoir. I was alarmed, too. For a moment I thought she was going to go to pieces or confess that she had burned it. I had a hard time getting her pulse rate back to normal and squash the memory of the pages turning to ashes in the fireplace. She recovered in time to lie and tell him she knew nothing about a second part. But she was rattled, and the anxiety showed in her face. Eliza immediately noticed it. She was the sensitive type, always fussing about other people's feelings. So, she took Adele's hand and patted it.

"You look unhappy," she said. "I know you worry about the need to rely on your landlord's generosity. But surely your qualms have been laid to rest by now. Mr. Prior impresses me as a man of excellent character."

"I am not sure," Adele said. "It may only be appearances." She pretended that she was still uneasy about Andrew, but she didn't trick me. I shared her thoughts, after all. She was anxious about the business of the Reverend's memoirs and uncomfortable accepting money from Andrew, but she liked him. In fact, she was falling in love with him. I could read her thoughts when she looked at him: *soft brown eyes, a manly jaw, lips like a Cupid's bow when he smiles*—and a lot of other romantic nonsense. Now she was afraid that he would pick up on the Hinxworth gossip and find out a few things she didn't want him to know, her affair with Francis, for example. And she was coy about her feelings for Andrew because it might look as if she was after his money. Well, with the lone exception of her pious friend Eliza, every young woman in Hinxworth was after his money. And Adele had the best claim to it.

I did my best to encourage her feelings for Andrew. Mr. Perfect didn't raise my pulse rate, but at least he wasn't disgusting like old Percy Stockdale. He was all right for the purpose at hand—getting back the Collingwood money. I wasn't going to stand in Adele's way if she wanted to go after him. Neither did Eliza. She kept praising Andrew, and Adele lapped it up, although she didn't put that into her memoir, I saw, going through Adele's version of the events:

"Come, come, Adele, Mr. Prior has a natural courtesy about him," Eliza said. "I believe he is a man incapable of meanness or dissimulation."

"You always see the best in everyone," I said. "I grant you he has an engaging manner, a way of putting one at ease. About his character we shall see, however. He has a lawyer's mind, it seems to me, and he may be more cunning than appears at first sight. It would not do to pass judgment after such a brief acquaintance."

"Then you shall have another opportunity to form an impression of Mr. Prior," Eliza said. "I mean to write him a note this very afternoon, requesting his company for tea at Grove Hall. And I intend to invite Dr. Worth as well."

My ears pricked up when I heard the doctor's name.

I had a crush on the man at the time. The doctor was about thirty then, a tall rangy man with a way of stooping and leaning forward when he talked, a mannerism he adopted unconsciously, I think, to be at eye level with his patients. Daniel Worth was certainly good-looking—thick wavy hair, a broad forehead, straight nose, sensuous lips. And his eyes absolutely fascinated me. I saw strength and determination in them, but I was wrong. It was obstinacy of the worst kind—the obstinacy of a scientist who thinks he knows it all. And that incurable melancholy of his! I completely misread that aspect of Daniel's personality. I thought he was being mysterious, holding back a dark secret, or thinking deep and absorbing thoughts. But it was just pessimism. That sort of mistake wouldn't happen to me now. I have learned how to read people's thoughts and honed my skills over the centuries, but back then I was a beginner, or I would have known better and kept my fingers from Daniel. He put a damper on everything—outings, dinner parties, dances, conversations. He ruined them all. But I didn't see his character flaws at the time. He had only recently set up practice in Hinxworth and lived in Pine Lodge, a small house inside the gates of the Florsham estate. It had originally been built for the groundskeeper and was enlarged to accommodate hunting parties, but Francis Florsham was short of funds and decided to rent out the premises. He needed money to support his extravagant lifestyle during his forced stay on the continent. But let's go on with Adele's account:

"I thought I should invite the doctor," Eliza said. "He must be lonely, living all by himself at the Lodge."

"The doctor lonely?" I said. "He chooses to be alone. He discourages company by his sombre bearing and dark looks."

"I see only melancholy," Eliza said. "His eyes speak of past suffering and invite sympathy. And what you call his sombre bearing, I would call a philosophical disposition."

"You are too good," I said and was about to say more about her inclination to see the best in everyone, but we were passing Mrs. Minton's cottage and were waylaid by the old gossip. She was out in her front garden, practicing her skill on passers-by.

"How are you, my dears?" she said, and put on a blithe smile. "And how is Dr. Worth, your distinguished tenant, Miss Florsham?—I believe I heard you mention his name just now."

"The doctor has settled into his new premises," Eliza said. "More I cannot tell you, for I have not spoken to him since."

"And are you not worried about what folks say of him?" Mrs. Minton said. Her eyes glittered with mischief.

"I do not know what they say and am not fond of listening to rumours," Eliza said in a reserved voice.

"They say he is cutting up dead bodies at night," Mrs. Minton said.

"Empty tales spread by idle people," I said impatiently. Eliza only bit her lip.

"That's as it may be," said Mrs. Minton, "but where there's smoke there's fire, I always say."

"That's a fine adage," I replied, "but I like 'innocent until proven guilty' better."

"Ah, Miss Collingwood," the old woman said. "I'm not up to matching wits with the likes of you." She turned to Eliza again, thinking she was an easier mark for her acid tongue. "Believe me, Miss Florsham," she said. I'm thinking only of your family's name, seeing that the doctor is your tenant. You would not like it be said that that there was anything improper—"

"You are right, Mrs. Minton," Eliza said. "I do not like it at all when people make insinuations."

Mrs. Minton closed her mouth and stared hard at us. She did not often find herself checked and looked pinch-mouthed as we turned to go, but she didn't allow us to escape without a parting shot.

"All the same," she called after us. "I'll be tying up my Rex, for they say the doctor is using dogs' bodies for his experiments."

When we were out of earshot, Eliza gave me a vexed look. "Can there be any truth in this, you think?"

"Who would give credence to Mrs. Minton's absurd tales?" I said, but the very idea of such experiments made my flesh creep. Lynne had no such qualms and whispered in my ear: "The doctor is a man at any rate, unlike your namby-pamby Mr. Prior. So what if he kills a few dogs for sport! There are too many strays as it is." I was appalled. You have a mean streak, I said to her under my breath, but the thought of Daniel Worth conducting bloody experiments only increased her interest in the doctor. I was afraid she would resume her pursuit of him. The death of the Reverend had quelled her taste for the wild life for a time, but there was no telling when she would go off again on one of her gypsy adventures.

That was certainly on my mind when we reached the gate of Grove Hall. I wondered whether I should pay the doctor a visit at his house at the first chance I had to escape the prison of Adele's body. We were about to say good-bye to Eliza and walk on to Three Oaks, when we caught sight of Joshua, the groom's son. He was leading a mangy dog by a leash and disappeared with it into one of the outbuildings behind the Lodge. A moment later we heard a blood-curdling howl. Mrs. Minton's sinister gossip came back to Adele in a flash. Eliza gasped. The two of them stood rooted to the ground. Then Adele took Eliza's arm and went to investigate what was going on. The howls came from an outbuilding, which had been used as a stable for horses in the old days. The eerie noise stopped as suddenly as it had begun, but the silence was ominous. Adele pushed open the door. A pungent chemical odour was in the air. In the dim light of the timbered barn we saw the dog lying in a pen, tearing at a piece of meat. Joshua was leaning over the railing, watching the animal. The dog stopped chewing when he heard us come in. He turned his head, gave us a vacant stare, and made a feeble attempt to scramble up, but he collapsed under his own weight and remained on the floor of the pen, motionless.

Joshua shouted triumphantly. "Aha! It's just as the doctor said it would be." Then he recalled his manners and pulled off his cap to salute us.

"Joshua!" I said. "What is the matter with that poor animal?"

"With your permission, Miss Collingwood," the boy said proudly. "Dr. Worth has gone and hired me as his 'prentice like, and I dosed the dog as I was told to. I can't hardly believe it, but that tincture put him down in a jiffy."

"And is that what the doctor told you to do? To kill the animal?" Eliza exclaimed.

"Ah, no, Miss Florsham," Joshua said. "He ain't dead, not likely. He's only sleeping, like." He reached into the pen and shook the dog's leg. "You can see for yourself, Miss," he said. "He ain't stiff nor cold—" He swallowed the rest of his words when he saw Eliza reeling.

She had turned very pale. "My head is spinning," she said, and leaned heavily on my arm. "I feel faint."

"It's the smell of the tincture, I warrant," the boy said. "The fresh air will set you right, Miss Florsham." He opened the barn door and accompanied us outside. I would have liked to ask him a few more questions, but Eliza had first claim on my attention. I led her into the house, made her comfortable in the drawing room, and called for smelling salts. When I saw her revive and the colour return to her cheeks, I offered to go back to the barn and speak to Joshua about his mystifying work.

"It would do no good to question the lad," Eliza said. "I must demand an explanation from Dr. Worth himself, and if the rumours of his experiments are true, I shall write to Francis. He cannot wish to continue an arrangement that is likely to be detrimental to the honour of the family, whatever the consequences might be of terminating the lease." She called for pen and ink, wrote a brief note to Dr. Worth asking him to see her at once, and handed it to her maid for delivery.

"Oh, but the doctor is in the house at this very moment," the maid said. "He is attending the cook, who can't get rid of her cough. Would you like me to ask Dr. Worth to come upstairs?"

"Yes, ask him to see me if he can spare the time," Eliza said. She turned to me. "And you must keep me company a little longer," she said. "I shall want a witness, for it would not do for anyone to say that I misunderstood or misinterpreted the doctor's answer to my question."

I agreed to stay for the interview.

I remember the doctor coming into the drawing room, looking dour as usual, but when he looked at Eliza, his expression changed dramatically, from hangdog to total devotion. That's when I realized why my gypsy act had been unsuccessful so far in attracting the doctor's interest. I had competition! Or rather, I was too late. Eliza was occupying his mind. My skill at reading people's minds was limited then, and the doctor's admiration for Eliza caught me by surprise. I was fuming.

"Did you see that mooning look?" I whispered in Adele's ear. "He is in love with the pious little idiot. So that's why I couldn't seduce him!"

"I assume you are referring to your gypsy adventures," she signalled back to me, "and I am heartily glad that they have been fruitless."

I would have liked to scream, but of course I couldn't. Adele was compressing her lips and silenced me. The helplessness I felt at that moment reinforced my determination to escape from Adele, and not just for an hour or two, but permanently. None of this, or very little, appears in Adele's memoirs, although she was well aware of my frustration. I know of course why she suppressed my views except when they served her purpose: to blame me for her actions. It's a case of selective recall. She puts down whatever makes herself and Andrew look good. And Eliza is a veritable saint, in this scene at any rate:

Eliza, meanwhile, asked the doctor about the cook's health. He assured her there was no reason for concern. With proper care, the woman would be well in a few days.

"By the by," he continued, "I recently had occasion to speak to a man who was once in your employ, Old Leonard, as he is called—"

"Dear old Leonard!" Eliza said. A nervous blush appeared on her cheeks. I was well aware of the reason for her embarrassment even before she offered an explanation to the doctor. "I cannot tell you, Dr. Worth, how sorry I was to let him go, but I was bound to follow my brother's instructions—" She faltered. She did not like to speak of her need to economize, and it distressed her that she had to let Leonard go without a pension. "I was obliged to send the old man away with only a small token of my appreciation, for he is a man who had earned his ease by his loyal service."

"There is no need to explain, Miss Florsham," said the doctor. "Leonard has already told me of your great kindness to him and shown me the present he received from you on his retirement."

Eliza searched for her handkerchief. She was close to tears. "My father's watch was all I had to give him," she said, "and I gave it in the hope that Leonard might realize a sum of money from its disposal. I meant no disrespect to my father's memory. On the contrary, I believe that he would not have wanted a faithful old servant to depart without a guerdon. I only hope that he did not importune you with a request to relieve him of the watch."

The doctor looked at her with a great deal of feeling.

"Allow me to say that I admire the nobility of your sentiments, Miss Florsham, and entirely approve of your motives," he said. "I can tell you, moreover, that Leonard has proved himself a worthy recipient of your gift, for the good old man could not bring himself to dispose of a watch that had belonged to his master and merely showed it me as he was reminiscing about his service. But giving Leonard the watch was too great a sacrifice on your part. I therefore took the liberty of buying it off the old man, assuring him that I would return it to the person most entitled to its possession—indeed this was the sole condition under which he would part with his treasure." And pulling the watch from his coat pocket, the doctor held it out to Eliza. "Here it is," he said. "I return it to its rightful owner with the greatest pleasure."

It was a regular soap opera: Eliza had tears of gratitude flowing down her cheeks. She thanked the doctor and mewled like a kitten. He was too kind, she could not accept his generosity, she had no means of repaying him. She went on and on. The doctor, meanwhile, couldn't take his eyes off the little idiot. She practically had him on his knees. "Seeing you happy is all the recompense I need, Miss Florsham," he said and snatched at her hands to kiss them. Adele sucked up the whole maudlin atmosphere and was gushing about the doctor's generosity. I was about to lose all patience, but he finally caught himself, returned to his usual reserve, and said briskly: "But I have no more excuse for keeping my patients waiting, and must take my leave." Only Eliza wouldn't let him.

She hesitated. "May I presume on your time a little longer, Dr. Worth?" she said.

"But of course," the doctor said. "If I can be of service to you—"

"After the token of kindness you have given me, Dr. Worth, I am almost ashamed to bother you with a question that may be awkward for both of us," she said, "but I cannot in good conscience forebear to ask it." She paused to gather her thoughts and continued. "There is talk in Hinxworth about certain experiments you are conducting at Pine Lodge—absurd gossip, no doubt. If you could enlighten me on the matter, I would willingly defend you against the rumour mongers."

"Rumourmongering is a popular sport in this town, I'm afraid. I hear a great many foolish tales, and I see I have become a target of rumours myself. I am sorry if talk of my experiments has given you occasion to conceive an adverse opinion of me, Miss Florsham."

I noticed how carefully he had worded his reply and wondered whether there was any truth to Mrs. Minton's tales after all.

"I can assure you, Dr. Worth, that I am not in the habit of forming an opinion unadvisedly," Eliza said, "but I must own that Miss Collingwood and I happened to see Joshua—your apprentice, we are told—experimenting on a dog, and you would much oblige me with an assurance that the animal will come to no harm. Indeed, can you promise me that the dog will recover its former health?"

"I am glad of the opportunity to provide you with an explanation, Miss Florsham," the doctor said, "but 'recovery of its former health' can only be a figure of speech in the case of the dog I am treating at present—a stray I found emaciated and covered with festering sores. I asked Joshua to administer an opiate to calm the animal and then to treat the sores with an ointment I compounded after reading of the effectiveness of the ingredients in a scientific publication. I expect the dog will recover his strength after being properly fed and treated with the ointment in question. I cannot, alas, guarantee the outcome. It is precisely the purpose of my experiments to establish the efficacy of the treatment, and to do so without risk to human beings."

When he had finished his explanation, he scrutinized Eliza's face as if he was searching her soul. He was desperate to find a spark of sympathetic interest there, but his courtship was off to a bad start.

It wasn't admiration that coloured Eliza's cheeks. It was indignation.

"I could never disregard the suffering of a creature for the sake of a theory,' she said. "Causing any kind of suffering goes against Christian charity."

"I see that I have offended your sensibilities, Miss Florsham," the doctor said. "My experiments, I am afraid, are no subject for delicate ears."

It was a clever move to buy the watch off Leonard. But the doctor didn't know how to follow up on his success, or he couldn't because he was in love with science as much as he was in love with Eliza. So the fool tried to justify his work and explain his theories to her. He explained that he was interested in the origin of pain, physical or emotional. He was rather ahead of his time and anticipated the findings of neurology. He wanted to prove that pain, indeed all sensibilities, originated in the brain and could be measured like any other organic activity.

That explanation didn't go anywhere. Eliza interrupted him. "Dr. Worth," she said. "I shall listen to your theories when you can show me the happy outcome of your practices."

The doctor bowed. I'm not sure that he understood where he had gone wrong, but he tried to stay on her good side.

"I shall inform you of the outcome in the course of time," he said, "and hope it will satisfy your concerns and re-establish me in your good opinion."

In this touching scene, I was the only person who remained unmoved, or let's say, I was moved only by jealousy. I saw that the man I wanted for myself was in love with Eliza. I realized why my efforts to attract his attention had yielded no result and why I couldn't hope for success in the future either. Adele was gleeful. She was happy that my intrigues were doomed and hoped I would give up and stop risking her reputation with my gypsy outings.

"What a sentimental lot you are," I said to Adele. "One is in tears over a trifling old watch. The other feels sorry for a gentleman in love! I was in love with Jack, and did I get what I wanted? And are you sorry for me? In any case, I liked the doctor better when he sulked and looked daggers at everyone, and when I thought he was killing dogs for sport. And even if that bit of mystery is cleared up now, there is something about that man, mark my word. I can't put my finger on it. It's something—"

"I tell you what you can't put your finger on," Adele said snidely when we were on our own. "He is a gentleman—a type of man with whom you have no truck."

"Well, Miss Hoity-Toity," I said and would have pinched her insides if I could have. "I can tell you this much: when it comes to rutting, a gentleman is no better than a dog mounting a bitch. But that Dr. Worth—he is different from the rest. It must be a black secret that gives him that gloomy look. I knew a fellow once, who got his jollies spanking me, and he used to look at me as sombrely as Daniel Worth."

"What a hussy you are," she said. "I wished I could close my ears to you." But she had no way to silence me. My voice was buzzing in her head, and I thought it was to her advantage to listen to me. She was too naïve for her own good. "I come over all hot and cold thinking of that fellow," I said. "He made me believe he cared, you know. He was the only one who ever wanted me to be good, or so he said, when he took the paddle to my bottom—In the end, he was just like all the others, though, and wanted to take his pleasure with me. So much for men."

Luckily for the doctor, his experiment was successful. A week later, he was in a position to give Eliza proof of his skill. It was a Sunday afternoon in late October. Adele and Eliza were walking in the park of Grove Hall. As they made their way past Pine Lodge, they ran into the doctor and Joshua, parading the experimental dog. The animal was wearing a large collar made of stiff cardboard and shaped into a funnel to keep him from licking his fur. Adele has included the scene in her memoir:

They stopped and exchanged greetings. Joshua introduced the experimental dog.

"The doctor has named him Lazarus, like."

"And why might that be, I wonder?" I asked, smiling at the boy.

"On account of his miraculous resurrection, Miss Collingwood," Joshua said earnestly.

"And I suppose the doctor played the part of Jesus in performing this miracle?" I said.

"Let us not be irreverent, my dear," Eliza put in. A frown appeared on her forehead.

"Or attribute to a miracle what can be explained by science," the doctor said.

"Suppose you explain to us why Lazarus is wearing a fancy collar, Joshua," I said, "and why his coat is all mottled."

"The funnel is so that he won't lick off the ointment," said the boy. "As for the dog's coat, Miss Collingwood, you remember what he looked like two weeks ago. He was all mangy, like, and near to death, and the doctor, if you please, has gone and worked a miracle with an ointment—"

"Which you yourself have compounded under my instruction," the doctor said, "as you might tell the ladies. Thus, you have done your part in curing the dog. And so let me hear no more foolish talk about miracles, Joshua, when I have taught you the composition of the salve and explained to you the effect of each ingredient. It will not do for you to transform science into miracles thus lightly. I have proposed to make a man of science of you, and you have promised me to pursue knowledge and truth to the best of your ability and leave old wives' tales to those who don't know any better."

The boy's cheeks reddened. He looked at the assembled company with embarrassment. "I own that I did," he said and shut his mouth. He didn't quite understand how he had given offense.

"You are too severe on the boy for using a figure of speech, doctor," I said. "And I dare say it was my fault for leading him on."

Eliza, too, came to the boy's aid. "You need not be embarrassed, Joshua," she said. "I am pleased to see that you are learning a skill and have applied it to such good purpose."

The storm clouds that had gathered on the doctor's brow dissolved, and he smiled on his lady love: "And I in turn am glad to see you pleased, Miss Florsham," he said.

In the meantime, Adele's, or should I say, our affairs were looking up as well. Andrew's visits to Three Oaks became more frequent. At first he pretended he was calling on business. He wanted to make improvements to the house, inspect the chimneys, discuss with Adele the construction of a greenhouse in the garden, and so on, but in the end he abandoned all pretense and talked like a man in love, which was pretty tame in his case and didn't go much beyond words. Holding hands and looking deeply into Adele's eyes was all he managed. He bored me to death.

Of course, Andrew's visits to Three Oaks didn't go unnoticed in Hinxworth and prompted a great deal of envy and surprise. How could a gentleman who had the world at his feet choose to give his admiration to a woman like Adele, who had so few attractions and so many shortcomings! Mrs. Minton did not neglect to inform Adele at the first occasion of all the unkind remarks she had overheard.

"I was shocked to hear them say those things about you, my dear," she said and showed her teeth to us which were as false as her smile. "They said you are determined to marry money, but I told them, no, no, I will never believe such a thing of Miss Collingwood."

No doubt, Andrew was given similar hints by well-meaning matrons, but that did not deter him. He kept up his visits. Several times he was on the point of proposing to Adele, and every time she discouraged him.

I was furious.

"What the hell are you up to?" I said. "I know you like him, so why don't you let him get down on his knees and say his piece and accept him? Instead you keep talking about the grocer and the apothecary and the gravedigger and other stuff that is certain to dispel any romantic thought."

"I can't marry him, Lynne," she said. "All you are thinking of are the material benefits of a wealthy husband, but how could I encourage the man I love—yes, I confess, I am in love with Andrew—how can I encourage him to marry a woman possessed by an evil spirit?"

"An evil spirit?" I said. "A rational spirit, you mean. Count your blessings that you have someone to talk sense to you."

"Your so-called sense does not include a sense of honour," she said. "I dare not confess my unfortunate condition to Andrew, and I cannot marry him without confessing. It is not right to conceal your existence from him or the role you played in the death of the Reverend, not to speak of my own scruples. No, my love for Andrew is doomed. There can be no happy ending to this affair."

I CHECK the time and put away Adele's book. Never mind the printed page. It's time to go to the Clarkson, read the new manuscript the library has acquired and have a hands-on commune with Adele.

As I drive to the Clarkson, my mind goes back to the time when I made my final escape from Adele's body and got the doctor where I wanted him. He fell for the new me, or rather the old me in a new body—Eliza's. Of course he did. I chose my victim carefully, and she in turn obliged me by falling ill at the right time. Adele and I stayed in touch after I left her, but not in a friendly way. When she visited Daniel and me—now Mrs. Worth—at Hamilton House, she brought along the manuscript of her memoirs and showed them to him. I don't know what she expected to get out of it—going behind my back, letting him in on our secret and telling him of my transmigratory powers. Did she think the doctor could force me out? She should have known better. He didn't have that power. And in any case, he didn't believe her. He questioned her sanity, but at the same time he felt threatened and feared for the family name. It would have been embarrassing if she published those memoirs. Adele called her book a "cautionary tale." I suppose she wrote it as a warning to others, but it would have taken a lot of nerve to publish such a story. And if that was her intention, it was a bad move to show a sample to Daniel Worth. He was a conservative man who observed etiquette, but in this case he lost his cool. He raged at Adele, confiscated the manuscript, and showed her the door. That's how those pages ended up at Hamilton House.

As I turn into the driveway of the Clarkson, I think about the mechanics of using the manuscript as a conduit to the past. I think of my fingers tracing Adele's writing on the page, of the ink entering through the pores of my skin, the words travelling to my mind and simmering in the coils of my brain. I hope it will work. The facsimile didn't do the trick, but it created the right mood, and for a few moments here and there as I read Adele's words, I could hear her voice and felt the sooty taste of London on my tongue. I was with Adele again, a speaker in her dialogue, an actor in the events she described. And today I'll be in her presence and join hands with her on the page. Will that touch have the power to transport me, not only in mind but also in body?

At the Clarkson, I park my car. The blinds at the Porter's Lodge are still down. I wonder when Sam will get back from New York. But why am I thinking of him? I should be thinking of Jack. I want to get back with *him*. What does that stray longing mean? Don't I believe in the success of my venture, in the possibility of being transported and reunited with Jack? Am I already casting around for a replacement just in case I'm stuck in this century? I pull myself up sharp. That sort of defeatist attitude won't do.

I get out of the car. The place has a narcotic pull on me, but I don't know what's pulling me. Is it Jack's name stored in the vault of the Clarkson, or is it Sam's name stored in a more recent memory file?

In the Reading Room, I go through the old routine: well, a slightly modified routine. They have tightened the security. Readers now have to enter the room through a ticking frame, the airport security type. That changes the game plan. Even if Patricia had given me access to Adele's memoirs, even if I had managed the sleight of hand of taking a page and concealing it, it would have been impossible to make off with it. No doubt the books are electronically tagged now. Alarms would go off, buzzers, rotating lights, whatever, but today I'm here on legitimate business. I have permission to handle the new manuscript. The question is: will a day spent with leftovers do me any good? Because that's what those pages are, leftovers, fragments of Adele's story. In his fit, Daniel burned some of the telltale pages, the ones reflecting badly on the Worth family. Were they crucial? Did they contain my name? Because it's the combination of our names—Adele and Lynne—that has the strongest pull on me. And of course, Jack's name. He is like a magnet, but the chances of his name appearing on those pages are slim.

The manuscript is waiting for me, as arranged. The librarian brings it over to my assigned desk and sets it up on a stand for me. The pages are in a paper sleeve tied with a string. I put on the cotton gloves provided, take out the sheaf of pages with Adele's handwriting, and begin to read. The first page starts midway through a sentence and keeps me guessing. Where are we?

> while she attended to her toilette, inspected the silks, ribbons, gloves, and hats presented for her approval, and sat in consultation with her dressmaker and milliner to master the latest tricks of fashion. Her toilet table was a marvel to behold. There were flasks with cosmetic water to carry off freckles, remedies for offensive breath and for the ill scents of the armpits, rice water to make the hair curl, delicate paste to smooth and whiten hands, red pomatum to plump and colour the lips, perfumes of all kinds, and a box of black velvet and silk patches. I was astonished, Adele. I had never seen the likes of it."

A conversation with Adele, I see. But who is the speaker?

> "I'm not surprised at what you are telling me, Alma. Lady Morecastle is well known as a woman of fashion."

Ah, the speaker is Daniel's sister, Alma Worth, telling Adele about her visit with Lady Morecastle in London. She got into trouble while there, committed some sort of indiscretion no one at Hamilton House wanted to talk about, except Alma herself. She had no brain, and once she opened her mouth, there was no stopping her. I soon found out that Francis Florsham had a part in the fiasco, and that Alma was out of her chaperone's sight for longer than was acceptable. Not her fault, she said. Francis trapped her. For all I know she was right. It may have been one of his desperate moves to get his hands on a woman with a substantial dowry, even if that woman was engaged to his own cousin. Alma was about to be married to Jonathan Bewdley, a model of a young gentleman and excellent husband material. He had only one flaw: he was related to Francis and made the mistake of introducing Alma to him.

"Every day in London was full of amusement. If the weather was fine, I accompanied Lady Morecastle on her carriage ride in Green Park and was told all about the eligible young gentlemen bowing to us. The evenings, too, were full of diversions, plays, balls, the opera—enough to make me dizzy with excitement. Of course, my governess, Miss Crawford, made a sour face at all the dancing and gadding and courting, as she put it. She called Lady Morecastle's house a den of iniquity and London a godless city, a modern-day Babylon! But she is an old spinster and averse to all amusement."

Of course, Daniel was annoyed when he read Adele's manuscript and saw that it referred to that London episode. He was protective of his little sister and worried about the scandal becoming public, although by the time he read Adele's manuscript, things were under control. Alma was safely married to Jonathan Bewdley. Her husband knew about the affair and blamed Francis. He acquitted his wife of any fault. Daniel didn't. He thought Alma's misbehaviour, if known, would leave an indelible mark on the family honour and took care to cover up the evidence.

I turn the page. There's something missing here, presumably the part Daniel fed to the flames. He would have thrown the whole manuscript into the fire if I hadn't interfered. The next page which escaped the holocaust deals with the consequences of Alma's misconduct.

The mood was of the gloomiest. Miss Crawford had already heard the tale of my misadventure from the house servants downstairs and was full of reproaches. Then I was summoned to Lady Morecastle's boudoir. I found her reclining on the bed, with a moist cloth pressed to her forehead. She fussed a great deal. 'I have passed a sleepless night in consequence of your horrid behaviour,' she said. 'And I was obliged to write to your father and decline all further responsibility for your conduct.' You can imagine how I felt when I heard that, Adele. I broke out in tears."

"Did you tell Lady Morecastle that Francis Florsham was a cousin of Jonathan and you had been properly introduced?"

"Of course, I did, but she wouldn't listen to me. She kept saying: 'You should not have left my side. There is no excuse for your behaviour. You should never have been left alone with that roué. The best thing will be to bury yourself in the country. I hope the world will forget about the affair, and your young man will honour his promise to you in spite of your misstep.' And that's what she put in her letter to my father. Oh, Adele, I was so ashamed and so afraid to face him."

"I can imagine your fears. I hope your father was kinder to you than

Another gap in the manuscript, but I know that the old man wasn't kind to Alma. He took Lady Morecastle's advice and buried his daughter in the country. That is, he sent her to Hinxworth to stay with her brother. It was the equivalent of a prison sentence because the doctor had the mentality of a jail guard, as I discovered eventually. But at the time when Alma arrived in Hinxworth, I was still twinned with Adele and still lusting after Daniel. He in turn was after Eliza, who loved only God and rejected his offer of marriage. In her situation, she should have jumped at the chance of marrying him. The consensus in Hinxworth was that she'd be a fool not to accept the doctor. Her brother had squandered her fortune and was facing bankruptcy himself. The doctor was a good catch. Why would Eliza refuse to marry him? Because she was "unworldly," as Adele put it. She was unfit for life if you ask me!

I turn back to the manuscript. So far it's been a disappointment. Nothing here to get me going and draw me into the past. Alma and her insipid talk won't do the trick:

When Alma arrived in Hinxworth, she did her best to promote her brother's cause and change Eliza's heart. I joined her in urging my friend to reconsider, braving my evil twin who was mad for the doctor and wanted him for herself. She need not have worried. Eliza had no interest in marriage. She looked at us with the meek eyes of a doe and spoke of the moral lesson her misfortunes had taught her.

"My dearest Alma," she said. "I learned how feeble are the efforts of human beings when set against destiny and the plans laid up in heaven."

"But it isn't destiny that's at fault," Alma said. "It's Francis who has ruined you."

"I know," she said, tears rising to her eyes. "God, in his unfathomable wisdom, allowed him to sink into the abyss of sin, and I hope that God will set him on the right path again."

"That's all very well and piously spoken," Alma said, "but what will you do when Grove Hall is sold and you are left with a pittance to live on?"

It was cruel of Alma to be so blunt, but Eliza showed her usual forbearance. "As grievous as it would be to lose Grove Hall," she said, "it will free me from worldly cares and allow me to embark on the spiritual life for which I have long yearned."

"And is this why you rejected Daniel's offer of marriage?" Alma said. "To live a spiritual life?"

It was clear that she was not in sympathy with Eliza's pious sentiments, and on that occasion, neither was I.

"God is my only comfort now," Eliza said and dabbed her eyes with a handkerchief. "I shall pray for Francis and trust that my prayers will be answered."

It seemed to me that more than prayers were required in the circumstances. Francis had squandered the Florsham fortune, and Eliza sat still, like a sacrificial lamb, and turned her eyes to heaven. She had in her a degree of goodness that approached sainthood.

Over the next weeks, Francis' monetary affairs went from bad to worse. At last he had no choice but to put Grove Hall up for sale. He was in Paris then and dared not return for fear of being dragged off to debtor's prison the moment he set foot on English soil. Eliza therefore called on their cousin, Jonathan Bewdley, to come and take the business in hand.

When he came, we were all assembled at Grove Hall— Eliza, Andrew, myself, Daniel, and Alma who blushed violently when Jonathan entered.

Yes, there was love in the air that day, enough to fill a romance novel. Daniel was dying for Eliza's attention—to my annoyance, since I was still keen on him myself. Jonathan and Alma were practically an item. And Andrew kept trying to propose to Adele, although in his case it was hard to say what motivated him: love or a sense of duty. Today I could tell exactly what he was thinking, but back then I got only a faint reading, a low level of radiation that could have been either love or a tender conscience. He felt badly about inheriting the Reverend's money and was principled enough to worry that the way Percy Stockdale got it wasn't kosher. In any case, he was ready to get down on his knees and ask for Adele's hand in marriage. It was her who put on the brakes. She had scruples accepting him.

"How can I marry Andrew, when I am encumbered with you," she kept saying—as if I was some kind of disease.

"What do you mean?" I said. "I'm no encumbrance. On the contrary, I'm good for you. I provide a counterweight to your mawkishness and I am sharing my good looks with you. You ought to thank me for correcting your natural disadvantages—a long nose and mousy hair." But she only sighed.

Jonathan in turn looked at Alma with languishing eyes, so that it was not difficult for the company to guess at the feelings that had sprung up between them. Indeed, Jonathan's arrival had the effect of an elixir on Alma. She became twice as flighty as before and blurted out more silly things than ever. At last, we arrived at the business that had brought Jonathan to Grove Hall.

He set about explaining to Eliza the situation she confronted. It was in the power of the creditors to foreclose at once, which would put her and Francis into a most disadvantageous position and leave them impoverished. If they had time to sell off the land and property in orderly fashion, however, they might salvage some of the assets and realize enough from the proceeds of the sale to pay their debts, allow Francis to make a new start in life and Eliza to live in a manner becoming to a lady, though of course a lady in reduced circumstances.

"Considered purely from the point of profit," Jonathan said, "a creditor might do well to wait and give Francis time to realize the full value of his property. The discounted sum fetched at auction might not cover all of his debt." But since there were many creditors, some more impatient than others, it was not likely that they would come to an agreement, he said. He had therefore consulted with his father and with Mr. Worth Senior—here he gave Alma a meaningful look, and she blushed becomingly as he continued: "And I am pleased to say that they are willing to satisfy the creditors and take possession of Grove Hall themselves."

In short, Jonathan had asked for Alma's hand, had been accepted as her suitor, and the two fathers intended to purchase Grove Hall with a view of making it the future home of the young couple. Jonathan, representing their interests, had all but completed the arrangements, which included an annuity for Eliza. How Francis would manage his life on the sum realized from the sale was left to his caution, but the general sentiment (always excepting Eliza) was that he would come to a bad end.

Alma meanwhile joyfully anticipated becoming mistress of Grove Hall. She declared with her usual surfeit of giddiness and lack of tact that if ever Eliza felt a longing for her ancestral home, she was welcome to visit. She was very pleased with herself for making this generous offer and naturally took the tears welling up in Eliza's eyes as a sign of deepest gratitude and

And what? I turn the page. The rest of the sentence is missing—another page destroyed by Daniel. His rationale isn't clear to me. He must have burned the pages indiscriminately, in a blind fury. We are on to a new scene, but I am sidetracked by a general movement in the Reading Room. The people around me are getting up from their desks and edging toward the electronic gate. I look at the wall clock and see that it's noon. Lunch time. I'm ready for a break, too. Adele's ironic retelling of Alma's story has kept me amused, but it's not my story. That's why the curlicues of Adele's handwriting have failed to work their magic so far, and the aroma of dried ink coming off the page has left me cold. My name is missing. I have no part in the conversations recorded. The words don't lift off the page for me.

I deposit the manuscript at the librarian's desk and make my way to the lunchroom. Patricia Baron is already there, her wheelchair wedged against a table. She waves to me. I join her.

She is eager to talk about the new manuscript. She hopes I'm hooked. This isn't the best place to tackle the question of sponsorship money, but her head is veiled in a cloud of money-raising thoughts. The titles of her projects are blinking, piercing the fog like search lights. She is on a scouting mission.

"So—how do you like it?" she asks while we eat our sandwiches. "Alma is an engaging character, don't you think?"

"I don't know about engaging. Silly, I'd say. I can't warm up to her."

The project lights around Patricia's head dim. She gives me a disappointed look. She expected more enthusiasm. As an experienced fundraiser she should know better. Even if I felt a gale of enthusiasm, I'd hold back for strategic reasons. In the money business, hesitation is a bargaining chip. But in this case I'm not faking it. I feel no enthusiasm. Not the slightest breeze. Sorry. I can't get off on Alma's story. She isn't good enough as a medium. I need a mention of my name. I need to put my fingertips on those letters to escape the present. I hope like hell Adele mentions me in the remaining pages. I don't even know if seeing my name is good enough. I need Jack's name as well. It's the combination that does it.

"You may find the second half more interesting," Patricia says on cue. "It's the part that ties in with Adele Collingwood's memoir."

She keeps on talking and drops the big word: sponsorship. The cloud of projects swirling above her head threatens to engulf me.

I smile at Patricia with all my teeth and start talking about the many worthy causes out there which have a claim on me, which compete for my attention: global warming, breast cancer, youth at risk, famine in Africa. Still, I say, there's no denying it: the Clarkson has a claim on my heart. She says that's good to hear and looks at me expectantly. The halo of projects around her head has stopped blinking. They hang in her firmament like stars, waiting for God's hand to move them, but I hold out a little longer. I want to see Patricia sit up and beg for money. I change the topic.

"What's with the tight security in the Reading Room?" I say.

"A lot of unnecessary expense if you ask me," Patricia says, "and all because of an old scholar who is in the early stages of dementia and tried to cut a page from a rare book with a razor blade. He didn't get far. Melanie, who was on supervision, jumped him and got cut in the process. After an investigation, it turned out that he'd stolen things from the library before."

"How did he manage that?"

"He took loose items from folders—bills, invitations, letters—and stuffed them up his sweater. When he brought the folder back to the counter, the supervisor checked it off as 'returned'. We've changed the procedure. The supervisor now counts the items in the folder or box before checking it out. And we've put electronic tags on the loose items. It's overkill, as I said, but everyone is paranoid after what happened."

At one o'clock, the crowd begins to thin. People go back to their offices or their desks in the Reading Room. I get up, too.

Patricia and I part at the electronic gate. I think about the information she has given me as I pick up the manuscript from the librarian's desk and return to my place. Making off with anything from the collection has become more difficult, if not impossible. Well, let's finish reading the manuscript. Maybe I can tease something out of the second half, although I'm not hopeful—Daniel may have burned anything mentioning an incubus.

I start reading, and hey, this looks promising. I can see my name a couple of lines down. *Lynne*—I'm glad I stuck with that name over the ages. It is like a beacon guiding me home.

It was at the time of Eliza's financial tribulations that my relationship with Lynne reached its nadir. After our return from London, she lay low for a while and was like a bad dream or a whispering conscience or a thought at the back of my mind. But soon she recovered her former power over me. My body was like a kingdom divided. She sat beside me on the throne, had her hand on the sceptre and issued her commands through my mouth. She made her escape into the world regularly, leaving me crippled and confined to my bed.

Her passion for Daniel Worth gave her new strength. Poor man! No sooner had the misunderstanding about his experiments been cleared up, a new rumour arose, that he was resurrecting the dead, had been seen in the company of a shadow figure resembling the late Reverend Stockdale, that he was keeping company with a black-haired gypsy woman, a mysterious creature costumed in voluminous, ill-matched clothes.

Adele knew of course that I was the mysterious woman and discreetly questioned the doctor about the "gypsy." He shrugged. "I see her sometimes when I return from my rounds at dusk," he said. "She seems to put herself into my way. I cannot imagine what she wants. She is a poor madwoman, no doubt, and I would gladly help her in any way possible, but no one in the village can enlighten me as to her name or tell me where she lives." I was furious at his put-down, but I didn't know how to get at him. He attracted and intimidated me at the same time. I never worked up the courage to proposition him in my gypsy guise. I was waiting for him to make the first move, invite me into the Lodge perhaps, but no luck. I was completely frustrated and gave Adele a hard time, banging around in her head, blowing off my anger.

"Will you calm down?" I said to Lynne. "Leave the poor man alone. Can't you see that he is pining for Eliza and has no thought for anyone else? But I know what you are after."

Lynne had infinite faith in the doctor's capacities. Was he not conducting experiments that brought about miraculous results? Might he not hold in his hands the secret of life and be able to give her a body of her own? She was no longer content to dwell in shared quarters and appear in the borrowed shape of a reluctant host. She wanted to have her own skin and bones, command a voice of her own, and experience her own feelings. I suspect she thought Daniel Worth was a kind of magician or necromancer and might make those wishes come true. That is why she sought him out. Her play for the doctor's attention left me anxious and disturbed.

A week before Christmas, Daniel Worth and his sister Alma left for Scotland to be with their widowed father at

Hamilton House, and Lynne became sullen and withdrawn. I saw my chance and reclaimed sovereignty over my body. I extracted a promise from her to abandon her gypsy act. She gave it readily and moped in a corner of my mind, showing little interest in the outside world.

Nonsense!—Did I just say that aloud? The librarian on duty gives me the irritated look reserved for people who disturb the graveyard silence of the Reading Room, and the grad student at the desk next to mine raises his head and blows a cloud of thoughts in my direction: *Getting a little carried away, are we?*

I clamp down my mouth.

Adele had no idea why I'd lost my taste for the outside world. I had a scare during my last escapade. I ventured out at dusk wearing my gypsy costume. The doctor had gone to Scotland, so I practiced my skills on a couple of guys at the local inn. At nightfall, I changed back into Adele's clothes and was just coming out of the barn where I kept my disguise, when I saw a man passing by on the far side of the road. There was something off-key about him. His figure wavered, drifting in the dusk. He halted and gave me a searching glance. His skin seemed grafted on to his face, and it was the face of Percy Stockdale. He looked like the Reverend and walked like him, soft in the knees and slouching. I turned abruptly and started running, but when I looked over my shoulder, I saw that he was coming after me. I caught the sound of words, or was it only a rustle of leaves in the wind? I should have stopped and found out: Was he man or ghost? But I felt vulnerable in my borrowed body. I had no strength. What if the man was a tramp out to rob someone? It wouldn't have taken much to knock me over, break my bones and turn me in a heap of I don't know what—ashes? air? Worse, what if he was the Reverend come back to life, a transmigrant like myself? I couldn't risk an encounter. Separated from Adele, I had only a half-life. I ran home and slipped back into her body, glad to have a hiding place. Over the next few days I kept my eyes open for the Stockdale look-alike, but I never saw him again, not through Adele's eyes at any rate. Still, the experience frightened me. I was more desperate than ever to be my own person and do what I wanted to do, to get away from Hinxworth, from Adele, from the whole Collingwood saga. For the first time it occurred to me that transmigration might not be a once-off thing, that I might be able to repeat the act and enter another person.

It was a wonderful feeling to see Lynne reduced to silence once more. Little did I know what this purported: she had her eyes on Eliza. With hindsight, I can see what she was up to. Her silence did not signal weakness or a willingness to yield to me. Her silence was a quiet watchfulness. She knew that Daniel Worth was in love with Eliza. She studied the object of his affection as a sculptor studies his model, scrutinizing every feature: the slant of her eyes, the curve of her mouth, the outline of her cheek, the movement of her hands. I should have felt the curling desire in my incubus, the tensing of her attention, her readiness to pounce, but her silence lulled me into a false sense of security.

In the meantime, the sale of the Florsham estate had been completed. Grove Hall was now owned by Jonathan Bewdley and would soon be undergoing renovations to accommodate the wishes of the future Mrs. Bewdley. The wedding was to take place in March. The thought of leaving her beloved home grievously affected Eliza's health. She felt very low, and took to bed with a fever. Alarmed, I wrote to Dr. Worth, begging him to hasten his return. Andrew, who was to spend Christmas with the Captain, delayed his departure and called in a specialist from London. The great man gave us little assurance, however. After examining the patient, he shook his head and said he had no means of effecting a cure. Eliza's illness was not of the kind a physician could dose. She was affected in her spirits, and it was a matter of rallying her will to live, he said, rather than fortifying her blood or lowering her temperature or prescribing medication. He collected his fee and departed.

I then put all my hopes in Dr. Worth and in the power of his love to save Eliza. He was on his way and expected to arrive in the morning, but that night Eliza took a turn for the worse. I watched by her bedside, read to her, and spoke softly of bygone times, taking care to touch only on pleasant memories—our carefree days at Miss Lee's establishment, our cheerful walks in the environs of Hinxworth, her father's library and the sages of antiquity. As the hours went by, however, Eliza wished to have only the consolation of Scripture and at last stopped speaking to me altogether. Her eyes and lips remained closed, her skin became translucent. In a word she was preparing to depart this world and be transformed into an angel of light.

I noticed that Lynne took a great interest in Eliza's state of health. Ignorant of her motives, I thought she felt pity for one who was about to suffer a fate much like her own—meeting with death at a young age. Although Lynne had shown no inclination to leave the confines of my body during those days, she made her presence felt, pushing to the forefront of my consciousness. She was positioned at the windows of my soul, looking out at Eliza with a steady watchfulness. If I touched my friend's hand, it was as if Lynne, too, put her fingers on her skin, and for a while I forbore approaching Eliza too closely. I feared that Lynne's presence was injurious to her or doing violence to her purity. But I could not abandon my friend at a time when her life seemed to be ebbing away.

The bed curtains had been looped back on the side where I was sitting. Suddenly Eliza moved, opened her eyes and parted her lips hesitantly as if she meant to speak. I feared they might be her last words. Bending over her, I took her limp hand in mine. As I touched my lips to her pale cheek, Lynne within me began stirring. Her blood bubbled and boiled in my veins. She came so close to the surface of my skin that my breath was infused with her outpourings, her moaning "Now! I must do it now."

I lean forward. My bare arms graze the pages of Adele's manuscript and thin them out. They melt away, or am I melting into them? I'm at Eliza's bedside. I enter her feverish brain. I begin the struggle with the dark forces, breathing strength into Eliza's flagging body. No, stop. What am I doing? I come to my senses and struggle to lift my arms and make my getaway into the present, back into the Reading Room of the Clarkson. This isn't the time or place to start my journey into the past. There must be nothing haphazard about it. I need to make sure I arrive when Jack is still alive, when there's still a chance of rescuing him.

I am breathing hard with the effort to wrench my arms off the page. I grip the desk and force my body to straighten up, pressing my spine against the back of my chair. I close my eyes, concentrating, pulling away from the past into the present and into the Reading Room. The page solidifies and the lines, which have faded to a thin transparent gray, darken again. When the crisis has passed and I open my eyes, the librarian is looking at me, thinking *Hot flashes?* I realize that I'm sweating profusely. Get up, I tell myself. It takes an enormous effort to move my legs, walk to the washroom, and splash cold water on my face to slow down my pulse. My system is frayed, as if it had gone through a heart attack. It has been a frightening experience, but at least I know now that I can do it. I can lose myself in Adele's pages. Now I just have to make sure the timeframe is right.

I lock myself into one of the cubicles and do deep-breathing exercises until my pulse normalizes and my system is working properly. When I get back to the Reading Room, I realize that it took me a while to recover. I've been in the washroom longer than

I thought. It's thirty minutes to closing time, the librarian tells me. People are winding up, unplugging their laptops, shuffling papers. I return to my desk. There are only a couple of pages to go.

The next moment I sensed Lynne hovering on the very border of my being. A spectre appeared before my eyes, a phantom woman, her hair colourless, her lips shimmering, her face of an indistinct shape, as if it was about to be reshaped and formed anew at that very moment. At the same time Eliza reared up, arching her back as if in agony. I reached for her hand and felt our fingers fused by an electric charge. A wave of pain undulated through my hand. I could not tell whether my pain was entering Eliza's body or her aching mind was communing with mine. We clutched at each other, until she fell back on her pillow seemingly lifeless. I was in a swoon myself. After a few minutes, I rallied and rose with difficulty to call for help. I feared that I had witnessed Eliza's death.

Before I could ring for a servant, however, I heard a commotion in the corridor, followed by a knock on the door. A moment later Daniel Worth entered the room, booted and spurred, for he had ridden through the night to be with his beloved. He stepped up to the bed with every sign of fear and alarm, put his hand on Eliza's pulse and, acknowledging my presence at last, motioned me to wait in the next room. I left to allow him to say his farewell to Eliza, thinking that was his purpose. When he emerged from the bedchamber an hour later, however, with tears glistening in his eyes, he told me that Eliza was breathing yet. The crisis had come, he said. We would know in a very few hours whether she was to live or die. He returned to the bedroom to do his utmost to save his beloved patient.

I sank into a chair exhausted and soon fell into a heavy sleep. I was drained—of strength I thought, but when I woke I understood that more than strength had gone out of me. There was a lightness in my heart, a self-possession that I had not felt in many years. Lynne had quit me, and I was once more the mistress of my mind and body.

It didn't take long for Adele to recover and take charge of her life. The day after my departure she accepted Andrew's proposal, and the morning after that she was at my bedside, or rather Eliza's bedside, gushing with happiness. She was a different woman. It was almost as if she and I had never shared a body. Of course, it's hard to gauge the impact I had on her mind, to what extent I shaped her and how she would have developed without me. I know that I have absorbed some of Adele's thoughts and memories. They have stayed with me throughout my lives. Physical features, I notice, have less permanence. I have retained a few of my own facial features throughout the years, and my red hair has a dominant quality. Sometimes I look into the mirror and see a glimpse of the woman I was two hundred years ago, but it is a fleeting impression, here one moment and gone the next. A core remains, I suppose. The rest fluctuates with each new admixture. Conversely, I wouldn't be surprised to find that Adele gradually reverted to her old features, her pointed nose and mousy brown hair.

I had a wonderful feeling of emancipation, but I could not give free vent to my joy. I sensed that my incubus had left me for another victim—Eliza. I could not help reflect on the circumstances in which Lynne had taken possession of me. She had slipped into my body when I was at death's door, much like my friend was on the night of Lynne's departure.

After a few weeks Eliza rallied and recovered her strength. Hinxworth credited the skills of Dr. Worth, but I knew better. It was Lynne who had breathed new life into her. Eliza rose from her sickbed a changed woman. She had the elegant bearing, genteel manners, and amiable smile of old, but the illness, or rather Lynne's nascent influence, had its dampening effects on her kindness and devotion and seemed to leave only her rational faculties intact. The change did not happen overnight. It was a gradual progression, and the first sign of Eliza's altered state was the increased favour she showed to Daniel Worth. It seemed only natural to the people of Hinxworth that she should change her mind and show gratitude to the doctor whose care had brought about her recovery. The doctor in turn did not take long to notice Eliza's change of heart and, taking advantage of this fortuitous circumstance, petitioned for her hand in marriage a second time. She accepted his offer without hesitation. All of Hinxworth thought of this as a happy ending, but I could not share the general opinion. When I tendered my congratulations to the engaged couple, I regarded Eliza with anxious eyes, expecting Lynne to glance back at me pertly. I met only the familiar gaze, but the telltale signs of Lynne's rule were there. Eliza was possessed of a new determination. She became livelier and cheerfully embraced Hinxworth society, whereas before she had been of a retiring nature. None of these changes were for the worse, and yet I could not help grieving the loss of Eliza, as she had been—my sweet and soulful friend. I could only hope that she would find Lynne more accommodating than I did, that her moral strength would keep Lynne from doing mischief, and that her modesty would combine with Lynne's ebullience and bring about a perfect equilibrium.

And that's the end of the notes Adele put into Daniel's hands when she visited us at Hamilton House, or at any rate the pages that survived Daniel's bonfire.

I look up and see that I'm one of two people left in the Reading Room. It's closing time. The librarian comes around to collect our manuscripts. Do I want to reserve it for another day? she asks. Yes, I say. I'll be back.

ON THE drive back to the villa, I can't help thinking of the last time I saw Adele. It was on the morning when Daniel sent her packing. She had shown him her memoirs to "save" Eliza. But I had done that already. I rescued Eliza from death. All right, I didn't do it for her sake, but she was the main beneficiary. She survived, even if not quite as herself. It's me who got the dirty end of the stick. I thought Daniel would suit me as a husband, but as it turned out we were incompatible, and Adele's interference made things worse.

I was on my way to the breakfast room when I heard raised voices and saw Adele storming out of the library.

"I never thought Daniel was such a brute," she said, brushing by me in the hall.

"What did he do?"

"Ask *him* what he did. I have nothing more to say about the matter. I have been asked to leave, and I am leaving this instant."

The doctor was just as stubborn. He refused to tell me what had happened between them. He didn't come to the door to bid Adele farewell when she was packed and ready to go. He sulked in his study.

After seeing Adele off, I went to him and demanded an explanation. I found him standing in front of the fireplace. He was holding a sheaf of papers in one hand and a poker in the other. Some papers were curling in the fire and slowly turning to ashes.

"What is going on for Heaven's sake?" I asked.

"This!" he said, holding up a clutch of pages. "Your friend Adele has been imprudent enough to commit certain recollections of hers to paper and provoking enough to ask my opinion of them."

And foolish enough to entrust the manuscript to him!

He fed a few more pages into the fire. For all I know he had already burned a good number of them.

"What is so provoking about those pages?" I said, fishing for more information.

"It is a disgraceful piece of writing and, if published, will cause speculation and may damage the good name of my family. She mentions Alma, you know."

He was worried about his precious sister Alma. *I* was worried about what Adele might have written about me.

"I don't know how she came by the information about Alma. If you tattled about her in your letters, it was very unwise." He gave me a questioning look. "Did you?"

"*Tattling*? What do you mean? We exchange letters. Adele tells me about her life. I tell her about mine. Is that wrong?"

"It is, if it involves my sister. I cannot have Alma's reputation ruined by your indiscretion or Adele's ambitions as an author. I asked her to destroy the manuscript at once."

"And she gave you permission to do so?"

He reddened. "She refused to accommodate my request."

"And you in turn refused to give back her property. Is that why she called you a brute?"

"I did nothing that would justify her calling me a brute. I had no choice but to confiscate those pages. If she ever decided to publish them—"

"Did she threaten to publish them?"

"Not in so many words. But she has unfortunately chosen to make it her calling to write for the public, and so my only recourse is to burn her crazed outpourings."

"Crazed?"

"I don't know what else to call them." He slapped the pages in his hand as if he wanted to shake out the crumbs of Adele's madness. "Indeed, their publication would embarrass no one more than Adele herself. My sister isn't the only subject of her ramblings.

She talks about Percy Stockdale making a ghostly appearance! She talks about an incubus that invaded her body and later seized upon you! She calls you possessed, Eliza—if that is not crazed, what is?"

I was as alarmed as the doctor now. I realized why Adele had come to Hamilton House: to betray me. To warn Daniel that Eliza wasn't the woman he thought he had married, that I had taken over her body. And what was that about Percy Stockdale "making a ghostly appearance"? He tried to scare me once. Did he haunt Adele as well? I took a deep breath and said: "That does sound rather far-fetched."

"To put it mildly. I had every right to ask her to leave."

I had to tread carefully. "I can see why you are upset, Daniel," I said. "I—possessed by an evil spirit? That *is* complete nonsense. You are right to want those pages destroyed, but what keeps Adele from re-writing them?"

He hesitated.

"Why don't you leave the matter with me?" I said. "I will write to Adele and ask her for a promise to keep the content of her notes private, for her own sake and for ours. I believe she would be open to a friend's appeal."

He shuffled his feet. "That may be the best approach. Perhaps I was too peremptory. And perhaps it is not right to destroy what is Adele's property after all. Write to her, offer her my apologies, and see what you can do. In the meantime, however, I shall lock away those poisonous pages."

He put them into his strongbox. And that's where they stayed, for two hundred years, until the Clarkson bought them. But even if Daniel had burned the whole batch, he couldn't reach into my brain and uproot the events I witnessed. They are still lodged in my memory. And they were lodged in Adele's. That is why she wrote her *Cautionary Tale,* even though she never published it or even bothered to rewrite the pages she had left behind at Hamilton House, as far as I can tell.

ADELE

ELIZA AND DANIEL moved to Scotland after their marriage. She had no wish to live in the shadow of Grove Hall, which was a constant reminder of her family's fall from glory. Daniel obliged, and circumstances favoured their move to Hamilton House, his father's estate. The local doctor there had reached the age of retirement, providing a suitable opening for Daniel to set up a practice. The newlyweds left for Scotland with my warmest wishes for their happiness and many promises to write and visit.

Lynne was slowly fading from my memory. At times she seemed no more than an illusion, a morbid fantasy driven out by Andrew's loving embrace. I tried to remember the night of the Reverend's death. Had I really been in Bishopsgate, I asked myself. Did I know of the murder before Mr. Merryweather told us the particulars? And my night vigil at Eliza's bed—did I really see Lynne hover above my friend? All I remembered with certainty was the fatigue I felt that night, and the desolation of my soul. And even those sentiments were hard to recall in my present state of happiness with Andrew. I embraced the idea that Lynne had been no more than a figment of my imagination because it absolved me from any responsibility for her dark deeds. If Lynne was an atmospheric illusion, so were her actions. The joyful events in my life—marriage to Andrew, a honeymoon on the continent—allowed me to keep unhappy thoughts at bay, but after my return to Hinxworth, the excitement and bustle of travel gave way to sober thoughts, and my doubts returned: Had my friend Eliza changed because her life had changed or because she was now possessed by Lynne? And if Lynne had really occupied my mind and body, were her sins my sins too?

To settle things in my own mind, I decided to write down my reminiscences, although it took great resolve to recall the dismal events leading up to the Reverend's death. How often I put pen to paper, only to draw back again, afraid of reliving the horror of those days, but in the end I convinced myself that putting it all in black and white might help relieve my doubts and clarify my situation. If I could make the story hang together without recourse to unnatural causes, if everything I had gone through could be explained in a rational fashion, if Lynne had no material bearing on the course of events, then clearly she did not exist. And if she was only a figment of my imagination, then I must overcome those disturbing fantasies with the help of reason.

The work of gathering my thoughts and writing them down kept me on an even keel for a time, but it took no more than a letter from Eliza to throw me off again. Her name, her handwriting recalled to my mind the peculiar circumstances of her illness, her miraculous recovery. My mind began to waver. I searched the lines of her letter for an underlying meaning. I examined every word, turned over every phrase, and asked myself: is this Eliza speaking, or is it Lynne? I argued first on one side, then on the other, but in the end I gave up theorizing, and decided on a practical test. I would visit Eliza at Hamilton House and let my eyes and ears be the judges of her condition.

I made a bargain with myself: If I could ascertain that Eliza was indeed possessed by Lynne's spirit, I would speak to Daniel, tell him all and plead for his help. He was a physician after all. He had shown a willingness to carry out experiments and explore new approaches. Perhaps he knew of drugs or treatments that might be effective in a case like this.

I arrived at Hamilton House and was warmly greeted by my dear friend. In the first joy of holding her in my arms again, I felt nothing but contentment. Eliza's words were as sweet as ever to my ears, her cheek as soft to my lips, her embrace as welcoming as I could wish. It was only when I listened more closely to the cadence of her words and examined her features, which the long years of our friendship had made so familiar to me, that I became uneasy. The changes in her appearance were subtle, but what convinced me more than anything of Lynne's pernicious influence, was the way Eliza looked at Daniel and spoke to him. There was none of the gentleness and warmth I remembered. She spoke firmly to her husband, almost coldly. There was no evidence of mutual love and understanding. On the contrary, there was an air of discontent such as I had never seen in Eliza before.

I began to ask her questions. Had the illness she suffered at Christmas left any lingering effects?

"Not at all," Eliza said. "I feel stronger than ever. Daniel has given me the best of care. Thanks to him, I have made a complete recovery."

"Thanks to Daniel and a merciful God," I said, noting that Eliza had omitted any reference to the Almighty—she who had always been so pious.

"That goes without saying. We are all in the hands of God," she said, but there was none of the old religious fervour.

"Still, it seems to me that the illness has changed you somehow," I said.

She lowered her eyes. "You are right," she said. "Sometimes I feel strange—" She stopped as if someone had shut off her voice.

"Strange in what way?"

"Oh, it's nothing really," she said, without looking me in the eye. "You are very kind to worry about me, Adele, but let me assure you, there is no reason for concern."

Alas, there was every reason for concern. With each passing day I became more convinced that Eliza was in a state of mental slavery, that she was no more than an instrument of Lynne's will. My gentle friend, I saw, had surrendered without a fight and meekly tolerated her intruder. I feared that she would soon be erased altogether and superseded by Lynne.

It was time to talk to Daniel and see what could be done. I had brought with me a few pages recounting the conversations his sister Alma and I had with Eliza before she fell ill. I meant to show Daniel how quickly and radically she had changed after she recovered from her illness. If he doubted my word, he could consult with his sister and confirm my impressions. In my notes I also described the night I spent at Eliza's bedside, so that he might compare his own observations with mine. I trusted in his judgment and put those pages into his hands, asking him to read them at leisure and give me his considered opinion in the morning.

To my dismay, he completely rejected my testimony and disparaged it in the most hurtful terms. His cold reception of my well-meant inquiries caught me entirely by surprise. I expected him to be more sensitive to the serious concerns I raised. Instead, he behaved in a most ungentlemanly fashion, telling me I had no business to record conversations that might compromise Alma's reputation or cast suspicion on Eliza's condition. My mention of ghosts and spirits was ludicrous. He only hoped I had not shown my notes to anyone else, as they were detrimental to the good name of his family, and mine. He carried on in this manner, spluttering and fuming, while I stood there, struck dumb by this unexpected tirade. At last, I gathered my wits and asked him to return my notes, seeing that he had no use for them. He demurred and threatened to burn my crazed outpourings, as he was pleased to call them. In these circumstances, I said, I would leave his house at once, never to return again. He showed no signs of remorse even then and offered no apologies for his insulting behaviour. Indeed, he did not deign to see me out.

In the hall I met Eliza (or should I say, Lynne), but I had no stomach to reply to her questions and directed her to the doctor for an explanation of my hurried departure.

It was on such terms that I left Hamilton House and returned to Hinxworth. The journey gave me time to compose myself, so that I was able to give a calm answer when Andrew asked about my holiday. I told him that I had found Eliza changed and feared that time and distance would cause us to grow further apart.

Soon afterwards, a letter arrived from Eliza begging me not to make public any of the things I had written and shown to Daniel. I readily gave her my promise. I had no intentions of rewriting the pages the doctor had confiscated. Indeed, I had lost interest in continuing with my memoir. The experience I had at Hamilton House quite discouraged me from the enterprise. I could see that my work served no purpose. It would neither provide me with a rational explanation to calm my conscience, nor serve as a warning to others. Readers would not believe the story of my life being blighted by an incubus. If Daniel—a physician obliged by the Hippocratic Oath to tend to the sick—could not be persuaded to deal with such a grave illness, an illness now afflicting his own wife, what hope was there of interesting others in my travails? I despaired of ever sorting out my strangely encumbered life and settling the question of my responsibility for Lynne's evil deeds.

Weeks went by. My memoirs—what was left of them—sat untouched, locked away in a drawer of my writing desk. But then a new piece of information came my way which determined me to make one last effort to arrive at a conclusive answer to the question of my conscience.

AT THE end of summer, we received an invitation, or rather a summons, from the Captain. He wished to speak to us on a matter of some importance, he wrote. "I hope you will indulge an old man and visit me," he wrote, "although I can offer you little in the way of luxury or amusement."

Of course, we obliged the Captain and set out for Agmondesham at once.

Although it was a warm and sunny day, the Captain looked rather wintry as he greeted us. His step was not as firm as I remembered, but his voice was as crusty as ever. He showed us into the house. The central entrance opened on a pair of stairs leading up to the bedrooms. The little parlour on the right was rather sombre in aspect, with heavy oaken beams overshadowing it. The decor reflected the indifferent tastes of an old man. The single shelf over the chimney piece, which occupied most of one wall, held a miscellany of objects: a tea canister, a ticking wooden clock, candlesticks, and a china Toby jug. A sabre hung in the place of honour above the shelf. A pair of plain fire dogs on the brick hearth completed the arrangements.

We sat down in the armchairs arranged around the hearth rug, and the Captain called for tea and cordials. Mary Watson came in to serve us. The cheerful young woman who had been Percy Stockdale's maid at the rectory and had attended the Captain during his illness there was now in his permanent employ and giving much satisfaction to the old man.

We conveyed greetings to Mary from her friends in Hinxworth, delivered a parcel with baked goods from her foster mother, satisfied her inquiries after her family's wellbeing, and promised to deliver her greetings in turn.

After she left the room, the Captain heaved a sigh and said: "Well, now that you are here, I mean to make you a long confession."

"A confession!" Andrew exclaimed. I too was surprised. The Captain was not a man to make admissions or retractions.

"It's such a tangled tale that it's hard to know where to begin," he said, "but it's time I told you the story. I am getting old. Who knows how much longer—"

"A very long time yet," Andrew said soothingly. "You feel a little low just now perhaps, but—"

The Captain held up his hand: "No need to soft-talk me, my boy. I know what I'm about. I can feel it in my bones. Time is running out, and I mean to talk to you about my last will and testament."

"Surely this isn't the time to talk about such a melancholy subject," I said, and Andrew added: "In any case, you need not worry about our future—"

"That's just what I was coming to," the Captain said, "if you'll let me say my piece. But first things first. As you get older, they say, you should take to heart the bit about, 'Forgive us our trespasses as we forgive those who trespass against us,' and that's why I want to make a confession to you and hope you will absolve me."

"I am more than willing to absolve you of anything you care to confess," Andrew said, "but would it not be better to ask God's forgiveness?"

"Zounds!" the Captain said, "I didn't ask for a sermon. Spare me your pious talk and let me tell my story."

Andrew apologized for interrupting, and we kept a respectful silence as the Captain went on.

"To begin with, Andrew, I confess that I concealed your whereabouts from Percy when he inquired after your address some years ago. I replied ambiguously, allowing him to think that you had gone to the colonies. You might wonder why I acted in this manner—I did it because I was afraid he would drive a wedge between us. I thought you might find Percy a more agreeable companion than me. And my resentment of Percy was so deep that I could not allow him to take up even a corner in the life of a young man whom I regarded as my special protégé."

The Captain's feelings for Andrew were touching, but his desire to be loved was, for me at any rate, unexpected. I had not thought of the old man as being overly sensitive in that quarter.

"And so, it's my fault that you didn't benefit from Percy's acquaintance during his lifetime," he went on, "although fate made sure you benefited from his death."

Andrew answered him kindly.

"The dispositions in the Reverend's testament must have been a great disappointment to you, Captain. You were Percy's closest relative and naturally expected to be the beneficiary of his will."

"Right you are. That's what I expected, and I was ready to dance on Percy's grave, so to speak. Well, let us say, then, that God punished me for my thoughts and heaped ashes on my head, for Percy died in the execution of a duty that I myself ought to have performed."

"I don't quite understand your meaning," Andrew said. "You regret that you didn't join the Reverend on his charitable errand?" The thought surprised us both. The Captain had never shown a propensity in that direction. In any case I had never put aside my suspicions about the charitable nature of the Reverend's business.

"You are not listening to me, my boy," the Captain said. "I was talking about duty, not charity. Duty toward a young woman I got with child some twenty years ago."

He paused and waited for our reaction, but we were stunned into silence by this unexpected disclosure.

"I dare say I was young and thoughtless," the Captain continued.

Looking at the crusty old man, I must say it was hard to imagine him young and in love.

"In my excuse I can only say: When I was posted on the Intrepid, I did not know that I had done more than broken the girl's heart, that I had ruined her life," he said.

"But how does the Reverend come into all of this?" Andrew said.

"Well, I suppose I can't get around acknowledging that there was a good side to Percy," the Captain said, wincing as if in pain. "But let me go on with the story. Alice Barland, as she was then, ended up marrying a worthless fellow by the name of Dodds, who was willing to give his name to the child she was carrying in return for a sum of money supplied by her father. Percy was the curate who married the pair. Later, when the man turned out to be a gambler and a violent drunk, who beat Alice and the child, she ran out on him, but soon found herself in great difficulties to eke out a living. It was then that she turned to Percy for help and told him that I was the father of her child. That's why he felt an obligation to come to her aid. When next I returned to England from my tour of duty, I found a letter waiting for me. It was from Percy telling me of Alice's predicament and appealing to my conscience. He said he had placed the child with a foster family near Hinxworth and was paying for her keep. To my great shame I rejected Alice's story as a fabrication and accused her of trying to foist her bastard daughter on me. I was a young hothead then and said a great many ill-considered things: that Alice was a hussy, which she was, that Percy had his pleasure with her and covered it up with pretended charity, which I said out of spite and had no proof of. But however much I denied my responsibility then, when Mary came to the rectory to look after me, she touched my heart with a force only Nature can impart. I loved her from the moment I set eyes on her, and I know now: She is the child Percy supported all those years and when she was old enough to work engaged as his maid. Mary is my daughter."

We could hardly believe our ears. We had been told that Mary was an orphan taken in by the Watsons.

"And how did you discover the truth?" I asked.

"Every time I looked at Mary, it was as if I caught a glimpse of the past and was once again in the presence of my old love. The striking similarity between Mary and Alice did not let me rest. I made enquiries and after explaining the reason for my interest in the young woman, was told the story by her foster mother. Had Percy not intervened and taken pity on my dear child, Mary might have suffered a fate similar to her mother's and ended up in the gutter. Percy met with Alice from time to time to give her news of Mary and a bit of money to look after herself, as she was in poor health. And it was in pursuit of this charitable mission that he was murdered."

Remorse and sadness were written on the Captain's face. He repented his heartlessness. I in turn felt a new regard for Percy Stockdale who had risked his name (and as fate would have it, his life) to relieve the want of a poor and downtrodden woman.

"But that's not the end of the story," the Captain said. "Alice Dodds was found at the scene of the crime, and now stands accused of murdering the Reverend. She denies it, and I for one believe in her innocence. Why would she kill the goose that laid the golden egg?"

We had heard that a murder suspect had been arrested, but nothing about any court action, for the wheels of justice grind slowly. Indeed, we expected the case to be dismissed for lack of evidence. I shuddered at hearing this added piece of information and discovering that the Reverend's tryst with the prostitute had been no tryst and no chance meeting, that there was a personal connection between the accused and the murder victim. If Alice Dodds was found guilty and hanged, another life would be on my conscience—*my* conscience, since I could not completely detach myself from Lynne's actions, even if our union had been a forced one, even if I was just another of her victims. It was clear now that she had not only murdered the Reverend and escaped punishment, but also entrapped an innocent bystander. I had assumed that the Reverend's death would be added to the long list of unsolved crimes in Bishopsgate, where violence and murder was the order of the day. I had regarded those events a closed chapter as far as the law was concerned. Now, to my alarm and consternation, I found that there was a sequel.

"Quite so," Andrew said. "The poor woman must be innocent. She had no motive to kill the Reverend and lose a benefactor, but once the circumstances are made public, the judge will come to the same conclusion and acquit her of the crime."

"If only it were as simple as that," the Captain said. "The moment I understood what had passed, I hired the services of a lawyer. He visited Alice in prison and found to his surprise that she was adamantly opposed to divulging her connection with Mary. She does not want the girl to suffer for the sins of her parent. She is ready to go to the gallows rather than revealing the illegitimacy of Mary's birth and the shameful profession of her mother."

"And she cannot be persuaded to change her mind, even if you were formally to acknowledge Mary as your daughter? For surely, you are willing to do that for her."

"That and more," the Captain said. "I have told Mary nothing as yet, but I naturally wish to look after her interests. And that's the other matter about which I wanted to speak to you, my boy. I'll say it without preamble: I have decided to leave my savings to my daughter rather than to you, as I had planned when I thought you were my only surviving blood relation. It may be a disappointment to you, but you are a wealthy man now and can do without my money. Still, I feel rather embarrassed about the whole business. I promised to make you my heir, and now I'm reneging on that promise."

His cheeks had turned russet, and he twisted uncomfortably in his seat. Andrew came to his rescue at once.

"Don't give it another thought, Captain," he said. "I quite understand your motives. You are doing the right thing. I respect the justice of your decision and don't begrudge Mary her good fortune. Indeed, it is as you say. I am well off already. Mary is your daughter and stands in need of support. And Alice Dodds may be amenable to telling her daughter the truth in these circumstances. It will of course be hard on the girl at first, but there is no other way out if we are to save her mother."

The Captain took Andrew's hand and thanked him. "It's a great relief to hear you say so, my boy," he said, "and we'll have to put our heads together and devise a way of breaking it to Mary gently and getting her mother out of prison next. It's a burden off my chest to have told you, but, alas, I haven't finished my confession."

We wondered what else was in store, as the old man continued. "I come to my last sin, for which I was struck down at once—perhaps it was fate, perhaps it was God's hand that brought me low that first night we spent at the rectory when you found me unconscious beside the writing desk. I had snuck downstairs in search of Percy's letters—the ones supposed to make up a second volume of correspondence. I was determined to discover what he had to say about me. You wanted to see those letters published, and I wanted to make sure he gave no false report about the Battle of Minorca. It was for the same reason that I had visited Hurst's printing shop earlier and introduced myself by a fictitious name. You will recall that I brought away with me the first part of Percy's correspondence, only to find that the volume ended where my interest began. When you invited me to come with you to the rectory, I eagerly accepted, assuming of course that the remaining letters would be found on the premises. After you had gone to bed, therefore, I began to search the rooms even though I did not feel well. I did not want to let the opportunity go by and told myself that I was merely suffering from the fatigue of travel. I began my search in Percy's study. The writing desk seemed a likely place in which to deposit a manuscript. I knew the secret springs and pulleys of the ancient piece of furniture, which had belonged to my father. I found no trace of the second part of his memoirs, but I did come across a piece of paper in one of the concealed drawers which had the aspect of a legal document, an addition to his will perhaps. It was labeled 'Codicil A'."

"Codicil A!" Andrew exclaimed and reached for my hand as if to declare his solidarity with me. We both had the same thought: the Reverend had meant to leave his money, or part of it, to me. I knew of course that there were conditions attached to his generosity, but Andrew, I fear, believed he had come between me and the Collingwood fortune through a legal sleight of hand.

"You know about the codicil?" the Captain said sharply.

"I know that it was to be appended to Percy's will, but I know nothing about its contents. The lawyer informed me that the conditions outlined in the document applied only in case I—the heir—could not be found. But the Reverend could not make up his mind about the wording of the codicil and so it was never appended. Whatever its contents, they do not apply in the circumstances. Yet I would be interested to know the Reverend's intentions and hope you will allow me to peruse the document."

"Too late, my boy. I destroyed it forthwith to avoid any mischief arising from it."

Andrew drew back in dismay. "But, Captain, shouldn't you have consulted a lawyer first, to clarify the legal situation?"

"The situation was clear enough to me," the Captain countered. "I don't need a lawyer to tell me that a document without signature or date has no legal force. It was a worthless piece of paper and would only have put ideas into the heads of certain people."

"But as the Reverend's heir, I feel morally obliged to act on his intentions, legally binding or not," Andrew said quietly and pressed my hand. "Suppose I hadn't presented myself at Merryweather's office, did the Reverend have another beneficiary in mind?"

The Captain twisted uncomfortably in his chair. "The paper was a draft, Andrew. You could barely make out the words with all the corrections and overwriting. I guess Percy had bad conscience about keeping the Collingwood money to himself and was thinking of giving a portion to Adele—"

"But then—" Andrew exclaimed. The Captain held up his hand and continued:

"—*if* she married the right kind of man. And I believe the fool thought of himself as a candidate for Adele's hand!"

He gave me a searching look, but I kept silent.

"So don't worry about your moral obligations, my boy," he continued. "Adele *has* found the right kind of man now that she is your wife, and she *is* sharing in her aunt's estate therefore, codicil or not. But if I had known you'd make such a stir about that wretched piece of paper, I wouldn't have mentioned it at all. Never mind that bit of legal skulduggery. I was more concerned with a bundle of letters I found in another drawer. Better have a look at them, I thought to myself, and put them in my pocket. I was curious to see if Percy had mentioned my name. You never know what rumours he might spread about me."

My heart nearly stopped. The Captain now in possession of Percy's letters. They were more likely to contain revelations about me than about his brother!

"And did you read them?" Andrew said. "I hope you found nothing in them to offend you."

"I never got around to reading them. I burned them together with the codicil at the first opportunity."

"Good God! Why would you do that?"

"Well, let me tell you what happened next. The moment I put those letters into my pocket, I felt a blow, as if someone had struck me. My heart began to race, and I could no longer think straight. I believe I was delirious, or how else can I explain the feeling that I was in the presence of Percy and thought it was he who struck me, that he was angry at me for taking possession of his letters. He shook me roughly by the shoulders then, or more likely, I was shaking with the illness that had taken root in me. In my fevered state, I thought Percy and I were face to face. There was a hungry look in his eyes, as if he hadn't eaten in a week, and was determined to make a meal of me. He was about to sink his teeth into my cheek and suck me dry, fill up on my blood. I can't describe it any other way, Andrew. I felt I was fighting him for my life."

I shuddered at the Captain's story. It made me relive my own experience, the shock of Lynne entering my body when I was in the grip of fever and fighting for my life. Had the Reverend turned into a spirit like Lynne, trying to take possession of his brother's body and come back to life? The very thought made me ill.

"Luckily, you appeared at that moment and brought me to my senses," the Captain said to Andrew. "I recovered sufficiently to go to my room, as you will recall. As soon as I was alone, I took out the papers I had removed from Percy's desk and threw them into the fire to rid myself of the cursed things."

"My dear Captain," Andrew said. "If you had been yourself, you would never have destroyed your brother's writings. But you were in the grip of a fever. You put on a brave face and went off to your room, I remember, but as it turned out, you were gravely ill. The doctor and I feared for your life."

It was the illness that made the Captain a perfect target for a wandering spirit, I realized. If the ghost of Percy Stockdale was looking for an opening to seize a body and embark on a new life, his brother's weakened state offered an opportunity to take over, but the old man was a soldier—a seasoned veteran—and successfully fought off the ghostly invasion. That is the only explanation I could think of for the Captain's story.

"Nay, you needn't make excuses for me, Andrew," he said. "I take full responsibility for my action. And I dare say, it did not come amiss for you. That codicil might have done a great deal of mischief. And who knows what poison was in those letters? It was a good thing I got rid of them." He pointed to the grate, as if the flames in the hearth were the very ones that had devoured the Reverend's letters. "So let us agree that my action turned out for the best."

Andrew was not convinced, I saw, but he held his peace. I myself seconded the Captain. It was indeed a good thing that he had gotten rid of the letters in the same manner that I had gotten rid of the second part of the Reverend's reminiscences. They were nothing but ashes now and would never haunt me again. Relief flooded my mind.

"And now," the Captain said to Andrew, "I need your help in persuading Alice to acknowledge her connection with Mary, tell the story of Percy's good deeds, and allow herself to be saved from the gallows. You might do better than the lawyer. That fellow likely frightened her with his officious language. You will say the right things and make her feel at ease, for you are the most agreeable man I know—I'll say that much for you, and I've never flattered anyone yet."

Andrew smiled at the old man's compliment. It was, for all I know, the first compliment the Captain had paid him or anyone else, for no one could call *him* an agreeable man.

"I shall apply myself to the task with all my energy," Andrew said, "and as you know I was halfway to becoming a lawyer myself and intend to complete my qualifications now that I have the necessary funds. My knowledge will come in handy in this case."

As soon as Andrew and I got back to Hinxworth and I had time to myself, I pondered the implications of the Captain's news. The situation in which Alice Dodds found herself as a result of Lynne's actions sent me back to my former question: was I a partner in her crime and responsible for the outcome? I had given up finding an answer by reasoning it out. It was a question of conscience after all, a spiritual matter, and now I saw a new and fitting way of settling the question: by ordeal. Andrew had decided to pay a visit to Alice Dodds at Newgate Prison to persuade her to go along with the Captain's wishes. I resolved to accompany him on his visit and test the effect of my appearance on Alice Dodds. Would she recognize me as the woman who stabbed Percy Stockdale? She had witnessed the Reverend's murder, and I too had been present in a mysterious way, a skin giving Lynne physical shape. I was a participant in her actions, even if it was Lynne's hand that held the knife and her willpower that propelled the murder. We were joined in a ghostly union. Were we two separate souls? Was only one of us to blame? No human being could answer that tangled question. I decided to seek divine judgment and take the result of my encounter with Alice as the final test of my guilt or innocence. Would Alice remain indifferent on seeing me or would she recoil at my sight, point a finger at me, and cry out: There she is—the woman who murdered Percy Stockdale! Whatever the outcome, I was willing to consider it a divine judgment and submit to my fate. If Alice did not recognize me, I stood acquitted of the crime. It was proof that I had remained a person separate and distinct from Lynne and was not responsible for her actions. If Alice recognized me, I would plead my case before the magistrate and let the world know about the suffering of a woman possessed. Thus, I might achieve my purpose after all: to warn others of the dark powers beyond our ken.

More than a year had passed since the night of the murder, and my face had undergone subtle changes. The features Lynne contributed to my appearance gradually became less pronounced. I looked the way I used to look in my younger years, that is to say, plainer. But it took a keen observer to perceive the shift in my appearance, and I had certainly not changed to the point where people no longer recognized me. Thus, I prepared myself for the worst. Of course, I was not the only one affected by the outcome of the ordeal. It had further implications. If the woman recognized me, what a toll it would take on Andrew! What shame I would bring on him! I would face the risk of losing his love—but those were considerations I left for another time. To go through with the ordeal and invite the judgment of God had become an imperative overriding all other concerns.

IT IS A well-known malaise of our judicial system that a person, once caught in its machine, will wait for years to see justice. This delay wears down honest people and gives criminals an opportunity to quibble and buy their way out of a scrape. If you have money, you can hire an unscrupulous lawyer and buy false witnesses at Westminster Hall, where they walk up and down with straw in their shoes, displaying the sign of their profession like a badge of honour. And even without clever lawyers and corrupt witnesses, a criminal may get away scot-free because the injured party fails to press charges or the jury takes a lenient view of his case or the judge pardons him on condition of him entering the army, which has been depleted by constant wars and stands in dire need of men. It has rightly been said that our laws were made for the protection rather than the punishment of rogues. Alas for poor Alice Dodds, who was caught in that maze and was languishing in Newgate Prison!

When I told Andrew that I wished to go with him to that den of misery, he tried to dissuade me.

"You will be exposed to horrible sights," he said, "to filth and disease."

"You will be exposed to the same horrors," I said, "and my place is by your side. The murder of the Reverend concerns me as much as it concerns you." Since I could not tell him my real purpose, I brought out lofty reasons, talking of my Christian duty and arguing at some length until I had overcome Andrew's reluctance and was allowed to join him on his mission.

The exterior of Newgate, which had been refurbished after the Great Fire of 1666, was almost distinguished-looking, but the interior was a filthy warren of broken-down rooms. It was a place of abomination. The corridors were gloomy and foul smelling. Not surprisingly, the want of air and cleanliness brought many an inmate low with the gaol fever. The prison was divided into the Common and the Master Side—or to put it another way between those without and those with money at their disposal—but there was no division between men and women, felons and debtors, convicts and those awaiting trial. The inhabitants of the Master Side lived in tolerable conditions and were able to hire beds and linens and keep a fire in the hearth. A public taproom supplied them with liquor, and the turnkey kept a store of tobacco and other luxuries for sale to the wealthy jailbirds. But Alice Dodds was confined to the squalid and overcrowded quarters on the Common Side.

Haggard faces looked up at us as we made our way past bodies rotting alive. The turnkey, whose help we had enlisted, pointed us to a woman lying on a straw pallet. Alice Dodds, we knew, was in her forties. The woman on the pallet looked like an old crone, with thin gray hair, sunken eyes, and a toothless mouth. Seeing her emaciated body and trembling limbs, Andrew whispered to me: "I fear there is little time left to procure her acquittal."

We stepped up and explained to the poor woman who we were and what we had come about. She listened to us in a kind of stupor. I was biding my time. I did not want to go about the divine ordeal in a haphazard manner and had decided to conceal my face until I could be sure I had Alice's attention. I pulled up my hood and pressed a handkerchief to my face, ostensibly to protect myself against the noxious smells, but my true purpose was to reveal my face suddenly and observe her immediate reaction. This was not the right moment to try her, I felt. She seemed too confused to be put to a test that was to determine my guilt or innocence.

The first order, we saw, was to provide for her physical comfort. Without the means to supplement the meagre prison fare, Alice was reduced to starvation. We had made inquiries and knew that the daily ration doled out to the prisoners barely kept body and soul together. We supplied the necessary "garnish," as the bribe was called, to satisfy the turnkey and ensure that Alice would no longer go hungry. No monetary contribution, however, could improve the general atmosphere of the prison, which was filled with riot and profanity.

On our request, the jailer's assistant brought soup, boiled beef, a penny loaf, and a jug of thin beer. While Alice ate and drank, Andrew told her of the Captain's willingness to acknowledge Mary as his daughter. She mumbled her thanks, but we could see that she was too weak and exhausted to understand the full extent of Andrew's words and to rise to any great hopes or expectations.

I hung back and confined myself to observing Alice, while Andrew talked to her about the charges she faced. Her overriding sentiment was one of dejection and fear at the prospect of standing before an unsympathetic judge. Andrew tried to reassure her.

"The main difficulty will be resolved," he said, "if you permit the lawyer to reveal the circumstances and explain the reason why you met with Percy Stockdale."

She nodded feebly. "But I was on the spot and I picked up the knife," she said. "Who will take my word when I say it wasn't me that killed him? 'She's a strumpet,' they'll say, 'and lying to save her life.' And then, in a cursed moment, I took the Reverend's money. I was desperate, and he meant me to have it, but they won't believe that either."

A look of stony horror covered Alice's face as she spoke of the fateful night, and I knew the moment for my ordeal had come.

"You saw Percy Stockdale being accosted by a woman," I said. "And it was her who stabbed him?"

"Aye," she said, "it was her."

I moved closer and pushed back my hood. Fear clogged my lungs and thickened my tongue, when I said: "Can you describe her for us?"

Alice had turned to me when I asked the question. She thought for a moment before she answered me. "She wore a hooded cloak, something like yours," she said, pointing to my coat. "She was—I don't know how to say it. I ain't got the words." She was looking straight into my face, but no glimpse of recognition showed in her eyes.

"Would you recognize her if you saw her again? If we brought her here, would you know that she was the woman who stabbed Percy Stockdale?"

"I saw her only for a moment, but I'll never forget her eyes—the eyes of a ghost, they were. She gave me such a fright. I'd know her if I saw her again, I'm sure of that, but it won't help me any. I was caught with the knife and the money in my hand, and I'll be on my way to Tyburn before long and hung by the neck."

Andrew soothed her fears, but his words were a blur to me. I was too light-headed to hear what he was saying. I was faint with relief. Alice had looked at me and given her verdict, or rather, God had passed judgment on me. I stood acquitted. The face and the eyes Alice remembered and would remember forever were not mine. The happiness I felt was almost too much to bear. My temples were pulsing. I hid my shaking hands in my coat sleeves. The doubts and the guilt that had blighted my life for so long left me feeling bruised, but now that I had passed the ordeal, I knew I would find peace and I had a presentiment of a future full of bright and exhilarating clarity.

I breathed deeply. Andrew's words began to register again. "It will be hard to explain away the evidence," he was saying, "especially the money in your possession—stolen goods in the eyes of the law, even if the Reverend had intended to give it to you. But justice will prevail in the end."

"It's no good, you talking about justice," Alice said. "There was a veteran here with a wooden leg, who shared my corner for a while. He was caught stealing two red herrings and he hung for it last session. Another fellow, who brags about robbing people on the highway, will never see the noose, I warrant. He walks around like a young cock and gambles and whores as if there was no God in heaven and no hell below."

The food and drink had rallied her spirits and made her talkative. "And look at the little maid over yonder," she said, pointing to a wan child across the room. "She's been acquitted of pawning her mistress' handkerchief, but much good it does her. The turnkey won't let her go before she pays his garnish, and where is she to get a shilling, the poor child?"

Andrew was able to put an end to the little maid's misery at once, but Alice was right. There were many cases of justice perverted, and we could not hope to settle them all.

As we prepared to leave, Alice asked when she could see her dear child. We kept an embarrassed silence. It was hardly advisable for Mary to visit her mother in these horrid surroundings and breathe the foul air rampant with disease. I was about to say as much, but Alice took the words out of my mouth. "No, but now that I think of it, I won't ask my dear lamb to come to this wretched place. She might catch her death here. And you shouldn't have come either. The air is like to make you ill."

The poor woman wasn't far off the truth, for when we reached Hinxworth in the evening, Andrew felt decidedly unwell. The next morning he had a fever and sent for the doctor. It was only a touch of the disease that was to ravage Newgate over the next fortnight, a virulent force striking down more than two hundred men and women. I was fortunate to escape without being infected, braced perhaps by the joy of knowing that I was innocent, a joy that filled me with a new zest for life.

Andrew weathered the fever and was soon on the mend, for he was strong in body and mind and in good hands, but Alice Dodds was not so lucky. Her wasted body succumbed to the onslaught of the fever. The only judge she had to face in the end was a merciful God in heaven.

And so, this affair has run its course. Now I must decide what to do with my memoir. Leave it to Jeremiah Hurst, to be published after my death? I dare not make it public during my lifetime. God has absolved me, but an earthly judge may take a different view of my role in the death of the Reverend. What's more, I cannot be sure that this will be the end of my tribulations. My conscience is clear at last, but a faint shadow remains to darken my life: the fear of Lynne's return.

LYNNE

ON MY way home from the Clarkson, I wonder why I even bothered to make an appointment to take another look at the pages Adele left at Hamilton House. How much can I achieve sitting in the Reading Room of the library? The manuscript stirred me, no, gave me a seismic shock, but the Reading Room of the Clarkson isn't a suitable place to execute my plan. Transmigration requires more privacy. I might not bring it off in public. It's not like making a wish and dissolving into thin air. Or perhaps it is in the case of reversing time. Who knows? I've never done it before and don't know what to expect. But let's assume my body—or rather Ginny's body which I took over—will be left behind. Will she resume control over her system and live on in her own persona? I doubt it. My take-over was complete. I wiped her out. So, what would be left on my departure? A corpse perhaps, since Ginny's system is still in good shape, or a heap of bones and a puddle of decaying matter, as in the case of her predecessor, who had pretty well reached the end of the line. The horrified reaction of bystanders could disturb the air or thicken it and hinder my escape into the past, changing the path of ascent. At least that is what I expect to happen when I leave Ginny's body: rising into the sky in a gentle arc, tracing a circle perhaps for a last look at the scene before turning my eyes to the far horizon. But perhaps I am wrong, and it will be a different journey this time, something more chaotic, a plunging through the centuries.

In any case, I need to be alone when I try the experiment. Adele survived my exit without suffering adverse effects, but she was the only one among my hosts who survived my departure. I had no experience when I invaded Adele. My take-over was botched and I never managed to get the better of her. In all other cases, my departure had dramatic effects on the original owners. They had what looked like epileptic fits, or fatal heart attacks, or aged rapidly and became terminally ill. In any case, they all died. In the present case it's me that's taking the risk. I may burn up in my attempt to dive into the past and resume life with Adele, but there is no other way leading to Jack, and he is worth the risk.

Jack's name is bound up with my last breath, with the despair I felt at the moment of dying as the distance grew between him and me and expanded into cosmic loneliness, until I found refuge with Adele.

"Jack!" I cried. "I don't want to die!" and that flailing beating cry of desperation clung to my soul and prevented it from completing its last journey. I was hovering in midair, swaying in the ether, skimming the void, waiting for a chance to be reborn, waiting for an opportunity to slip into the body of another and be resurrected, and Adele gave me that chance. She was at death's door when I rode in on a strangled breath, entered her core and began battling the dark forces together with her. We won the crucial fight. We survived, she and I. But we never congealed. It was my maiden voyage—I made mistakes, and Adele was stubborn.

I don't want to be unfair to her. I know: I came like a black horsefly, buzzing up from a squalid puke-covered doorway. The stench of death was on my skin, the harrowing knife wound gaping in my neck, leaching a history of violence. I came up from that black hole of a slum with nothing but the wild desire to live again, to find shelter in a functional body, to dissolve the nastiness of my life and death in Adele's white flesh. She felt my brutishness, but there is no such thing as instant transformation from beast to beauty. There are rules of operation, even for transmigrants—especially for transmigrants. To begin with I had to battle death and make myself mistress of Adele's body. It is a wrenching experience for invader and host. Some bodies are easier to conquer, some minds easier to bring to heel than others. I was all willpower when I entered Adele, a ruthless charging force. I needed all my strength to overcome death, and secure my new locale, to bully my way past my host's defences. I admit it: I was a brute when I took up residence inside Adele, but then she didn't provide the ideal habitat either. Unlike the other women, whose bodies I colonized over the years, Adele frustrated me at every turn. I was willing to adapt, to learn her boarding school manners, to take over the knowledge accumulated in her brain, to become Adele, but she wouldn't let me. There are limits to what a transmigrant can do in a case like that. I didn't make a good first impression, and I didn't expect Adele to love me, but I expected some give and take. We shared a body after all. I did my part. I picked up on Adele's feelings—yes, she retained them. I did not realize then how rare it was for an invaded body to keep her own feelings. Unlike the other bodies I invaded, she did not scorch the earth. She allowed love to blossom, but she kept the harvest to herself. I tried to take my cue from her infatuation with Francis. I tried to empathize and share her crush on him, which is more than she ever did for me when I talked about my love for Jack. *But, Lynne, he is a criminal!* she said. Adele never understood me. It was always me who had to give. I modified my behaviour. I worked with what she had to offer. I tolerated her intellectual interests, which didn't play well in Hinxworth. It was a handicap in those days to inhabit a brainy woman like Adele, but I took it in stride. Why did she not show me the same consideration? Didn't I deserve sympathy—I died young, I died for the man I loved. I became a target and was murdered because Jack was my lover. It's not my fault that my feelings went flat over the centuries.

No, Adele never understood me. She was far from an ideal hostess, but I've made up my mind. I'm going back to her, and this time it will be different, I swear. I'll put my experience to work and make her do what is needed to make me whole: rescue Jack. My memory of Jack has become an immovable shadow that stalks me from life to life. I will get back to him and feel passion again. All I need is an entry point into the past that has the essential ingredients to conjure up an atmosphere of dread and foreboding. A scene set in a bleak night, a scene of illness and despair. Those are the elements that thin out the flesh and fissure the skin. They produce the right consistency for spirits to pass through and float down the genetic stream. The breakthrough-and-enter action is pretty much routine for me, I've done it so often, although I never allow myself to become careless and underestimate the danger of entering a foreign body in its weakened state. The enemy is lurking within: death and dissolution. I can deal with that, but in this case, I can't predict what will happen. I'll have to manage a double feat—travelling back in time and recolonizing Adele's body. It's a first for me. I've always migrated to an available body without changing the calendar date, a young body, mind you, to extend my life by a generation with each leap and move on into the future. Transmigration is an ambitious project. You need stamina to do it successfully. And nerve. Luckily I have both. I've learned a great deal since my death and have pulled off more than a dozen successful transformations. I really should draw up a list one day, a transmigrational resume.

I do a quick timeline in my head. It would make an excellent PowerPoint presentation!

First came Adele Prior, neé Collingwood—the only one who held out against me, who refused to become one with me. Instead we ended up cobbled together like a mythological monster, half Adele, half me.

Next, Eliza Worth, neé Florsham. That was a mistake. Eliza was one of those maudlin and feeble girls who are pious because they don't have the brains to think outside the Ten Commandments, and if her thoughts ever strayed into forbidden territory, she wouldn't have had the guts to translate them into action. My take-over was a desperate move, the only way I could manage to attract the doctor. But desperation isn't a good basis for making decisions. It was the kind of move an inexperienced transmigrant would make. Eliza was contemptibly weak. She had no resources. Her mind was like water. I couldn't make anything of her. She kept losing shape. And life with Daniel—the man for whom I accepted Eliza's inferior system—didn't turn out as expected. I thought of him as a mad scientist ready to play God and create me anew, but he was a morose man without enterprise, stuck in the mud of a tender conscience, always feeling guilty about something or other—not doing his Christian duty or lacking the heroic will to do it. If he were alive today, he would think it was his duty to join Doctors Without Borders and save babies on drought-ridden continents, then feel guilty for dragging his feet about doing it. That's the kind of man he was.

We made a reasonably good beginning in our marriage, when I was still infatuated with him. He wasn't a bad lover, I'll give him that, although he lacked imagination, and when I took the initiative and showed him what I liked, he clamped up. To begin with, he thought it was immodest to keep on the lamp in the bedroom, but I could tell his thoughts even in the dark. They practically burned holes into my chest. What a bold woman, he thought, I never dreamed Eliza could be so shameless. Of course, he never said that out loud, but I took him up on his thoughts.

"What's the matter, Daniel?" I said. "You don't like it that way?"

He winced. As far as he was concerned, you didn't talk about sex. You shut your eyes tightly and took your guilty pleasure.

"I think we shouldn't indulge too much," he said after swallowing hard. "Everything in moderation, my dear!"

I persisted. "But it's your marital duty. Even the church says so."

"I know," he said, looking pained.

"And it's no sin to take pleasure in sex."

"Only if it's done for the purpose of procreation," he pointed out.

He got the hang of it eventually and even started to enjoy sex, but when he couldn't get me pregnant he sunk into a deep depression. He blamed himself for the situation, although it was my poor reconstituted body that wasn't up to the feat of procreation. I could have told him so, but not without giving myself away, and I did at any rate try to convince him that it wasn't his fault.

"It was my illness," I told him. "You said it yourself. Brain fever can cause infertility."

"I should never have gone away that Christmas," he said. "You were in very low spirits at the time, and that is when the body is most vulnerable to disease. I should have stayed and watched over you."

"No one could predict my illness. It wasn't your fault, Daniel."

"It was, and I will always blame myself for it!" he said and went on and on about it, making me unhappy as well. I don't know whether there was a residue of motherly feelings left in the body I inherited from Eliza—a hormonal trace that left me hollow and discontented. Perhaps it wasn't that at all, and I was merely bored at Hamilton House. The only visitors we had were Daniel's staid relations and a couple of dour neighbours. Or else it was the wind blowing off the Scottish moor that made me miserable, but I think Daniel had an inborn tendency to kill all joy in those around him. Alma, the lucky girl, had made her escape and was determined not to allow her brother to spoil her fun again. She kept her duty visits short. When Adele announced her visit, I was looking forward to a change of pace, but she ended up complicating things for me. Daniel started bickering about "my" family, my no-good brother Francis who almost ruined Alma's prospects and pushed me into bankruptcy. Then Adele—"who calls herself your friend," he sneered—wanted to bring shame on his family by writing and gossiping about those sad events! Of course, these considerations brought on another bout of ill humour. He crucified himself. He should have kept an eye on Alma, he should have protected me and prevented Francis from squandering my fortune. I hung in for a little longer, hoping for a change or an improvement, but Daniel stayed the same, fussing and bellyaching over everything. So, I gave up and abandoned Eliza for a body I thought offered better prospects, or let's say, for a body that was at hand:

Eleanor Worth, Daniel's niece. She was staying with us at Hamilton House and, as luck would have it, felt suicidal. She almost managed to kill herself—and me. It was a desperate struggle. She had used rat poison, one of the nastiest means of committing suicide, but we survived. Although Eleanor was only seventeen, her nerve ends were in poor shape from years of depression. I managed to inject a bit of joie vivre into her brain, but it was an uphill battle. At least she provided a springboard to a more advantageous position. In 1811, I landed in Madam Lola's sturdy body.

1811–22. Lola (changed to "Lynne") Stinton, proprietess of a London whorehouse and active herself in the profession. We had an interesting life, but all that romping was hard on my borrowed physique. Sex is good when you're hot, but acting hot and talking dirty, and making it up on the go makes for a tough life. I had to leave Lola behind. Life with my next hostess was just as tough. She was a dressmaker and freelanced as mistress to wealthy men—but then came Mary Ann.

1839–59. Mary Ann Evans, writer—now that woman was fun. I would have stayed with her longer, but she was getting uglier by the day, and turning into an old woman. I had to move on.

There was a lot of puddle hopping after Mary Ann—short, unsatisfactory stays, and an especially dreary immigrant experience, sailing to North America and roughing it in the Canadian bush. The twentieth century was more interesting, especially after I married an American and moved with him to California. I had a good time in the fifties as a film star (stage name: Lynnette Savoy), living fast in twinkly Hollywood—posing, primping, bantering, big smiles and air kisses in public, and deal making in private, using sex as my currency. After that, I went through a few troughs until I lit into the Addington girl.

1999–present. Virginia (renamed Lynne) née Perosa, briefly married to her high school sweetheart John Addington, then taking up graduate studies. She was working on her thesis, "Entertainment in 18th century London," when I made her acquaintance. I liked the topic, needless to say. Ginny had brains worth preserving and a trim little body that defied germs, viruses, and other malignant intruders, except me. She had a weakness for horror flicks. After a night watching snuff films with her, I took my chance. She had a lively imagination, and that was her downfall. On screen or in the flesh, it was all the same to Ginny's brain. When I pounced, she (like the on-screen victim) was defenseless, shackled in her mind to a bed, about to be gutted. Her empathetic dread was as good as the real thing. I slipped into Ginny while the ghoul on screen turned the knife in his victim's guts. Done. I clicked off the VCR and made myself at home in Ginny's brain. The horror film had prepared her well. She was a natural victim and knuckled under within a month. It had been high time for me to take the leap. My pre-Ginny body was all but used up. Once I had taken over my new host body, nothing remained of the old one except a foul-smelling hide filled with bones. I held my nose, shoved the pile into a garbage bag, and chucked it into the bin out back. All that was left to do was wash the floor, throw out the area rug where my old self had landed in the take-over, and spray room freshener to cover up the odour with pine scent. By now I have Ginny diluted to the point of non-existence. We are ninety-nine percent Lynne and one percent Ginny. And I like the body she left me. It's still in good shape fifteen years later despite the added mileage. But in my present nostalgic mood, I'd give up her body in a minute, exchange it for Adele's—and this time I'm going to have it my way. I have the skill now, and I will be more persuasive than I was the first time round.

AS I DRIVE back to the villa and mull over my planned escape into the past, I realize that I am missing an essential piece of information for timing my re-entry. I need to know what happened to Jack. Was he put on trial, and if so, what was the verdict? Did he get away with jail time, or was he sentenced to death and died on the scaffold surrounded by a jeering crowd of spectators? If I arrived back in London at that point in time, there was no hope of rescuing him. I had to be there beforehand. I expect Patricia has done the necessary research into the trial records. She is nothing if not thorough. I'll check her edition of Adele's *Cautionary Tale* first thing I get home.

In the lobby at the villa, I don't bother to wait for the elevator. I run upstairs, slam the living room door shut behind me, drop the keys on the coffee table and pick up the book, scanning the footnotes for the relevant information. Yes! Here it is, at the first mention of Jack's name: "He may be identical with one Jacob Spence, 'tried for the murder of a serving girl in Bishopsgate and sentenced to be hanged by the neck until he be dead.' The judgment was executed 2 October 1771."

I tear up reading it. There is a noise in my ears, and a pulsing around my temples. It's like losing Jack all over again. The date, 1771, comes at me like a flash bulb, blinding. I can only save Jack if I get to him before October 1771. That settles it. I phone and cancel my appointment at the Clarkson. No need to reread the pages Adele brought to Hamilton House. They won't help me. They don't offer the right time frame. The events describe there are from a later period. I need to get my hands on the original manuscript of the *Cautionary Tale,* which deals with the earlier years, and I need to concentrate on the lines that bear Jack's name. I know of course that my plan will only work if it is possible to undo history. That's the big question lingering in my mind as I consider possible scenarios. Can a transmigrant change what has already happened? What if the past is unalterable, and I have to go through the same dreary moves all over again? The bickering with Adele, the joyless marriage to Daniel. What if I can't rescue Jack and, after getting back to the eighteenth century, am condemned to live the next two hundred years a second time, including all my mistakes?

No, let's have some positive thinking here. Let's think about the alternative life I'll live once I'm back in Old England. A walk on the wild side, with Jack. I'll turn him around. He's got brains. He's got potential. Together we'll do great things. Our life will be a blast of colour and light, an explosion of fireworks. But there's work to be done. Step Number One: obtaining the manuscript of *A Cautionary Tale*. Step Number Two: slipping into the past, gliding through the loops in Adele's letters. And: minimizing the risk of error, eliminating the chance of a mishap during the journey back. I'll simplify the expedition down the river of time by starting in the right place. I'll fly to London, drive to Hinxworth and execute my plan there. It's hard enough to cross timelines. I don't want to complicate matters by adding another dimension: space. What if I land in the right time zone, but fail to navigate the spatial dimension and stay in California by mistake—in the camp of Gaspar de Portola staking claims for the Spanish Crown or at a Franciscan mission converting Indians to Christianity? No need to take a chance when it comes to hitting the right place. I'll consider the rest of the expedition when I'm in Hinxworth. I wonder how much or how little it has changed. In Adele's time it consisted of some forty houses clustered around the church of St. Nicholas. A quick check online tells me it has 300 inhabitants now—still a village. There are several images of St. Nicholas, with its interior as I remember it: plain, whitewashed walls under a dark beamed ceiling. Grove Hall, where Eliza lived, no longer looks as grand to me as it did then, although it's still impressive. I wonder who lives there now, and if they rent it out for filming soap operas of the *Downton Abbey* kind.

But first: How do I get my hands on Adele's memoirs, those pages of her *Cautionary Tale* that contain Jack's name? Patricia won't let me touch the manuscript. She can't be bribed, I've seen that. The promise of a donation didn't sway her. I don't think I can get at the manuscript legitimately. I need a burglar, someone to break into the Rare Book vault and retrieve the manuscript for me. This isn't a task I can delegate to staff at the Dream Villa, and I don't know any burglars.

Then it strikes me: I do. Sam Kelley. He is a night traveller, or had the reputation at any rate. He is where I need him to be, on the premises of the Clarkson, at least until the end of the month. He can hang around the library at night without arousing suspicion. It's his business to hang around. And he has a master key. Sam is the solution to my problem. The question is: will he collaborate with me? I've never been good at reading his mind, but I think there was something between us, a gray area where our thoughts bumped up against each other and became entangled. They remained garbled and unintelligible, yes, but we shared common ground.

Sam's my man. Or not. I call the Porter's Lodge at the Clarkson, listen to his taped voice, and leave a message, telling him I'm in town and would like to see him—on business, I say, so as not to scare him off. He doesn't return my call. Not that day, not the next. Perhaps he is still in New York. Maybe I'm mistaken about that intersecting gray area where our thoughts met, or too much time has passed, and my name no longer means anything to him.

I wait another day for Sam to get back to me. When he doesn't, I call again. I know it's strategically wrong to phone him a second time, but I have no choice, really. I absolutely have to talk to him before the month is out and he leaves his job as caretaker at the Clarkson. I need him to have access to the library—if he takes on the job I intend to offer him, to steal the manuscript for me. I call him first thing in the morning, and this time I get him on the phone in person.

"Lynne," he says, turning the name over in his mouth, as if he couldn't make up his mind: does he like it or not? He doesn't say hello, or how are you, or good to hear from you. He says: "I got your message, but I haven't had time to call you back."

His voice raises my pulse. I catch my breath. I'm afraid my pounding heart will be audible over the phone. What are his feelings? I couldn't read his mind under the best of circumstances, and definitely can't over the phone.

"I'm in town for a couple of weeks," I say. I keep a tight grip on my voice, managing my words carefully, bringing them out in a neat and even lineup. "Want to get together?"

Pause on the other end. "Okay," he says. He doesn't sound enthusiastic, but I follow up nevertheless.

"How about a drink?"

"All right."

He's making me work for every word. "When?" I say. "Where?"

"Here, after work. Let's have a beer. Nine o'clock work for you?"

"I'm not into beer."

"Lynne, I don't have time to chat. I've been away. This is my first day back—I've got a ton of work to do."

"All right," I say, taking what's on offer. "See you tonight. I'll bring a bottle of wine."

"Whatever."

I'm not reaching him. It doesn't sound good for my plan to enlist his help or for my lingering desire to get together, a desire that puzzles me, no, makes me uneasy. I can't rationalize it. It doesn't fit my usual train of thought: purpose, plan, action. I am spooked. Nostalgia mixed with memories of Jack are messing me up. The desire in me isn't merely physical, which would be explicable. There are shreds of sentiments floating in my mind. If I didn't know better, I'd call it romantic longing. It must be a temporary malfunction of Ginny's system. Perhaps I need to check the neural pathways.

I GIFTWRAP the special boxed edition Patricia gave me. I'm going to regift it, present it to Sam, as a peace offering. I promised him a copy of *A Cautionary Tale* twelve years ago and never delivered on that promise. Better late than never.

At nine I'm at the gate of the Clarkson. It's like a rerun of the year I started to work there. I press the intercom and hear Sam's gravelly voice. He comes to the door. He still has the red-hot aura and, my God, he's impossibly good looking. Men do come into their own when they hit the mid-thirties. There is a sparseness about him now, the silk-blue eyes have acquired an edge, a quality of single-mindedness. The buzz cut is gone. His hair has grown out into tight curls. There's light-n-sexy stubble on his chin, a silver stud in one ear, and are those designer jeans he's wearing? But I'm more interested in Sam's inside. It's maddening. I still can't get a clear reading. He's as good as ever at disguising, scrambling the few words spiralling up from his head like smoke from a joint, keeping his thoughts down. On his mental screen: a snowstorm of pixels, like an old malfunctioning TV screen.

He waves me past the door. My shoulder brushes against his, and it's like an atmospheric particle collision. Fuck! I'm in love with this man, I mean it's the whole can't-fight-it thing. I'm in meltdown. But of course it's not love, not the actual sensation, only an incredibly vivid recollection of my helpless, hopeless infatuation with Jack. It's a bloody amazing thing to happen to a transmigrant. I feel endangered. I have no idea what that degree of emotion can do to an artificially constituted body like mine. Dissolve the tissue, separate the white from the red blood cells? That's what it feels like. I'm working hard at holding together and standing up to Sam's scrutiny. His eyes are on me. He's checking me out. I feel faded, far gone into the thirties.

We stand in his living room. I haven't actually said hello, just nodded to him, speechless. I don't know whether to offer him my cheek for a kiss. No, I'd better keep my body to myself. He stands back, as if he, too, was vulnerable and needed distance.

The living room is empty except for a few sticks of furniture and movers' boxes lined up against the wall, ready to go.

I pretend I don't know that he has been asked to leave and say:

"You're moving?"

"In a couple of weeks. I got fired."

"What for?"

He shrugs and looks past me, unsmiling. I feel a surge of irritation. Why is he holding back like that, feeding me little scraps of information, making me ask follow-up questions?

I stand in the middle of his stripped-down living room, holding the gift-wrapped box of books and the bottle of wine I've brought. I hand them to him.

He puts them down on the coffee table beside an open can of beer.

"Okay," he says. "I'll get you a glass." He points in the direction of the shabby sofa. "Sit down."

There is a trail of crumbs from a bag of potato chips, ending at the crack between two sofa cushions. I envision a layer of crumbs down below. The TV is on, flickering an action movie, sound on low, a rumble of crashes.

Sam comes back from the kitchen with a glass and a corkscrew. He opens the bottle and pours wine for me. He gives me a probing look. His eyes are cloudy now, as if the colour was in transition.

He clicks off the TV, takes a swig of beer, looks thoughtfully at the dead screen, and says: "So what do you want from me, Lynne?"

"I wanted to see you again," I say, but I feel backed into a corner.

"You said something about business in the message you left me."

So I did. Like an idiot. I guess I'll have to go with that theme now.

"Yes, business too."

"Let's get it over with, then."

"Okay," I say, "business first." I take a deep breath and jump in at the deep end. "I understand you are good at breaking into places."

"Says who?"

"Just a rumour floating around when I worked here."

"And?"

I lean forward. I practically breathe in his aura, which has gone from red to cautious amber. I get a faint reading, encouraging enough to cut to the chase.

"I'd like to hire your services as a burglar," I say. "I need someone to retrieve a manuscript for me. Are you interested?"

He laughs and shakes his head, as if he couldn't believe his ears.

"What manuscript? Where?"

"Here at the Clarkson."

"Is it valuable?" he asks.

"It may be valuable, but that's not why I want it. It's more of a collector's thing. An obsession. I've been after that manuscript for some time."

"What's so special about a piece of paper with writing on it?"

"I want it as a souvenir. It's the manuscript I rescued when Patricia Baron had that accident. Remember? It was my moment of glory. The LA Times called it a 'heroic rescue'."

"Yeah, I remember. They gave you a champagne party for being crazy enough to risk your life to save a handful of pages."

"They are of historical interest. It's a woman's life story."

"A woman with an incubus called Lynne."

I draw in my breath. How does he know?

"How do you know?" I ask.

"Doris Langer used to come by with treats for Gordie. I asked her how Patricia Baron was doing and what happened with the manuscript. She said they repaired the damage, and Patricia was going to publish an edition of it. Later she gave me a complimentary copy, 'since I had expressed an interest,' she said. So I'm up on the story of Lynne, the incubus."

I hold his gaze. I don't back off.

"In that case I'm too late with my present," I say. "I brought you a boxed set of the books."

I nudge the package on the coffee table.

Sam's hand moves to the packet. He spins it around a few times before taking off the wrapping. He slips *A Cautionary Tale* out of the box and opens it to the title page. "No dedication," he says. "You promised me a dedication: To Sam my friend and fellow gambler, if I remember correctly."

"That was then," I say. "Maybe I should find something more appropriate, to describe our present relationship."

A pause, as we contemplate our present relationship. Sam's arm is resting on the back of the sofa, an inch away from my shoulder. I turn to him. I look at his curvy, sensuous mouth and imagine what it would be like to run my tongue over his lips, but it's only a fantasy. There's a warning in Sam's eyes. He removes his arm and backs away. The moment is over.

"Something more appropriate?" he says. "Like: To Sam the burglar?"

The colour of his aura has turned an orangey hue, like the first rays of the sun at dawn. What does it mean?

"Okay, if that's what you want me to put there," I say. "Does it mean you'll do the job?"

"Depends," he says.

"On what?"

"The pay. What's in it for me?"

He looks at me. A thought is rising from his forehead, dark and foggy, and I am afraid he will say no if I don't offer him enough.

"How does fifty thousand sound?" I say quickly. Shit, I should have waited with my offer. As the words come out of my mouth, Sam's thoughts break through the fog, and for the first time, for a split-second, I can read him: *Maybe I should do it for nothing.* Then his thoughts are just a puff, and he says:

"Make that two-hundred thousand."

I blew it! Maybe I misread him, but I don't think so. He just went from zero to 200,000 in less than thirty seconds.

"Where does that figure come from?" I say.

He laughs. "My life has changed," he says. "I'm an artist now." He pronounces "artist" with an ironic twist. "Hard to believe, huh?"

"No, I always thought you had a creative side."

"I should show you a copy of the write-up the gallery did on me: Sam Kelley, conceptual artist. You know what my paintings sell for?"

"No. What do they sell for?"

"The dealer in New York priced my pieces at twenty thousand to fifty thousand, depending on the size. That's risk-free, legit money, you know."

"Have you actually sold any?"

"The show sold out, and the gallery wants more. So I'm not taking any shit from you, Lynne. You want my services? You pay. And you've got the money. I've been keeping tabs on you."

"You have? For personal reasons?"

"We're talking business here, right?"

"Business, yes," I say reluctantly.

"So what do you say?"

There isn't much to say. I accept Sam's terms.

"Two-hundred thousand. It's a deal."

"Cash. You show me the money, I show you the manuscript."

"What—you don't trust me?" I say, trying to make it sound like a joke, but he doesn't smile.

"You don't have a good track record," he says. "You promised to give me a copy of that book twelve years ago, and you never did."

"I left before it was published. My boyfriend was transferred to New York, and I went with him."

"And how did that work out?"

"We got married, and then we got divorced. And you? Are you married?"

"Nah, never met anyone I liked enough to live together with. Except Gordie. It broke me up when that dog died. First I thought I'd get another one. But why set myself up for disappointment? I wouldn't have found another one like Gordie."

"No, you get lucky only once."

"You got lucky every time when we bet on that window frame coming down. You won all bets, didn't you?"

"I lost out on the big one."

He contemplates that remark for a moment, then tips his head back and drinks the last of his beer. "Okay," he says, "enough of the memory trip. Let's talk about the job. You have a plan?"

"I want you to go to the Rare Book vault, take the manuscript out of its box and replace it with a facsimile, the one in the set here."

"As simple as that?" he says with a lopsided grin. "And no one will catch on to the switch?"

"Not for a long time. That manuscript isn't brought out very often. Once in a couple of years, maybe, for an exhibit or to show to someone on special request. And the facsimile looks real enough to the untrained eye. It will feel real to the gloved hand—no one ever handles a manuscript without gloves."

I'm not sure I believe what I'm saying. Sam looks doubtful as well.

"Let's say it works, but what happens if you try to sell the manuscript, get caught, and start talking?"

"Why would I sell it?" I say. "I wouldn't make any money on it. It isn't worth two-hundred thousand except to someone who has an emotional attachment to it. I told you I want it as a souvenir of my 'heroic' deed."

I describe the location of the book to Sam and give him the combination for unlocking the door to the vault.

"They've changed that combination," he says, eyeing me with something like pity. "They reset it every six months, but I keep a record of the numbers."

"So you won't have any problem."

"I'll get the manuscript for you," he says. There's a slight move, a closing of air between us, a rapprochement. It's a done deal. The business part of the evening is over.

We look at each other. For a moment I think he is going to put his arms around me and draw me close. I tense up. I realize I'm not prepared for anything physical, but he doesn't move. His aura dissolves and goes misty. A thought is bubbling up. Before I can get a reading, he withdraws it.

"I guess I know all I need to know for now," he says and gets up from the sofa. I get up too.

"I'll be in touch when I have the manuscript or if I need more information," he says and hustles me out the door. He doesn't step outside. He doesn't accompany me to the parked car. He shuts the door on me before I'm even down the steps and on the walkway.

BACK HOME, I google Sam's alias, JOHO, read up on him and his "relational art which reflects a deeper set of contemporary concerns than street art." I look at images of Sam's paintings. They are like walls on walls, huge squares, some of them covered with tags, others empty expanses with tiny scribbles that remind me of the canvas I saw at the Shearers' place in New York. I text Dan Shearer and ask him: *Who did the large painting in your dining room?* He texts back: *LA artist Sam Kelley aka JOHO. Buy into him now. Excellent investment.*

Well, I hope my $200,000 investment will pay off.

Nothing to do now except wait and get together the money to pay Sam. I visit a number of bank branches to collect the cash in amounts that won't trigger the computers keeping track of spending patterns. When I get home, the afternoon sun is slanting into the room. I go out on the terrace, sit in a lounge chair and look at the ocean, the scalloped waves rolling in, the mauve line of the horizon. I am restless, move back inside, and do a few stretch exercises while I go over the scenario: what will I do with the manuscript if and when I get it? (Right foot forward and lunge) Where is the best place to insert myself? (Left foot forward and lunge) I keep reviewing my life with Adele, the arguments with her aunt, the trysts with Francis, the failed elopement, Percy Stockdale running interference. I need a spot that is ghoulish or at least dark and desperate. Those are the catalysts facilitating re-entry. (Right lunge) There are only two scenes to work with in the manuscript. (Left lunge) The moment when I first entered Adele has all the ingredients, but I wasn't at my best then, just out of my own death throes. I wouldn't want to go through that again, not if there is another viable scene. (Clasp hands overhead, bend right) Then there's the murder of the Reverend, but I'd left Adele's body behind that night and carried only a vestige of her with me. Not surprisingly, Adele's narrative of the events that night is short on the essential details. She wasn't quite there. But the scene would do if necessary. (And bend left) Percy Stockdale's resurrection and my own sighting of him would serve very well, but Adele doesn't mention it because that, too, happened when I was on an outing. In any case, that encounter probably happened too late in the game. It wouldn't give me enough time to rescue Jack. (Clasp hands behind back, hang forward)

A new butler, by the name of Evan, serves me dinner on the terrace. The new hire is more professional than James the bit player. Evan comes and goes without leaving a trace on my mind—I'm too preoccupied to watch his moves or read his thoughts. My head is full of what ifs. I need to find a point of entry into the past that will work for me. A definite time, place, and event. The night I visited the Bullfrog and talked to Nellie is the most promising spot after all, I decide, even if Adele doesn't provide a full description of it in her memoir. At least Jack's name and mine are on one page. It's a hypnotic combination. The scene is suggestive enough to serve as a conduit to the past. And then what? Once I'm back, twinned with Adele and woven into her life again, will I be able to persuade her to take an interest in Jack's case? I need to talk her into going back to London, to the Bullfrog, and to ask Nellie to serve as a witness and swear that she saw me alive, that the corpse they found wasn't me. That would get Jack off the hook, unless they stick him with one of the crimes he actually committed. Will it help if I work out a detailed scenario now and practise it before diving back into that night, if I block out my steps and learn my lines so I won't go wrong when it comes to the crunch? The answer to all those questions depends on Sam delivering the manuscript, and I haven't heard from him since we made the deal.

IT'S THE END of the month. In twenty-four hours Sam will hand in the master key that gives him access to the library, and he still hasn't contacted me. Tonight is the deadline, his last chance to pull off the heist. Tomorrow someone else will be caretaker at the Clarkson.

I'm pessimistic. I don't think it will come off. My thoughts keep circling back to the manuscript and what comes next if Sam manages to steal it after all. I feel queasy thinking of the unknown risks of reverse-time travel. What if I get stuck en route without a suitable body and drift about, a rudderless spirit? The nostalgia that has brought me back to L.A. is ebbing. I'm suddenly having second thoughts about the possibility of diving back into Adele's life. Maybe I should stay on here for a while. The present is beginning to overshadow the past. I feel a weakening in my heart, in Ginny's heart, the thing at the centre of the present me. What do I really remember of my first life—perhaps only the way I was burning with desire, bursting with the will to live the fast life. My nostalgia is a longing for the intensity no borrowed life can match. What do I really remember about Jack—the sound of his voice, his hands, the roughness of his skin, the muscles moving under his skin? I'm no longer sure. His name is like the chiming of a distant bell. My memory of his body no longer has clear contours. It blends with other memories that don't match. I remember a muscular body, a scratchy voice and a red-hot aura enveloping me. But I suspect it's Sam. Could it be that he made me forget Jack? Maybe I should stay in the present and give Sam a chance. I've never had an artist lover before. No, the question is, can I make Sam forget whoever he's seeing now and give *me* a chance. I'm sure he's in a relationship and I'm up against competition.

I wish my body was better and I had some of that buffed centrefold glamour, something to hold Sam's attention. I phone downstairs and ask the concierge to make an appointment for me at a spa. I have a long day of waiting ahead of me and may as well use it to advantage. The concierge calls back to say he has made an appointment for me at The Crystal Touch, "the spa of the stars."

I follow the GPS to Coral Canyon Road. The spa is tucked into a ravine, a low-slung building with a round foyer topped by a blue glass dome. Beyond the marble reception desk, it's all white gauzy curtains, Greek urns, and flower arrangements—a kind of ethereal funeral home if I read the iconography correctly, a place where you deposit your old skin and emerge a new woman. Not that different from the concept of transmigration, but without the life-and-death battle. The sweetly dorky receptionist twists her hair and consults the schedule. She taps the screen of her computer and informs me that Tonya will look after me.

I relinquish my body to a perfectly toned, bouncy-haired woman, only I don't know how to let myself be pampered by a personal assistant. The massage doesn't go well. I can't stand Tonya's hands on my body, which is a delicately reconstituted thing and sensitive to touch. Tonya's kneading hands woggle my kidneys. I tell her I want to skip the massage. Tonya stops reluctantly and suggests a loofa scrub instead. Absolutely essential, she says, to renew my surface cells. She won't let me off that punishment. Dull skin is anathema at The Crystal. I suffer warm stones being placed on my spine and try not to listen to Tonya's patter, the ceaseless drip of words about rejuvenation and revitalization. Tonya carries on like a one-woman shopping channel, looking down on me with her doe eyes, speaking pleasantly, evenly, cheerfully, soft-breathing recommendations of lavender aroma therapy to increase circulation and assist lymphatic drainage, or hydrotherapy with purifying algae to battle my congested and (she insists) hyperpigmented skin. At the very least, I need a mud pack to detoxify my body, she says. I try to read Tonya's thoughts, but her mind is completely filled with ready-made phrases that leave no space for personal preferences.

I escape, finally, and get dressed in a room that is a hall of mirrors. In spite of my annoyance with the screen-perfect Tonya, I have to admit: my body has a certain sheen it did not have before. In the car, I check my phone. A text from Sam. He's on his way to the villa. My heart starts up violently, but I won't allow myself to go there and start thinking of the future, or rather the past, no, it might all evaporate into a dream or turn into a disaster. No, hold the enthusiasm, I tell myself, but it's remarkably difficult to rein in my heart, get my pulse and breathing back to normal. I didn't know I had that much residual passion, or whatever that flutter means.

Back at the villa, I call downstairs and order up two bottles of Cristal Brut from Evan. "Special occasion," I say, although I don't owe him an explanation. I'm running over at the mouth with anticipation. Evan immediately seizes on my weakness for a bit of one-upmanship and suggests Armand de Bignac instead. Apparently Cristal Brut is totally yesterday and Armand de Bignac is the right stuff for "special occasions" if you know the scene. Evan doesn't say that of course. His voice is perfectly civil, but he manages to inject a little hauteur into his suggestion. Another B-movie actor like James? But when he brings the two bottles and ices them, his gestures and movements are impeccable. Maybe he is a real butler.

For the next twenty minutes I am finger-drumming, bum-shifting restless, waiting for Sam. When Evan shows him in, my throat doesn't allow for hello. I'm in Sam's electric field. I do a soundless acknowledgment. He doesn't say hello either. He just nods.

"Nice place," he says, looking around.

He stands in the middle of the living room, holding a plastic bag with a drugstore logo. I assume it contains the stolen manuscript, but I can't be sure. Sam is his usual enigmatic self, keeping his thoughts tucked in.

He does a slow half-turn, studying the walls. It looks as if he's taking their measure, gauging their potential for graffiti. His eyes come to rest on me.

"Posh," he says. I take it he means the villa.

"I don't own the place," I say. "I rent it by the week."

I take Sam out to the terrace and show him the view, or what remains of it, because it's late, and twilight is shifting into night.

He looks down on the strip of beach, turns his eyes to where the horizon would be if you could see anything, and says "Nice view" like a polite guest.

He is holding on to the plastic bag as if it contained his life. It must be the manuscript, what else could it be? But he makes no move to hand it over.

We go back inside.

"So how did the operation go?" I say.

"No surprises," he says. "The manuscript was where you said it would be. I took it out of the box and replaced it with the fake. Let's hope you are right and no one finds out. Even if they do, there's no way they can pin the switch on me. You got the money?"

I nod and reach for the manila envelope with the money in hundred-dollar bills. It's like Academy night. We've both played well. And the winner is—? It's a draw, I suppose. I give him the envelope. He hands me the bag. I can feel the manuscript through the plastic, a curl of pages. I want to take it out, get my fingers on it, run my eyes over the naked lines, but I politely wait for Sam to count his money. He doesn't. He puts the envelope down on the counter of the wet bar.

"Don't you want to count the bills?" I ask.

"Okay," he says and picks up the envelope again with a tolerant half-smile, the kind you give a child. He opens the flap, takes out the hundred-dollar bills and stacks them on the counter. But he still doesn't count the notes. He divides them into two piles, tucks one half back into the envelope and hands me the other. "Here," he says, as if it was surplus.

"Do I get a discount?" I say.

"I've kept a couple of the pages for myself," he says.

My skin crisps. What pages? Are they vital pages? Will this unexpected move spoil my plan? Is this another hurdle I have to jump?

"I want all the pages," I say. "That was the deal. What's the idea anyway? I thought you aren't interested in manuscripts. You couldn't see why anyone would pay that kind of money for a few pieces of paper with writing on it. That's what you said."

He shrugs. "I wanted a souvenir. Like you." Yes, that's the fake explanation I gave him, and now he is parroting me with an ironic smile. But I suspect he kept the pages for another reason, which I can't guess. His thoughts are closed to me.

He holds on to the bar counter, as if to steady himself. Is he drunk? I don't think so, although an atmosphere of drinking surrounds him, a pub atmosphere, something foggy and Londonish, I can't make it out. It surrounds him like a ragged gray cloth. The fog is interfering with his defense mechanism, making his cranial walls porous. I see, not exactly his thoughts, but their object, a knife. Why is Sam thinking of a knife? Words are seeping through the barrier now. *Hanged for murder.* No, those aren't Sam's thoughts. Those are words out of Adele's memoir. It's a quote. He may have looked at the manuscript, but why would he recall those particular words? Why now? And they don't explain why he has kept back part of the manuscript.

"What are you going to do with those pages?" I say.

"That's what I was going to ask you," he says and gives me a mute look full of things I don't understand. "What are *you* going to do with the manuscript? And don't tell me you wanted a souvenir. That's bullshit."

Neither of us is willing to confess what we're up to.

I take the manuscript out of the bag and rifle through the pages to find out what's missing. The last page ends with the scene in the Bullfrog on the night of my return to London and Nellie's prediction: He'll hang for murder.

The rest of the manuscript is missing, but I know what happened next, I know what's on the next page: I couldn't stop sobbing and crying out Jack's name.

I see everything through a film, Sam, the stack of money, Nellie in the kitchen of the Bullfrog. I can no longer tell what's real and what's coming off the manuscript in a ghostly stream. The air is suddenly full of vibrations and sets my heart pounding and my body trembling. Touch is the test. My fingertips will tell what is real and what isn't.

I go up to Sam and touch his shoulder. A shock runs through my fingertips and up my arm. There is a white explosion in my head. I am reeling.

I lose my balance and lean into him. I expect him to step back, recede like a ghost—surely he is an apparition, Jack's avatar—but his body is solid. I put my head against his chest to listen: does he have a heartbeat? It's a slow drum. He puts his arms around me, and the truth comes rushing at me like the wings of an eagle.

"Jack!" I say. The name breaks out of my mouth, a supersonic stream that engulfs him so he can't get away.

"Lynne," he says. His voice is suddenly soft at the edges, eroded by a wash of feeling.

He holds me close, and we kiss, chastely, like virgins.

It's all new to us, being alive to each other.

"I've run after you for two centuries and a dozen lifetimes and missed you every time," Jack says. "Don't give me the slip now. Don't go back—because that's what you wanted the manuscript for, didn't you? To slip through the lines into the past."

"I'm not going anywhere."

I have no reason to slip back into Adele's life. This is it. The last leg of my journey. *LA to NY. NY to LA.* Those were Jack's directions, the signposts he planted on the painting in Dan Shearer's dining room, so I'd know where to find him. I put my arms around Jack to arrest him, to make sure of him.

I won't ever let him go.

POSTSCRIPT

AND SO Lynne and Jack live happily ever after.

No, that's not how the story goes. They move into a smart condo in Santa Monica and are happy in each other's company for about six months. Then they get bored, or nostalgic, or both. Jack is tired of the gallery circuit—the art world is not criminal enough for his taste. He misses the hands-on approach to earning money, the breaking and entering, cracking his knuckles on a man's chin, flooring the gas pedal on a get-away car. That sort of thing. Sometimes he slums it in downtown LA. He wanders the tent city, enjoying a little physicality when someone tries to rob him. He considers an offer to become a drug dealer, but not seriously. The lower ranks in the drug trade are pathetic. You get in a few snarling threats. You get to pistol-whip customers who don't pay their debts or, at best, nick them with a knife (but don't kill the golden goose). No, there is no excitement in dealing drugs, not at the street level and it takes time to penetrate the upper echelons. Jack doesn't have the patience to work his way up.

"You know the last time I got a kick out of anything was when I stole the manuscript," he says to Lynne, "and even that was a tame affair. No risk to it, really."

"Maybe you should try the stock market. The stakes are higher there."

"Nah," he said. "*You* haven't gone back to it, and I know why. Because you are bored with that sort of hustle, right?"

"It's more like: Been there, done that. I'd like to try something I haven't done before. Maybe a podcast or a blog on investing, but I'm still looking for the right fit."

"What about your idea of going back to the eighteenth century?" Jack says. "That's something we haven't done before: travelling back in time. Besides, there is potential for making it big in Old London if we apply our experience, the knowledge we've picked up in other centuries. Are you still up for it?"

They are lounging on the balcony, looking out on a fiery sun sinking into the dark waters and spreading a half-light over the bay. Lynne takes a sip of wine and thinks: His boredom has nothing to do with his art work. It's personal. I am boring him.

"I didn't think the excitement would wear off so quickly," she says, keeping her voice level. She doesn't want to come across as a bitch.

"Yeah," he says, "how does the old song go? 'Life goes on but the thrill of living is gone.' You have to keep moving to keep it interesting. So are you up for it or not?"

"Are you sure we can pull it off and travel back in time? Using Adele's manuscript as a channel is dicey, don't you think? But if you want to take the risk, okay..."

"You almost sound as if you didn't want to leave here, but you know how that song ends? 'You aren't missing a thing.' So let's take the risk."

"All right," she says because she has never been able to say no to Jack, or to a dare. "We'll go to the bank tomorrow and get the manuscript out of the safe deposit box."

"That's my woman!" he says and raises his glass of whiskey to her in a toast of appreciation, but he doesn't get up to kiss her. He drains his glass and says: "We'll get the manuscript and take it from there."

ACKNOWLEDGMENTS

I would like to thank my friends Karin MacHardy and Roberta Johnson for reading my manuscript at various stages and giving me their advice. Sincere thanks to everyone who helped shape my book—Jennifer Hale, Kimmy Beach, Ashley Rayner, and Beate Schwirtlich. I also have fond memories of Luciana Ricciutelli and still miss her warm hugs!

OTHER NOVELS BY ERIKA RUMMEL

Playing Naomi
Head Games
The Effects of Isolation on the Brain
The Painting on Auerperg's Wall
The Inquisitor's Niece
Three Women and Alfred Nobel
The Road to Gesualdo
Evita and Me